Murder at Deadline

by
Thomas Canavan Jr.

authorHOUSE™

1663 LIBERTY DRIVE, SUITE 200
BLOOMINGTON, INDIANA 47403
(800) 839-8640
WWW.AUTHORHOUSE.COM

© 2005 Thomas Canavan Jr. All Rights Reserved.

First published by AuthorHouse 11/29/05

ISBN: 1-4208-8282-1 (e)
ISBN: 1-4208-8283-X (sc)
ISBN: 1-4208-8284-8 (dj)

Library of Congress Control Number: 2005908001

Printed in the United States of America
Bloomington, Indiana

This book is printed on acid-free paper.

Cover illustration and design by David Vandeventer and Dennis Pellicano.

To Tom, Brian, Brendon, Sean, Jake and Josh, the six greatest nephews in the world; and to Jaclyn, even though you may be my only niece doesn't mean you can't be my favorite.

2006

Mrs. C.
Thanks for all
those delicious
holiday dinners.
Your pal,
Dave Van Deventer

Acknowledgements:

Special thanks to Diane, for that extra set of eyes; to David Vandeventer and Dennis Pellicano for an amazing cover to this book; to Ann, a very special lady; and to all, or maybe most, of the newsroom staff I've worked with these last eighteen years. Every one of the hundreds of them know who they are.

CHAPTER ONE

The air around him was stale, but he knew he was the only one who could smell it.

On any other day when the air was this bad, he'd tuck his nose under his armpit and sniff, in an intentional yet casual way so as not to be noticed, to be sure the smell wasn't emanating from his body.

But that day was different. The smell was different, perhaps unique to others, but not unfamiliar to E.G. Lord, a reporter who could smell a story a mile away, and this, he knew, was going to be a big one.

The voice on the other end of the phone was as familiar as the smell. And of all the words E.G. jotted in his notebook as his source spoke, the words "dead" and "bodies" jumped off the page. His source did not know how many dead bodies, nor how they died, but sources didn't necessarily know the whole story. Their information, as vague as it sometimes was, usually was enough to give a reporter direction. A good reporter, on the other hand, knew how to follow direction.

"And they're there now?" E.G. asked his source, referring to the police. He looked at his watch, then, pulling the cord on the telephone, stepped out of his cubicle and glanced at the clock on the wall at the front of the office, as if he expected the time to be different. "I'm on my way."

E.G. patted the ass of his jeans and felt the rectangular spiral notebook he kept in the rear pocket. The extra one, he thought, which no reporter should leave home without. He checked his left ear; the pen was there, and E.G. was off.

He debated whether or not to tell his editor about the tip, but it was a short-lived debate because by the time he reached his car in the rear of the parking lot, it had ended, with secrecy prevailing for the moment. After all, he told himself, he knew his editor. Despite all his years in the business, Mel Shepard couldn't handle breaking news, and if it were going to happen, he'd give Mel the least amount of time to worry about it. E.G.'s adrenaline was pumping faster than his heart was beating. It was rare that a breaking news story with this kind of timing was dumped in the lap of a reporter working for a weekly newspaper. He only had a few hours before the presses would roll, and he could taste the ink that would give his story life.

Besides, he would tell Mel later, he was on his way to see dead bodies, and how many people would interrupt that?

E.G. slipped into the late afternoon traffic and, as he did every time he got behind the wheel of his car, cursed the fact that he lived in New Jersey. Whether it was nine in the morning, nine at night, or three in the afternoon, the one thing a driver in New Jersey could count on was traffic.

But on that day, he used the traffic to his advantage. As he maneuvered his 1981 Toyota Tercel through the onslaught of cars in downtown South Orange, he flipped the sun visor and jotted questions on the notepad fastened there with two elastic bands. Question number two almost came at the expense of a gray-haired man in a Honda, who, for no reason E.G. could explain, came to a complete stop on South Orange Avenue, leaving the Tercel resting only inches from his rear bumper. He cursed the driver, knowing it was his own fault for not paying attention to the road, and returned the visor to its original position. He remained behind the Honda until the road opened to two lanes, then swung the Tercel into the left lane and accelerated up the hill. He was on his way to see dead bodies, and he didn't have time for traffic.

There would be dozens of them, he told himself, and swore every reporter would think the same based on the tip. Mass murders. He pictured the front page of *The Sentinel* the following day, with his story at the top of the fold, declaring mayhem and carnage in the South Mountain Reservation. Funny, he thought, how one family's agony becomes a journalist's Milk Bone. But that was how it always happened. Death, especially murder, ignited a slow news week, and, like it or not, sold newspapers.

An exclusive would be the angel at the top of the Christmas tree, and as E.G.'s Tercel chugged up the hill despite the accelerator pressed against the floor, he knew he had a chance of publishing the story without any other newspaper finding out about it in time to meet their own deadlines. As the excitement grew and he neared the entrance to the Reservation, he unconsciously pushed against the erection that pressed against his jeans. "This is going to be big," he told himself.

But the one thing he didn't expect when he reached the top of the hill was the roadblock. Three police cars, linked like a kiddy ride at an amusement park, sat guard in front of the narrow road that led to the top of the mountain. The emergency lights on the patrol cars were dark, and as E.G. inched closer, he could have mistaken the four officers as being on a break. Three sipped coffee despite the temperature that afternoon reaching ninety degrees, and the other drank from a bottle of water while holding a cigarette between two fingers in his other hand. As one officer spoke, the other three laughed. It didn't look like a murder scene.

E.G. approached the roadblock, and one of the officers stepped into the middle of the road, his hand in the air indicating he wanted E.G. to stop. He did. He had no choice.

Bending slightly and peering into the driver's side window, the officer said, "No visitors here today, sir. I need you to turn the car around and head on back out." His voice was calm, as if he had uttered the same words dozens of times already that day. The three other officers remained near the cars, but the laughter had stopped as they watched their colleague try to direct the driver out of the Reservation.

E.G. lifted the sunglasses from the bridge of his nose and rested them on top of a head of blond hair that was cut above the ears, but hung to his shoulders. He smiled at the officer as he fished through a pile of papers on the passenger seat before removing a three-inch by seven-inch placard that displayed the word PRESS in large, bold type, and E.G.'s name below it in smaller type.

He presented the card to the officer and said matter-of-factly, "I understand some dead bodies were found up here not too long ago."

"Oh, Jesus Christ," came from one of the officers in the background. E.G. didn't know which one. "They're not even cold yet, and the fucking press knows."

The placard boasted the words *The Sentinel*, a local weekly newspaper that served the entire Essex County, New Jersey, and as the officer handed the identification back to E.G., he said, "We have nothing to report at the moment. I need you to turn your vehicle around and head on back out of here. This is a police investigation, and I can't permit you to go beyond this point."

"I came up here because I heard there was a murder," E.G. said. "Apparently, according to your friend back there, it involves more than one body."

"I don't want to have to tell you again, sir, so for the last time, I need you to turn around and head on out of here." The voice had begun to change, almost like a father's voice when he finds himself delivering the same instructions to his child for the third time. The badge on his shirt identified the officer as Shawn Collins of the Essex County Sheriff's Department. He stood more than six feet tall and was stocky, but that didn't intimidate E.G. He'd been in the business too long not to know his rights.

"You know as well as I do, Officer, that as long as I'm on this side of your roadblock, I'm not interfering with a police investigation. I'm on public property," E.G. said, nodding behind him. "I'll even pull my car back to one of those public parking spaces, and I'll just sit and observe."

Without waiting for a response from the officer, E.G. backed the car a few yards into one of the six empty parking spaces. He turned off the engine and got out of the car.

He stood about six feet tall and, in his jeans and button down Nautica shirt whose sleeves were rolled up to the elbows, anyone could see that he worked out regularly. Broad shoulders defined the rest of his body, which included a muscular chest and a lean waist.

As he leaned against his car, he flipped the sunglasses back over the bridge of his nose, checked for the pen over his left ear and again patted his ass where the notebook was tucked in the pocket.

E.G. watched the officers, but that wasn't the reason he went to the Reservation that day. He was there for a story, and he was determined to get something from his visit. He pushed himself off the car and began walking toward the officers, but Collins saw him coming and stepped back into the middle of the road. He started to say something, but E.G. beat him to it.

"I'm not looking to cause trouble," he said, suddenly sounding desperate. After all, it was Wednesday afternoon, and if he wanted a story for that week's edition, he was going to have to get it within the next couple of hours. And leaning against his car wasn't going to get him anywhere. He lowered his voice so the other officers couldn't hear him. "Obviously, something did happen up there. Otherwise, I wouldn't have gotten a tip and you guys wouldn't be barricading this roadway. Can't you tell me anything? I swear I won't quote you as a source. I'll use the information only as background."

Collins just stared at him.

"I've been in this business for ten years," E.G. continued. "You can trust me. Word will get out anyway, and I'd like to at least have something in the paper tomorrow if the dailies are going to have it. Otherwise, my story doesn't come out for another eight days. I know that doesn't mean squat to you, but it means a lot to me. And if you do me this favor, I swear I won't screw you by revealing you as my source. I know you don't know me, but..."

Collins turned his attention away from E.G. From behind the reporter, he watched a vehicle pull into the entrance to the Reservation, the only occupant a male driver. Collins raised his hand and the vehicle stopped. "No visitors here today, sir. I'm going to need you to turn your vehicle around and head on back out of here."

The driver looked beyond Collins and saw the police vehicles barricading the road into the Reservation. He put his car in reverse, turned the vehicle around and, as Collins requested, headed on back out of the park entrance.

Collins turned his attention back to E.G. "I do know you," he said. "I know of you, anyway. I read the papers." And by reading the papers, Collins had seen E.G.'s byline hundreds of times, even having remarked a few times of his fair and balanced coverage. A reporter gave birth to his reputation based on how he wrote articles, and reputation, good or bad, was the key ingredient to whether people trusted him enough to talk to him. E.G.'s reputation sparkled in Essex County where *The Sentinel* was published and it was the reason Collins felt at ease to begin sharing information.

As quietly as E.G. had spoken, Collins did the same. "Off the record, they found two bodies up there."

E.G. removed the notebook from his pocket and the pen from his ear. There goes the theory of the dozens of bodies, he thought as he flipped open the notebook and began writing. "2 bodies," he wrote with his left hand.

"Try to be a little more discreet, will you?" Collins demanded through clenched teeth as he glanced back at the other officers.

E.G. turned slightly, hiding the notebook from the view of the other officers. "Male? Female? Both? Ages?" he asked.

"Both were male," Collins said. "Twenties, maybe thirties."

They were about his own age. E.G. wrote the letter "M" and "20s, 30s" under the line where he wrote "2 bodies," then stopped and looked up at Collins as if someone had slapped the back of his head for taking this long to realize the obvious. E.G. knew about the Reservation. He had been told of the events that had occurred within the woods, and was given names by anonymous sources. The road-blocked path led to an area of the South Mountain Reservation frequented by men who engaged in homosexual activity. That section of the Reservation was a twenty-acre bathhouse, with men lingering near vehicles, and going into and out of the woods, either alone to find a partner, or with a partner they had just met. Sex in the Reservation was performed in cars, in the woods, just about anywhere a guy could whip out his penis for someone in waiting. And there was always someone in waiting.

"Were the bodies naked?" E.G. asked.

"Look, I think I've said enough," Collins said.

"No, you haven't. Come on. Tell me. Is this related to the stuff that goes on up there when you guys aren't looking?"

E.G. didn't have to explain what he meant, nor did Collins have to ask him to explain it.

"We're not sure about that yet," he said.

E.G. made another note in the book, then asked when the police thought the incident occurred.

"I can't answer that. Medical examiner is on his way. I don't know how the hell you got the information so fast that you got here before him."

"I've been in this business for ten years," E.G. said, continuing to scribble in his notebook. "I'd be embarrassed if I *didn't* get here before the medical examiner." He smiled at Collins, whose gaze told him he didn't think that was funny. "Just trying to add levity, Officer," E.G. said as he looked around and scribbled some more in his notebook. "Specifically, where were the bodies found?"

"Can't give you that information."

"Were they naked?" he repeated.

"No comment."

E.G. wrote as he spoke. "What kind of weapon was used?"

Collins did not respond.

E.G. continued to write.

"Are you sure it was a double murder, and not a murder-suicide?"

Collins still did not respond.

"What did you have for breakfast this morning?"

Collins creased his brow, and E.G. said, "I just want to make sure you're paying attention. You've stopped answering my questions."

"Any further information will have to come from the spokesman at the Sheriff's Office," Collins said. He moved closer to E.G. "And anything I've already told you better not have my name attached to it."

"You've got my word on that," E.G. said as he closed the notebook. "Off the record" was as sacred to E.G. as "I swear to tell the whole truth" was as sacred to a court of law. "But just between you and me, Officer, what will the medical examiner do when he gets here? How long do you think he'll be up there?"

The questions could pertain to any case, so Collins answered them. "He'll officially pronounce them dead, take notes on what the bodies look like, load the bodies in his vehicle and take them to the county morgue. A little more involved than that, but that's it in a nutshell."

E.G. wouldn't give up. "And how long will the police be up there?"

Collins was losing his patience. "No more information," he snapped. "If you want to stand by your vehicle and stay out of the way, do so. Otherwise, you'll give me no choice but to charge you with interfering with a police investigation."

Collins turned and walked back toward his colleagues, who had separated from the pack they had formed and walked around by themselves near the road into the Reservation. "When will that goddamn coroner get here?" Collins said, opening the door to his cruiser and grabbing hold of the handset of the radio.

E.G. returned to his own car, not bothering to try to hear whom Collins was calling, assuming it was the coroner's office. He looked out upon South Orange Avenue. Cars passed the entranceway at about thirty-five miles per hour. Some, with their directional indicating they wanted to enter the Reservation, slowed to turn into the entrance, but turned off their signals and continued with the flow of traffic once they saw the police vehicles inside.

E.G. wondered how many men actually visited this part of the Reservation for sex. He had heard some of the stories, but didn't have the desire to see first-hand what the storytellers had shared. When he had first heard the stories, he thought it would make a good expose for the newspaper. "Cruising in the '90s: Anonymous sex in an age of AIDS." He had the title and everything. Even a willing photographer to accompany him. But then the idea died, revived only by the tip he received less than an hour earlier. A new expose formed in his mind: "Cruising in the new millennium. It could get you killed."

He opened the passenger door of his car and removed a cell phone from the front seat and pressed the key pad. The voice on the other end of the line was familiar. *"Sentinel,"* Margaret said. "How may I help you?"

"Margaret, it's E.G. Is Mel around? It's important."

While he waited for his editor to come to the phone, E.G. recalled all the reasons he disliked Mel. The first was the fact that he would have to explain the importance of the story even though "dead" and "bodies" should be enough. Mel was regimented, and a story this close to deadline could push him over the edge. He pictured Mel completing his pages in the composing room, hovering over each of the paginators as they followed his layout instructions. To the paginators, that was no different than if he were to stand over them as they urinated. Mel had difficulty adapting to change, and E.G. was certain that by this hour of the day, the front page had been completed and it would be a struggle to convince him that a change was necessary.

But the publisher liked Mel, E.G. knew, because he was, for the most part, neutral, and neutrality didn't jeopardize advertising revenue. Mel also always completed production early, and by doing so, published on time and saved credits to the accounts of advertisers.

E.G. prepared himself for the argument that was about to ensue and thought of the words he was going to use when Mel came to the phone.

"I'm surprised you're not at the bar already," Mel said. "Or are you?"

"Someplace better," E.G. responded, thinking it would be wiser to ignore the remark. "I've got a great story for tomorrow's edition. If we don't go with it this week, we should get the artist to draw a big asshole on the front page of next week's paper because that's what we'll look like." Hit him with the guilt first and be diplomatic later, E.G. thought.

There was silence on the other end of the phone, and E.G. imagined Mel panicking.

"What is it?" Mel asked, barely audible, and E.G. wondered if it was disinterest or if it was the noise of the passing cars along South Orange Avenue that made Mel's voice seem low.

E.G. stuck a finger in his right ear to block any noise and leaned inside the car. "I'm at the South Mountain Reservation, and I just had the police confirm that two dead bodies were found up here. You know the spot where the guys go to meet each other?"

"Meet each other for what?" Mel asked.

E.G. shook the phone in the air in frustration. "To swap recipes," he said sarcastically. "To get blow jobs!"

When he heard silence on the other end of the phone, E.G. pictured Mel's face reddening and imagined that he came from around his desk to close his office door.

"Oh, that area," Mel said.

E.G. again wondered why the company kept Mel on its payroll. "Yes, that area. They were naked, so it's probably tied to all that activity. I don't have much to go with, but they're waiting for the coroner to get here. I may have something after that. How much time do I have to file a story?" He posed the question as if there were no doubt the story was going to happen.

As E.G. looked at his watch, he pictured Mel looking up at the Yankees clock that hung on the wall in his office. Mel wasn't a Yankees fan. He didn't even like baseball. But when the mayor of one of the towns the newspaper covers presented it to him for some kind of "outstanding" coverage, the topic of which E.G. couldn't remember, Mel accepted it and hung it on his wall.

It was 3:15 p.m.

"Hey, Mel, are you there?"

"And what makes you think we'll hold the paper for this story?" Mel asked.

It should have been Mel's turn to ask E.G. if he was still there because the phone went dead. But after a moment, E.G. said, "Are you kidding me?"

"You have little information. We can't go with a story based on what you've just told me. You know as well as I do that it's not enough."

"I'll get more. But you need to tell me how much time I have to get it."

After a moment of silence, Mel said, "You've got until 5:30. That's thirty minutes after deadline."

A flashing red light reflecting in his windshield caught E.G.'s attention. He turned to find the coroner's black van glide into the entrance to the Reservation and stop near the police barricade.

"Thanks, man," E.G. said to Mel. "I'll be back by five to write the story. If I'm delayed, I'll call and feed you my lead." He hung up without waiting for Mel to respond.

E.G. closed his car door and watched as one of the police vehicles reversed to allow room for the coroner to make his way up the narrow road.

As Officer Collins returned his vehicle to secure the barricade, he looked in the direction where E.G. had parked his car. The Tercel occupied one of the six parking spaces just inside the entrance. But there was no sign of the reporter.

CHAPTER TWO

E.G. could have waited at the bottom of the mountain to get his story, but that would have been the easy out. And costly too, he told himself as he made his ascent through the woods into the Reservation.

As he turned onto a dirt path that ran parallel to the road the county medical examiner took, E.G. pictured the story in the following day's daily newspaper, his competition, and began to jog to the top of the mountain. He wasn't about to let anyone beat him to this story, and he knew the only way he would get it by deadline was to get it himself. He could trust his source not to share the tip with anyone else, including reporters from the daily newspaper. And, based on the anger of one of the officers after hearing the press knew of the murders, he felt safe that he was the only one who had the information.

The woods were cooler, at least ten degrees cooler than it felt at the entrance to the Reservation, where the sun had hammered its heat upon him and the officers. Collins. By that point, Collins had to have noticed he was missing, E.G. thought, and wondered if he should return to his car. The last thing he wanted was a night in jail for interfering with a police investigation, especially when he had only two and one-half hours to get and file his story.

He dismissed the thought, knowing he had friends in high places he could contact if necessary, and continued up the dirt path.

The woods were too quiet for the amount of noise he was making with his shoes. Dried leaves and frail branches crumbled under his feet with every step he took, the sounds amplified by the silence all around him. He hadn't been to this part of the mountain since he was about thirteen years old, when he and a group of friends had hitchhiked to the Reservation to swim in the fresh spring at the bottom of the waterfall. That was twenty years earlier, and E.G. thought it funny that he hadn't recalled that day until now. He was with Larry, Pat, Michael and Daryl, friends he hadn't seen in almost as long, but their names rolled right off his tongue.

He stepped off the dirt path and onto the grass alongside it and immediately noticed how invisible he had become. He didn't know the location of the crime scene, nor if police would be combing the area, but he was sure he wasn't going to let the sound of his footsteps give him away. So much litter, he thought, as he grabbed hold of a branch for support. Beer cans, empty and crushed McDonald's food boxes, faded newspapers and condoms — were they used? — laced the grass. Safe sex with a stranger, E.G. thought. There's something wrong with that picture.

He felt a bug crawling on his arm and swatted at it, splattering its blood on his fingers. It was a tiny bug and he instantly thought of deer ticks and Lyme disease. The Reservation was overrun with deer, too many, he knew, from all the stories he had written about the subject. So it must have been the power of suggestion that made him swing at a loose branch that brushed against his leg, causing him to jump away from what he was sure was a deer.

"Jeez," he shouted, then looked around to see if anyone was close enough to hear him.

Satisfied that he was alone, he continued along the path, glancing at his watch and realizing he was down to two hours to deadline. If he blew this, and even if the daily newspaper didn't have it the following day, they'd still have seven days to publish a story before he could.

"Eight days," he said aloud, almost stomping up the hill. "No way am I waiting eight fucking days to write this story."

No sooner did he pick up speed than he stopped in his tracks. The rustling of leaves. He ducked behind a tree and a wall of overgrown weeds, imagining Officer Collins on his trail. The rustling drew nearer, and when it seemed he could reach out and touch it, it stopped. E.G. waited a few moments, even trying to slow his breathing so as not to be heard, and listened for the noise to resume. The sun poked through the tops of the tall trees. He checked to his left and then to his right, but could see no one. Worse than the police, he thought, it could be the person responsible for the dead bodies at the top of the mountain.

A bird sang in a tree high above him and its soft chirping blanketed E.G. with a certain calm. Slowly, he rose, and just as his face cleared the fence of weeds, he felt his underwear moisten. There, within inches of his face, was the face of a deer, its eyes big and round and just as surprised to see E.G. as E.G. was surprised to see it. They stared at one another for a moment, the deer positioning itself to run on a moment's notice, but they both remained frozen. It was like a face-off, and neither wanted to be the first to blink.

But realizing how stupid the situation appeared, E.G. slowly backed away, uncertain whether the deer would run or strike at him. At a safe distance away, E.G. stomped his foot and pretended to lunge for the deer, and that sent him deeper into the woods and out of sight. It wasn't until that moment that E.G. discovered how fast his heart had been beating. It was also then that he discovered the urine stain he left on his jeans.

Running up the dirt path this time, and glancing at his watch, E.G. reached a clearing and found himself on a part of the road that encircled the section of the Reservation that men used for sexual encounters. On any other day, the road would be lined with cars, parked half on the road and half off as the drivers waited for a potential score. But that day was awfully quiet and empty, thanks to Officer Shawn Collins and his patrol at the foot of the mountain.

E.G. crossed the road and entered the next set of woods, but did not go as deep into them. Instead, he went in about twenty feet, just enough distance to keep himself hidden and with the knowledge that if he was going to come across something, it would be soon.

He heard the sound of a police radio in the distance. His heart began to race faster as he pushed through the woods, swatting at flies and fighting branches that hung in his way until he reached another clearing. From there, he saw at least five police cars, the coroner's van, an ambulance and about fifteen police officers, uniformed and plain-clothed, gathered at what he assumed was the scene of the crime.

He peered through trees. A man in a white uniform was kneeling on the grass over what appeared to be a body. E.G. was too far away to confirm that, but he was certain the man was looking at the bottom of someone's foot. The man in the white uniform stood, motioned to a police officer, then walked approximately twenty-five feet to his right and stepped off the blacktop road and into the grass before kneeling once again. It looked to E.G. as if the white-uniformed man was talking into a tape recorder which he held in his left hand, while his right hand, from what E.G. could see from where he crouched, was poking at something in the grass.

E.G. looked back to the left and watched a uniformed officer trace the outline of the body. When he was finished, two emergency medical personnel took his place at the site. They laid a stretcher on the ground and lifted the body — yes, it was naked, he noted — onto it before lifting it higher onto a gurney. On the gurney was a plastic bag, and they placed the body inside the bag as easily as if they were placing a sandwich into a Ziplock. They zipped the bag — airtight for freshness, E.G. thought grimly — and wheeled the gurney to the coroner's van, where they transferred it and waited for the next passenger.

E.G. crouched once again, this time behind a tree. He removed his notebook from his pocket and jotted some notes. *Bodies are twenty-five feet apart. Five police cars: two Maplewood, three Essex Sheriff. One ambulance. Officers walking the area, obviously checking for clues? No other activity, such as civilians detained for questioning. Both bodies were taken from the scene naked.*

As he wrote, the emergency medical personnel zipped up the other body and wheeled it on the gurney to the coroner's van. Another outline had been traced, and by now, the coroner was speaking to a plain-clothed man. The emergency medical personnel had gotten into the ambulance and pulled back slowly from between two police cruisers before making its way passed E.G.'s hiding place and down the blacktop path to the exit of the Reservation, where E.G. assumed the three police cars still kept wake.

E.G. made a mental note to call Officer Collins the next day and remind him that he had kept his word, which was that his name would be kept out of the story.

Within minutes of the ambulance leaving, a brown Buick made its way up the same road and passed him. E.G. couldn't see inside because the windows on the car were tinted. It passed him slowly, and E.G. watched as it stopped near the police vehicles. A short, stocky man who looked to be in his 40s got out of the passenger side of the vehicle and lit a cigarette as he made his way to a group of officers huddled under the afternoon sun.

From the driver's side emerged a tall man, early thirties with brown hair and wearing a short-sleeved, white dress shirt with light beige pants and loafers. He was a striking man who, as he walked toward the same group of officers, carried himself with confidence.

E.G. knew how confident the man was. He was an investigator with the Essex County Prosecutor's Office, he was one of the best detectives the office had, and, most importantly, at least to E.G., the man was his cousin.

"Shit," E.G. muttered under his breath when he saw Raymond Vanderhoeven.

Raymond had taken over the scene, moving from one officer to another, asking questions, surveying the location, speaking with the coroner and viewing the outlines that only a few minutes earlier contained the bodies of two naked males in their late twenties to early thirties. Raymond was directing an officer to collect something that was lying on the ground near the outline of the first body. While the officer removed a plastic bag from his pants pocket and knelt, Raymond had backed onto the grass and began combing the area for other clues.

He was good at what he did, E.G. thought. He knew Raymond's investigations had resulted in the office solving at least three tough murder cases in the eight years he had been an investigator with the Prosecutor's Office. He knew Raymond was relentless, almost to the point of obsessive, when he was working on an investigation. That was nothing new for E.G.'s aunt's third son, who was born six months after E.G. When they were 14 years old, he remembered Raymond's bike was stolen from the side of his house, and he spent days conducting his own investigation before, less than a week later, he found the bike and turned over the thief to police. "He's going to be a cop," E.G. remembered his uncle saying when he saw Raymond coasting down the street toward home on his bicycle.

Now, twenty years later and both thirty-three years old, Raymond had conducted hundreds of investigations that resulted in the arrests of as many people during his tenure with the Prosecutor's Office, and before that, with a local police department. His citations and commendations filled a wall in the den of his comfortable home in Livingston. Surrounding them were pictures of Raymond with New Jersey's governor, the state Attorney General, and President George Bush, when the president had come to the city of Newark as the guest of honor at a re-election fund raiser in the early 1990s. E.G. was there that night, having been assigned to cover the event for *The Sentinel*. He remembered how Raymond eased his way through a crowd of Bush supporters while Raymond's wife, Elizabeth, followed with a camera practically glued to her face, hoping for a snapshot of her husband with the president.

E.G. recalled that there was no one more embarrassing at the event than Elizabeth, an obsessive-compulsive who left the dinner table at least six times that night to call home to see if the answering machine would engage. If it did, her logic dictated, the house wasn't on fire and she indeed turned off the gas burners on the stove. E.G.'s date that night, who eventually became his wife who eventually became his ex-wife, Rachel, tried to convince Liz that her unfounded concern was ruining a festive night, but that didn't stop her.

She did manage to get the picture, though, of her husband with the president, but it came at the expense of a Secret Service agent, who made the foolish mistake of standing in Liz's path while the camera was pressed against her face. It took four people to get the agent untangled from Liz's pocketbook strap as they both lay on the floor in front of hundreds of shocked onlookers. As much as E.G. didn't want to laugh that night, he found it hard not to burst at the seams.

Raymond had met Liz a few years after his and E.G.'s relationship deteriorated. That started back in 1985, and, like most teenage boys, it began over a girl.

They were born six months apart, went to the same schools, and shared most of their classes together. The Vanderhoeven house became a second home to E.G., and the Lord house became a friendly port for Raymond, who docked there when E.G. wasn't at the Vanderhoeven's. They were the sons of sisters who raised their seven collective children as one family.

But that year, on Raymond's seventeenth birthday, Danielle came between them. She was a sixteen-year-old girl who had blossomed by fourteen and was introduced to E.G. by Raymond. E.G. had fallen head over heels for her and expressed his feelings to Raymond, who did the noble deed of playing matchmaker. E.G. took Danielle to a movie, showing off in the first car he had just purchased, and kissed her on the mouth when he dropped her off for the night. They had set up their next date before saying good night, a trip to the Jersey Shore during the day and the boardwalk at night.

Bursting with excitement about his first "real" date, E.G. couldn't wait to tell Raymond all about it. So, the following morning after slipping into sweatpants, a T-shirt and a baseball cap, and collecting the gift he purchased for his cousin, E.G. raced to the Vanderhoeven house and drove up the long driveway toward the side of the house. There were no cars in the driveway, but that didn't stop E.G.

He walked to the back of the house and reached into the pot of a hanging plant and removed the key to the back door. He was convinced Raymond was asleep and knew that ringing the doorbell wouldn't be enough to awaken him.

The house was silent, and E.G. swiftly moved through the kitchen and living room, then up the stairs to the second floor. He walked to the far end of the hallway, to the next flight of stairs that would take him to the attic, and as he put his foot on the first step, sounds, muffled voices came from the top floor.

Slowly, he crept up the stairs, the birthday gift hanging from his right hand. There was laughter. It was a girl's voice, and E.G. didn't need to see her to know it was Danielle.

The door to the attic was ajar, and E.G. peeked inside. At first he didn't know what to make of what he saw, probably because it was the last thing he expected to see. But as he stared through the crack in the door, the picture became clearer. Raymond lay on his back on the floor, one leg resting against the carpet, the other bent at the knee. Danielle lay between his legs, her face pressed against his crotch, his fingers tangled in her hair. Raymond moaned. Danielle giggled. And then she took him in her mouth and Raymond gasped.

E.G. stared for a moment, eyes glued, as if he were watching a porno film for the first time. But as reality set in, he slowly backed down the stairs, praying a board in the steps wouldn't creak. He trotted lightly along the carpet on the second floor and took the stairs two at a time to the first floor.

At that moment, he wanted to knock something over, to ring the doorbell, something that would make his presence known and force them to stop, to panic and scurry down the stairs.

But he chose to do none of those things. He decided to walk out of the house as quietly as he had come in, but before doing so, he left the gift on the kitchen table. The card on the package was addressed to "Ray," and it was signed, "Your best bud, E.G."

E.G. never took Danielle to the Shore. In fact, he hadn't called her again, and refused to return the calls Raymond placed to him that afternoon. He must have called twelve times that day and the messages he left with his aunt sounded frantic. E.G. knew Raymond was trying to find out when he had left the gift and imagined his surprise when he and Danielle came downstairs and found it on the table.

E.G. and Raymond had distanced themselves after that day. It had taken a natural course, with E.G.'s disappointment over what his cousin had done to him, and Raymond's guilt over what he had done to his cousin — and getting caught. They were boys still, and they both found it easier to hide how they felt, rather than confront it.

Even their family visits together were strained, and the subject never came up.

Throughout his ten years in the newspaper business, E.G. managed to produce his own wall of honor in his house, and as he recalled Raymond's, he recalled his own. In a room in a finished basement that he turned into an office, E.G.'s wall of honor included more than twenty-five awards from the New Jersey Press Association, Society of Professional Journalists and National Newspaper Association for investigative reporting, breaking news writing, feature writing and public service.

Now Raymond was on a case that E.G. called his own from the moment he got the tip earlier in the day. Could be a blessing in some ways, E.G. thought, thinking it might be easier to get information, off the record or not, from a cousin in the investigator's office rather than calling blindly and trying to get the same information. Could also very well be a curse, he thought, knowing how stubborn Raymond could be.

As he observed the scene before him, E.G. guessed that Raymond was finding several things in the grass he was combing. Raymond would pick up dog shit and try to squeeze a clue out of it. When he saw his cousin disappear into the woods, he turned his attention to the marked police vehicles that began to pull out of the Reservation one after another. Ducking to avoid being seen, E.G. turned the page of his notebook, looked at his watch and began writing more notes: *Police vehicles left scene at 4:15. Investigator in the woods (probably pissing behind a tree somewhere). No arrests made — yet.*

He knew it was time to call Mel, whom he envisioned pacing the newsroom, ready to release the existing front page instead of waiting for E.G.

E.G. removed the cell phone from his shirt pocket and flipped it open when he felt the smack on the back of his head. Startled, he jumped from his spot at the bottom of the tree, dropped the cell phone, and instinctively swung behind him.

CHAPTER THREE

He connected with something that stung E.G.'s hand, and when he opened his eyes and turned, he saw Raymond falling backward over an uprooted tree. Raymond landed on the ground with a thud, and as angry as E.G. was that someone had come up behind him, he nearly fell over with laughter at the sight of his cousin lying on his back in dirt with his legs sticking up over a tree stump.

Controlling himself, E.G. rushed to Raymond and took his hand.

"What the hell did you do that for?" an embarrassed Raymond demanded, trying to maneuver to get up without looking more like a fool than he did.

"You snuck up behind me," E.G. said, still holding Raymond's arm and realizing that by holding his arm, Raymond had a more difficult time getting his bearings. "I didn't know who it was."

E.G. pulled Raymond up so that he could sit on the tree stump. Raymond rubbed the back of his neck, which was covered with dirt and leaves.

"Are you all right?" E.G. asked.

"I'll be fine," Raymond replied rubbing his neck.

"What are you doing over here? I just saw you a few minutes ago disappear into the woods over there?" E.G. said, pointing in the direction he had seen Raymond.

"I was looking for you," Raymond said, brushing the leaves and dirt from his neck and suit.

"For me? How did you know I was here?"

"I saw your car at the foot of the hill when I pulled into the Reservation. I didn't have to be a detective to figure out it was your car. STET on your license plate. And you're not good at hiding, either. I spotted you as I drove up the path."

STET was a copy-editing term, meaning "Let it stand," and he had ordered the personalized plates about three years earlier.

E.G. searched for the cell phone and found it near an empty beer can. He flipped it open and dialed. Margaret's voice on the other end of the line seemed drained. It was, after all, near the end of the day. She put him on hold and within seconds, Mel came to the phone.

"It's about time you called me. I have a gaping block of white space at the top of the front page waiting for a story from you. Is there going to be one? Where are you? What time are you coming back? I need to get this paper ready for the press."

"Mel, please," E.G. responded, brushing dirt from areas of Raymond's sport coat that Raymond missed. "I've got a story, one of the best you've seen in a long time." He shot a glance at his cousin, then glared at him as he continued to speak. "And it'll be an exclusive. The dailies won't have it tomorrow because no one from the law enforcement community is going to be talking to the press tonight."

E.G. went silent for a moment, still looking at his cousin as he listened to Mel on the other end of the phone. Finally, he said, "I'll be back to the office in twenty minutes." He flipped the phone closed and returned it to its spot in his shirt pocket.

"Am I correct, Ray? Nobody's gonna be talking to the newspapers tonight?"

"I don't plan to issue any statements to the press until tomorrow afternoon. And that includes you, E.G., so don't start asking me questions about this mess."

"Can you just tell me what kind of weapon was used?"

Raymond stood and shot a resigned glance at his cousin, but said nothing.

"Oh, come on, Ray. It's one question. The cop down the hill said it was a gun. A 38. How many bullet wounds did you find on each body?"

Raymond reacted to the question. "There were no bullet wounds," he said before realizing he was being set up.

"Then it wasn't a gun?" E.G. asked.

"E.G., what are you doing up here? Who let you up here? Or should I even ask?"

"Actually, no one gave me any information. I'm just going to report what I've seen so far unless, of course, you can tell me what kind of weapon was used. I'd hate to report erroneous information. It could make you look bad in the end."

Raymond started to walk toward the clearing. "I'm going to ask you to leave now. You're interfering in a police investigation, and I won't tolerate that — even from you."

"Interfering? I was minding my own business. As I recall, you were the one who approached me and struck me in the head." E.G. grabbed the side of his head as he followed his cousin into the clearing and onto blacktop. Grimacing, he held the back of his head. "I would hate to see a lawsuit."

"Stop fucking with me," Raymond screamed into E.G.'s face, and it attracted the attention of the remaining officers who stood approximately one hundred feet away from them. Raymond raised a hand in their direction, seeing that they had begun to approach him.

"Listen, Ray. I've got five minutes before I have to leave here to get back to the office and put together a story about this. After tomorrow, my paper doesn't come out for another week. You're going to announce tomorrow, I would expect, what happened up here, and included in that announcement is going to be the weapon used in the murder. Why can't you just tell me that today and let me get an edge on the daily newspapers? I won't say you told me."

Raymond knew E.G. wouldn't give up. He knew that five minutes would turn into ten minutes, and in those extra five minutes, he would ask more questions, diverting his attention, yet gaining more information that he shouldn't have. "All I can say is that it was a blunt object to the head."

E.G. opened his notebook. *Blunt object to the head,* he wrote. "On both victims?"

"Both victims."

E.G. continued writing. "When will an autopsy be conducted?"

"I told you, E.G. One question. You've already got answers to two questions. Don't you have to put a newspaper out tonight?"

E.G. closed his notebook. "Between you and me, you have no clue who did this, do you?"

"I've been here less than an hour. Even Sherlock Holmes couldn't figure it out in that amount of time."

E.G. winked at his cousin. "That's three answers."

Anger reddened Raymond's face, and E.G. held up his hands. "I'm leaving," he said, as he began to back away and walk down the blacktop path toward the Reservation exit. "But I'm sure I'll be talking to you tomorrow."

E.G. turned, and as he walked down the path, he knew Raymond was watching him. He felt it. He knew that if he turned back around, he would see Raymond glaring at him, probably muttering under his breath. But he didn't turn. Instead, he opened his notebook, reviewed his notes, and began writing the story he would, a few minutes later, enter into the computer for Mel to read and publish the following morning — exclusively.

He imagined the expressions on the faces of the reporters who worked for the daily newspaper in the area when they discovered that he had a story they didn't have. Exclusives always made his job more fulfilling.

As he neared the bottom of the path, he noticed the three police cars still laying in wait near the entrance to the Reservation. Before ducking into the woods to get to his car without being seen, he noticed that although there were still three cars, they were a different set of vehicles. They didn't belong to the Essex County Sheriff's Department, but instead to the local police department. E.G. chose not to use the detour through the woods.

He continued walking along the blacktop road, recognizing at least two of the officers leaning against the hood of one of the cars. E.G. waved to the officers, and the two he recognized waved back, almost as if they expected him to be at the scene.

It wasn't until he got behind the wheel of his Tercel and pulled to the exit of the parking lot that the same familiar thought fluttered into his head: one family's tragedy becomes a journalist's Milk Bone. And each time that happened, he had to remind himself that this was a job, a combination of fact finding and storytelling told to record history.

And that reminded him how much fun he had doing it.

CHAPTER FOUR

"Two found dead in Reservation" read the headline in *The Sentinel* the following morning.

"Police found the bodies of two men in the South Mountain Reservation yesterday in an area frequented by men who engage in gay sex," began the story. "The men, found unclothed and lying approximately 25 feet apart from one another on the cusp of Crest Drive, both died from wounds to the head after being hit with a blunt object, according to police sources."

As he read the newspaper at his desk, E.G. felt a pair of strong hands rest on his shoulders and begin to massage them. "Great story, E.G.," the voice said. E.G. didn't have to look up to see who it was, not even when the shoulder rub began.

"Thanks, man," E.G. replied, lowering his head and inviting Conor Headley to rip the knots from below his neck. "I can't believe the timing of it."

"Talk about a fast ball down the middle," Conor said. "One might believe you went up there and killed those two guys just in time for deadline and a great scoop on the dailies."

"Do I detect jealousy?" E.G. asked as he pointed to an area just below the shoulder. Conor pinpointed the area and, with both thumbs, massaged the sore muscle.

"Yeah, I'm jealous that I wasn't one of the bodies they found up there," Conor said sarcastically. "Don't you know by now, E.G., that my dearest wish is to have you write my obituary, and I couldn't think of a better way to have gone. I can see the lead," he said, looking up at the ceiling while raising his arms. "Conor Headley, star reporter for *The Sentinel*, was found bludgeoned to death this week in the South Mountain Reservation. Blah, blah, blah. Police said they found a note in Headley's wallet that read, 'If I'm found dead, please donate my organs to the National Organ and Tissue Association and be sure E.G. Lord is assigned to the story.' Just be sure you find out who did it. I'd hate to be featured on 'Unsolved Murders,' or whatever the hell that show is called that I never watch."

Conor had been with *The Sentinel* for a little more than six years and covered the Essex County court beat, a position to which he ascended three years earlier. It was a move the ownership of the newspaper never regretted making, especially after the first year, when Conor brought home six awards from the New Jersey Press Association. It wasn't necessarily the topics that won him the honors, since most of them were dry, but more so how he wrote the articles that he generated from the halls of the Essex County Courthouse. Conor was an offbeat kind of writer who put so much detail into trial stories that he turned some of the most boring hearings into soap opera material. He would give more prominence to a witness' body language and eye movements than to their testimony, and, to give the story more appeal, would pour over writing the reactions of as many onlookers in the chambers as he could remember.

It was a little less than two years earlier that he began to change his writing style, after he came to the realization that news writing was, plain and simple, extremely boring. The reader needed additional elements to offset the tedious reporting of facts to be coaxed into finishing an article. That was called flavor. Within months of the change, he developed a following that was unprecedented for a weekly newspaper. Despite what some readers called the theatrics of the report, none of them could say Conor was less than objective in his coverage. He reported what he saw, albeit in non-traditional journalistic form, and he did what he was supposed to: let the reader draw the conclusion.

Conor was twenty-nine years old, having joined *The Sentinel* fresh out of college as a stringer. Stringers weren't considered staff members — more like the people a newspaper called upon when a town meeting needed to be covered and none of the full-timers were available to handle the assignment. Town meetings were the bread and butter of *The Sentinel*, since the daily newspapers consciously ignored them, and Conor showed that sometimes even the barest agenda provided the most substance. Within two months of joining the newspaper as a stringer, he developed a list of sources any veteran would envy, and was given his own beat, one that landed him in a cubicle next to E.G. Lord in the paper's South Orange office.

Conor and E.G. had a great deal in common, and it didn't take long for them to discover the favorite pastime they shared. It came in pitchers, sat on a table between them in the bar and became the catalyst for many heated debates. They loved their beer, and most nights of the week, especially Wednesdays when the paper was put to bed for the week, they'd think nothing of sharing five pitchers between them.

Most of the patrons at The Brew, a local tavern in South Orange where they migrated after work, knew E.G., and through him, came to know Conor. They were inseparable, and The Brew became their court. From politicians to civic leaders to just about anyone who had a story to tell or a complaint to lodge, they dropped into The Brew and dropped their dime. Sometimes it was with E.G., other times with Conor, who connivingly timed the order of the next pitcher of beer with the impending departure of one of their visitors. "Do you have enough for another one?" E.G. would ask Conor innocently, peeking into his wallet. It was a subtle hint, but it was usually enough for the guest to call the waitress to the table and proclaim, "I'll get the next one," while fishing for the cost of the pitcher in his own wallet.

So if they shared five pitchers between them, it wasn't unusual that they were only paying for three. They loved journalism as much they loved their beer, and it was no surprise to anyone that they had become such good friends so quickly.

Conor had sandy brown hair that always looked as if he had just rolled out of bed, matted on the sides and back, and unintentionally spiked on top. A few freckles dotted his cheeks, and he stood about an inch shorter than E.G.'s six feet. He took E.G.'s copy of *The Sentinel* from his desk and looked at the story again. "Seriously, damn good job. How did you get the tip?"

E.G. remained silent.

"I see," Conor said.

E.G. swiveled in his seat. "There's a press conference today at 2. The prosecutor's office is going to announce what I basically had in my story, and I don't think they'll be telling us anything new. I took a ride up to the Reservation this morning, and they still have it blocked off from the public."

"That didn't stop you yesterday from getting in. Did you get inside today?"

"I think the cops were waiting for me. I didn't get halfway into the parking lot before all eight of them lifted their rifles and pointed them at me."

Conor glanced down at E.G.

"I'm kidding," he said. "They may as well have done that, though, because they didn't even let me get near the place. It was probably my cousin's doing. He was pissed that I had written so much about something I was supposed to have no information about."

"Who's that? Ray?" Conor asked.

"Yeah. He called me this morning at home, and I'm not exaggerating when I tell you I could have left the phone on the table, got into the shower and still heard him screaming."

"Screaming about what?"

E.G. began to mock his cousin. " 'You're gonna fuck up my investigation. I didn't want any of this information released until I could do it formally.' "

"What did you say?"

"I asked him if I could quote what he had just said." E.G. shrugged. "I can't give a shit about what he wants. This is news. People have a right to know what's going on in their back yards."

"You're preaching to the choir, man," Conor said as he rolled up the newspaper and swatted E.G. on the shoulder with it. "Don't let him get you down." He handed him the newspaper.

"Oh, he's not getting me down. I live for this."

"I know you do. Think how pissed he'd get if you did some investigating of your own and found out who offed those guys before he did."

E.G. smiled coyly at Conor. But before Conor even finished his sentence, he knew the wheels had already been turning inside E.G.'s head. Cousin or not, E.G. always was happiest when his stories contained leads that even the police didn't think to check.

"What are you working on today?" E.G. asked Conor.

"I'm heading to the court house," Conor said as E.G. turned to his computer and flipped the power switch. "Typical stuff today. Cases of criminal burglary. Nothing major. Oh, and I also have this wonderful feature story Mel assigned me for this week." He pulled a sheet of paper from his shirt pocket. "What does this sound like?" he asked as he began reading. "These are the symptoms: sudden weakness or numbness of the face, arm or leg in one side of the body; sudden dimness or loss of vision, particularly in one eye; loss of speech, or trouble talking or understanding speech; sudden severe headache with no apparent cause and unexplained dizziness, unsteadiness or sudden falls."

After a moment, E.G. said, "Sounds like our staff on deadline night."

"Yeah, I thought that too," Conor agreed and laughed. "I have to write about this new program for stroke victims at one of the hospitals we cover. I'm not particularly happy about it, but I'll survive. Hey, listen, maybe I'll catch you at the press conference. It's at the courthouse, right?"

"Yeah," E.G. said, signing on to the Internet. "2 p.m. Let's say we catch a beer afterward."

"You got it." Conor slipped out of E.G.'s cubicle and disappeared.

The familiar "Mail call" tone sounded as E.G.'s computer connected to his ISP. It took about 40 minutes before he reached his last piece of e-mail and, having responded to *The Sentinel* reader who inquired how she could contact a particular council person in the town of Irvington, E.G. closed the mailbox, turned and reached for his coffee.

No sooner did he have the cup to his lips that the "Mail call" tone drew his attention back to the screen.

Clicking on his mailbox, the screen opened. One piece of mail beckoned him, and was from a person called "Dirtdealer," a name unfamiliar to him. The subject line read, "The murders." He clicked on the entry. The message was one line long: "Call Travis Boesgaard from West Orange and ask how he's doing." West Orange was the next town from where the paper's office was located.

E.G. creased his brow and read the message again. Who was Dirtdealer, he thought, and why was he passing him this information? He moved his mouse to the member list and searched for Dirtdealer. There was a match, but all it told him was that Dirtdealer was a male, 25 years old and single. He was also online and on a live board.

E.G. had a choice. He could join Dirtdealer on that board, he could initiate a conversation with him online, or he could ignore it. He didn't want to ignore it, but he also didn't want Dirtdealer to know he took the bait and followed him onto the board.

E.G. had two accounts with his ISP, the most known being eglord2541. His other name, one he used when he didn't want to be disturbed by anyone while he was online, was Stetson165. Neither account revealed any identification about the reporter.

As Stetson165, E.G. followed the same path to the live board and joined Dirtdealer.

There was a list of names on the board, his at the top, but no one was posting. He scanned the list until he found what he was looking for. Dirtdealer was still on the board, nestled between two other strangely crafted names. The name of the board was Murders in New Jersey.

EG waited. For about three minutes, no one on the board said a word. Finally, conversation began:

Musicat62:   "Boy, this room is dead this morning."

No one instantly responded to Musicat62's statement. About two minutes later, another person spoke.

Dirtdealer: "Yeah, about as dead as those two guys they found in the woods yesterday."

E.G. took note of Dirtdealer's statement. He wondered if the e-mail about Travis had anything to do with the incident in the Reservation. He kept his eyes glued to the screen, although he could see new members appearing above him as other members, their owners obviously not interested with the dead board, moved on.

The chat continued:

Musicat62:   "What two guys? What woods?"

Dirtdealer: "The newspaper said this morning that two guys were found in the Reservation up in Maplewood. Both were killed with a blunt object.

E.G. got a kick out of knowing that at least one person had read his article that morning and was already referring to it. It had to have been his article because he knew no other newspaper carried the story that day.

Musicat62:   "Were they gay?"

Dirtdealer: "Don't know. Police haven't said anything about the situation yet. According to the newspaper article, both guys were naked. It's gonna be a while before guys can go to the Reservation because of all of this."

Dpthrote90:   "Hey, guys, what's going on? Anyone want to meet now? I've got the place if you've got the time."

Apparently, no one had the time to meet this deep-throated individual, E.G. guessed, because none of the people in the room responded to his invitation. In fact, no one was talking, even about the two bodies found in the Reservation.

While E.G. waited, he checked outside his cubicle to be sure no one was hovering. No one else knew Stetson165.

E.G. returned his attention to the board, where more conversation had taken place.

25Traveler: What's the Reservation?

Dirtdealer: One of the best cruising spots in the state.

Musicat62:   Some of my fondest memories come out of the Reservation.

GPI534:   Just think, Music, I may have given you at least one of those memories.

Dpthrote90:   Anyone want to meet now? I've got the place if you've got the time.

Damn, E.G. thought, Dpthrote90 must be desperate. He noticed that the conversation had shifted from the two dead bodies to less-than-stimulating conversation about adventures in the Reservation and wondered if he should join in and put it back on the track on which Dirtdealer had directed it. Funny, he thought. Dirtdealer was being quiet. And it was he who started the topic only minutes after he e-mailed E.G. to inquire about Travis. E.G. wondered if Dirtdealer was thinking that Stetson165 was, in this form of camouflage, E.G. Lord, reporter for *The Sentinel* who broke the story about the two dead bodies in the Reservation. But he convinced himself quickly that there could be no way Dirtdealer knew.

The conversation continued.

Musicat62:   We were talking about the two guys who were found dead in the Reservation. It's scary.

Dpthrote90:   When did that happen? I didn't hear about that.

Musicat62:   Yesterday. Two guys.

Dirtdealer: Have their identities been revealed? Are they from the area?

The e-mail he had received from Dirtdealer couldn't be tied to the Reservation incident, E.G. thought, because if it did, why would he ask if the two men were from the area? Something told him not to draw premature conclusions. Just as Dirtdealer was lowering the bait for him, he also may be lowering the bait for the guys on the live board.

"E.G!"

The voice behind him sent him into a panic. E.G. stood, his back to the computer monitor to prevent anyone from seeing what he was doing, and glared into the eyes of his editor.

"Mel, you scared the shit out of me," E.G. said, backing Mel out of the cubicle and into the newsroom. "How long have you been standing there?"

Mel chuckled at the sight of E.G. jumping. "Not long," he said with a grin. "Just wanted to tell you I thought your story was pretty damned good for a forty-five minute turnover."

E.G. tensed. Mel was complimenting him. He waited for the lightning to brighten the sky and pierce him in his heart. Mel never complimented anyone. In fact, in all his years with the paper, Mel never had a kind word for anybody. The primary feedback Mel offered was that his reporters were late with their stories. And that was only because Mel couldn't handle pressure. E.G. had never met anyone like him: The editor of a newspaper that served more than one hundred thousand readers and he couldn't handle pressure.

E.G. knew that to be in the business of deadlines, which is the foundation of any newspaper, one had to be an extremely organized individual. To be the top guy, even more so did organization play a major role. But Mel went to the extreme. E.G. recalled the time Mel had issued a directive that all stories for a given week's paper had to be filed by Monday afternoon, even though the newspaper published on Thursday. It took a while for the staff to convince their editor that the paper was missing some good, timely stories for the week based on their new schedule, but Mel eventually did rescind the order. And ever since, he hovered over any reporter like a fly over an open box of cake at a picnic if they wrote their stories on Tuesday. He did the same with the Advertising Department, whose responsibility was to deliver pages to Mel by the end of the day each Monday. By three o'clock, he paced between the Advertising Department and the newsroom, sometimes clearing his throat to send a message and sometimes standing under the clock that hung above the door to the photography room to get their attention. But he never came right out and asked for the pages.

There came a time when everyone became so used to Mel's presence at the end of the day on Monday that they stopped looking up and continued with their work. That didn't stop Mel, though. Suddenly he began helping get the pages ready for composition, and when that started, Advertising made sure they were completed by 3 p.m.

If one thing didn't bother Mel, another did. He was responsible for twenty reporters and four editors, and on any given day, he would find something wrong with the way at least one of them was doing his or her job.

"He's going to snap one day," E.G. had told Conor a few years earlier. "And it's not going to be a pretty sight."

No, Mel hadn't snapped yet, but it was something everyone in the office awaited. He stood about five feet seven inches tall and maintained a thin physique. For a man in his sixties, Mel managed to get around the newsroom as if he was thirty years younger, but the newsroom was really the only place he ventured. He no longer wrote his own stories and, at least for the past ten years, had gradually clung to the confines of his desk.

"I appreciate the comments," E.G. replied to the praise Mel had bestowed upon him. "I've got a few ideas that I'd like to go over with you at some point tomorrow after I go to today's press conference and hear what they've got to say. Obviously, throughout the week, there may be other developments."

Mel removed the cigarette that rested above his left ear and a lighter from his shirt pocket. "I have a meeting at 8:30 a.m., a conference call at 11, then lunch at 12. How about 10?"

Conor waved to E.G. as he passed Mel. That surprised E.G. because he thought Conor had left a while earlier.

"Ten is good," E.G. replied, thinking how typical it was of Mel to give every detail of his day before narrowing down a time to meet instead of just telling him the time he was free.

As Mel headed toward the front exit of the building to smoke his cigarette, E.G. slipped back into his cubicle and returned to the live board.

More conversation had taken place in his absence, and most of it was about the murders in the South Mountain Reservation. E.G. scrolled up and picked up where he had left off when Mel had come into the cubicle.

Musicat62:   Paper said they didn't have the identities yet.

Dpthrote90:   How did they die?

Musicat62:   Paper said blunt object to the head.

Musicat62:   They really didn't have many details. Apparently, police found them late and the paper had an exclusive on it. I guess more details will come tomorrow.

25Traveler: Haven't been to the Reservation, but I know for sure I'm not going there today.

Musicat62:   Stop making jokes, 25. This is serious.

GPI534:   Guess 25 couldn't handle it. He left the board.

E.G. looked among the list on the live board. Not only did 25Traveler disappear, so did Dirtdealer, who must have signed off while Mel was talking to his ace reporter.

"Who are you, Dirtdealer, and what kind of dirt are you trying to feed me?" E.G. asked aloud.

With Dirtdealer out of the room, E.G. felt safe to start talking.

Stetson165:   Did the police close the Reservation, or can anyone still go up there?

Musicat62:   I drove by this morning. Police have it blocked off.

Stetson165:   For good reason. They need to search for clues.

Musicat62:   Doubt they'll find them. It's a big place up there.

Stetson165:   Do you think the guys were killed there or were they just dumped there?

GPI534:   Why so curious, Stet?

Stetson165:   Didn't think I was any more curious than you guys.

Musicat62:   What's the difference? I mean, if they were killed there or just dumped there?

Stetson165:   If they were dumped there, it would have nothing to do with cruising. We'd be safe to keep going there.

E.G. couldn't believe he was including himself among those who cruised the Reservation for sex. But he knew that to get information, any information, he needed to gain their trust.

Musicat62:   I guess you have a point, Stet.

GPI534:   Too bad 25 left the room. He could have taken comfort in your theory.

Musicat62:   You come in asking a lot of questions, Stet.

Stetson165:   Just as curious and concerned as you guys.

Musicat62:   You a regular up there, Stet?

Stetson165:   Not at all.

Musicat62:   Cool.

Suddenly, a new box, an invitation from Musicat62, appeared on E.G.'s monitor. E.G. accepted.

Musicat62:   You sound pretty cool. And intelligent. Don't get that much on these boards.

Stetson165:   Thanks. You sounded very concerned about what happened in the Reservation. Any particular reason?

Musicat62:   Could have been me, if I was there at the wrong time. Would be very embarrassing to be identified in the newspapers as one of the dead guys in the Reservation, especially when no one knows I'm bi.

Stetson165:   How often do you go to the Reservation?

Musicat62:   About twice a week. I was there two nights ago.

Stetson165:   The night of the murders?

Musicat62:   Yup.

Stetson165:   Did you see anything?

E.G. waited for a response. None came. He viewed the board, and while conversation had continued among the remainder of the men on the board, Musicat62 had not been participating. While he waited, E.G. added Musicat62 to his contact list.

Stetson165:   Are you still there? Did you see anything?

Finally, Musicat62 answered.

Musicat62:   Why are you so curious?

Stetson165:   Because if you know something, I'd be interested in knowing too.

Musicat62:   Why? Are you a cop?

Stetson165:   No, I'm not a cop. If I had information about this, wouldn't you be interested in knowing it?

Musicat62:   I guess. But I don't even know you.

Stetson165:   One of the joys, I guess, of these boards. We can both remain anonymous to one another and get to know each other better than if we lived next door.

Musicat62:   That's funny.

Stetson165:   What's funny?

Musicat62:   What you said is so true. I'm more open with people I talk to on these boards than I am when I'm face to face with people.

Stetson165:   It's the security of anonymity. Why can't you just tell me what you know?

Musicat62:   How do you know I know something?

Stetson165:   Call it instinct. You've been hedging. You wouldn't be this evasive if you were in the Reservation and hadn't seen anything. It would be easier for you to say you saw nothing.

Musicat62:   I guess you're right. You're a smart guy. What's your name?

E.G. slapped the monitor in frustration. "Tell me what you know, jerk off," he yelled at his computer. But he continued to play along, even providing a fake name, choosing the first name of a journalist he emulated, Barry Farrell.

Stetson165:   The name's Barry.

Musicat62:   Matt here.

Stetson165:   Nice to meet you, Matt. By the way, Matt, do you realize you're driving me crazy over here?

Musicat62:   Sorry, man. Don't mean to be doing that. I guess it's just difficult.

Stetson165:   What is?

Musicat62:   Telling anyone what I saw.

Stetson165:   So you did see something?

Musicat62:   Yeah.

Stetson165:   Have you thought of calling the newspaper? You said you saw the story there.

Musicat62:   No. Wouldn't want to do that. It's too risky.

Stetson165:   Then tell me. I swear I won't tell anyone about it. You can trust me.

Musicat62:   I don't even know u.

Stetson165:   You've told me this much already. Why not continue?

Another box and another invite to talk privately appeared on the monitor. This time it was from Dpthrote90. E.G. accepted.

Dpthrote90:   U like the hats or the cologne?

Stetson165:   Huh?

Dpthrote90:   Ur name. Is it after the hat or the cologne?

Stetson165:   Neither.

Dpthrote90:   Whatever. Sounds real masculine.

E.G. laughed at the computer. In his thirty-three years, he had never had this kind of conversation. While he waited for Musicat62 to respond, E.G. decided to play along with his new friend.

Stetson165:   What kind of experience do you have?

Dpthrote90:   Not much. But I have this special kind of curiosity about enemas.

Stetson165:   Are you kidding me? Of all the guys I've chatted with, I've never heard anyone say that.

Dpthrote90:   I have...I look on the boards and I see topics that rub me the wrong way. Beastiality, for example. For some reason, it's some kind of taboo thing.

Stetson165:   What is it about enemas that makes you curious? You'd get turned on by giving one to someone, or getting one?

Dpthrote90:   I don't know why it turns me on. But that's my secret fantasy.

Stetson165:   Hey, role playing can be a good thing.

Dpthrote90:   Do u have any secrets like mine?

Stetson165:   No. Nothing like that.

Dpthrote90:   Ever try it...ever get one?

Stetson165:   Never had an enema. Have you?

Dpthrote90:   No...given a few, though.

Stetson165:   You mean to fulfill a sexual fantasy?

Dpthrote90:   Yup.

Stetson165:   Wow. What do you do for a living?

Dpthrote90:   Attorney. U?

Stetson165:   Retail. Hey, listen, the phone's ringing. Gotta go.

Dpthrote90:   Keep my name handy. I'm George, and I'm always curious and available.

Stetson165:   Will do. Barry here. Talk soon.

E.G. still had not received a response from Musicat62. Even the office outside his cubicle seemed to be miles away and in another world. No sign of Mel lingering. Hell, for all E.G. knew, the phones could have been ringing off the hook the whole time he spent chatting with Musicat62 and Dpthrote90.

E.G. glanced at his watch. Shit, he thought. Time was closing in on the press conference. He knew it would be time to go soon, and as much as he wanted to rush Musicat62 to an answer, he felt it would be better if he gave the man some time. E.G. clicked himself out of the board, asked Musicat62 if he was still there, then leaned back on his chair and folded his hands behind his head.

Finally, there was an answer.

Musicat62:   I saw the car.

E.G. leaned forward and typed.

Stetson165:   Whose car?

Musicat62:   It was very dark. After 10. I never go up there that late. Honestly. My girlfriend was out with friends. I was horny. Actually, I was surprised to find anyone up there that late. I mean, have you ever seen how dark that place gets?

Stetson165:   No. Never been there that late.

Musicat62:   Met a guy and went for a walk. Didn't go too far into the woods. I let him do oral, and when he finished, he walked out ahead of me back to his car. Kind of stupid, don't you think? It's pitch dark, and I want to make sure no one sees me walking out of the woods with this guy.

Stetson165:   And what happened?

Musicat62:   By the time he got to his car and left, I saw another car coming around the circle down the road. I figured I'd hang back in the woods and wait for it to head out of the Reservation before I left, but the damned thing stopped not one hundred feet from where I stood.

Stetson165:   Jeez. You must have been shitting in your pants.

Musicat62:   I thought it was the cops. Figured I was busted.

Stetson165:   What happened?

Musicat62:   Guy got out of the right back door and started pulling another guy out. He was already naked. And crying like a son of a bitch. Begging for his life. When he got out of the car, he broke away from the guy holding him and started to run, but the driver got out of the car and chased him down. Hit him across the back of the head with what looked like a hammer. Fucking guy dropped like a sack of potatoes.

E.G. hung back and let Musicat62 continue. He wasn't about to interrupt him now. He glanced at his watch. He had some time, but not much.

Musicat62:   The driver hit him again, like three more times, before he just stood over him and waited, as if he was waiting for some sign of movement so that he could knock out whatever bit of life remained in him.

Musicat62:   In the meantime, the first guy who got out of the car comes around to the other side and pulls out a second guy from the back seat. This guy was already dead. You could tell from the way he was being pulled out. Did you ever watch a kid pick up one of those Raggedy Ann kind of dolls? It was just like that. No life. Dumped the bodies. The two guys got back into the car and took off.

E.G. waited for something more, but nothing came.

Stetson165:   What did you do then?

Musicat62:   You mean after I vomited up against the tree?

Stetson165:   Sorry to hear that, man. I don't envy you.

Musicat62:   I waited another few minutes before coming out. All I kept thinking was that car was going to back around the circle and catch my ass there, and I would have been found lying there with my head bashed in too.

Stetson165:   Did the car come back?

Musicat62:   Not while I was there. I checked the two guys, and I was right. Both were dead.

Stetson165:   So they were dumped there? It wasn't like they had sex there and were both murdered in the Reservation.

Musicat62:   No, they were murdered there. I know that because when I first got there, I walked around the park, and I saw the same car on the other side of the circle. The car had to have been there for about   twenty-five minutes before they dumped those bodies.

Stetson165:   You get the make of the car? A license plate?

Musicat62:   Black TransAm. Got a partial plate number.

Stetson165:   What did you get?

Musicat62:   Would rather not say. I said too much already.

Stetson165:   And I appreciate what you've told me. Tells me you trust me.

Musicat62:   I'm not so sure about that. When you're online, you reveal some of your most intimate thoughts without even realizing it. But I do feel better for getting some of it off my chest.

Stetson165:   Did you call the police?

Musicat62:   Yeah, but I waited until about noon the next day. I don't know. I was too scared. Kept thinking that if I called them sooner, they'd find me somehow and think I was responsible.

Stetson165:   You mean this happened on Tuesday night, and the police didn't find out about it until after you called them that late the next morning? Nobody saw the bodies lying there?

Musicat62:   If you knew where they were lying, you'd understand why no one saw them. If you were cruising the park, you wouldn't have seen them in the grass. And that's not an area where guys would go for sex during the day. Even though it's a bit hidden, it's too close to the road.

Stetson165:   Did you tell the police what you saw?

Musicat62:   No. Called them from a payphone, told them about the bodies, then hung up. Felt I gave them enough information.

E.G. wanted to know so much more from Musicat62, but he had to leave for the press conference. He told Musicat62 that he was at work, which was true, and that he had to go to a meeting, which was also true, but he told him that if he didn't sign off now, his boss would have his head, which was not true.

Musicat62 understood, or so he said, and thanked E.G. for listening. Before signing off, E.G. said he would be back online at six o'clock that evening, and wondered if Musicat62 would be available to talk then. He'd like to hear more. Musicat62 told E.G. he'd try, but if he wasn't online, then he could find him online at around eleven o'clock that night, most likely on the same board.

E.G. dragged the cursor across the entire text in the private message box and copied and saved it to another program.

E.G. signed off, collected a couple notebooks from his desk, took a copy of that morning's *Sentinel,* tucked it under his arm and left for the press conference, wondering how much his cousin had learned in the almost twenty-four hours since he had seen him. He was certain it was nothing compared to what E.G. had just learned, and left the building smiling, thinking he was a step ahead of the police in the investigation into the murders in the Reservation.

CHAPTER FIVE

E.G. took the long way into Newark. Any way into Newark, New Jersey, was the long way because no matter which route one took, he would face traffic, double parking, kids in the streets and traffic lights whose cycles lasted only long enough for about four cars to move through an intersection.

He glanced at his watch and panicked. He was ten minutes away from the building in which the team from the county prosecutor's office would be conducting a press conference in five. He said a silent prayer that Conor would already be there, able to fill him in on the details he was sure he was going to miss. Would it start on time, E.G. wondered. Of course it would, he told himself. Once his cousin saw he wasn't in the room, Raymond would purposely — no, spitefully — ensure the conference would begin on time and end early.

As his car slipped through the Orange Avenue intersection, the street opened to two lanes and E.G. maneuvered into the left lane and toward the jury parking lot, where he knew he could park despite not being a juror that day. As he headed into the lot and saw the familiar face of Juan Estevez, E.G. remembered the words Musicat62 told him. "...but the other guy caught him and hit him across the back of the head with what looked like a hammer. Fucking guy dropped like a sack of potatoes."

"Can I park here, Juan?" E.G. asked. "I'm late for a press conference."

Two minutes late, to be exact. Juan escorted E.G. through the wooden ticket gate and indicated an empty parking space toward the back of the lot.

Connections, E.G. thought as he pulled into the space. He could buy them for as much as a sausage and pepper sandwich from a vendor outside the courthouse, which he made a mental note to buy for Juan on his way out.

E.G. raced through the front door, pausing to remove keys and any other metal objects that had to be personally escorted through the metal detector, and climbed the stairwell to the fourth floor, believing he'd get there faster than if he took the elevator.

When he burst through the doors that would bring him into the fourth floor corridor, the last person E.G. thought he would run into was Raymond. And run into him he did.

Papers floated around Raymond's head and onto the floor where he sat after being struck by the swinging doors. Raymond looked up and saw his cousin standing over him. Second time in two days, Raymond thought. E.G. bent down and gathered some of the papers around his cousin.

"I'm really sorry, Ray," E.G. said. "I thought you'd have already started the press conference, and I was late."

"Leave everything alone, E.G.," Raymond snapped. "I can pick it up myself."

A crowd began to gather, one woman leaning over to help Raymond to his feet. E.G. was struck by the cleavage she exposed and had the urge to push Raymond back down, just to get a longer glimpse of the woman's breasts.

"I'll help him," E.G. said, reaching down and grabbing Raymond's arm.

"I'm not helpless," Raymond said, brushing off E.G. and the woman. He collected the spilled papers and got to his feet — by himself — before shooting a menacing glance in E.G.'s direction and heading into the conference room.

"Hi, I'm E.G. Lord," he said to the woman whose breasts had him standing in the hallway with a semi-erection.

The woman ignored E.G. and pressed into the conference room behind a small group of staff from the prosecutor's office. E.G.

watched her enter the room, realizing that from behind, she looked just as good as she did from the front.

Inside the room, television cameras lined the back walls, while microphones identifying networks and call letters sat in a cluster on a podium toward the front of the rather expansive conference room. Big stuff, E.G. thought. A large oak table was pushed to one side of the room and, in its place in the center of the room, were three rows of chairs, taken by the local press corps and national broadcast stations.

E.G. slipped to the back of the room, taking notice of the people from the media. He felt a sudden jealousy creep inside him, knowing that most of these reporters would be able to file their stories and release them to the public in a matter of minutes. Those except for the daily newspapers, of course, which would have to wait another fifteen hours, but that was better than seven days, the first opportunity he had to publish his next story.

The jealous feeling waned, though, as quickly as it had surfaced, because as he looked more closely at the reporters in the room, he knew none of them could possibly have the information he had just received within the past two hours. E.G. had no respect for any of the reporters in the room, as a matter of fact. He had read their articles, had seen their broadcasts. As far as TV reporters were concerned, E.G. couldn't even call them reporters. He was sharing a room with people who wanted glamour, and that's how they portrayed the news today. News was not glamorous, he knew. It meant getting your feet and hands dirty, something that cannot be done when you have a make-up artist following you around half the day.

As far as the daily newspaper reporters in the room were concerned, E.G. knew they only surfaced when something major was to be reported. Otherwise, they could be found sitting at their comfortable desks in their comfortable news rooms, with their archives and tear sheets all filed nicely because they had the people, time and resources to do it. At a weekly, the editor or reporter usually did the filing themselves.

So he stood in the back of the room, as he always did when he covered an event or town meeting. You get a better perspective, he had been known to tell new reporters, because you get to see everything that occurs except the fly that's shitting on the wall behind you.

Raymond approached the microphone, and the room grew still. His hair was combed neatly and he wore the small-frame glasses he needed for distance. The cream-colored short-sleeve shirt he wore showed rings of sweat under his armpits, but E.G. knew it was a result of the weather and not anxiety about the press conference.

"As many of you may be aware," he began after identifying himself as the lead investigator in the case, "the prosecutor's office is investigating a double homicide in the South Mountain Reservation in the town of Maplewood. The unclothed bodies of two men were found yesterday afternoon, and, we believe, based on a preliminary examination by the county medical examiner, that the cause of death to both men was as a result of a blunt object to their head. Until results of the autopsies are released, we can't be sure of the exact time of death, but preliminary reports indicate that the men may have been dead for at least nine hours before their bodies were found."

As E.G. took notes, he couldn't help but feel a certain pride for his cousin — his professionalism and how tall he stood in front of a group of people while cameras flashed around him. Raymond had to be aware of the television cameras capturing his every word, his every gesture, yet he was smooth. He commanded this office as if he were sitting at the head of his dinner table discussing a routine day's events with his wife and children.

"At the moment," he continued, "we have no suspects, but we have collected many items during our search of the Reservation that may be useful in assisting this agency in its investigation. The results of the autopsies are expected to be completed by Monday, at which time this office will have more information for the public."

As E.G. expected, nothing new came from the press conference, but he knew that Raymond, if he had pertinent information, would not reveal it this early in the investigation.

A reporter from a daily newspaper raised her hand and asked, "We know that this part of the Reservation is an area frequented by men for gay sex. Is there any connection between that and these murders?"

Fair question, E.G. thought. But it was way too obvious. He wondered if the reporter stayed up half the night thinking of it. Or, at the very least, saw his story in the paper that day. But if she had, she would have known that E.G. answered that question.

"At this time, we have no connection, although we are exploring that avenue," Raymond said, acknowledging another reporter with a hand in the air.

This time, the reporter stood. From the bag near her chair that was covered with the DHM radio call letters, E.G. didn't have to guess which news organization she represented. "Who discovered the bodies? How did the police learn of this double homicide?" she asked.

E.G. was impressed, and even raised an eyebrow as a salute to this obviously well-thought question.

Raymond responded. "Police received an anonymous phone call late Wednesday morning from an unidentified male," he said, and, anticipating the obvious follow-up question, added, "We are investigating that phone call."

E.G. wanted to shout to the room that he knew where the call came from, that he knew more information about the murders than anyone in the room. But he couldn't, and he grew restless. He wanted to be back online chatting with Musicat62 and learning more about what he had seen.

As another reporter began to ask a question, E.G.'s eyes were drawn to the door, where he saw Conor enter and search for him. Conor, slipping a notebook into the back pocket of his pants, moved to the back of the room and stood in an empty spot to E.G.'s right.

He whispered into E.G.'s ear. "How goes it?"

"I got an invitation today to have an enema performed on me. But other than that, things are going well."

Conor's brow creased.

"I'll tell you about it later."

"Can't wait," Conor said. "How's it going here?"

"It's bullshit. Nothing new," E.G. whispered back. "At least they're not saying anything new."

"I had a bullshit day myself," Conor said. "Court sucked."

"Usually when you say that, you write stories that get the most feedback."

"That's because people are fucked up. Murder stories, there's no feedback. Burglary stories involving 14-year-olds knock a community on its ass. I'll never be able to figure it out."

As they talked, reporters had been asking questions of Raymond, but Raymond cautiously hid behind the protection order that allowed him to withhold information if it meant releasing anything he deemed to be news that could harm his investigation.

The next question set E.G. on his heels.

A reporter from a daily newspaper, his competition, stood and asked, "We noticed that *The Sentinel* carried a story this morning that included very specific details about this case. Is there any connection between that story and the fact that you and the reporter are cousins?"

E.G. rolled his eyes and leaned into Conor as several of the reporters turned to look at E.G. He whispered, "If the National Enquirer was here, their story would be that my cousin and I are in an incestuous love affair."

Conor elbowed E.G. and laughed.

"There is no connection between the news report in *The Sentinel* and the fact that the reporter and I are cousins," Raymond said.

"Then how did the reporter obtain all this information?" the same reporter asked.

E.G. shook his head in disbelief at the question. Once again, he leaned into Conor. "'Cause I'm good," he said sarcastically, not realizing he had said it loud enough for many in the room to hear. The laughter that followed embarrassed the daily reporter enough that he took his seat, not expecting Raymond to answer.

But Raymond did. "In the state of New Jersey, the governor's Executive Order mandates that law enforcement officials release certain information to the public within 24 hours after a crime or an arrest. This press conference is in accordance with that order. And I have no intention, or even desire, to answer on behalf of the reporter."

"I think the reporter just did," came a voice E.G. couldn't identify. The statement, though, was greeted with more laughter.

Raymond stepped away from the podium. Half listening to Conor and half listening to Raymond during the press conference, E.G. learned that clothing had not been found, identification for the two men had not turned up anywhere in their search of the Reservation, and no one had come forward reporting a missing person.

His thoughts returned to Musicat62. He held some of the pieces to the puzzle, and E.G. wanted to find them before Musicat62 broke down and went to the police voluntarily.

"You want to have a beer tonight?" Conor asked as the press corps began filing out of the conference room.

It was Thursday. E.G. and Conor hadn't missed a Thursday night at the bar for as long as he could remember, but tonight would be different. It had to be different. He had a story that needed investigating. And as much as he wanted to trust Conor with the information he had received earlier in the day, E.G. felt he couldn't. This one, he knew, he had to do on his own.

"I'm going to take a rain check, guy."

Conor expressed surprise.

"I know. I know. But there's something I have to do tonight."

"Want to fill me in?" Conor asked.

"Sorry, but I can't."

"Something to do with this case?"

"Yeah. Kind of. I hope you understand."

"Yeah, sure," Conor said. "I can go dry for three consecutive nights." He laughed. "I understand."

Funny thing was, Conor understood more than E.G. realized.

CHAPTER SIX

7 p.m.

E.G. paced the floor in his cubicle, frequently sending an invite to Musicat62 for a private talk to find out if he was online. The invites were rejected, indicating he was not online. The office was quiet that night, his shoes against the floor the only sound in the building, other than the Yankees clock ticking on the wall in Mel's office.

As he paced, he thought about the phone call he made earlier in the evening regarding Travis Boesgaard. Apparently, Travis was alive and well, according to a contact E.G. had called upon from the West Orange Police Department. He didn't reveal why he was inquiring about Travis, nor did the contact ask. That was just the way it worked.

He thought about going back to the Reservation. Hell, he had about ninety minutes before the sun would go down. He remembered the old police theory that criminals always go back to the scene of the crime. Maybe he would see the black TransAm that Musicat62 said he saw the night of the murder. He dismissed the thought, knowing the police would still have the area cordoned off from the public, and it would be the last place the criminals would go. And going there now, even if it just meant confirming that the police were still there, he knew he could miss talking to Musicat62, who may sign on while E.G. was gone.

So he waited.

E.G. crossed the empty newsroom and slipped through the Advertising Department on his way to the kitchen, where he brewed a pot of coffee. He knew he'd be alone that night. By Thursday night each week, the day the newspaper was published, most of the editors and reporters were coming off their high from the grueling deadline days of Monday, Tuesday and Wednesday. Tuesday was the most grueling of the three, when reporters sometimes worked sixteen-hour days, including E.G. But it was something he had grown accustomed to many years earlier. He had even remarked that a month earlier, when he had taken vacation during the third week of July, he had seen baseball's All-Star game live on television for the first time in ten years.

As the coffee dripped into the pot, he returned to his cubicle and again offered the private invite to Musicat62. Of his two new "friends," both were offline. Before returning to the kitchen, he turned on the radio that sat on a shelf he installed just above his computer monitor. Marvin Gaye's "Sexual Healing" was the latest fare from the oldies station to which he was tuned. The seventies, he thought, and they're calling them oldies, as he went to fill his coffee mug.

He set the mug on the table to the left of the keyboard, next to the picture of his daughter, and his heart raced as he checked the member list and found Dirtdealer had signed on.

E.G. signed off, and re-signed on under eglord2541. Within seconds of signing on and hearing the familiar "Mail Call" tone, E.G. added Dirtdealer to his contact list, and at the same time added Musicat62, but when he completed the action, he checked the list again and noticed Dirtdealer had signed off.

"Damn," E.G. said aloud while closing the extra windows on his monitor. He clicked his mailbox and saw that among the mail he had received, one was waiting for him from Dirtdealer.

He opened the mail and read the contents. Again, similar to the first piece of mail, this contained a one-line message. "Is Travis still shaking?"

E.G. creased his eyebrow. He clicked REPLY, and a new box appeared on his monitor. He began typing: "Dear Dirtdealer. I appreciate the e-mails you have been sending me. Obviously, you're trying to lead me somewhere for some reason that only you know. Can you at least tell me where this road is leading, or give me some hint as to the nature of the search? I love a good puzzle, but I need certain pieces to be able to complete it. Thanks for your help."

E.G. sent the e-mail to Dirtdealer, then changed accounts and returned to Stetson165. He sent an e-mail to Musicat62. "Dear Matt. It's about 7:30 p.m., and I've been waiting to talk to you. I was hoping to find you online, but, alas, you haven't shown up. I will sign back on at 11 p.m., as you indicated earlier that that is when you expected to be on. If you're on earlier and do not hear from me, please wait. I'm sure to arrive. Thanks. Barry."

E.G. felt embarrassed signing his name as Barry, but he wasn't prepared to reveal himself to Musicat62 just yet. E.G. signed off, downed the cup of coffee that sat near his terminal and went into the kitchen to pour himself another, this time using the thermal travel cup. He turned off the pot and left the building, heading west in his car toward the South Mountain Reservation.

CHAPTER SEVEN

Six miles to the east, Raymond stood alone in his office, nursing a half-cold cup of coffee while staring out the window at the evening sky and the streets below. Martin Luther King Jr. Boulevard. Broad Street. Springfield Avenue. They were as busy at 7:30 at night with vehicles and pedestrians as they were at any time during the day. And just as hot, he imagined, feeling the air conditioning blowing from the vents over his head. He hated the heat, had very little tolerance for it, and instinctively, wiped what he thought was a bead of sweat from his temple. His shirt, the same cream-colored shirt he wore at the press conference, remained tucked in his pants. He tried to push up the sleeves further than they were, but the defined bicep prevented them from going any higher up his arm. With hardly a soul in the building, he still found it necessary to keep his tie fastened around his neck.

He turned back to his desk and surveyed the notes that sat atop it. There was much written on the sheets of paper, but none of it was leading anywhere. The phone call came from a phone booth in South Orange near Seton Hall University, and surveillance using unmarked police cars and off-duty police officers was in place. Raymond was hoping that the man who had made the phone call alerting police to the two dead bodies would call again – and, if they were lucky, use the same phone booth. So far, he hadn't even called again.

He picked up a sheet of paper with a name on it. By now, the woman whose name was scribbled on that paper was in the morgue a few blocks away to confirm whether or not the son she had reported missing was one of the men lying on a cold slab in the county morgue with a ticket attached to the end of a cold, lifeless toe. "Wait until the press gets wind of this," Raymond said aloud, dropping the paper back onto the desk, hoping, for her sake, that it would not be her son. But he also hoped, for his own sake, that it would be, and he would have his first true lead in the case.

It was less than an hour after the press conference that Raymond received a phone call from the South Orange Police Department alerting him to a woman in town reporting her son missing. The description of her son matched the description of one of the men in the county morgue. The son's friend, a very close friend, from what the woman told police, hadn't returned the calls she had placed to his house since early Wednesday morning.

CHAPTER EIGHT

Anytime Nathanya Berns entered a room, heads turned. If you didn't know her, your head turned because of her beauty. If you did know her, your head turned because you wanted to be the first to kiss her ass. She was a tall woman, always impeccably dressed, and she moved through a room so lightly and briskly that one would think she moved on a conveyor belt. An owner of several pieces of prime real estate in South Orange, Nathanya was arguably the wealthiest woman in the village, her home, which sat on five acres of land at the top of the mountain, a testament to the power she held.

Nathanya served for more than a decade on the village's governing body in the 1970s and 1980s. Politics to Nathanya was like a fine wine. Once you tasted it, rolled it around your palate for a while, and savored it, you wanted more. In addition to the taste, there was the buzz. And there was nothing greater than the buzz. Politics intoxicated her. Even when she returned to her role as a private citizen, she remained active behind the scenes. Acting behind the scenes meant throwing as much money around to as many people as possible to win an election. She had businesses in her pocket as well as senior groups, the theater crowd and most of the university personnel who lived in town. It was safe to say Nathanya controlled South Orange.

But the voting public did not see that side of her. They saw her charitable work, whether it was donating candy and toys to children during the annual holiday celebrations, or opening the courtyard of one of her buildings each year for the summer concert series on the lawn, where free refreshments were served courtesy of Nathanya Berns. It made her a pillar of the community, and when it came time to publicly support a candidate, most people in town remembered her selections and answered her call, not once stopping to think that she could be playing them as pawns in her political games.

Nathanya Berns always walked with her head held high.

Even on that hot summer night, the night after her son did not return home and repeated calls to his friend's house went unanswered, Nathanya Berns entered the county morgue in Newark with her head held high, her white suit neatly tailored, and the smell of her perfume drifting into the humid air.

A plain-clothed investigator from the prosecutor's office escorted her into the room, one, she thought quickly, looked exactly as she had seen hundreds of times in the movies. It was a cold room, and she wasn't sure if the air conditioning made it that way, or if its sterile appearance made her shiver. Along the far wall were rows and columns of drawers, each looking like its own icebox. They were the color of steel, and she could see her blurred reflection in each one. In front of one of those drawers stood a short, balding man wearing a three-quarter length white lab coat.

Nathanya got halfway into the room before she stopped and noticed that as she got closer to the far wall, the number of reflections decreased. She said nothing; simply looked in the direction of the man standing in front of her. The man looked beyond Nathanya and at the investigator, who, with a simple nod of the head, cued the man to open the drawer he seemed to be guarding.

The man pulled the drawer, and instantly exposed the soles of two feet. He covered the feet with the white sheet that was crumpled around it, and pulled further until the drawer was fully opened. Nathanya stepped forward, closer to where she knew the face of her son would be. And yes, it would be her son, she thought. She had seen those feet for the last 30 years and recognized how the third toe on each foot extended well beyond the others around it.

She leaned closer as the coroner lifted the sheet from the body. She couldn't tell if the lab-coat wearing man had been excessively slow, or if time was playing a trick on her, because everything seemed to move in slow motion. First, the brown hair, much like her own when she was younger, and then the face, the boyish looks he had had all his life suddenly wiped away with death.

Nathanya closed her eyes and leaned against the drawer. Her head dropped, and a hand moved to her temple. She stood for a few moments as if she were the only person in the room, and as she drifted into a world of her own and separated herself from the lab technician and the investigator, she recalled the day she gave birth to Mickey, the day she sent him to school for the first time. A host of memories flooded back, and as much as she tried to contain herself, she began to sob, quietly at first. As the sounds became louder, the investigator stepped toward her and put a hand around her waist.

Nathanya jumped, forgetting she had been in this room, wanting to return to the safe world where she had just been, a world where her son was alive, young, and with his future ahead of him.

"I'm sorry," she said, trying to regain her composure. Although upset, her voice maintained control.

Beside her, the man in the white lab coat opened the drawer next to the one in which Mickey Berns lay and revealed the body of another man, who looked a few years older than her son.

"That's Steven Conroy," Nathanya said in the same controlled voice, slowly shaking her head. "What were they doing up there?" she asked herself aloud, referring to the Reservation. She looked back at Mickey and almost fell against the drawer.

The investigator was quick to respond. He again held her at the waist. "Why don't you have a seat back here?" he suggested.

"No," Nathanya said firmly and shook herself free from his clutch. She stood erect. "This is my son. I have arrangements to make."

CHAPTER NINE

E.G.'s trip to the Reservation was futile. He drove up the hill to the entrance of the park, and, upon making a left turn into the parking lot, was greeted by cement barricades guarding the entrance to the path. Next to the cement stood a uniformed officer reading a book.

E.G. pulled into a parking space at the edge of the Reservation and got out of his car. The officer rested the book on the hood of his patrol car, open to the page he was reading, and approached E.G. E.G. flashed his press pass, but it didn't impress the officer.

"You know I can't say anything," the officer said curtly. "All information has to come from the prosecutor's office. And no one, not even the press, can get by here."

E.G. wouldn't go away.

"Can you just tell me if any police are up there now?" he asked, pointing to the road into the Reservation that was blocked two days before by Officer Shawn Collins. "It's only out of curiosity."

The officer stood firmly, but did not say anything.

"I get the hint," E.G. said. He took a few steps to the right and looked beyond the officer. Then, he decided to change his tone, putting the reporter persona away and acting like a regular citizen. "Amazing what happened up there, huh? Nothing like that should happen to anyone."

He waited for a response from the officer, but did not get one. "How about those Yankees?"

E.G. kept his eyes on the officer, hoping to get a reaction, and he did. The officer, after seeing the expression on E.G.'s face, chuckled sourly and shook his head.

"Come on. Give a guy credit for trying," E.G. said.

"You people are all alike," the officer said, but not angrily.

"Who? The Irish? The English?" E.G. asked, smiling.

"Reporters. Do you even care about the people who were killed in this park? Or is everything just information, information and more information? Those guys have families, you know. And it seems to me when stuff like this happens, you guys in the press don't seem to care about that. All you want is your story."

The last thing E.G. expected that night was to find himself in a philosophical and moral discussion with a police officer about news reporting.

"That's not true," E.G. defended. "You and I are after the same thing — finding the person who did this. The only difference is I get to publish what I learn."

"And when did you become a cop?" the officer asked, his tone becoming defensive.

"And when did you become an analyst for the news business? I'll agree that there are reporters in this business who have no concern for the subjects they write about, nor do their publishers care. To them, it's the bottom line that matters. I'm here to gather information about a crime that took place so that, through my stories, I can alert the public to whatever information becomes available, either through law enforcement officials, or from my own investigating. Wouldn't your wife, or your kids, or your brother want to know what happened up here and if there's any information about the person who did this? Knowing that, they can be more careful if they're out alone and they come across the wacko."

The officer wouldn't back down. "That's a holier-than-thou attitude that reporters have," he said. "Leave the police work to the police. If anything new comes up, we'll let the papers know."

E.G. began to respond, but decided against it. It wasn't worth it, he told himself, to debate the merits of good journalism with this officer. Instead, it made him more determined to learn more about the case – and report it as fairly and objectively as possible.

"It's obvious we're getting nowhere," E.G. told the officer. He headed back to his car and pulled out of the Reservation into the evening traffic.

His first goal, he told himself, would be to meet Musicat62 - even if it meant staying up all night waiting for him to get on the Internet.

CHAPTER TEN

"We've confirmed the identity of the two men."

Raymond kept the phone to his ear and listened as the investigator who accompanied Nathanya Berns to the morgue confirmed that the woman identified one of the men as her son, Mickey, and the other as Mickey's friend, Steven Conroy.

"Shit," Raymond said, not completely understanding his reaction, but fully knowing that once the media heard the name, life would become a circus for Nathanya Berns as well as the law enforcement community. The press hovered for a few days before going away, he knew, but he didn't expect that to happen in this case. Not when Nathanya Berns was involved.

"Where is she now?" Raymond asked.

"We had someone take her home."

Raymond's watch read 8:15 p.m. "At least we can hold off until tomorrow before alerting the press. That gives me an opportunity to visit Ms. Berns."

Raymond returned the phone to its cradle, paused for a moment, then pressed a programmed button on his telephone. After two rings, his wife answered. "I'm on my way home," he said into the mouthpiece. "What a long day. And they're only going to get longer."

CHAPTER ELEVEN

E.G. lifted the lid from his Dunkin' Donuts cup and sipped, rather than gulped, the coffee. The store was the only stop he made on his way back to the office from the Reservation. As he expected, the newsroom was empty, and he was pleased.

He slipped into his cubicle, turned on the computer, and listened for whether or not Stetson165 had mail. He did, and it was from Musicat62.

"Dear Barry," it began. "I signed on to check e-mail and found yours. You sure do have an interest in this case, one I can't completely understand. Are you involved somehow? If so, please be up front with me." That was the end of the e-mail. No indication of whether or not Musicat62 would be online later that night, or if he even wanted to discuss the case further.

E.G. wondered if he should be up front with Musicat62 as his new friend had indicated in the e-mail. But he was afraid that if Musicat62 learned he was talking to a reporter, he could shut down completely, change his name so there would be no way to locate him, unless, of course, E.G. befriended someone from his ISP, like he did at the phone company, and could find out who registered the name. Or he could just refuse to respond to his requests for information.

While he thought about how to respond to Musicat62, E.G. signed off, then signed on as eglord2541. He found another piece of e-mail from Dirtdealer, and when he opened it, he read the one-line passage: "Travis most likely will be at the funeral."

"Keep throwing the dirt, jerk off," E.G. yelled at his computer.

"Who's throwing dirt?"

The voice behind him took him so by surprise that E.G. jumped and spilled most of the coffee onto his desk, and it had begun dripping to the floor.

"Sorry about that," Conor said, taking the cup from E.G. and handing him a fresh cup. "I thought you would have heard me come in. I saw your car in the lot, and the lights were on. I thought you'd be here, so I stopped by Dunkin' Donuts. Good thing I did, huh?"

E.G. scrambled to turn the monitor off so Conor could not see what was on the screen, then fished for the tissues he kept on a shelf to wipe the desk. "Get me some paper towels, will you?" E.G. barked.

Conor left the cubicle, and returned a few seconds later with a roll of towels. He tore off a long piece, handed the roll to E.G., who was moving papers out of the way of the trail of coffee that began to run like a river across his desk, and wiped the floor.

"I'm really sorry, man," Conor said again, not knowing if E.G. heard him the first time.

"It's all right," E.G. said. "I'm just a little edgy."

"Obviously. What the hell are you involved in here? You've been so mysterious ever since your story came out." Conor stood and placed his wet and dirty towel into E.G.'s trash basket.

"Not there!" E.G. barked again. "You'll have the whole damn place smelling!"

Conor took the wet paper towels from E.G.'s hand and threw them into the trash basket, freeing E.G. to remove some more from the roll. Conor disappeared, and returned with an empty basket, just in time to accept more wet towels from E.G.

"You've got leads?" Conor asked, trying to return to the subject.

"Yeah, but they're playing with my head," E.G. responded.

"I'm not sure what that means."

"It means I'm being led somewhere, and I'm not so sure I have the patience to be teased this way."

"You want to let me in on it?"

"No," E.G. shook his head. "Not yet. Part of me is excited about how this guy is feeding me information. Yet, another part of me feels like a dog that pulls on its leash to reach that scent of another dog's urine near a tree. You know? He can smell it for ten yards, and he can't wait to get to it, but he's struggling because his master keeps pulling on the leash?"

"Oh yeah, I know exactly how you feel," Conor quipped. "Happens to me every time I pass a ladies room and I know I can't go in there." Conor flashed a strange look on his face that E.G. caught as he glanced over at him. They both laughed, but it didn't do much good for the frustration E.G. was feeling. That frustration was mounting, and he knew his ego and desire to get the story had a lot to do with it.

E.G. stopped wiping. "Did you ever want something so bad you can taste it?" he asked, putting the last of the wet paper towels into the basket Conor still held. He didn't wait for Conor to answer. "Well, I want to be able to publish a story telling exactly what happened up there in the Reservation, who the guys were, and who did it to them and why - all before the police find out."

Before Conor disappeared again to empty the trash basket, he said, "I have no doubt that you can do that. Convince yourself of that, and we can have a Pulitzer Prize adorning this office next year."

"I'm that good?" E.G. asked.

"You're better."

It was no surprise to E.G. when Conor peppered him with the confidence he needed. It was a habit of theirs to praise one another at least once a week, even though within that praise sometimes came criticism. Constructive criticism, the kind that made their interviewing skills sharper and their writing more clear and crisp. E.G. and Conor made a good team in the newsroom, but as E.G. patted his friend and confidante on the shoulder for the comment, he told himself that this story was going to be a solo venture.

Without having to be told, Conor said good night. His footsteps echoed throughout the empty newsroom, stopped near the front door, and then he was gone.

.

E.G. turned back to his computer, flipped the switch on the monitor and sat back in his chair, knowing that while his wait for Matt might take all night, he was prepared to keep the fires burning.

CHAPTER TWELVE

For the life of him, E.G. couldn't figure out where the ringing noise was coming from. He looked under a table in a room he had never seen, and not seeing anything there, he checked behind the refrigerator that stood in a corner of the room. Nothing there, so he looked on the floor of the car. Still nothing.

Suddenly, the ringing noise came closer, and just when he thought he discovered its origin, he awakened and sat upright in bed. The telephone on the night table rang once more, and E.G. reached over and lifted the receiver out of its cradle.

"Yeah."

Mel's voice on the other end was coarse. "I knew it. I knew I'd catch you sleeping off a bender. Is Conor somewhere on the floor too, or is he lying out in your yard because he couldn't make the stairs?"

E.G. knew it was best, most of the time, to ignore Mel and move on with a conversation. "What can I do for you, Mel?"

"The prosecutor's office is holding another press conference this morning at 11, and I'm wondering if you could grace it with our presence. Or should I call the copy boy in for the assignment? At least he's here."

Sarcasm, E.G. thought. Mel always resorted to sarcasm. "What time is it now?" As E.G. asked the question, he looked on his dresser at the clock, which sat next to a framed picture of his daughter. He squinted and read 10:02. "Oh, shit." With the phone still resting on his shoulder, E.G. jumped out of bed and removed clothes from his dresser drawers. "Did they say why they're holding the press conference?"

"Yes, they thought you did a wonderful article yesterday, and they want to throw a surprise party for you. Only now, oops, it won't be a surprise."

"Mel, dammit, did they say what it's for?"

"Of course they didn't. You know by now how these agencies operate. They beckon you, and you come."

"I'm showering and heading straight to Newark," E.G. said.

"And will you be taking a siesta when the conference is done, or will you be coming into the office?"

E.G. thought twice about responding, knowing if he opened his mouth, he'd be fired. So he did the next best thing. He hung up the phone, but not before he heard Mel start to say something about Conor.

Twenty minutes later, his hair still wet and a green button-down shirt draped over the waist of his pants, E.G. slipped into a pair of moccasins, grabbed a reporters notebook from a stack of notebooks on the food cart in the kitchen, and left the house.

In another twenty minutes, ten minutes before the press conference was to start, he was knocking on Raymond's door at the prosecutor's office. A brown-haired woman in her fifties glanced up from her computer and, seeing the blond-haired man through the window, reached under her desk and pressed a button that automatically unlocked the door.

"Is Raymond here? I didn't see him in the conference room." E.G. said.

"You're his cousin, aren't you? The reporter," she said politely.

"Yes. I was hoping to see him before the press conference begins."

The woman stood and moved to the door behind her. She knocked, put her ear against the door, waited a few seconds, opened the door, then closed it behind her. Less than a minute later, she emerged, with Raymond in tow.

"What's up, E.G.?" he said as if he didn't feel like making the time for him.

"Do you have a minute?"

"Just about." Raymond moved from the middle of the open door and motioned E.G. to go inside. He closed the door behind him when they were inside.

"No special favors," Raymond said when they were in private. "You'll find out why we've called this press conference when every other media person finds out."

"If I wanted to know that, I wouldn't wait ten minutes before the press conference to ask." E.G. leaned against Raymond's desk. "I've been getting some leads, and I..."

Raymond cut him off before he could say more. "This is my investigation, E.G. You're going to tell me you've got leads, and all you're going to do is recount everything you've done since Wednesday, but somehow, all you're really going to be doing is fish for information. I know your style. I fell for that once a long time ago, and I'm not going to fall for it again."

"Raymond, all I'm trying to do is get your professional advice on something."

"I've got a press conference to conduct in less than five minutes," he said, looking at his watch. "Talk to me when it's over."

Raymond picked up a folder from his desk and started for the door, but when he realized he would be leaving E.G. alone in his office, he stopped, held the door, and motioned for E.G. to leave first. E.G. walked passed him, looked him in the eye, and grinned. He didn't say a word, but continued out of the outer office and into the hallway.

Raymond didn't like E.G.'s smile. He knew it only too well, and he wondered if he should have allowed his cousin to tell him what he knew.

E.G. moved slowly down the hall, allowing Raymond to move swiftly passed him and into the conference room, the room that was growing more familiar to E.G. as the days passed. Inside, media outlets again filled the room, and E.G. recognized most from the day before, even the reporter from the daily newspaper who was convinced that being Raymond's cousin got him the exclusive. E.G.

glared at the reporter as he moved to the back of the room. The reporter maintained a dumb look on his face as E.G. passed him.

Raymond took his place at the head of the room and began to address the media. "We have identified the bodies of the two men found in the Reservation Wednesday afternoon. Their names are Michael Berns and Steven Conroy. Mr. Berns resides in South Orange, while Mr. Conroy resides in Montville. As I said yesterday, both men died from wounds inflicted to the head. At this point, we do not know why they were in the Reservation."

"Will you speculate?" The question came from a TV news reporter.

"We don't speculate in this business, nor should you in your business," Raymond said dryly.

Cheap shot, E.G. thought as he scribbled in his notebook. He watched the faces of the other reporters when Raymond announced Michael Berns as one of the men who died. Not one of them recognized the name, but E.G. knew Michael was the son of Nathanya Berns. He mouthed the words "holy shit" when Raymond mentioned the name because E.G. knew Nathanya, had interviewed her for many stories during the last ten years at *The Sentinel* and knew how powerful a figure she was in South Orange. E.G. refrained from asking anything about Nathanya, hoping the reporters in the room wouldn't discover the connection, and he'd have first dibs on Mrs. Berns.

They asked questions about the men's occupations, their ages, whether or not the police had learned anymore about the case, and if arrests were planned, but they didn't ask about Nathanya. The press conference ended by 11:30 a.m., and Raymond disappeared before any of the media could get to him.

E.G. remained until all the news representatives left, then went to Raymond's office. His secretary buzzed the door open again for him, and when E.G. entered, she said, "Your cousin is not in. He had to run out."

"And from which door did he leave?" E.G. asked, knowing he had not seen Raymond depart from what he knew was the only exit into the hallway.

"The same door you're standing in," she said in the same tone E.G. used. "He dropped his folder on my desk and said he had to leave."

E.G. believed the woman, especially after seeing Raymond's file sitting half on the desk and half off. The secretary, noticing it the same way, collected the folder and placed it on a table to her right.

"Tell him I stopped back after the press conference to finish our conversation. He knows where to find me."

By the time E.G. got to the office, it was after noon, and most of the staff was either out to lunch or on assignment. Conor and Kasie, a reporter who began working at *The Sentinel* about a year earlier, were engrossed in the stories they were writing. Conor came out of his cubicle when he saw E.G. pass, and followed him.

"I need coffee. Desperately," E.G. said, carrying the Dunkin' Donuts cup, the 20-ounce size, and leading Conor to the kitchen. They passed through the Advertising Department, where a sales representative was speaking, in E.G.'s opinion, too loudly to a potential client on the telephone. "How does he get sales?" E.G. asked Conor, not expecting a response. "That would turn me off if I had to listen to that."

"You're grumpy today. Did you go to the press conference?" Conor asked as they turned the corner and entered the kitchen.

"Bad morning. I haven't even had coffee yet," E.G. said. "They identified the bodies. Check this out. One of them is the son of Nathanya Berns."

"No shit." Conor also knew Nathanya Berns. "Wow," he said. "She wasn't there, was she? At the press conference?"

"No, and I'm thrilled she wasn't," E.G. said, removing the gallon of milk from the refrigerator and placing it on the counter. "I don't think anyone in that room made the connection, or if they even cared at that moment, but once they find out, I'm going to feel bad for the illustrious Mrs. Berns. The fuckin' press can be hawks."

E.G. poured his coffee, accentuating it with a decent amount of milk and the slightest touch of sugar. "I wonder if she's home right now. I'd like to see her."

"It's not too soon? I mean, she just learned her kid was murdered. I'm sure she knows by now if they announced it."

"You think I can worry about that?"

"Yeah, the fuckin' press can be hawks," Conor said.

"I'd bet there are press crews on her front lawn as we speak," E.G. said, feeling the need to justify his desire to be on the front lawn with them - assuming they had made the connection.

E.G. again led the way back to the newsroom where, once there, he set his coffee on his desk and flipped on his computer. "I'm so tired," he said.

"How late did you stay last night after I left?" Conor asked.

E.G. looked at Conor, but did not say anything.

"That late, huh?"

E.G. paused before answering. "I was here until 3:15. By the time I got home and into bed, it was after 4. When Mel called this morning to tell me about the press conference, I had no idea where I was, what day it was. All I wanted to do was bury my face deeper into the pillow and sleep for another five hours."

"Why were you here so late?" Conor asked. "Come on, E.G. You've never held anything back from me in all the years I've known you."

E.G. waited a moment before answering. He knew he could trust Conor, and he also knew that what he was about to tell him wouldn't jeopardize his investigation. "I was online and on boards all night."

"Why?" Conor had an odd look on his face.

"I got some tips about the Berns story. I was supposed to talk to someone at eleven o'clock, and he never showed up. So I waited. And then I waited, and I waited. Before I knew it, I found myself on these boards and talking to guys I had never met before. Do you know what occurs on those boards?" E.G. didn't wait for Conor to answer. He moved some papers on his desk so he had room to sit and continued. "I'm sitting at my terminal searching boards, and all of a sudden I get this invitation to privately talk. The guy asked how big I am. And if I'm cut or uncut. You know, circumcised or not. What the hell is that?"

Conor laughed. "Did you tell him?"

"At first, I was, like, what do you want to know that for? No guy has ever asked me those questions. And here I am at two o'clock in the morning revealing information about my privates."

Conor laughed again.

"It's not funny," E.G. said. "Do you know that these guys spend almost the entire night on these boards? Some of them were there at ten-thirty when I went onto the boards, and they were still there at two-thirty, three a.m."

"With you," Conor was quick to say.

"Hey, I was there for a reason," E.G. said defensively. "I wound up getting into two arguments."

"With whom?"

"I don't know who they are," E.G. said. "They were pissed because I was on the board not saying anything. And then when I said I wasn't interested in meeting anyone, they were telling me I needed to search within myself to find out why I was here, and how they could help me." E.G. took a sip of coffee. He started talking faster. "Yeah, help me. Right. Another guy asked if I'd be interested in having phone sex with him. And married men. You wouldn't believe how many married men are on these boards looking to hook-up with another guy. It's unbelievable."

"Sounds like you were on some bizarre boards," Conor said. "How does all of this have to do with the murders in the Reservation?"

E.G. didn't want to reveal anymore, but once he got started, he felt the excitement creep up on him. And he was talking to Conor, he justified. "On Wednesday night, I got to talking with someone on a board who gave me a couple leads. I've talked to him since then, and I thought I would get to see him online last night. At least, I thought we had a tentative date, so to speak."

"Does this person know the Berns kid?" Conor asked.

E.G. shrugged his shoulders. "I have no idea. Talking to him is like pulling teeth. He's really afraid." E.G. wouldn't reveal any more details, such as Musicat62 being in the Reservation and witnessing at least one of the murders. He trusted Conor, but wanted to keep his promise to Musicat62. E.G. protected his sources. He also declined to tell Conor about Dirtdealer and the e-mail messages his other "friend" was leaving for him.

He realized that he hadn't been online at all that day, what with waking up late and running to the press conference without even eating breakfast. "Is Mel out to lunch?" he asked.

"I guess," Conor replied. "I saw him for about five minutes this morning. I got in kind of late myself today."

"I know. Mel thought you were with me after a bender last night." E.G. emphasized the word bender, a word he knew was a favorite of Mel. "I have to get some work done." It was E.G.'s way of sending Conor back to his cubicle so he could get online. And it worked. Conor excused himself, telling E.G. he had a story to file, and within seconds, E.G. was alone in his cubicle with his e-mail window maximized and staring him in the face.

He signed into Stetson165, hoping he had received an e-mail from Musicat62, or, better yet, to find him online. He would sign into eglord2541 afterward, he told himself, to see if Dirtdealer had also tried to communicate with him.

Musicat62 was offline, and there was no mail from him. E.G. found himself growing concerned for Matt, a man he had never met, but who potentially held some keys to solving a double murder. He wondered if Matt talked, and if his identity had been discovered. He imagined Matt meeting with the killers under false pretenses and being hit upside the head as well, left to die in a place similar to the Reservation. He wondered if Matt had gone to the police and told them what he saw. He wondered where the hell Matt was, and why it appeared he hadn't been online in almost eighteen hours.

E.G. signed off, then returned as eglord2541. Among his mail was a piece from Dirtdealer, so he clicked on that first, eager to find out what Dirtdealer was revealing this time.

Dirtdealer did not address the e-mail E.G. had sent to him after his last one. Again, there was only a one-line passage: "Travis is so upset."

E.G.'s mind raced. So many thoughts moved in and out: Could Dirtdealer's real name be Travis, and was he somehow trying to reveal to E.G. that he, Travis, was involved in the murders? Was Travis one of the men in the Reservation that night, one of the men who put the hammer to Mickey Berns' skull? Was this a friend of Travis who knew what had happened that night? If so, how did Travis know?

E.G. knew it didn't take a ten-year veteran of the newspaper business to realize he had to find Travis. He removed a reporters notebook from a drawer in his desk and opened to the page where he had been writing Dirtdealer's passages. He added the latest, and they read: "Call Travis Boesgaard from West Orange and ask how he's doing." "Is Travis still shaking?" "Travis will most likely be at the funeral." And, "Travis is so upset."

E.G. made a mental note to check the obituary columns in the newspapers the following day to get details of the services for Mickey Berns and Steven Conroy.

He returned to Stetson165 and prepared another e-mail to Musicat62. "Matt," he wrote, "I hope everything is all right with you. I haven't communicated with you online in a while. Please send me an e-mail telling me you're OK." E.G. began to type his own name, but realized that to Matt, he was Barry.

As he signed off, he called out to Conor, who entered E.G.'s cubicle within seconds.

"What's up?" he asked.

E.G. grabbed his sunglasses, a folder, his cup of coffee, and a notebook from the desk and said, "If Mel is looking for me, tell him I'm on assignment."

Before Conor could ask where he was going, E.G. was out the front door.

He pulled out of the parking lot and entered the traffic heading west on South Orange Avenue, the same direction as the Reservation. Cars crawled through the center of town along the single-lane road. Just beyond the train station, where the street opened to two lanes, he darted into the left lane and up the hill. If only the stupid people of the world slept in, E.G. thought, three-quarters of these cars wouldn't even be on the road. At the top of the hill, he approached the entrance to the Reservation. E.G. glanced to his left and noticed the concrete barricades still in place with two police officers standing near them, but he did not stop.

Instead, he continued to the next traffic light and made a right turn onto Glenview Road.

E.G. knew where Nathanya Berns lived. As the reporter for *The Sentinel*, he had occasion to visit her house several times, most of which were to collect information she wanted the reporter for the local newspaper to have.

He drove the almost two miles to the end of the street and made a left turn into a dead end street. The Berns residence was the last house on the block, and the street was unexpectedly quiet. As E.G. coasted to the front gate, he wondered where all the news crews were. He was sure they would have been there, that someone would have made the connection between one of the dead men and arguably the most powerful woman in South Orange.

But apparently nobody had.

E.G. stepped out of his car and approached the gates. Locked, as he expected. Gripping two of the iron bars, he looked beyond the gates and onto the property. Except for the paved road that disappeared into a forest of trees, he could see nothing. Talk about privacy, he thought.

To the left of the gate, set within a marble pillar, was an intercom E.G. had used before to gain entry to the Berns residence. He pressed the button and waited.

There was no response.

A few minutes later, he pressed it again, and within seconds, a voice sounded.

"Can I help you?"

It was Clara's voice. Clara was a live-in maid who had been with the Berns family for at least four years. Perhaps she didn't recognize E.G., he thought, because he knew she was watching him from the camera that rested above the gate.

E.G. looked into the camera and smiled. "Hi, Clara. It's E.G. from *The Sentinel*. I'm looking for Mrs. Berns."

"Mrs. Berns is not in at the moment."

"Do you expect her back soon?"

"I can't say."

Clara was loyal. She expressed no hint that Nathanya might be too upset for visitors, never mind a reporter who wanted to question her about her son's death. Nor did Clara reveal that this was not a good time to pay a visit.

"Clara, can you tell me how she's doing?"

The question drew no response, although E.G. thought he heard a sigh on the other end of the intercom. "You know that's why I'm here. I know about her son."

Clara's response was simple: "Mrs. Berns is not in at the moment, and I can't speak for her." The response was not rude, although perhaps carefully constructed in the event she was to be quoted in a newspaper article. E.G. received it as a matter-of-fact no comment.

"Will you please tell her I stopped by and would like to talk to her?"

"I can do that," Clara said, sounding relieved that the conversation was about to end.

"Thanks, Clara."

E.G. heard the intercom click, and Clara was gone.

As he stuffed his notebook into his back pocket and pushed his hair out of his face, E.G. heard the sound of a car approaching the quiet street. He turned and saw an emerald green Mercedes 450 turn the corner and approach the front gate. It was Nathanya, alone, and for a moment, E.G. froze.

E.G. didn't like raising the dead. That's how he referred to articles that involved shoving a notebook in the faces of family members and asking them to comment on the loss of a loved one. "Wasn't it obvious how they felt?" he had argued with one of his editors early in his career. He learned two things from that conversation: one, editors always win, and two, quotes from grieving family members do enhance a story and sell more papers. As his career developed, E.G. tried as often as possible to conduct "raising the dead" interviews on the telephone.

From the other end of the phone line, he could hide some of the things that displayed his discomfort, such as his shaking legs, his need to straighten his desk, his rapid heartbeat.

But this time was different. This time, there was a murder involved, there were no suspects, to the best of his knowledge, and the mother of a victim was Nathnaya. Somehow, he told himself, he had to talk to Nathanya in person.

The Mercedes slowed to a crawl as it approached the front gate. Nathanya peered through the tinted windshield at E.G., trying to identify the man standing near the entrance to her property. As she reached the gate, the driver's side window hummed open, and E.G. got a glance of a woman who looked battered, as if she hadn't slept in days.

"Mrs. Berns?" E.G. said without identifying himself. "Do you have a moment?"

"This is not a good time, E.G.," Nathanya said, her voice strained, yet oddly deep and forceful.

"You know me, Mrs. Berns. I'm not going for sensationalism. I'd just like to talk to you for a few moments about your son. I'll respect your privacy and leave when you ask me to leave, but please, give me a few moments and take the opportunity to tell a real reporter the story before the rest of the media come flying up here."

E.G. waited a moment and watched Nathanya, who seemed to be registering what he had said, as if her brain were on a different speed, and she needed to catch up to him.

"And they will be here," he added with certainty, knowing that even if other reporters didn't make the connection, they would drop on her house the moment he published the connection in his next story.

She beckoned him to follow her, and E.G. did so. The front gates opened, and the Mercedes disappeared onto the property and the road that led to the Berns residence. Once inside the gates, E.G., through his rear view mirror, watched the gates slowly close behind him.

All the questions E.G. wanted to ask Nathanya were stored in his head. A skill he developed a few years into his journalism career was to write the questions he wanted to ask in a notebook, memorize them and ask them casually throughout the interview so his subjects would gain his trust. That method was better, he thought, because instead of an interview, the interaction felt more like a conversation and put the subjects at ease. It also made them comfortable enough to reveal more information than what the question sought.

About thirty seconds after entering the road inside the gates, E.G. came upon the Berns residence, the most magnificent home ever to be built in South Orange. E.G. pulled his Tercel behind the Mercedes and got out, hurrying over to Nathanya, who had reached into the back seat of her car and removed several bags bearing the name of the local supermarket.

"I had to get out of the house," Nathanya said, as if she were making excuses for going to the supermarket while the help stayed home.

E.G. took two bags from her, which allowed her to fish for her keys to the front door before picking up the two other bags that rested near the car.

"I'm expecting company tonight," she said as she approached the house. "I guess I'll be having company whether I want it or not."

She laughed, and E.G. realized Nathanya was really talking to herself out loud. "Let them make fun of my hair. I'm supposed to look this way under these circumstances."

E.G. didn't think anything was wrong with Nathanya's hair. It was combed neatly, pushed back and held in place with what looked to him like an emerald hairpin in the shape of a butterfly.

"I just wish it wasn't Friday," she said. "If it were any other day of the week, everyone would be working, and they wouldn't have the time to visit. Now, everyone will be able to come to the house because it will be the weekend."

She slipped a key into the front door lock and turned it. She stopped, as if she were hit with a revelation. "But you know," she began, this time addressing E.G., "being that it's the weekend, at least Mickey will be here to help me with the guests."

With a smile, she pushed open the front door and stepped inside. Again, she stopped, this time dropping the bags of groceries on the floor with a thud. E.G. stopped behind her and heard the sobbing, but dared not confront her.

"He's really gone," Nathanya said. And that's when E.G. felt the pain of a mother who had just lost a child.

CHAPTER THIRTEEN

He had felt the pain before.

Almost a year into his journalism career, E.G. was assigned to interview the mother of a seven-year-old girl who was killed after she ran into the street and was struck by a car. He had seen the pain in the eyes of the young girl's mother, had heard it in her voice, one that trembled as she gripped the wallet-sized photo of her daughter in her left hand. But deeper than the pain was the anger; and it twisted her face every time she said the word drunk.

"He was drunk," she choked through gritted teeth. "Where is the justice? For a lousy good time on that stupid man's part, my baby is gone." It was almost as if the words created the beads of sweat that formed along her dark brown forehead. Unconsciously, she wiped them away with the back of her equally dark brown hand, but they formed anew. Not even the table fan that blew directly in her face could keep her cool in what felt like a ninety-degree kitchen.

The woman flattened the wrinkled photo against the table and gently rubbed two raw fingers against the image. More tears fell.

All E.G. could do was sit across from the woman and watch. It was all he could do to prevent his own tears from falling. It would be about five years before he would have a daughter of his own, so he had no words for the grieving woman.

He glanced at the open reporters notebook that lay in front of him on the table, the pen covering some of the few words he had scratched when he arrived. He wondered what kind of business he was in that would require someone to relive what must certainly have been a nightmare, only to sell those words for fifty cents on a newsstand.

He slid the pen off the notebook and closed the pad. For the last time, he expressed his condolences to the woman and slipped quietly from the kitchen.

For what seemed longer than the interview, E.G. sat in his car, unconsciously wiping the tears that built in his eyes. He looked back at the house from which he had just emerged and, until then, did not know that the woman had followed him outside. She stood on the porch, clinging tightly to her two surviving children, and all of them were crying. He had caused their tears, he told himself.

As he pulled away from the curb, he decided he was in the wrong business. He wondered if the profession he had chosen was unsympathetic, too unsympathetic, and as he returned to the office, he mentally drafted the resignation letter he would hand to Mel before he collected his belongings and left the office forever.

Luckily for E.G., Mel was not in the office when he returned.

Instead, Patrick Crowe, an associate editor at *The Sentinel*, watched as E.G. stepped into his cubicle and slapped his notebook against his desk.

"Tough day?" asked Patrick, a white-haired man who had guided E.G. through many stories during his rookie year.

"Tough story," E.G. said quietly.

"The Wilson girl?"

"Yeah," E.G. said flatly, finally looking Patrick in the face and wondering if he could accept a resignation.

"If it's any consolation, we get stories like that at least five times in our career," Patrick said, hoping to cheer up E.G. "They're not easy, and they're never going to go away. The fact is, death is a very real part of life, and it's our job to report that. If we are to succeed in accurately portraying community life, then it's a newspaper's responsibility to include in that journal any deaths that occur, regardless of how they happen."

"But do we need to invade one of the most private moments a family endures?" E.G. asked. "I mean, do we have to stick our notebooks in the face of a woman who just lost her child? Don't you think the reader is intelligent enough to guess how the woman feels?"

"No, we don't need to quote her," Patrick shrugged, "but any words that woman expresses and how you report them have a powerful impact on the reader. If a reader walks away from that story with tears in his or her eyes, you as the reporter and writer brought the readers closer to that woman, perhaps even allowing them to share her pain."

While E.G. absorbed the philosophy, Patrick wheeled a chair into the cubicle and sat across from him.

"We come across as being such a cruel and unsympathetic industry," E.G. said.

"For the most part," Patrick agreed. "Your reaction to the interview tells me you've got what it takes to strengthen our profession. We're human beings; we're not robots. Who says we can't be sympathetic to someone who just lost a child? Who says we can't cry with that person when she tells us her story, shares her feelings, her pain?"

Patrick wheeled the chair closer and tapped E.G. on the knees as he spoke. "I can tell you were crying. What that tells me is that someone whom you had never met had a tremendous impact on your life today. And now you have an opportunity that most people do not have. You get to tell that story to more than one hundred thousand people. If you report it well, the story will give readers not only a better insight into the life of someone whose daughter had just died, it will give readers a better understanding of you — the reporter and the human being. And they'll respect you more. That's how you develop a good reputation as a reporter. Report your story as a reporter, but write it as a human being."

E.G. did not respond.

"Did you complete all the interviews you need to write your story?"

E.G. tapped his notebook and nodded.

"Good," Patrick said as he stood and pushed the chair out of the cubicle. "Then write your story now. Close the door and don't come out until it's completed. My bet is that this will be one of the finest stories you'll have written since you've been here."

***   ***   ***

As E.G. followed Nathanya through the living room and into the yard, he thought of the Wilson girl. He also thought of Patrick, who had since died, and how the story he had written that day garnered him a first place award from the New Jersey Press Association from a writer with less than one year of experience at a professional newspaper.

E.G. knew that the lessons he learned that day from Patrick and the subsequent lessons he had learned until Patrick died was the reason he stood in the Berns' yard watching Nathanya, who was squatting and clearing her flower beds of leaves and twigs. Nathanya respected him not only as a reporter, but as a human being, someone who, when he made a promise, kept it. That was probably the best gift he had received from Patrick.

The August sun was beating down on them, but at least Nathanya had E.G.'s shadow to hide in. E.G. felt sweat form on his back and slowly drip down to the waistband of his pants. He wished he was back inside the house, but knew, without asking, that Nathanya was probably more relaxed tending to something she enjoyed.

"When was the last time you saw Mickey?" E.G. asked.

"Tuesday morning," Nathanya said without hesitation. "He was leaving for work when I asked him if he had plans for dinner that night."

"And he said?"

"Mickey ate out most of the time. Tuesday was no different. With whom he was having dinner I don't know. I stopped asking questions a long time ago."

E.G. thought that was a curious remark from Nathanya. It also beckoned his next question. "Mrs. Berns, was Mickey gay?"

Nathanya looked as uncomfortable as E.G. did for posing the question.

"I realize it's none of my business," E.G. continued, "but the fact that he was found where he was found would make any reporter want to ask the question. If I don't ask it, someone else will."

Nathanya paused, then shifted position, maneuvering herself into a sitting position on the decorative wall that enclosed the garden. "The only wish I requested of Mickey was that he not flaunt it. He could do whatever he wanted, just as long as he kept his private life private."

"Did he have enemies?" E.G. asked.

Nathanya chuckled. "We're the Bernses. You don't live this high on the hill without them."

"Does anyone stand out in your mind who would want to cause harm to your son?"

Nathanya shook her head. "As I said, I stopped asking questions a long time ago."

"When did you report your son missing?"

"Wednesday evening." Again, she answered without hesitation as she went back to work on the flower bed. "The morgue is not a very friendly place to visit."

"You were there Wednesday night?" E.G. asked, knowing the answer.

Nathanya gathered the debris she removed from her gardens and scooped them into a plastic bag she removed from a pocket. "I feel as if I'm answering the same questions I answered when the police asked them. If you want to talk about my son and how I remember his life, fine, but I don't think I'll be able to provide any revelations that will solve this murder. I'm growing bored."

"I'm sorry, Mrs. Berns. I know it sounds like I'm prying, but all I'm trying to do is find information that the police may not find."

"Leave the criminal investigation to the experts," Nathanya said. "I'm sure you wouldn't want them to edit your stories." She smiled as if to say the interview had ended.

E.G. understood that Nathanya had more to do than to answer a reporter's questions. "I'll find my way out," he said and turned to walk down the path.

Nathanya's voice sounded behind him. "He was a very good son." E.G. turned to face Nathanya, who returned to sitting on the rocks. "He didn't deserve to die."

E.G. returned to Nathanya's side and sat next to her. He placed a hand on her shoulder and rubbed gently, hoping the human touch would make her feel at ease.

"I'm so afraid of what the press is going to do to the memory of my son," Nathanya said. "The Reservation is not a very clean place. Will you at least treat him with dignity?"

"You know I will."

E.G. waited a moment, he thought out of respect, before standing. "A colleague once told me to treat the subject of every story as if I were writing about my mother. I'll give him the dignity he deserves."

Nathanya did not respond, nor did she look up at E.G., who turned and walked down the path toward the front of the house.

He slipped into the driver's seat of his car and slowly pulled around the circular drive that led back to the path surrounded by woods. At the end of the drive, as if someone had been watching him the entire way, the gate automatically opened and E.G. drove out into the street. He made a left out of the property, then a right onto Glenview Road on his way to the main road. Driving the two miles along the quiet street to the traffic light at South Orange Avenue, E.G. thought about Nathanya and decided she would have no trouble standing up to the press scrutiny she was about to endure. He knew she had courage and strength, and he had no doubt she could handle the media.

On the passenger seat was the folder E.G. had taken with him when he left the office. He reached over and opened it to reveal a file of articles about Nathanya Berns. He scattered them on the seat hoping he could find an article that contained a picture of her son. It would be easy reference, he thought, if he found an article among the pile that included information about Mickey because he really didn't know anything about him.

As E.G. scanned the articles, he heard the sound of a horn and looked up. Without realizing it, he had drifted to the other side of the street and was facing an oncoming car. He gave the steering wheel a quick jerk to the right and avoided hitting the black Camaro that, to E.G., seemed to be traveling too fast the other way on the quiet street.

The Camaro's brakes squealed, just as E.G. slammed on his own brakes, and the folder and its contents flew off the seat and onto the floor. The cup of coffee that was nestled in the console jerked loose, and if it wasn't for E.G. grabbing hold of it in time, the Berns file would have been a pile of soaking wet, coffee-stained newsprint.

By the time he got his bearings and secured the coffee cup back in the console, E.G. was only able to watch the Camaro disappear in his rear view mirror. If they're not stopping, I'm not stopping, he thought, and continued to the traffic light.

He needed to talk to Mel. He needed to tell Mel to take him off his regular beat so he could focus on investigating the murders in the Reservation. He had leads, he had clues. The only thing he didn't have was the time to put the pieces of the puzzle together before detectives in the law enforcement community could do it.

E.G. knew he was kidding himself. He wanted the time to be able to investigate so he could beat his cousin to the punch.

By the time E.G. got back to the building, Mel was in his office slinging a jacket over his shoulder, ready to leave for the day. E.G. laid his coffee mug and folder on his desk, then pushed into his editor's office.

"I need five minutes," he pleaded.

Mel looked at his reporter with such disdain that E.G. wondered if he was doing the right thing asking to be relieved of other assignments.

E.G. waited for Mel to say something, but Mel only stared. "We've got an opportunity to do something that no other newspaper has yet to do, and that's to help solve a murder."

E.G. waited for a response from Mel, but none came.

"I've got leads, Mel. I've got people on the Internet talking to me and feeding me shit that I don't think the police are getting. If I can spend every hour of every day working on these leads, I'll give you stories like you've never seen before. But I can't do that if I'm locked up in some council chambers covering meetings or going to grand opening events just to see a mayor cut a ribbon. Mel, this is good stuff. Take me off the other assignments and let me work on this exclusively."

Mel laid his jacket on his desk. "How do I explain to your publisher that he's got a reporter who does nothing all day but visits the Reservation and talks to people on the Internet while the rest of his staff is busting their butts writing seven, eight, nine stories per week?"

"You've got to be kidding me," E.G. responded. "Doing nothing all day? This could be the story of the century for this newspaper, and you're worried about what your boss is going to think about a reporter's production value? Mel, this story is worth its weight in gold. If I solve this murder..."

"*If* being the operative word," Mel interjected, his voice rising slightly. "Be realistic, E.G. You don't have the first clue how to solve a murder."

"But I've got the brains to try." E.G. pulled the door over and continued in a whisper. "Two days ago, I stumbled upon a good story. Two days later, I'm talking to someone who witnessed what happened. You're my editor. You need to know this, but I ask that you don't repeat that to anyone. And I mean anyone. That's why I'm asking you to let me pursue this. I was just at the Berns home, and I know Mrs. Berns trusts me. I've got this guy online who said he was there when the bodies were dumped. He wouldn't tell me that if he didn't have the slightest desire to want to talk."

"A witness?" Mel asked. Now he seemed interested. "What did he see?"

"I'm not at liberty to reveal that, Mel. Even to you."

"Is it information you should take to the police?"

"Not yet. I almost said something to my cousin Raymond this morning at the prosecutor's office, but the son of a bitch wouldn't listen. So to hell with it. I want to gather this information on my own."

"You're a civilian, E.G. If you have information that can lead to an arrest in this case, and you withhold that, you could face charges too. And you won't have the Shield Law to protect you."

"What I have would not lead to an arrest. Yet. So I'm still safe," E.G. responded.

The New Jersey Shield Law protected journalists from revealing information they accumulated in the news-gathering process. E.G. knew the law, and knew he was walking the fine line between gathering news and obstructing justice, but he wasn't about to argue the points of the law with Mel, who, E.G. believed, was trying to intimidate him into backing down from pursuing the story.

"Give me some time with these people," E.G. said. "Let me determine when, or if, I should go to the police."

"And in the meantime? What do I do? Pay you in the hopes that you'll uncover something?"

"Mel, this is great research."

"I still can't justify that to the publisher," Mel said.

"I'll get other stories out of this," E.G. countered. "When the police barricades come down, you know damn well the cars will be flowing through that Reservation like a river in a rainstorm. I'll get reaction pieces. I'll do a history of the place. Someone, somewhere connected to this county should have an idea as to when cruising began there. I can take the reader on a journey of that area of the Reservation. This is award-winning stuff."

Mel picked up his jacket, indicating he was ready to leave. "I'm not interested in awards. I'm interested in publishing a good, local newspaper."

"Without controversy," E.G. added, as if to finish Mel's sentence. And he knew they were two words that would elicit reaction.

The words stopped Mel, whose face began to redden. "That's it, E.G. I don't want to hear another word about this or you'll have nothing to write, ever again, for this newspaper."

"I was trying to get you pissed, Mel, so we could argue about this. You know me. At least let me do this: During the weekend, I'll come up with story ideas that would guarantee reader interest for the next several weeks. Share them with the publisher and see what he thinks. This is a business, too, and I'm sure he'll support anything that sells more newspapers...as long as it's done objectively and in good taste. And that's the kind of reporter I am."

For a moment, the only sound in the room was the sound of the clock ticking on Mel's wall. It was at that moment that E.G. realized just how loud it was. To him, it seemed as if one hundred ticks had sounded before Mel broke the silence.

"Fine," was all Mel said.

"You mean it?"

"Don't push it, E.G. Have that list on my desk first thing Monday morning." Mel slung his jacket over his shoulder and pushed beyond E.G., stepping out of his office and into a newsroom filled that afternoon with staff. Mel wasn't the kind of person who took the time to say hello or good-bye, so it wasn't a surprise to anyone in the office when he brushed by each of the desks and cubicles on his way out the front door.

When he was gone, E.G. emerged from Mel's office and darted for Conor's cubicle. When he entered, he did so with a "Hey," half startling Conor, who grabbed the monitor on his computer and spun it to hide the contents on the screen.

"Oh, it's you," Conor said, looking up with an odd look on his face at a smiling E.G., but still blocking the monitor. "You scared me. What's with the shit-eating grin?"

E.G. ignored the look. "I think I just talked Mel into giving me the Reservation — exclusively. This is a fucking dream come true."

Conor listened as E.G. recounted the meeting he had had with Mel only minutes earlier. He was conscious of omitting the information about his sources, because, as he had said to Mel, he did not want anyone to know how much information he had gathered during the last two days. When he finished, he returned to his own cubicle, signed on to the Internet as Stetson165, and found a lone e-mail from his online friend. He opened it and read the contents.

"Barry, everything is fine here. Thanks for your concern. I spent most of last night wondering what I should do next. I know I have a lot to lose if I come forward, and as much as I know it's the right thing to do, I'm not prepared to do that. Any suggestions?"

The e-mail went unsigned. Instead of replying, E.G. closed the piece of mail and left his account live, hoping Matt would return and invite him to a private talk. While he waited, he looked up Travis Boesgaard in the phone book. He jotted the address on a page from his notebook, then tore the page from its spiral clutches and slipped it into his shirt pocket.

Ten minutes later, E.G. found himself reviewing the notes he had taken from the two days' worth of press conferences at the prosecutor's office. When he heard the familiar shut down tone, he looked up at his monitor to see if his account had signed off automatically. It had not.

"Conor, were you just online?" E.G. called over his cubicle.

"Yeah, why?" Conor called back. "I was checking mail."

"Just checking. I thought my computer had signed off on its own."

"You've been online? How come you didn't show up on my member list when I tried to invite you to a private talk?"

E.G. scrambled for a reply. Conor knew only the eglord2541 account, which wasn't the one E.G. was using at the moment. "Oh, sorry. My mistake. I wasn't even online." He lowered the volume and quickly signed off, not knowing if Conor would join him in his cubicle to continue the conversation and see the other account on the monitor.

But Conor did not join him, nor did he respond to E.G. And that was fine by E.G. It gave him time to think of any suggestions he could share with Matt. Of course, any suggestions he offered, he knew would serve his own interests, not those of the law enforcement community. He wasn't about to become this involved, only to hand every bit of information he had to the police.

E.G. wondered if he should tell Matt that he was a reporter, and that his only interest in continuing the communication between the two of them was to advance his career. Forget it, he told himself. Knowing Matt — or anyone, for that matter — he would just as quickly clam up and disappear.

Meet. That was the next suggestion that occurred to E.G. It wasn't a far-fetched idea, he thought. After all, he recalled a gentleman on the live board the day before requesting a meeting of no one in particular on the board. "If you've got the place, I've got the time," he had said. That could be a dangerous proposition, he thought, because what would happen if he came face to face with Matt and discovered that he was someone he had known all along? He didn't know any Matts, but as he had thought earlier, Matt may not be Musicat62's real name, just as Barry was not his own real name.

And then what? Musicat62 would know that Stetson165 was *Sentinel* reporter E.G. Lord, someone who had lured him from the security of the Internet closet under false pretenses. E.G. didn't want to take that chance, nor did he want to risk revealing himself this early if it meant losing the strongest lead he had.

He needed to build a trust in Musicat62 first. That he knew, but did it mean spending every hour of every day online waiting for Musicat62 just to be able to talk to him? E.G. reminded himself that it had been only two days since the story broke, and convinced himself that as it unfolded, the key to keeping one step ahead of the police was to keep Musicat62 within arm's reach. And the key to ensuring that, he added, was to build trust between them.

When Conor entered E.G.'s cubicle, he found his colleague seated in his chair with his legs stretched across a pile of papers that lay on his desk. E.G. didn't hear Conor come in.

"A penny for your thoughts," Conor said.

E.G. swiveled his neck so he could face Conor. He left his hands folded on the back of his head. "Don't start throwing cliches at me."

"What'cha thinking about?"

E.G. wanted to tell him, but knew he couldn't. "Life," he said, then noticed the briefcase slung over Conor's shoulder. "Heading out?"

"Yeah, it's been a long week."

"Usually, long weeks find us commiserating over open spickets of beer. Why no invite?"

"Tired too. I need to take a break this weekend. Get some things done around the apartment."

E.G. removed his legs from his desk, taking some of the papers with him. As he reached to the floor to collect them, he said, "I wouldn't be able to do anything tonight anyway. This is my weekend with Erin. I have to pick her up at her mom's after work."

"Enjoy it," Conor said as he backed out of E.G.'s cubicle. He waved once, then vanished, but not before belting a "Good night, everyone," as he made his way out the front door.

The responses ranged from a cheerful "Have a good weekend" from the always optimistic Andrea Gray, to stifled mumbles of "night" from a few of the other reporters, to the always expected race to the door by Will Edmonds, who, without fail, believed good night meant it was time to talk.

This time, though, Conor beat Will out the door and left him at the entranceway talking to, E.G. could only assume, the glass pane in the front door. Oh, the personalities we meet in the world of journalism, he thought.

Knowing it would be only a few minutes before he would leave for the day, E.G. returned to the Internet one more time, hoping for another piece of mail, but there was none. He opened the last e-mail Musicat62 had sent and clicked Reply.

"Matt," he wrote, "Believe it or not, I feel the pain you must be enduring at this point. That's some burden you're carrying. I really hope you give me the opportunity to talk to you about this. You asked if I had any suggestions. I do, and I would be interested in sharing them with you. But I can't do that unless we get to talk. And hey, maybe something positive would come out of those discussions. I'll be back online tonight at eleven p.m. Please do your best to be there." He typed Barry, and clicked Send.

His mail sent, E.G. signed off, then returned as eglord2541. He found a piece of mail from Dirtdealer, who had sent it only ten minutes earlier.

In typical fashion, the one-line note read, "Where is Travis going?"

"How the fuck do I know?" E.G. yelled at the monitor. "What are you trying to tell me?"

The outburst left the newsroom silent, and drew a young female reporter with dark brown hair to E.G.'s cubicle. Kelly Kelly stood silent for a moment before saying, "Everything all right in here?"

Kelly Kelly had joined *The Sentinel* two years earlier upon graduation from college. Six months later, and only three months after E.G.'s divorce had become final, he and Kelly were fucking. Three months after that, without any explanation, they stopped. Since then, both maintained a cordial relationship in the workplace.

E.G. convinced himself that his attraction to Kelly developed at the same time his daughter told him about her mother's new friend, Jason, who had been coming to the house more frequently since the divorce became final. He was aware of the coincidence, but also was aware that it had been months since he had gotten laid, and Kelly

Kelly, who seemed to exhibit an attraction toward him, happened along at a time when he needed someone.

Kelly's beat at *The Sentinel* included Essex County's western suburban towns, the beat normally given to new reporters, who, once they had begun to show signs of maturity, were moved to towns with more complex issues. But Kelly, who hailed from the West Essex town of Livingston, provided the kind of coverage that garnered an increase in circulation among the four towns she covered.

As she stood at the opening of E.G.'s cubicle, E.G. couldn't help but remember that the outfit she was wearing, a beige skirt and white top, was one he had peeled from her body in his bedroom on a cold winter night.

Half aroused thinking about that night, E.G. smiled at Kelly and said, "Everything's fine. Just a little frustrated."

"How's your daughter?"

E.G. glanced at his watch. "She's doing great, and actually, I have to get out of here to pick her up."

E.G. signed off the Internet and turned off the monitor on his computer. He glanced across his desk, collected a couple folders and notebooks, slipped his hand inside his shirt pocket to be sure the note he had written to himself was there, then brushed past Kelly out of his cubicle. "Have a great weekend," he said, then disappeared out the front door.

In his car, E.G. thought about Dirtdealer's most recent e-mail. "Where is Travis going?" he said aloud. He concluded that it could mean only one thing, and that was that Travis had plans to go somewhere. He wondered if Travis' vacation plans, or whatever they were, had something to do with the murders in the Reservation. Considering Dirtdealer's e-mails had begun just after the murders took place, and they had tied Travis Boesgaard to at least one of the victims, or perhaps both, he figured Travis had to have some knowledge of what took place.

As he pulled his car into the late afternoon traffic, E.G. decided that a visit to Travis would come sooner than even he anticipated.

CHAPTER FOURTEEN

Raymond had an aversion to returning calls from the press. It wasn't that he couldn't handle their questions; it was how they asked their questions that he didn't like. Reporters were filled with distrust, he had decided, as if Raymond, or anyone in the prosecutor's office, for that matter, had more answers than they were willing to give the media. Leave them with a "no comment" or "I can't discuss that," and he becomes the bad guy once the newspaper hits the stands.

"I decline to give information, not refuse to give information," he had corrected reporters many times, but their stories always used the word refused.

But E.G. was unique. Returning a call from E.G. Lord meant preparing for a game of mental ping pong because, not only would E.G. ask questions, he would listen, truly listen, to the answers, something he realized few reporters did. And it was from those answers that E.G. would develop more questions — questions that would sometimes stump him, put a wrench in some of his theories and lead him in a new direction.

So he wasn't disappointed when Margaret, the receptionist at *The Sentinel*, told him that E.G. had left for the day. In fact, he was thrilled that he could leave a voice-mail message telling his cousin that he had honored E.G.'s request to call him back after missing him following the press conference. Raymond also did not get into the habit of calling E.G. at home related to business, nor did E.G. expect it.

Raymond quickly left the press conference to visit Nathanya Berns, only to be told by the voice in the intercom that Nathanya was not home. From there, Raymond drove the two miles back to the Reservation, was let through the barricade set up by the two police vehicles, and parked his Buick near the area where the bodies of the two men had been found.

He didn't expect to find anything new on this trip. In fact, if Nathanya Berns had been home, he wouldn't have made the trip into the Reservation. He convinced himself that this trip was made because, for the first time, he hadn't a clue as to how this happened, who could have done it, or why. Revisiting the scene only made him feel closer to the case, as if his presence there would spark some inspiration.

Raymond found himself at an area in the Reservation where, legend had it, the first president visited more than two centuries earlier. He couldn't help but imagine George Washington marching his troops through the Reservation, only to be propositioned by a young man on a horse. He laughed aloud and unconsciously looked around to be sure he was alone.

The view from that spot was magnificent. Set high on South Mountain, Raymond looked out beyond the waist-high, stone wall and saw the tops of thousands of trees that acted like a blanket over the town of South Orange and, just beyond, the city of Newark. Through those trees, he saw some of Newark's tallest buildings, before looking into the horizon and seeing the New York City skyline.

He turned his back to the view, leaned against the wall and surveyed this area of the Reservation. To his right was the path where visitors entered. He imagined a car coming up the path, the driver just a blurred image because it was dark, the only lights coming from his headlamps. The car slowly drove along the path, passing where Raymond was standing, and continued until it reached the turn in the path, not that far from where his own car was parked. The brake lights came on, and then he could see the reverse lights flash as the gear went from drive to reverse to park. The driver stepped out, looking around before opening the rear door and pulling a passenger out of the vehicle. The passenger was naked, and was being dragged across the pavement into the grass. The driver returned to the car, slipped into the backseat once more and removed a second passenger. Also naked, the second passenger was dragged like the first, being left not too far from his friend in the grass.

The driver, looking around one more time, closed the rear door, got back into the driver's side, reversed, and turned the car around, this time accelerating as he passed where Raymond stood and continuing at a high rate of speed down the path and out of the Reservation.

That was Raymond's theory. The killings took place elsewhere, and the bodies were dumped in the Reservation. There were no vehicles belonging to Mickey Berns or Steven Conroy found in the Reservation since the night of the murders, which, to him, meant they had to have entered the park in another vehicle.

At the same time, he became curious about the alleged leads E.G. had hinted at just before the press conference. It would kill him to learn his cousin knew more than he knew and wondered if now was the right time to extend an olive branch. He'd take the branch back once the case was solved because, he told himself, the only reason he'd extend it in the first place was to find a way to end this case before E.G. captured the glory for it. Raymond reminded himself how E.G. had burned him once before with his reporter's investigation, and he wasn't about to let it happen again.

Out of the corner of his eye, Raymond was distracted by a figure moving toward him from his right. Dressed in light green shorts and a white tank top, the man, a jogger, slowed to a rapid walk. He removed a small towel that had been tucked into the back of his shorts and wiped sweat from the back of his neck. He was oblivious to Raymond's presence until Raymond stepped from the concrete stairs and into the path of the runner.

The runner stopped short, obviously taken by surprise.

"Sorry to have frightened you, sir," Raymond said as he removed a badge from his breast pocket and displayed it for the runner.

"What can I do for you, sir?" asked the runner, slightly out of breath and glancing at the piece of silver.

"I'm curious to know how you got in here. We have a police barricade at the entrances to the park."

The runner pointed in the direction of Raymond's car. "The Reservation is my back yard," he said, his breathing becoming more even. "I come up the dirt path to do my jogging here. It's been a pleasure running up here the last couple days. Nobody here to bother you, if you know what I mean."

"Yes, I do," said Raymond, realizing from the man's fairly toned body that he was probably bothered many times during his attempts at exercise. "You didn't happen to see or hear anything on Tuesday night, did you? Anything unusual?"

"No, I didn't. I was up here Tuesday afternoon, and only saw what usually goes on up here."

"Can you show me this dirt path you take?"

"Sure." The runner began to walk in the direction of Raymond's car. "It's this way."

Raymond kept pace and walked alongside the runner, who wiped the sweat that had begun to drip from his temples to his jaw.

"I gather you run here often," Raymond said.

"Been doing so for about ten years now," the man said. "Best way to keep in shape. You wouldn't guess that I'm forty-eight years old."

Actually, Raymond pegged him as being in his late forties or early fifties. "You look great for forty-eight," he lied.

They were near Raymond's car when the runner asked, "They know who the guys are?"

"As a matter of fact, yes," Raymond said. "We released the names this morning. Mickey Berns and Steven Conroy."

The runner stopped walking and turned to face Raymond. Raymond also stopped. "You've got to be shitting me. Mickey Berns?"

"You know him?"

"He went to school with one of my kids," the runner said, looking away for a moment with a perplexed look on his face, one Raymond noticed instantly.

"Are you okay?" Raymond asked.

The runner looked back. "Yeah, sure, I'm okay." He smiled sadly. "I just didn't expect to hear that name, is all."

"What about your kid? Were they still friends?"

Again, the runner looked away. "Nah. No, they haven't been friends for a long while. You graduate from high school, go separate ways. That was about ten years ago."

Raymond found it difficult to believe the runner, but played along with him. "I see." He nodded in the direction of the woods. "Is this the way to the path?"

The runner nodded and started to walk again. Raymond followed him into the woods, where, approximately one hundred feet away, blacktop had turned into a dirt path that led down the mountain before splitting into several paths that spilled into the yards of some of the finest homes in Maplewood. On a few occasions, Raymond had to grab hold of tree branches to stop from sliding on the dirt.

At the bottom of the path on which the runner led Raymond, they stopped. "This is my house," the runner said, pointing to a yard equipped with a built-in swimming pool, marble statues and lush gardens.

Raymond looked around. "So anyone can basically come down these paths and scurry through these yards to get out of the Reservation," he said, more as a statement than a question.

"That's exactly true," the runner said. "The spotlights go on from time to time at night. It's either a deer, or I'll catch someone coming from the yard onto the street. It doesn't happen often, but I don't think too many people know the path is there or where it leads."

Raymond glanced between the runner's house and his neighbor's house, taking note of the maroon Chevrolet parked on the street in front of their houses. "What street is that out there?" he asked.

"Sagamore Road," the runner said.

"I want to thank you for showing me this path," Raymond said. "You've been a great help."

"Do you think it will help in your investigation?"

"Can't comment on that. But knowing there's another way out of here gives me some more answers – and questions." Raymond shook the runner's hand and made his way back up the dirt path. Before disappearing into the brush, he turned back and noticed the runner was still watching him. "Now I understand the importance of exercise," he called back as he loosened his tie and gripped tree branches for support to get up the hill.

By the time he got to his car at the top of the path, Raymond was almost out of breath. His tie in hand and his shirt unbuttoned at the top, he walked slowly to the Buick. He leaned into the backseat and removed a briefcase. Placing the case on the trunk of his car, he opened it and removed a map from an inside pocket. He spread the map across the trunk and searched for Sagamore Road in Maplewood, trying to find the most direct route to the street from the Reservation.

Finding it and making a mental note, he returned the map and briefcase to the backseat and got into the driver's seat. Seven minutes later, Raymond was slowing his car near the maroon Chevrolet parked on Sagamore Road that he had seen from the runner's yard. He glanced up at the front of what he knew was the runner's house and made a note of the street address. As he pulled away, he didn't notice the curtains in the front window move, and the runner's face take their place.

CHAPTER FIFTEEN

"I'm on my way home," Raymond said into the phone. "How about we just order a pizza and watch a movie?"

"You're coming home early?" Liz asked, with disbelief in her voice. "How about if I send the kids to my mother's?"

"That's not a bad idea. We can have the house all to ourselves."

"Can you think of something we can do all by ourselves?" Liz asked, speaking softly to prevent the children from hearing her.

Raymond spoke equally as quiet. "I can run a nice warm bath, fill the tub with bubbles. You can slip in and sit in front of me with your back resting against my chest as I slip my arms around your waist. My legs will press against yours, and I'll kiss the back of your neck." As he spoke, he doodled, and when he closed the folder, he didn't take the time to erase the breasts he had drawn, or the erect penis that he placed between them.

"That sounds wonderful," Liz said. "You can't imagine what you're doing to me right now."

"And you me," Raymond said.

He leaned back in his chair and rested his hand against the bulge in his pants. "I have to get off this phone before our evening ends too early."

They both giggled like two school kids who just discovered flirting.

"Why don't we drop the kids off and go out to eat?"

"Sounds like a plan, Mr. Vanderhoeven."

"I love you, Mrs. Vanderhoeven. I'll be home soon."

As he hung up the phone, Raymond put his crotch back in order before standing and coming around to the front of his desk. The Sagamore Road address appeared on a printout Raymond searched for on the Internet. Ian Winter was the runner he had met earlier that day in the Reservation. He was the runner who, Raymond remembered, seemed concerned when he heard that one of the murdered men was Mickey Berns; the runner who said one of his kids knew Mickey Berns but who hadn't seen him in, what, ten years.

Raymond picked up the phone and pressed one button. When his secretary answered, he said, "Find out what year Mickey Berns graduated from high school, Columbia High School in Maplewood, and then get me a copy of that year's yearbook." After a pause, he said, "First thing Monday morning ...Thanks." But as quickly as he hung up the phone, Raymond picked it back up and pressed the same button. He looked at his watch while he waited for his secretary to answer.

"Never mind," he said when she responded. "I'm leaving the office now. Call Columbia High School, get the school librarian on the phone and tell him or her that a representative from the prosecutor's office is on his way to pick up the book. Find out the year he graduated from the guidance office before talking to the librarian. It'll save time."

Raymond again hung up the phone. He slipped the printout of the Winter residence into his briefcase, grabbed his jacket from the coat rack and left the office.

Twenty minutes later, he was seated outside the principal's office at Columbia High School next to a boy who looked no older than fifteen years old. Acne had begun to stretch across his cheeks. "What are you in for?" Raymond asked.

"Huh?" the boy asked, almost disinterested.

"What's your crime?" When the boy continued to stare at him, he tried to make it as simple as possible. "Why are you here?"

"Had my radio playing too loud in the hallway."

"Oh," Raymond replied, then said, "That doesn't seem like it deserves punishment — unless, of course, the music was Soul Daddy

Pup, or one of those groups whose music I just don't understand anymore."

The boy continued to look up at him, as if to wonder who the hell this guy was.

"I remember a time I had to go to the principal's office," Raymond said, not interested in whether or not the kid wanted to hear the story. "I was a junior in high school. I went to Catholic school, and I was in religion class. The priest — we had priests teach us too in addition to the nuns — was calling roll and one of the kids wasn't answering, but he should have been in the class. He wasn't absent or anything, so the priest asked if anybody knew where this kid was. I think his name was Michael. Remember that I'm going back about twenty years here, so the name may not be the right one. A lot has happened since then, so the name of the kid I got out of trouble is kind of lost in here, you know?" Raymond said, tapping his temple.

The boy continued to stare.

"So anyway, of course no one knows where Michael is. I mean, you really didn't expect someone to say, 'Oh, he decided to cut your class.' So this priest starts looking around and stops when he gets to me. He calls me to the front of the class and asks me to go to the office to find out if Michael went home sick, or if the office knows his whereabouts. They didn't like when you cut classes in Catholic school. You know why he chose me, don't you?" Raymond asked the boy.

"No," the boy said. "Why?" Suddenly the boy was interested.

"Because I was such a nerd in high school, and everyone knew it. Well, it angered me that he chose me, so when I left the classroom, I didn't go to the office. I went to the gym, which was in a separate building, because that's where I left Michael the previous period. We were in the same gym class. I caught up to him, and found him hanging outside the building getting high with some other kids, and I told him that the priest, Father Bill or something like that, was looking for him in religion class, and that he sent me to find him. So I told Michael that I would go to the office and tell them that he was sick and lying down in the gym, and then when I get back to the classroom, I would just tell the priest that Michael is sick and the office is aware of it. I wouldn't have been lying, really, because if I said it that way, it would be accurate."

The boy, waiting for the outcome of the story, didn't hear the secretary when she called him into the principal's office.

"Charles," the woman called.

Charles turned and placed his index finger in the air, indicating that he needed more time with the stranger.

Raymond, realizing that the boy was surely on the brink of more trouble, summed up his story. "Turns out that when I got to the gym, I didn't realize that in all my zeal to get this guy out of trouble, I forgot that my religion class faced the gym, and the priest watched everything I did from the window. I wound up getting into trouble trying to get someone else out of trouble. So that was the last time I had to go to the principal's office. I know, a boring story, but it passed the time."

The boy got up without saying anything and followed the secretary into the principal's office, leaving Raymond sitting alone in the waiting room. Within minutes, though, an anemic looking woman entered the room and smiled curtly at him.

Raymond stood and accepted the book the woman presented to him as well as a slip of paper she asked him to sign.

"We'll have this back for you next week," he said, signing the paper on top of the book and returning it to her.

The woman, still smiling, left the room as quickly as she had come in.

Tucking the yearbook under his arm, Raymond followed her out the door.

***   ***   ***

Brian Winter wasn't a bad looking guy, at least during his senior year in high school. Raymond noticed the military style haircut first, and then the small pursed lips on a somewhat stern face. Instead of a yearbook photograph, he thought, Brian looked as if he should have been sitting for a Boot Camp graduation picture.

Brian had blond hair and slightly resembled his father, Ian. Raymond guessed that he probably stood about five feet nine inches tall. He couldn't help but wonder if Brian was gay, and if that was why Ian seemed reluctant to talk about him during their conversation in the Reservation. Brian played the piano; enjoyed good times with friends who, according to the profile in the yearbook, knew who they were; listened to the music of Talking Heads and Queen, and visited Shipbottom on Long Beach Island during the summers.

Flipping back several pages, Raymond stopped at the photo of Michael Berns. The first thing he realized was that Mickey had not aged that much between the time the yearbook photo was taken and how he had looked just before he died. He had maintained a boyish look, one that included a smile that seemed to say, "I just got away with it." Beneath the name line under the photo was a listing of Mickey's interests, which included drinking with friends at the quarry, several acres of unused land not too far from the Berns residence, clubbing in New York City, and good times with Adam, Melissa and Brian. He had also listed several charitable organizations to which he claimed to be an honorary member, and suggested that everybody donate to them.

So Mickey was a party guy with a good heart, Raymond thought as he flipped through the pages of the yearbook looking for other photos of Mickey or Brian. There was Mickey in what appeared to be a Chemistry lab with other students, but no other pictures in the few pages he had managed to view before his cell phone rang.

Raymond instinctively reached over to the passenger seat and clicked the phone.

Liz didn't sound too happy on the other end.

"Where are you? I thought you were coming home early," she said.

Raymond closed the book and tossed it into the backseat of his car on a pile of newspapers that he had collected that carried stories about the Berns murder. He realized he hadn't even left the high school parking lot. "I'm sorry, hon. I made one stop and got delayed." As he talked, he started the car and backed out of the parking space.

"How long before you're going to be home? I have the kids all ready to leave..."

"I'll be home in twenty minutes," Raymond said, cutting off Liz before she could begin the usual guilt trip. "Twenty minutes." In his rear view mirror, as he made his way out of the parking lot, he saw

Charles emerge from the front door of the school. Short detention, he thought.

There was a moment of silence, which Raymond took to mean that Liz had no more to say, but then, "I knew this was going to happen. You set me up for a nice night for the two of us..."

"I said I'd be home in twenty minutes. I'm already on the road. Nineteen minutes, and I'm hanging up the phone now," Raymond said.

He waited, and after a few seconds, heard Liz's voice. "Nineteen minutes. Good-bye."

He couldn't help but wonder if Liz had multiplied the sixty seconds in a minute by the nineteen in which he said he would be home and began counting down from the one thousand one hundred forty seconds it would take to reach the front door. She had done stranger things, so he wouldn't have been surprised if he got home and she alerted him that he had made it with thirty-seven seconds to spare.

When he heard the click on the other end, Raymond hung up his own phone and placed it back on the passenger seat of the car. Taking back roads, he made his way out to South Orange Avenue toward his home in Livingston, passing streets that he knew would lead him to Sagamore Road. Since looking at the yearbook photo of Brian Winter, Raymond had wanted to pass the Winter house one more time before heading home, but knew he couldn't. Liz didn't sound happy, and the last thing he wanted to do at this hour was get delayed, something he predicted would happen if he visited Sagamore Road.

Raymond wasn't the kind of person who could satisfy himself with a quick drive near the house. He knew himself well, and that meant he would have parked his car several houses away from the Winter house and waited for Brian to either come in or go out, and he would have waited hours, if need be, for that to happen.

Liz. She could be a bitch at times, he thought as he leaned over and picked up the cell phone again, but he loved her more than anything in the world. "Hi, Mary, this is Ray Vanderhoeven. How are you?" he said when he made the connection. "That's great. Listen, can you put half a dozen red roses together for me? I can pick them up in five minutes." After a pause, he said, "You're the best." Then hung up the phone.

Raymond looked at his watch as he pulled into the driveway of his home. Despite the onset of rush hour traffic and the quick stop at the florist, he had made it home in eighteen minutes. Liz couldn't be angry with him now, he thought.

He collected the pile of newspapers, the yearbook and his briefcase from the back seat and cradled them in his right arm, closed the car door with his knee, and hid the flowers behind his back in his left hand. At the top of the stairs outside the front door, he carefully laid the pile from his right hand on the wooden bench that adorned the porch. The house was quiet as he entered, except for the sound of the television in the family room at the back of the house.

"Hon," he called out. "I'm home. And I'm on time."

"I'm up here." Liz's voice came from the top of the stairs. No mention of the time.

He found his wife in their room, the door partially closed, as she sat in front of a mirror brushing her shoulder length brown hair. She wore only panties, and as Raymond leaned into the room, she caught his reflection in the mirror and smiled. "Did you fly home?" she asked, putting the brush down on the table and picking up eye-liner.

Raymond remained in the doorway, only his head actually in the room.

Liz held the eye-liner near her face as she stared at Raymond through the mirror. She was intrigued, to say the least. "What are you doing?" she asked.

"I can never get enough of you. I can stand here and watch you all day."

"Did you break this case you've been working on? You're awfully flirtatious." Liz said it with a smile, feeling flirtatious as well.

"I've got a new case I'm working on," Raymond replied. "And it's a tough one. I've been assigned to watch a gorgeous young woman, but every time I lay eyes on her, I find it so hard to control myself."

Liz put the eye-liner down and stood from her make-up table. She turned to face Raymond and slowly walked toward him. "Should I be jealous? I mean, can she compare to me?"

Raymond looked down at Liz's breasts, then further down at the dark imprint that appeared through her white panties. Her long legs, tanned from the last two months of sunning in their yard, were toned from her daily morning jogs. And the closer she got, the more turned on Raymond got.

He eased his way into the bedroom and, just as Liz was close enough to reach out and touch his face, he revealed the long-stemmed roses. "Nothing can compare to you," he said, placing his right hand on her hip and drawing her closer to him. "God, you are so sexy."

Liz took the flowers from Raymond and nonchalantly dropped them to the floor. "They're beautiful," she said, placing a hand behind Raymond's neck and drawing him closer to her. They kissed for what seemed like an eternity. Raymond's right hand slipped from Liz's hip to her buttocks, and his left hand found its way to her breast. Liz slipped her other arm around Raymond's waist and held him tightly. Their breathing grew heavier.

With one swift movement that caught Liz by surprise, Raymond lifted her and carried her to the bed, where he lay her head gently against the pillow. He climbed onto the bed with her and kissed her neck, her breasts and her stomach. Liz lay back, moaning with each touch. Instinctively, she reached for Raymond's shirt and pulled it from the waist of his pants. Her hands found his skin, the soft fingers leaving Raymond tingling.

Liz moved her hands across his stomach and then to his chest, where she dug into the hair that crossed his pecs. She slid her hands down to his pants and began to unbuckle the belt, but stopped when she heard, "Are we leaving yet or what?"

It was Julien's voice coming from the bottom of the stairs.

Liz nearly kicked Raymond in the crotch in an effort to break away from him, fearing their five-year-old son would come upstairs and into the bedroom. Raymond rolled to the other side of the bed as Liz jumped from her side and approached the door, prepared to close it if Julien had climbed the stairs.

"In a few minutes," Liz called. "Get a couple toys ready." She closed the door and turned to face Raymond, who had begun to laugh.

"Shit. I completely forgot where I was," Liz said, reaching for the closet door, where the dress she decided to wear to dinner hung.

"I'll take that as a compliment," Raymond said.

"Get in the shower, so we can get out of here," Liz snapped.

Raymond continued to laugh. "You're so horny right now, you're absolutely beside yourself."

"I didn't see you yawning with boredom," Liz retorted as she picked up the roses from the floor. She laid them across the make-up table and slipped into the yellow dress.

Raymond undressed and disappeared into the master bathroom, and as he stepped into the shower, Liz still could hear him laughing.

Liz approached the bathroom door. "I can turn it off as quickly as I can turn it on," she said, loud enough for Raymond to hear.

Suddenly, the only sound that came from the bathroom was the water pouring from the shower.

CHAPTER SIXTEEN

There were few things in life that E.G. dreaded. One of them was picking up his daughter at his former wife's house. It wasn't that he and Rachel Lord ended their marriage acrimoniously. On the contrary, they remained very good friends after their divorce became final nearly two years earlier. What he dreaded was seeing his wife because it reminded him how much he still was in love with her.

The rain pounded against the windshield of the Jeep the night Rachel told E.G. she had fallen out of love with him. They were on their way home from a weekend in Washington, D.C., a friend's wedding, and were about thirty minutes into the four-hour drive when she broached the subject, picking then, as she had said, because he had nowhere to escape. E.G. was a terrific person, a wonderful father, she reinforced, but Rachel emphasized that she needed a husband who was there when she needed him. She convinced herself that she could never get used to the schedule he kept, rarely seeing him three nights out the week and, when he was home, he was either dissecting notes or talking for hours on the telephone with news sources. That was his life.

Cars sped by, and E.G. was surprised to discover that he had been driving only 45 miles per hour. Surprised because he wanted the trip to end as quickly as possible, to be home, to pick up his daughter and hold her, to forget that this conversation had even taken place. Yet he told himself that the longer he was in the car with Rachel, the better chance he had to convince her that she was wrong.

Although everything Rachel had said was true, E.G. didn't think it was enough to dissolve their marriage. "Is there someone else?" he had asked.

"It's not about anyone else. It's about us," Rachel had replied.

"I can't give you 9-to-5 in this business," E.G. had said. "Journalism is not a job, it's a lifestyle, and you knew that marrying me was marrying a lifestyle. We talked about that."

"And I thought I could accept it and adjust, but I've discovered that I can't do that."

For what seemed like an eternity, both were silent. Rachel stared at the blackness on the side of the highway, occasionally blinking when the lights from exit signs appeared in her path. E.G. kept his eyes on the road in front of him, drawn deeper into thought by the constant motion of the wipers slapping against the windshield.

"I could change careers. I mean, I could find something where I could still write, but not in the news business," E.G. had offered. "I could do public relations," he said, feeling his body involuntary shudder at the thought.

But Rachel wouldn't have that. "You were born to be a reporter, and you're damn good at what you do. Despite the way I feel, I am very proud of you and all you've accomplished. I would never ask you to give this up. And even if you did, I know you wouldn't be happy."

And she was right. E.G. could not imagine dressing each morning in a shirt and tie at a certain hour in order to be at a desk by nine a.m., the same time the rest of the nation would join him. He was not the corporate type, and had no desire to fit into the corporate mold. To E.G., the corporate world was one in which humans turned to robots for an eight-hour period five days per week, and each night, they would return to their homes, their only happiness being in the paycheck that was directly deposited into their cushioned savings accounts. They had their 401Ks, their health benefits plans, four weeks of vacation after one year of service, and somebody to come to their homes to tend to their lawns and pools.

But they didn't have the one thing E.G. had in the newspaper business, the one thing that was more important to him than anything material — an impact on human life. Through his stories, E.G. had united neighbors, mourned with families whose lives were shattered in the blinking of an eye, rallied community groups that formed after reading about development proposals that had the potential to change entire neighborhoods, and put children on the pedestals on which they belonged.

No, he knew his option of leaving the newspaper business was nonexistent. And the more he and Rachel discussed their future, and crossing Maryland, Delaware and into New Jersey, the more realistic it had become for the both of them that their only option was to separate — but to do so amicably, if only for Erin's sake.

When they divorced, they divided everything equally, including custody of their daughter. There was no alimony, no ordered child support payments. As a certified public accountant for a Fortune 500 company, Rachel did not have to rely on a stipend from E.G.'s salary, which she knew was moderate to begin with and would put him in a difficult enough position living on his own.

As he did each time he drove onto the street where Rachel lived, E.G. tensed. He knew one of these times he would see an unfamiliar car in the driveway, a car belonging to a man who would enter Rachel's life and lock the door on any chance of a reconciliation. E.G. held out hope, although he knew his chances were slim to none. Yet after two years, he also knew that when the time came for him to meet the new man in his ex-wife's life, he would be just as jealous as if he were married to her and found out she had been having an affair.

But that day, just like every time he had come down the street for the last two years, only the blue Jeep Grand Cherokee that became hers in the divorce occupied a space in the driveway. E.G. pulled in behind it, and stepped out of his car.

The August sun peeked over the top of Rachel's light blue Cape Cod home, casting a shadow over most of the front yard. The lawn, dark green despite more than a week without rain, was evenly manicured. Flowers of nearly every color in the spectrum adorned both sides of the brick path that led from the foot of the property to the front porch. Centered on either side of the walk were two small elm trees, and at the foot of the trees were more flowers. Shrubs were lined neatly on either side of the porch, some high enough to prevent seeing into the front windows. In front of the property stood one of South Orange's landmark features — a gas lamp.

Erin was daddy's little girl, so E.G. had been told many times. She was blond like her father, shared the same light complexion, and could be as bold as he could be during his toughest interview. And when she opened the door before he could even ring the bell, she smiled the same bright smile that would grace E.G.'s face as he tried to put at ease one of his interviewees.

"Hi, daddy," Erin said, stepping back to let E.G. into the house.

"How's my little girl?" he asked, stepping into the doorway and picking up Erin. Their faces only inches apart, Erin whispered, "Mommy's upset."

"She is? Why is that?" E.G. asked, his voice also a whisper.

"I don't know," she continued whispering. "But when we got home and she looked in the mailbox, she read something and said 'Oh, Christ.'"

E.G. kissed his daughter on the cheek and put her down, holding one arm over her shoulder. He looked into the house and, not seeing Rachel, asked Erin to find her mother and to tell her he had arrived. Erin disappeared, and a few minutes later, returned with her mother in tow.

Rachel was, as Erin described, upset. While to a casual observer she didn't show it, E.G. learned to read his former wife. Rachel had light brown hair that she almost always wore braided, and big round brown eyes. She came to the door in her stocking feet, the heels she wore that day resting against the side of the stairs, where E.G. knew Rachel had kicked them when she came home from work. It was always the first thing she did when she got home from work.

Rachel forced a smile, and E.G. returned it, albeit with a sincere one.

He bent to come face to face with Erin. "Why don't you run upstairs and get some of your toys ready?"

"OK, daddy." Her voice was cheerful as she turned and scooted up the eleven stairs and toward her room.

E.G. stood and looked at Rachel. "What's wrong?"

She didn't hesitate to tell him. "Somebody must think you still live here," she said, putting her hand in a pocket in her skirt and pulling out a folded sheet of paper, which she handed to E.G. "I found this in the mailbox."

E.G. unfolded the paper and read the cut out letters taped to the white piece of paper. "Stop asking so many questoins," it read.

Seeing how upset Rachel was, E.G. tried to inject humor to ease her mind. "They spelled questions wrong."

"E.G., this isn't funny," Rachel said. "What have you gotten yourself into?"

"Why do you assume this has anything to do with me?"

"I get the paper each week. I saw your story yesterday, and from the tone of it, it reeked of E.G. Lord on the prowl. I can only imagine what you've been up to since you scooped everybody else."

If there was one person E.G. could count on to support his journalism career, it was Rachel, E.G. thought. As long as it was from afar, he added sadly to himself.

"Just your basic snooping," he replied, trying hard, through the process of elimination, to figure out who could have written the note. "I know," E.G. said. "It's that guy in your office you always turn to when you're stuck on some tax question."

The second attempt at humor did not go over well with Rachel. "Cut the shit," Rachel said. "Someone came to this house today, in broad daylight, and put something in our mailbox. Whoever that was has a lot of balls, and I'm not too comfortable with that."

"I'm sorry," E.G. said. "You're right. I guess I was just trying to ease your tension."

E.G. followed Rachel into the living room and sat across from her on the couch. The note hung between his fingers, and they both stared at it. "Did you call anyone about this?"

"Who was I going to call? I got home ten minutes before you got here."

"Okay, okay, relax. I'm asking because I don't want anything to happen to you or to Erin while you're in this house. Let me call the police just to have something on record. I'll get my contacts at police headquarters to have patrol cars drive around here tonight."

"I don't need this, E.G."

"I'm sure it's nothing. A scare tactic. I just want to be on the safe side."

As E.G. left the room to use the phone in the kitchen, Erin came down the stairs. In her hands were two dolls and the latest Barbie house E.G. had recently bought for her. She dropped everything by the front door and jumped on the couch next to Rachel. "Where's daddy?"

"Making a phone call," Rachel said, reaching over and straightening Erin's shirt. "He'll be right back."

They could hear E.G.'s muffled voice through the door he pulled over when he entered the kitchen.

"Who's he talking to?" Erin asked.

"Just a friend," Rachel lied. "Something to do with one of the stories he's working on. You know daddy. He never stops working."

They heard the phone be placed back on the receiver, and soon after, E.G. emerged from the kitchen and joined them. "Are we ready to go?" he called out to Erin. "Where's your bag?"

Erin rolled her eyes and got up from the couch. "I left it upstairs."

"Well, hurry up and get it."

When Erin disappeared at the top of the stairs, E.G. turned to Rachel. "A patrol car will be checking out the house tonight from time to time. Leave the front light on all night."

"What did you tell the police?"

"That you were sent a note that was meant for me telling me to stop asking questions."

"Bullshit," Rachel said.

E.G. stood frozen.

"Do you expect me to believe that you told the police there's a possibility that killers were at my front door today and all they said was they would check out the house from time to time? Do you think I'm stupid, E.G.?"

E.G. was caught and he knew it. But as much as he was embarrassed that he was caught, he was tickled that Rachel had grown to become so analytical and logical. Only he would never tell her that.

"All right, all right," E.G. said. "I told them you were being harassed at work today, and that while I'm sure it's nothing to be worried about, you'd feel safer if a patrol car went by the house a few times tonight. It was the police who said to leave the light on unless you want to get their attention."

Rachel stared at him, not saying a word.

E.G. collected the dolls and Barbie house and looked upstairs, but Erin still was not coming down. He was growing uncomfortable.

"It's a scare tactic," E.G. repeated. "Nothing is going to happen. A note like this is their way of trying to put fear in me, to get me to stop doing my job. And besides, if they left the note today, do you think they'd come back to the house this soon after? They have to believe we would have called the police to report it."

Rachel moved to the stairs and looked up to the second floor. She could hear Erin in the bedroom. "I'm not comfortable with this. I don't want you to let her out of your sight for one minute this weekend. Am I making myself clear?"

E.G. called up the stairs for Erin, and she came bouncing out of the bedroom and down the stairs. He whispered to Rachel, "Call me on my cell phone if you have to. And I gave the number to the police as well, so relax."

Rachel bent and kissed Erin on the cheek. "I'll see you Monday after work," she said.

"Bye, mommy. I love you," Erin said, taking E.G. by the hand and leading him out the door. As they pulled out of the driveway, E.G. saluted Rachel, who remained in the doorway waving good bye to Erin.

It wasn't until they reached the end of the street and turned onto the main road that E.G. let his fear show, something he refused to do in Rachel's presence. The image of Rachel waving good bye remained etched in his mind, and instinct told him to turn around and return to the house. Rachel was right. Killers could have been at her front door that afternoon, and if, as even she said, they were bold enough to go to the house in daylight, what would stop them from going to the house during the evening, or the middle of the night, when they would assume everyone in the house was asleep?

He laughed aloud at what he called his own foolishness. The laughter caught Erin's attention in the back seat, and she stopped playing with the doll's hair. E.G. caught her in the rearview mirror and looked quizzically at her.

"What did you laugh at?" she asked.

"Someone in another car," was his response. "They looked funny."

He reached into his shirt pocket and removed the two slips of paper from inside. One, he recognized instantly as the note Rachel found in the mailbox. The other, folded twice, he had to open. It contained Travis Boesgaard's address, and E.G. remembered he had put the note in his pocket just before leaving the office.

He laid both notes on the passenger seat, his eyes returning to the cut-outs, and each time he saw it, anger rose inside him. Nathanya Berns, Matt from the Internet and Dirtdealer were the only three people who knew he was doing more than his job of writing stories. He eliminated Matt from the list because Matt didn't know he had been talking to a reporter, and he eliminated Dirtdealer because Dirtdealer, after all, was the one who was leading him somewhere with the information he had been supplying. Would Nathanya Berns have sent the note, E.G. wondered, and if so, why?

E.G. turned to face Erin when he reached a red traffic light. "How would you like to get burgers and fries and then go on a mission with me?"

Erin's face brightened. She had been to court with E.G. when verdicts had come in; she had been to Board of Education meetings with E.G. when residents loudly traded barbs with their district leaders; she had been to accident scenes with E.G. that horrified her, and she got to pet and hug a monkey whose owners were being forced to remove it from their home after it was discovered they kept it as a pet.

So anytime E.G. suggested they go on a mission together, Erin was ready and willing.

"Where are we going?"

"Tonight, we'll be spies," he said, grinning, hoping to build her interest enough so she wouldn't grow bored.

"Who are we going to spy on?"

"I'll let you know that when we get there."

Forty-five minutes later, with two double cheeseburgers, fries and a soda for E.G., and a kid's meal for Erin, the two of them sat in E.G.'s car down the street from where Travis Boesgaard lived. The Boesgaard house was magnificent. Built entirely with brick, the three-story home was set back on an expansive piece of property that included a mini-waterfall cascading down a slope in the front lawn that was filled in with huge boulders. That was to the right of the steps, which began at the sidewalk and wound their way to the top of the lawn, stopping at a walkway that led one way to the front door and to the driveway on the other side. To the left of the staircase was a well-tended garden, whose plants were colorful for a dry and hot August day.

With the exception of a few cars passing E.G.'s Tercel, the street was awfully quiet for a summer evening. Where were the kids, E.G. wondered, running around the street like they'd be doing on his own block? And the longer they waited, nothing changed.

By seven o'clock, Erin began to grow restless. "How long are we going to sit here? This is a boring mission."

"Yeah," E.G. sighed. "It sure turned out to be that." But just as he was about to start his car, E.G. noticed a figure moving near the Boesgaard house. A man who looked to be in his mid to late twenties sat on the porch and held a cordless phone to his ear. Bracing the phone against his shoulder, he reached into the pocket of his short-sleeve pullover shirt and removed a cigarette.

"Stay low," E.G. said to Erin, who, after more than one hour of waiting in the car, was not about to pass up the chance to discover what this mission was about. She picked her head up, glanced at her father, and shifted her eyes in the same direction as his.

"Is that who we're waiting for?" she asked, whispering.

"Could be. I've never seen the person before," E.G. replied.

Travis Boesgaard sucked on his cigarette while he yelled into the telephone. E.G. couldn't make out what he was saying, but knew, from the facial expressions he was making as he spoke, that he wasn't happy. Travis stood about six feet tall, was lean with a long, thin face that was lined along the jaw with a narrow beard that reached up to dark brown hair along his ears. He wore a baseball cap whose peak

131

was bent to the point that it looked as if it spent more time folded in his back pocket than resting on his head. The short gym trunks he was wearing revealed legs belonging to a runner.

Travis dropped the phone from his ear and disconnected the call. He took one more deep drag on the cigarette before flicking the butt into the waterfall. He stood and went back into the house.

"What do we do now?" Erin asked.

"We wait. That's if it's okay with you. Are you feeling all right? I know we've been sitting here a long while."

"Well, what do you think is going to happen?"

"Your guess is as good as mine. I'm hoping that with the phone call he just made, someone will be coming to the house. I'd love to go right up there and ring that doorbell."

"Why don't you?" It was an innocent question coming from an innocent seven-year-old.

"If only it were that easy, sweetheart," E.G. said. "But I can't, because I don't want him to know I'm from the newspaper."

"What did he do?"

"Only the Dirtdealer knows for sure."

Erin looked up at E.G. with a confused look on her face. "I don't even know if that's the person I'm looking for," he said, without explaining the Dirtdealer reference.

They didn't have to wait long because within ten minutes, the man who E.G. assumed was Travis appeared again at the front door, this time inserting a key into the lock and heading toward the driveway. E.G. heard the sound of a car engine starting and, a moment later, watched a black Audi back out of the driveway and onto the street. E.G. gently pulled Erin down and leaned over to hide the both of them if Travis were to drive by the car. Glancing just over the dashboard, he watched the Audi move in the other direction.

E.G. started his own car and pulled away from the curb slowly, allowing some distance between his and Travis' vehicle. Travis turned onto Northfield Avenue and headed west along the main thoroughfare out of West Orange, through the town of Livingston and into Morris County, continuing west on Route 10. It was a twenty-minute ride that ended for Travis in the parking lot of a bar on the highway. E.G. watched the black Audi leave the highway, and he continued, finding the next available turn-off, a gas station, where he guided his Tercel into an empty parking space near the bathrooms.

E.G. had a clear view from where he was sitting. Travis got out of the car and went inside the bar.

"I have to go to the bathroom," Erin said.

E.G. knew that when a seven-year-old declares she has to go to the bathroom, that means she's had to go for quite some time.

"C'mon," E.G. said, releasing Erin from her seatbelt. "Climb over and come out this way."

Erin did as she was told, and the two of them marched into the office of the gas station, where a tall, heavyset black man sat with his feet on the desk.

"My daughter needs to use the restroom. Would that be all right?"

"Key's up on the post," the man said without moving.

E.G. grabbed the key for the men's room and led Erin out the door and toward the side of the building, all the while looking into the parking lot next door for any sign of Travis. He unlocked the door and ushered Erin inside, looking around first to be sure they were alone. The tiny room, complete with a urinal, stall, sink and garbage pail, smelled of urine, and E.G. could think of at least one thing the man in the office could have been doing instead of sitting with his feet on a desk.

When Erin began to slide her pants down, she was met with a "Wait a minute" from E.G., who had stepped into the stall and pulled pieces upon pieces of toilet paper from the roll that clung to the side of the stall wall. He must have lined the toilet with three inches of paper before he allowed Erin inside.

"Don't let your fanny touch anything but this toilet paper," he said, closing the door and allowing her some privacy.

"Why?" she asked.

"Because I don't want you waking me up at three o'clock in the morning crying because you have a rash on your bottom."

"Why would I get a rash?"

"Because."

"Why because?"

E.G. opened the outer door and looked into the neighboring parking lot. The Audi was still there.

"Because you don't know who used the toilet last. It could have been a dirty person."

"And they would give me a rash?"

"Erin, please. I'll explain it to you when you're fifteen."

E.G. could hear Erin fussing inside the stall. "Daddy, I'm done."

"Then flush the toilet and come on out of there."

"But if I flush the toilet, I might touch something and get a rash."

"Then just stand up and pull your pants up. I'll flush the toilet."

Erin came out of the stall and instinctively moved to the sink. Before she could turn the faucet on, E.G. rushed over and turned on the water using a piece of toilet paper.

"Will I get a rash here too?" she asked.

"Everything in this room reeks of a rash, sweetheart," E.G. said, flushing the toilet and disposing the toilet paper he used as a seat liner.

Outside, dusk was beginning to settle, and E.G. thought how early it began to get dark in late August. Across the lot, the Audi still sat in the parking lot of the bar.

"Are we going to sit here and wait some more?" Erin asked.

"No. I have an idea," E.G. said, leaving Erin at the corner of the building while he went into the office to return the key. The black man was in the same position as he was when E.G. went in to borrow the key, and he wondered if there had even been one sale since they had arrived. He nodded to the man, who nodded back, and E.G. was out of the office.

He led Erin to the car and backed out of the parking space. "I hope this works," he said aloud to himself as he entered the traffic on Route 10.

"Where are we going?" Erin asked.

"How would you like to play with Julien and Josh?" E.G. asked, his voice trying to make the offer sound tempting. "We can take a ride to Uncle Raymond's and you can see them. It's been a long time since you've seen them, right?"

"They were at my birthday party last month, remember?"

"Oh." She had him on that one, E.G. thought. "But still, a month is a long time."

He explained that he needed to go into the bar, that it was important for his story, but he couldn't take her with him. At a traffic light, he turned and, with a pleading look on his face, he begged his daughter to work with him on this one.

He stared until, finally, the driver behind him pressed on his horn. The light had turned green and traffic moved all around the Tercel. E.G. turned and moved with the traffic, glancing in the rearview mirror at an obviously upset Erin. "I promise, somehow, I'll make it up to you," he said.

"I guess so," she gave in. "But if Julien messes with me, I'm gonna hit him."

"Just like I taught you," E.G. replied, then added, enunciating his words, "But you have to swear to me that you will not tell Uncle Raymond where I'm going."

Erin rolled her eyes and simultaneously crossed her heart. "I swear."

He estimated that the drive from the bar on Route 10 to the Vanderhoeven house would be about ten minutes, fifteen at the most. He made it in twelve and sighed with relief when he saw the Buick in the driveway.

CHAPTER SEVENTEEN

The Audi sat exactly where he left it, and E.G.'s heart began to beat faster when he saw it. He slipped the Tercel into the parking stall next to the Audi and when he got out of his car, he peered into the passenger's side window of the other car. It was another way to look for information. The inside of the car was a mess, E.G. thought. Cigarette butts spilled out of an open ashtray, and ashes spread along the console and carpet between the two front seats. On the back seat lay that week's *Sentinel* among a pile of assorted papers, and among them, E.G. saw a piece of an envelope addressed to "Tra" as it rested underneath an overturned piece of paper.

He knew that if he could see the entire envelope, the Tra would become Travis. The beginning of Travis' address also was visible on the next two lines. A man who looked to be in his early thirties crossed the sidewalk in front of E.G. and looked back at him before entering the bar. E.G. closed the door to the Tercel and followed.

The room was dark, lit only by dim overhead lamps. Music from a jukebox played in the background, drowning the sound of the television that sat perched over the bar. Of the approximately fifteen people in the bar, the first person E.G. saw was the thirty-ish man who had given him the once-over outside. The man nodded and smiled, and E.G. nodded back, offering a phony smile in return. Two other men sat together at a table in a corner of the bar, and as they talked, their eyes remained fixed on one another. Neither looked over when E.G. entered the bar. A group of four men sat three tables over, and each looked in E.G.'s direction when he entered. Two of the men locked eyes with E.G. as his eyes scanned the table. E.G. guessed they were all in their early forties, as were the three men toward the back of the bar, where a pool table had their attention. At the bar itself, four more men sat, none of whom was Travis Boesgaard.

E.G. mounted an empty stool at the bar near the entrance and waited as the bartender approached. "Evening," was all the bartender said.

E.G. nodded and asked for a Corona. He shook his head when the bartender offered a glass, and laid a ten dollar bill on the bar.

Two stools over, a half empty glass sat orphaned next to a pack of cigarettes, an ashtray and a small pile of dollar bills. The occupant, however, was missing, probably in the men's room, E.G. thought.

The bartender, a stocky man in his forties, returned and placed a mug of draft beer on the bar in front of the seat next to E.G. and the Corona in front of him. The thirty-ish man got up from his table and moved to the bar, opting for the open seat next to E.G., and swallowed half the mug of beer.

"You're new here," he said to E.G. "Welcome." He lifted his glass; E.G. lifted his bottle.

"Name's Bill. Are you from around here?"

"I'm Craig," E.G. replied, picking the first hard C name that came to mind as he looked at the word Corona. "And close enough."

Bill got the hint. It wasn't unusual for a guy to come into The Lucky Leaf and want to remain anonymous. Some guys, he told E.G., were married and therefore had to remain discreet. Others, he said, came in to find a partner for an hour and never step foot into their lives again. "It goes with the territory," he said.

E.G. looked around the bar once more and realized then that there were no women inside. He realized which territory he had invaded.

"Do you fall into the married category or the quickie? I hope neither because you definitely look like relationship material," Bill laughed.

E.G. returned a smile and thought fast, realizing for the first time he was in a gay bar. With his left thumb, he unconsciously massaged his left ring finger, adorned once with a wedding band. "Let's just say I'm very new to this and need to go slowly," he lied.

"Looking for anything in particular?"

Just then, E.G. heard what sounded like a telephone being slammed into its cradle and, from around the corner near the pool table, Travis Boesgaard emerged and headed toward the bar.

"Be a little more careful with the phone," the bartender reprimanded.

"Yeah, yeah, yeah," Travis responded, taking his seat on the stool in front of the drink and cigarettes. Bill sat between them. Lighting a cigarette, Travis glanced in E.G.'s direction long enough to lock eyes. He appeared to be the youngest guy in the bar. E.G. prayed that he wouldn't recognize him as a reporter for *The Sentinel.* The anger had disappeared, and was replaced by a flirtatious smile. "Smile," Travis said. "We could be married in the morning."

E.G. froze.

"The man wants to be left alone," Bill intervened from between them.

"And is that why you've slithered up here?" Travis asked. "If the man wants to be left alone, he'll have to tell me that himself."

Neither Bill nor E.G. replied.

Hearing no reply, Travis said to Bill, "Take your sorry ass back to your table and take a number."

Obediently, Bill slid off the stool, but leaned toward E.G. before leaving. "I'll just be over here if you need me."

E.G. remained frozen as he watched Bill get up from the stool as if on command.

"Bill would settle for Mr. Right, but he'd never turn down Mr. Right Now," Travis said, leaning toward E.G. as if he were a confidante in the middle of a secret, but speaking loud enough for even the two men in the far corner to hear him. "What's your name?" he slurred.

"Craig," E.G. said, wondering how many drinks Travis had consumed.

"It's a pleasure to meet you, Craig. I am the one and only Travis Boesgaard, and I would like to buy you your second drink tonight, if you'll let me. Then after that, we can talk about the third, fourth and fifth drinks. The sixth, I'm hoping, will be at my place."

"Are you always this forward?" E.G. asked.

"Only with guys who look as hot as you do. How's that for honesty?"

"That and flattery will get you everywhere." E.G. played along apprehensively. He raised his bottle toward Travis, and Travis returned the gesture with his own glass, sliding onto the stool next to E.G. He then chugged the remainder of the contents and asked Henry the bartender for another.

As if on cue, Henry filled a glass with ice and, under E.G.'s careful eye, mixed Jack Daniels and ginger ale in the glass and set the drink in front of Travis.

From his few moments with Travis, E.G. didn't see any signs of someone holding key information in a murder case as Dirtdealer was suggesting. To the contrary, Travis was in control, despite the reddening eyes and slurred speech. E.G. thought of Dirtdealer's e-mails and couldn't help but think he was led on a goose chase.

"What's your story?" Travis asked. "What brings you to The Lucky Leaf?"

E.G. lied. "At first, I was looking for some quiet time. But I didn't realize I was going to meet someone as charming as you." He smiled a fake smile hoping to win over Travis. "I just lost someone very close to me."

Travis raised his eyebrows, and E.G. knew his new friend went for the bait.

"I'm sorry to hear that," Travis said, looking somber for the first time. "But don't they always leave us?"

"They? Who's they?"

"Lovers," he said, and growing pensive, continued, "I used to write the names of lovers within the shape of a heart. Now I'm going to write them in a circle. Circles don't break. Hearts do, and I'm tired of having a broken heart."

A melancholy drunk, E.G. thought.

"Did you lose someone too? Is that why you're drinking?"

Travis picked up his drink and swallowed a mouthful of the Jack and ginger. He also lit a cigarette and, unconsciously, blew the smoke in E.G.'s direction. He held the pack of Marlboro Lights to E.G.

E.G. waved him off. He hadn't had a cigarette since Erin was born.

"So who died?" Travis asked.

"I don't know what you mean."

"You said you just lost someone very close to you. Who died?"

"Nobody died. It was a break-up."

"I don't know what's worse: losing someone in a break-up or having them die on you. At least in a break-up, they're still with us, and there's that chance you'll get to see them again, even if it's only to stir the memories of the time you spent together."

E.G. instantly thought of Rachel and how he would give his left arm for a reconciliation.

"Did that happen to you?" E.G. asked. "Did a lover die?"

Travis shifted his gaze from the bottles that lined the wall of the bar to E.G. "You ask a lot of questions."

"You look hurt, and you sound as if you need a friend. I'm a good listener. Sometimes, the people you don't know often give the best advice."

"You have a beautiful smile," Travis said, staring at E.G.'s mouth. "Has anyone ever told you that you have a beautiful smile?"

"A few times." Never another man, E.G. thought.

"And those eyes. It's as if they look right through you, into your soul."

E.G. grew uncomfortable, for as much as he was trying to gain Travis' trust, no man had ever spoken to him the way Travis did. Guilt built inside him, and he knew he had already stepped over the line of deception to gather information. He thought of Patrick Crowe, his late editor, and wondered if this was what he meant when he posed the question, "How far would you go to get a story?"

"What do you see when you look into my soul?" Travis asked, gazing into E.G.'s eyes.

E.G. directed the course of the conversation. "Someone laughing on the outside, but crying on the inside. Someone who needs a friend."

Travis swallowed another mouthful of his drink and took another drag on his cigarette. He returned his gaze to the bottles on the wall and blew the smoke in the same direction. E.G. watched the smoke drift into the air and dance under the lamp above the bar. "I was a lover, not a friend," he said.

"To whom?"

"I'm going to a funeral in the morning," Travis said in a happy tone laced with sarcasm and smelling of anger.

E.G. remained quiet, waiting for Travis to spill all about his relationship with Mickey Berns.

"The toughest part is going to be blending with all the other funeral goers and saying good-bye from afar." He shifted his gaze to E.G. "Nobody knew about us," he said somberly.

E.G.'s sad smile was sincere, and he realized that the longer he listened to Travis, the more he felt sorry for him. He wondered if Nathanya Berns knew about her son's relationship with Travis.

"You may have read about him. It's been in all the papers," Travis said.

"Who?"

"Steven Conroy. He was found dead this week. Police have been investigating it for the last three days."

E.G.'s mouth dropped, and Travis questioned his surprise.

"Of course I heard about it," E.G. said quickly. "I never expected to run into the guy's boyfriend." He was certain Travis was going to say Mickey Berns. "Now I can see why you're so upset."

Travis finished his drink and asked for another. Like magic, a new Jack and ginger appeared. E.G. took a long swig of the Corona and finished the beer. He also asked for a refill.

"He was found on the mountain, right? With another guy?" E.G. asked.

Travis sneered. "Yeah. That mother fucker deserved to die, but not Steven." Travis stared into the new drink left by the bartender. As he took a swig of his beer, E.G. wondered when the bartender would decide Travis had had enough.

"Did you know the other guy?" E.G. asked.

"Mickey Berns?" Travis called to the bartender: "Hey, Henry." When the bartender turned and approached Travis, he said, "The man wants to know if I knew Mickey Berns."

Henry shook his head. "Bad news," was all he said.

Travis turned back to E.G. "If you had something Mickey wanted, he did his best to take it from you. The man sucked."

"And he did that well," Bill said from the table behind them.

E.G. ignored the comment and focused on Travis. "If you and Steven were a couple, why was Steven with Mickey that night?"

"I had something Mickey wanted." Travis suddenly grew bitter. "He took it from me, but that's the last thing he'll ever take from anybody, isn't it?" he said, sounding almost satisfied that Mickey was dead. He even sounded as if he were gloating.

E.G. had the follow-up question resting at the tip of his tongue, dying to ask it, but The Lucky Leaf was the last place he wanted to ask Travis if he was responsible for the deaths of Steven and Mickey.

So he ran around the bush for a bit. "Is that why they're dead? Did somebody not want them together?" He knew there was no difference between the way he worded his question and if he had come right out and said, "Did you kill them?", but stated with quizzical eyes to a drunk man, the words emerged with a vastly different meaning.

Travis rubbed the rim of his glass with his finger. "Steven is dead because he was with Mickey. Steven wasn't high profile. For Christ sake, he was so deep in the closet, he hung out with the dust balls. He was looking only for quiet companionship with a guy. You know who's going to be in the church tomorrow with his family? His girlfriend. She had no clue that half the time he was kissing her good night, he was leaving to come to my place."

E.G. could believe that, if only for the recent experiences on the online live boards with married guys who were looking to cheat on their wives with men whose secret lives were built around online aliases.

"Nobody was after Steven," Travis was saying. "He was the kindest guy you'd ever want to know. He just happened to be in the wrong place at the wrong time."

"How long had you two been involved?"

"About four months."

"And you accepted that kind of relationship? The secrecy?"

Travis chuckled. "It's a turn-on for me." He looked at E.G. and noticed the perplexed look on his face. "A masculine guy looking to break the barriers and explore his sexuality? They're more real than any queen you could pick up in a place like this. Present company excluded, of course."

Travis winked at E.G., and E.G. felt the discomfort warm his reddening face.

"But then again, you're no queen," Travis said, not hiding the fact that he was looking down at E.G.'s crotch. "Besides, I've been there before. The last guy I was with was the same way. And we were together for about two years. Nobody at work knew, nobody in his family knew."

Travis seemed to disappear into a world of his own. With bloodshot eyes, he stared into the glass in front of him, the cigarette dangling between his fingers.

"You okay?" E.G. asked, leaning closer to Travis.

Travis blinked, then looked up at E.G. "Would you take me home? I don't think I can make it on my own."

It wasn't difficult to figure that out. "What will you do about your car? Your car is parked outside."

"It'll have to stay there." Travis pushed the drink away from him. "I had too much."

"I'll agree with you on that. Can you stand?"

Travis smiled. "Are you really going to take me home?"

"If there's a choice between driving you home and reading about you in tomorrow's obits column, I'll give you the ride."

"Hopefully, it will be the ride of my life," Travis said, winking.

"Not only are you very drunk, you're also very horny," E.G. replied, getting up from his stool.

"Come on, we're men. Aren't we always horny?"

"I suppose you're right," E.G. said, taking Travis by the arm and assisting him off the stool.

At first, Travis wavered, but after a moment, he got his balance, collected his cigarettes and lighter from the counter, and allowed E.G. to lead him out of the bar. As they walked, E.G. looked back into the room and realized that half the bar was watching them. He gave one final look at Bill, the man who had tried to come on to him when he first arrived, and noticed Bill give him the thumbs up.

Outside, Travis pointed out the Audi, telling E.G. that was his car and asking whether or not he thought it was beautiful. Feeling E.G.'s arm around his waist, Travis slipped his own arm around E.G.'s waist as they walked one car over to where E.G. had parked the Tercel. He opened the passenger door and helped Travis inside. As E.G. leaned in to fasten the seat belt, Travis kissed his cheek, a move that forced E.G. to jump back and hit his head on the rearview mirror.

"What did you do that for?" he asked.

"To see if you're really gay," Travis replied. E.G. backed out of the car. "You don't look gay, and you don't act gay. So what's your deal?"

E.G. closed the passenger door, stepped around the car and got in on the driver's side. The five seconds that it took gave him time to think. "My deal is that I don't have to act gay to be gay. Aren't you sick of the stereotypes? Did you know that when I looked at you, I didn't think you were gay either?" He turned on the engine, then laid his right hand on Travis' thigh. "I'm new to this," he lied. "Cut me some slack."

Travis instinctively rested his hand on E.G.'s, and E.G. decided it would be best not to pull it away quickly.

"It's all right, man. I'm patient."

E.G. took Travis' hand in his own, laid them on the gear shift, put the car in reverse and slowly backed out of his parking space. Still keeping his hand in place, he shifted into drive and pulled out of the parking lot, heading west on Route 10 until he came to the first jughandle to get back onto Route 10 East. Travis had given him the street address, and E.G. said he knew exactly where it was, not mentioning, of course, that he had sat in front of the drunk man's home for a couple hours earlier that night with his daughter waiting for him to come out.

Erin, he thought. His instructions before he dropped her off at Raymond's house were for her not to say anything to her uncle or aunt about what they had done that night. It was for a news story, he had told her, and when he investigates news stories, he always has to keep his information private.

Of course, Erin said she understood. She enjoyed the mystery that surrounded the missions she embarked on with her father — knew it was his job and knew that he could get hurt if his secret information were revealed to the wrong people.

That night probably wouldn't have been the best time for her to reveal anything, though. He recalled the anger on Raymond's face when Erin greeted him at the front door. Liz came right behind him and opened the screen door for her niece. From his idling car in the driveway, E.G. yelled, "I hope it's okay. It'll just be for a couple of hours." And as he rolled back down the driveway and into the street, he extended his arm in a gesture of thanks and continued, "I need to meet Rachel somewhere."

Blocking their opportunity to respond, E.G. pulled away from the house and was gone.

A part of him wanted Erin to say something to Raymond. He thought of it as an indirect way of informing the police, to protect his own ass, and to relieve himself of some of the guilt he was feeling because of withholding the information.

The doubt that had crept inside him now, he knew, stemmed from the fact that he was in a car with someone who could be a double murderer. What was it, he wondered, jealous rage that pushed Travis to this? Had he discovered them together? Did they laugh at him, taunting him to the point of taking their lives? And where does Dirtdealer fit into this, he continued to wonder.

But the more he re-examined his conversation with Travis that night, the more he believed Travis was innocent. At least in the actual murders. Call it good reporter's instinct, or one of the lessons Patrick had taught him: Watch your subject's behavior, Patrick Crowe had told E.G. People always reveal more than they intend to reveal.

Travis didn't exhibit the behavior of a killer, especially one who struck only four days earlier. If he was, E.G. thought, he was a good actor.

At the very least, he might hold information, and that was equally important. But to gain that, he knew he had to scale the wall of ethics and pretend to be gay to build a trust in Travis.

E.G. wondered what Patrick Crowe would be thinking as he looked down from heaven's newsroom and watched him crossing the line of journalistic ethics.

He glanced at Travis, seated in the passenger seat with eyes closed and head bobbing. How far would he go for a news story, E.G. asked himself as he crossed into Livingston on his way to Travis' house in West Orange.

Halfway into the ride home, Travis opened his eyes and looked around, trying to get a grip on his surroundings. He sighed heavily, shifting in his seat.

"Looks like someone's going to get a good night's sleep tonight," E.G. said. "You're already passing out."

"Sorry, man," Travis said, and E.G. distinctly heard the slurring in the two words. "I drank more than I should have."

"Hey, you're upset. It's understandable. It's not every day you lose someone in such a horrible way." After a pause, E.G. asked, "Do you know anyone who would want to do this to Mickey Berns?"

"The easier question to answer is if I know anyone who *wouldn't* want to kill Mickey Berns," Travis said. "The only one I can think of is you — and that's because you didn't know him."

"Well, think. When you were with Steven, did he say anything to you that might have caught your attention? Something that you didn't realize was significant until you look at it in retrospect? Like mentioning someone else's name, or referring to something maybe Mickey had gotten involved in."

"He never talked about Mickey. He never let on that he was seeing Mickey. And I never even got a chance to confront him on that."

As they crossed into West Orange, the two men sat silent. Travis continued to drift in and out of consciousness, and E.G. grew concerned about what would happen once he got Travis home. Travis didn't seem like a bad guy, he thought, as he made his way down Northfield Avenue, convincing himself once more that he couldn't have been responsible for the double homicide.

E.G. turned into Travis' street and made his way up the long driveway, bringing the car to a halt on the side of the house and out of view of anyone from the street. He got out of the car and dashed to the passenger side, opening the door and releasing Travis from the seat belt. "Hey," he said into his ear. "You're home."

Travis flinched before waking up, and once again, looked around to capture his surroundings. "Man, I appreciate this," he said, accepting a hand from E.G. to get out of the car. "Come on in, Craig. Have a beer with me."

E.G. put his arm around Travis' waist and directed him up the driveway toward the back of the house. "I'll come in, but we can skip the drinks," he said. "You have your keys handy?"

"They're in my front pocket," Travis said, continuing to slur his words, but beckoning E.G. to get them himself.

E.G. reached into Travis' pocket and caught hold of the keys. He also caught hold of an erection and was amazed that as drunk as Travis was that he could still sustain a hard-on.

Travis grinned as E.G.'s hand brushed against his erection. E.G. ignored it, and removed the keys, leading Travis to the back door. After a few attempts, he found the right key and the door opened.

Inside was one of the most magnificent kitchens E.G. had ever seen, swearing to himself that it was as large as his living room and kitchen combined. "Come this way," Travis said, ushering E.G. through the kitchen and into the living room. "I live alone, so don't worry about waking up anyone."

Travis led him to the staircase, where he turned on a switch that dimly lit the room. Another switch lit the second floor. At the bottom of the stairs, E.G. saw a set of luggage and was reminded of the e-mail Dirtdealer had sent him earlier in the week. "Is Travis leaving town?" it had read. Apparently, Dirtdealer was accurate, he thought, as he stepped over the luggage and followed Travis. What else did he know, he wondered.

"How did you manage to get a house like this all to yourself?" E.G. asked as he followed Travis up the winding stairs.

"I'm rich," he said bluntly. "Blessed by two wealthy parents. When my father died, he left me a shitload of money."

The second floor boasted five bedrooms and a bathroom. They passed each of the rooms until they stopped in front of a door at the end of the hall, which, E.G. guessed, was actually at the front of the house. Using a key, which he dropped once before slipping it into the lock, Travis opened the door and led the way inside. Once inside, he turned and reached out to E.G.

E.G. held out his hands and rested them on Travis' arms, first, to prevent him from getting any closer than he already was, and second to make it seem like he was returning the affection. "I don't think you want to do this," E.G. said.

"Do what? Fool around?" Travis replied. "You bet I do."

E.G. shook his head. "I'd feel like I was taking advantage of you, and I don't want to feel that way. You just lost a lover, and I can't be a replacement for him. Not now."

If it wasn't for E.G.'s hands on his arms, Travis would have fallen to the floor. He was swaying and he barely was able to keep his eyes open. E.G. led him backward to the bed and sat him down at the foot of it. He sat next to him and put an arm around Travis' shoulder. Travis, in turn, rested his head against E.G.'s chest.

E.G.'s heart beat faster, and he wondered if Travis felt the pounding, thinking that he would never know guilt was playing the drums in his chest.

"I was beginning to fall in love with him," Travis said, resting an arm on E.G.'s stomach just above his crotch.

E.G. found himself comforting Travis like a friend would do to another. He knew he wasn't getting any more information from him, so E.G. helped him back to the pillows at the head of the bed, where he removed his jeans and laid them on a dresser next to the bed. "Steven's funeral is in the morning. You need to sleep this off if you want to make it."

"Stay with me," Travis said into his pillow, and E.G. was reminded again of his daughter. He used the same tone of voice that Erin used when she wanted E.G. to read to her at bedtime. It wasn't a question, nor was it really a statement. "Read to me" meant she wanted to go to sleep, but she didn't want to descend alone, that the sound of her father's voice would ease her into a new land, one filled with the unknown. Those three words uttered by Travis spoke volumes — that he didn't want to be alone, and that, albeit he had only known E.G. for a few hours, there was something about E.G. that made him trust him, especially in his own home as he was about to descend into a tranquil unknown.

Reluctantly, E.G. put his hand on Travis' shoulder and began gently rubbing his back. With each stroke of his hand, he thought, "This is all for a story." Once Travis was asleep, he would leave the house. He would take the key and return in the morning to make sure Travis was awake to attend the funeral. E.G. watched his hand rotate on Travis' back, watched as his hand met with the pullover shirt. Until five minutes ago, he had never been this close to another man, and he kept telling himself again and again that he was doing it for a story.

A short time later, E.G. heard the rhythmic breathing that meant Travis had fallen asleep. Passed out was a better word, E.G. thought, and he leaned over Travis' body and watched him breathe. As he looked at him, E.G. saw the child behind the tough facade Travis displayed when he first met him at The Lucky Leaf that night.

He felt sorry for Travis. He would attend the funeral the next day of someone with whom he had spent the last four months, but as Travis had said earlier that night, he would be seated in the rear of the church, a mere spectator as far as Steven's family was concerned. Perhaps a friend from the gym, or someone from the office, they would think. But certainly not someone whose heart had been damaged by their loss.

Or would they think otherwise, E.G. thought. Would Steven's family have been told of the place the Reservation had become, and would they already have become resigned to the fact that their son, brother, nephew, uncle enjoyed a life that he had kept only to himself? Would they look around the church in the morning and wonder if the faces of the unfamiliar men belonged to Steven's other life?

He'd come back in the morning, E.G. promised. To be safe, though, he moved to the dresser where he had placed Travis' pants and reached for the alarm clock that sat on the left side. It was enough distance from the bed that would require Travis to get out of it to turn off the blaring radio once the alarm sounded. Unfamiliar with the rectangular shaped clock, E.G. lifted it to determine how to set the alarm, and when he did, he uncovered a photograph that sent him reeling back to the bed.

The scene was a picnic grounds, with a barbecue pit burning on the right side of the photo and a man in an apron and chef's hat flipping what were probably hamburgers on a barbecue grill. A volleyball net was set up in the background, and a group of people — men, women and children — seemed to be having a good time playing. The focus of the photograph, in the center, was Travis with his arm around the shoulder of another man. They were both smiling. E.G. had to look twice and continued staring at the picture to convince himself that the other man indeed was Conor Headley.

It seemed to be a recent photo, and E.G. checked Conor's haircut and clothing to determine when the photo could have been taken. He guessed it was about a year old because he didn't remember seeing Conor in those clothes during the most recent summer, and his haircut was the same as it was now. E.G. stepped out into the hallway and turned on a light so he could search the photograph for familiar faces. There were none.

He returned to the room, searched the top of the dresser for other photos, looked in the frame of the mirror for the same, and, seeing none, placed the photo of Travis and Conor back under the alarm clock. He leaned over Travis' body. He remained fast asleep.

E.G. slowly opened each of the dresser drawers and skimmed them for more photos. As he rummaged — of course careful not to upset the arrangement of underwear, socks, condoms, and a few adult videos — he thought of something Travis had said at The Lucky Leaf: "The last guy I was with was the same way. And we were together for about two years. Nobody at work knew, nobody in his family knew."

Could he have meant Conor, E.G. wondered. He dismissed the thought of Conor being gay, or even bisexual, because, to the best of his recollection, neither of them had ever gotten into a discussion about sexuality. If Conor had been in a relationship with another man, E.G. thought, he would have seen some kind of sign regardless of how secret he wanted to keep it: a frequent caller at the office; unexplained hickeys on his neck; something that would prompt E.G. to ask a question. Wouldn't he?

But there was no sign, except for the photograph that lay under the alarm clock.

Shaken, E.G. wanted to call Conor for the answer and instinctively reached for the cell phone in his pants pocket. But he decided against it, preferring instead to handle it another way. In another drawer, he saw other photos, mostly Travis with men, but he didn't recognize any of them. A few seemed as if they were from the same picnic — close-ups of guests playing volleyball, one of the men wearing the chef's hat standing over the barbecue grill, and two handsome men at a picnic table with their lips locked in what seemed like a tender moment between the two of them captured forever, no different than the photo of Travis and Conor.

CHAPTER EIGHTEEN

The South Orange patrol car slowly turned onto Meadowbrook Lane, its headlights brightening the otherwise dark street. As he cruised along the narrow street, Officer Richard Duffy placed his coffee cup in the console and reached over onto the passenger's seat for the note he wrote to himself containing the address of Rachel Lord. Halfway down the street, he checked the numbers of the houses against the number on the piece of paper and realized he must have passed the house. A strange feeling stirred in his stomach as he looked into his rearview and side mirrors. He couldn't recall a house with a porch light on. He threw the car in reverse and inched backward, keeping his eyes on the right side of the street, the side with the odd numbers, the side where the Lord house would be.

The red brake lights glowed on Meadowbrook Lane when Duffy stopped in front of the Lord home. He knew it was their home because the number above the mailbox to the left side of the front door matched the number on the piece of paper he held in his hand. He had difficulty seeing the number because, just above it sat the porch light, but it was turned off.

CHAPTER NINETEEN

Conor knew Officer Richard Duffy of the South Orange Police Department. Duffy frequented The Brew and many times had purchased a pitcher of beer for Conor and E.G.

"As long as you guys aren't drinking and driving, this one's on me," he'd say, as if that would somehow free him from liability if one or both got into a car accident when they left the establishment.

But as much as Duffy could recognize Conor on sight, he had no idea what kind of car Conor drove, and didn't know that the silver Cutlass that pulled out of Meadowbrook Lane only seconds before he turned the patrol car into the street belonged to the reporter.

Conor casually pulled out of Meadowbrook Lane, then watched in his side-view mirror as Officer Duffy made a right into the street. He swallowed hard and continued driving to Ridgewood Road, where he made a left and headed to South Orange Avenue. At the traffic light, after lighting a cigarette, he picked up a cell phone and entered a phone number. "Shit," he said, when the voice mail picked up. He disconnected and tossed the phone onto the passenger seat, then slipped onto South Orange Avenue.

Within five minutes, the Cutlass turned onto Sagamore Road, and as he approached the Winter residence, Conor slowed the vehicle and looked around. A dimly lit living room was the only sign of life at the front of the home, but as he passed the house, he looked toward the side and saw one lone light coming from a second floor room toward the rear of the house. Below the window, parked in the driveway, was the Jeep Grand Cherokee that belonged to Brian Winter.

Conor again picked up the cell phone and pressed redial. Again, as he watched the window for sign of movement, he got the voice mail. He threw the butt of the cigarette out the window and took his foot off the brake as he disconnected the call.

As he pulled further up the street to turn his car around and debated whether or not he should go to the front door and ring the bell, headlights pierced his rearview mirror. He squinted from their unexpected brightness and then watched through his side-view mirror as a vehicle pulled into the Winters' driveway.

Able to see through the rearview mirror again, Conor watched as Ian Winter got out of his BMW and raced to the front of the house. He carried what looked to Conor like a duffel bag, but from his distance, he couldn't be sure. It was too dark. He waited for Ian to get inside before he turned the car around and parked it on the other side of the street. Turning off the headlights and engine, Conor waited in the dark and watched the Winter house. He lit another cigarette and took a deep drag that filled his lungs.

From where he sat, he could see Brian's window on the second floor. The light remained on, and within seconds, a light appeared in the kitchen window below. Conor knew it was the kitchen, just as he knew the upstairs bedroom belonged to Brian. He knew the layout of the entire house because he had been inside many times.

Of all the nights he wanted to be in there, he couldn't. He wasn't permitted in the house when Ian was home. It was a rule Conor had accepted when he met Brian. And even though Brian wasn't taking his calls, any calls it seemed, he was prepared to bang on the door until Brian had no choice but to open it and let him in.

The kitchen light went dark, and Conor sat upright in the driver's seat. He watched the front of the house for a sign that Ian might be leaving, but after waiting for about an hour and smoking four more cigarettes in that time, he assumed Ian was in for the night. He had so desperately wanted to be with Brian that night, and he discovered that the longer he couldn't be with him, the more frustrated he grew. He was prepared to tell Brian everything, and felt Brian was the only person who would understand what he had to do. He knew he couldn't turn to E.G. this time, despite their years of friendship, because he wasn't prepared to reveal the lifestyle he had hidden from his best friend all these years.

Conor started the car and slowly pulled away from the curb, unaware that one town over, his best friend had uncovered one of the secrets Conor had been keeping.

CHAPTER TWENTY

E.G. closed the last dresser drawer and checked Travis once more before searching the closet in the bedroom. He looked for a familiar piece of clothing, a shirt, pair of pants, that he might recognize as Conor's. After all, he justified, if Conor and Travis dated for almost two years, and their break-up was recent, chances were there may be something of his left in the house.

With no luck in the closet, E.G. stepped from the room and stood in the middle of the hallway. One by one, he peered into the four remaining bedrooms. Each held just the right amount of furniture to be considered guestrooms — a double bed, dresser with a mirror, night table and lamp, and a couple paintings each on the walls. The rooms were immaculate, as if they were exhibits in a museum instead of bedrooms in a home. Each of the drawers in each of the dressers was empty with the exception of random packages of mothballs in some of the drawers. The closets were the same, empty with the exception of a few clothes hangers in each.

E.G. couldn't help but wonder who cleaned the house, noticing instantly the difference in cleanliness between Travis' bedroom and the four others on the floor. He held the banister of the staircase leading to the third floor of the house, but decided, although his curiosity peaked, not to ascend the stairs. Instead, he used the bathroom, emptying the few beers that had filled his bladder since leaving The Lucky Leaf.

When he returned to Travis' bedroom, he found Travis had shifted, still asleep but now lying on his back. He pressed his hands against Travis' back and gently rolled him onto his side, fearing that on his back, he could get sick and choke on his own vomit.

E.G. lifted the alarm clock and, once more, looked at the photograph of Travis and Conor as he figured out how to set the clock for 6:30 the next morning. Conor had to have meant something to Travis, E.G. thought. Otherwise, why would this photograph be separated from the others?

The vibration of his cell phone in his pocket distracted his attention. As E.G. fished for it, he made his way back into the hallway, where he pulled over the door to Travis' room and turned on an overhead light. He recognized the phone number as one he had dialed hundreds of times in his career — the South Orange Police Department.

"Yes," he said into the mouthpiece and acknowledged that he was E.G. Lord to the familiar voice on the other end.

"You should get to your wife's house," the man said.

E.G. didn't think it was the time to correct the officer, to say, "No, you mean my ex-wife's house." Instead, he said, "I'm on my way," before hanging up the cell phone, checking on Travis once more and then racing out of the Boesgaard residence.

CHAPTER TWENTY-ONE

The distance between Travis' house and Rachel's house was a little less than three miles, but E.G. felt like an eternity had passed by the time he reached his former home. He maneuvered around sparse late-night traffic on Northfield Avenue and Gregory Avenue in West Orange and cut through side streets down the steep hill before crossing the border into South Orange. He heard at least one horn sound as he passed a car, and thought of returning the signal with the flip of his finger, but reacted differently. There was no time.

He chose not to ask the officer on the telephone to reveal what happened at his ex-wife's house. He didn't want bad news sooner than he had to hear it.

As he turned onto Meadowbrook Lane, E.G. saw a patrol car parked in the street in front of Rachel's house and the tail end of another police vehicle at the foot of the driveway. Neither had lights flashing, although, as E.G. got closer, he heard their engines still running. He parked on the street in front of a neighbor's house and bolted from the car, ignoring the walking path up the center of the property and dashing across the front lawn.

E.G. tried to open the front door at the same time as he pounded on it, but found it locked. "Rachel," he called out, pressing his ear against the door. He pounded again. In a moment, the door opened and he was greeted by Officer James Webb, someone he had seen many times, even talked to a few times, but did not have a close relationship with him.

"Where's my wife?" E.G. asked. No time for technicalities, he thought, as he pushed his way passed the officer and stepped into the foyer. On the couch in the living room, E.G. found Rachel sitting next to Officer Duffy. She looked startled toward the front entrance until she saw it was E.G. who had come in. Then, her fear turned to anger and she stood to confront him. She had changed from her skirt into a pair of sweat pants and T-shirt since he had left earlier in the evening, E.G. noted.

"What the hell have you gotten yourself into? Are you happy to have been called here?" She was only inches from his face.

"Are you all right? What happened here tonight?" The concern was sincere, and E.G. did all he could to refrain from reaching out and holding Rachel.

"Where's my daughter?" Rachel asked, concern growing in her voice.

"She's all right. She's with Raymond and Liz. She's spending the night there."

"How did she wind up there?" Now Rachel was yelling.

"It's a long story, and I'll tell you later. I want to know what happened here tonight."

Duffy came between them, resting a hand on E.G.'s elbow and guiding him to one of the chairs. "She got a fright tonight," he began. "She said she heard someone, or some thing, on the back deck. She turned off the porch light as you instructed her to do, and then she called us. We searched the property, but found nothing out of the ordinary."

Still standing in the center of the living room, Rachel glared at E.G., now seated in an easy chair in front of the large bay window.

"Will you be staying for awhile?" Duffy asked E.G.

"Yes," E.G. said, shifting his gaze from Rachel to Duffy. "I'll stay with her." He rose.

"Then we'll be on our way. There's nothing else we can do here. But if you think of something you may have forgotten to tell us," Duffy said to Rachel, "come outside. I'll begin writing my report in the patrol car."

"I'll do that," Rachel said and ushered him to the door.

She didn't waste a breath once the door was closed. She rushed toward E.G. and banged her fists on his chest. "Talk to me right now. Who is after you?"

E.G. held onto her arms as she tried to break free from his grip. "I don't know who's after me. Punching me is not going to help, though, so would you sit down and get hold of yourself." He let go, and Rachel refrained from hitting him again. She rubbed her wrists where E.G. held them and turned away from him.

"Whoever it was drove a black Camaro, or some kind of Camaro-looking car," she said quietly.

E.G. leaned toward Rachel. "What?"

"You heard me," she retorted.

"Did you give the police that information?"

Rachel shook her head. "No."

"Why not?"

"Because I'm a jerk off," she said, turning back to face him. "I'm a big fucking jerk off because I know that's the kind of information you'd be looking for, am I right?"

"That is important information, but it doesn't make you a jerk off," E.G. replied. "Big or small."

"Who are they, E.G.? And are they out there to try to scare us, or will they cause harm? Was this the first in a series of visits?"

"I don't have the answers for you. I just have a feeling, though, that I may be learning more than I really want to learn about this case, you know? It's getting kind of scary. I wish I could tell you about it, but I have to keep it to myself."

"What about Raymond? Why don't you tell Raymond what's going on? He's the lead investigator in this case."

"I'm not telling Raymond shit," E.G. said, and his response caught Rachel's attention.

"Is that what this is all about?" she asked. "Are you putting my life in danger for some kind of one-upmanship?"

E.G. remained silent.

"How dare you, E.G.! How much do you know that you've been keeping to yourself? And why is Erin at Raymond's house tonight? Where were you?"

"Following up on a lead," E.G. replied, and Rachel rolled her eyes. "And I learned so much more, babe. I've got hold of such a story that I have no idea where it's going to take me next. As far as Raymond, I tried to tell him what I know. He wouldn't listen. He thought I was buying time just to fish for information. So I'm doing this on my own."

"And in the meantime, I have to worry about Camaros pulling up in front of the house and people walking around my property. That doesn't seem very fair, E.G."

"This Camaro," E.G. said. "Did you actually see it in front of the house?"

"It was parked in front of the Bloombergs' house," Rachel said, nodding toward the house next door. "It pulled up a little before eleven o'clock."

"How do you know that?"

Anger grew once again in Rachel's voice. "Because I was sitting upstairs watching out the bedroom window all night. In case you haven't noticed, the note that I found in the mailbox when I got home tonight scared the hell out of me."

***   ***   ***

Rachel sat in the rocking chair that she had kept in the bedroom since she and E.G. purchased it seven years earlier in anticipation of Erin. It was a chair she clung to since, using it as her security blanket. The rocking eased her, especially after frequent feedings, and later, after arguments with E.G. or just a bad day at work.

And it was where she sat on that Friday night, the rocking growing faster and faster as she waited, terrified, telling herself nothing was going to happen as a result of the note in her mailbox, but not wanting to let her guard down. The bedroom was in darkness, except for the faint glow of the street lamp that sprinkled tiny spots of yellow, through the narrow openings in the mini-blinds, on the walls behind her. She thought of Audrey Hepburn in the movie "Wait Until Dark," the blind woman who overcame her attackers by creating an environment such that they would be on her level playing field. Suzy, Hepburn's character, smashed all the lights in the hallway of the apartment building and removed the bulbs in each of the lamps in her apartment to ensure there would be total darkness when or if her attackers arrived to the flat.

Rachel thought of the movie because she admired Hepburn's courage in the film, courage she hoped she could muster in a similar situation.

She never realized just how quiet her street became late at night. Few cars passed, and even fewer people walked the road, especially for a hot August night. She did spot a police cruiser on two occasions pass the house, slowing to a crawl when they reached her property, then continuing once they saw the front porch light glowing.

It was a little before eleven when Rachel got out of the rocking chair, stretched and prepared to go to the kitchen when the headlights of a car entering the street caught her attention. She expected to watch the car pass the house on its way to who knew where, but when it slowed and eventually stopped in front of the house next door, she stood against the wall to hide herself.

She ducked under the front windows and crawled to the set of windows on the side of the house, where she knew she could watch without being seen. She employed the same strategy when she had watched her neighbors arguing on the front lawn one night a few years earlier. That night, she was captured by the topic, the husband's lost job, and the language, words she would only use in the privacy of her own home. E.G. had come into the room that night, and as soon as he entered, Rachel pressed a finger against her lips, urging him to keep quiet and listen.

And so they did. They listened until the husband finally stormed from the property, got into his car and sped down the street, the wife throwing more of the same language at him as he disappeared onto the next block.

"And you oughtta fucking die," she yelled before slamming the front door on her way inside the house.

E.G. and Rachel couldn't control their laughter, despite both thinking what a tragedy it would be if they learned that Mr. Bloomberg had died that night.

"If we ever get into an argument that bad," E.G. had said, "please promise me we'll stay inside and close the windows. I wouldn't want our neighbors hiding in their bedrooms and listening to us."

As she remembered assuring him she would, Rachel wished he had been there with her now. The car outside the house was one she did not recognize, and she couldn't tell whether or not she knew the occupant because he, or she, stayed inside. Her instinct was to call the police, but she dismissed the thought instantly, thinking it would be an overreaction.

Rachel waited, and about five minutes later, she heard a clicking sound and then a creaking sound, and when she peered through the blinds, saw that the passenger's door had opened and a figure was emerging. The man — she knew it was a man because he was too tall to be a woman — looked in the direction of the house, and for a moment she believed he looked right into the window where she stood. She backed away, hoping to hide a shadow, hoping not to be discovered, and heard the same creaking sound. It was the door again, she thought. He had closed the door. She didn't recognize the face. In fact, in the darkness in front of the Bloombergs' house, she couldn't see a thing.

By the time she slid her face back to the corner of the window with the car in view, the man had disappeared. Not sure if he had gotten back into the car, Rachel stood in the middle of the window, glancing up and down the street as far as she could see, and looking below her at the narrow path of grass that separated her house from the Bloombergs'.

The man was nowhere in sight.

She felt her heart racing and willed the driver of the car to leave. But the vehicle remained, engine turned off and no movement from any occupants. Slowly, she bent to the bottom portion of the window, which she had opened a crack, and put her ear against the blinds. She heard nothing from the side of the house, but jumped when she heard a thump come from what she thought was downstairs, in her living room.

For a moment she froze, not knowing what to do next, but instinct dictated that she collect the baseball bat which she had left on the edge of the bed and tiptoe into the hallway. There, she waited, listening in the silence. Nothing.

She tiptoed back into the bedroom and to the front window, hoping the car would have left in the few minutes she had walked away. But it still sat there, as if it had joined the other cars parked on the street for the night, asleep on their pavement bedding.

Holding the bat against her shoulder, her left hand gripping the bottom and her right hand right above it, she looked as if she were in the on-deck circle waiting for the batter before her to get his turn. Again, she stepped lightly into the hallway, but this time, still hearing nothing, moved along the top of the staircase and slowly descended the steps. The first floor, except for the porch light that shone through the glass design at the top of the front door, was dark, but, like Audrey Hepburn in "Wait Until Dark," Rachel knew she could navigate the rooms with ease even if she was blind.

She moved through the living room and the dining room behind, making her way to the family room at the back of the house, where, she figured, anyone trying to break in would try there first. That was something she learned having dated and eventually marrying a reporter. "I cover the police beat every week," E.G. told her every time she prepared to leave the house without checking the windows on the back of house. "The cops should make one of those stamps and stamp it on each of the reports — entry gained through rear window. It would save a lot of writing time because it seems to be on every break-in report." It took a while, but Rachel eventually made it a part of her daily routine to check windows on the first floor every time she left the house.

So as she entered the family room, Rachel knew the windows and sliding door were secure. And although she recalled only hours earlier checking the locks, she felt compelled to do it again. Better safe than sorry, she thought, as she approached the drawn drapes that graced the sliding door.

Even in the dark, she knew where the drapes parted. As she reached for them, a sense of security drifted over her, as if the time it took to get from the top of the stairs to the family room gave her a chance to think rationally and realize she was letting fear possess her. So when she parted the drapes enough to double check the bolt on the door and was greeted by the silhouette of a man reaching for the handle on the other side, the sense of security quickly disappeared. Before the drapes fell back into place and the bat had fallen from her hands, Rachel saw that the man had been as frightened by her presence just as much as she had been frightened by his.

She saw him leap from his place on the deck before he disappeared behind the closed drapes. Screaming, she collected the bat, reached for the couch, guided herself around it and fled the room, instinct telling her to run for the living room and turn off the front porch light. After she did, she turned and felt for the stairs, bracing herself against the bottom of the banister and feeling her way to an end table that stood a few feet away. On the table, she knew would be the telephone. Once she dialed 9-1-1 by feeling for the three numbers on the keypad, she carried the phone with her to the front window, where, through sheer curtains, she saw the male figure jump into the passenger seat of the black car parked in front of the Bloombergs'. A moment later, the car disappeared from view.

As she spoke to the dispatcher, Officer Richard Duffy was turning his cruiser onto Meadowbrook Lane, placing the cup of coffee in his console and reaching for the note on the passenger seat that contained Rachel Lord's address. Duffy had missed the black vehicle's exit from Meadowbrook Lane by only minutes.

***   ***   ***

E.G. waited a moment before speaking when Rachel stopped. She had calmed enough to sit on the couch as she told her story, and E.G. had felt comfortable enough to sit beside her. He fought the urge to reach out and hold her, press her against himself and assure her that everything would be all right. He fought it, because he didn't think she'd like it.

Instead, he reached over and laid his hand on hers, and when she didn't pull away, as he expected her to do, he tightened his hold. He was even more surprised when Rachel shifted her hand to lock her fingers inside his.

"I need to be honest with you, hon," he said, and he told her the story.

E.G. began with the tip he received about the murder, the first e-mail he received from Dirtdealer and being lured into the Internet live board, where he engaged in discussion about the murders in the Reservation. He told Rachel about the private online conversation he had had with Matt, and how Matt had been an eyewitness that night. He related his visit to the Berns residence, where he allowed himself to be the shoulder on which Nathanya Berns needed to cry. And finally, without mentioning him by name, E.G. detailed his encounter with Travis Boesgaard earlier that night.

"Is there something else you want to tell me?" Rachel asked, learning that her ex-husband was in bed with a gay man.

"I'm not gay, if that's what you're asking," E.G. said. "I wasn't in bed with him; I was with him while he was in bed." When Rachel merely looked at him, E.G. continued. "Why are you looking at me like that? I didn't sleep with him."

"Why are you getting so defensive?"

"I'm not being defensive. I'm trying to explain to you that I followed up on a lead, and it led me to the bedroom of a man who may or may not have had something to do with what happened in the Reservation. And he happens to be gay. It's no different than when I covered the child sex abuse trial and interviewed the girl who was charged with the assaults. Did that make me a child abuser because I was with her?"

"E.G., would you calm down?" Rachel stressed. "I'm teasing you."

"Well, I'm not into that kind of lifestyle, and if you insinuate that, you're insinuating a lot more."

Rachel changed the subject. "I know you're not gay. Believe me, if there's one thing I miss about our marriage... More importantly, we need to talk about what happened here tonight. We can rule out your lover because you were with him tonight..." Rachel rolled her eyes the minute she saw E.G.'s reaction, but cut him off before he could speak. "Who knows that you've been investigating this?"

E.G. thought for a moment. He cited Nathanya Berns, who he said seemed genuinely upset about the death of her son; Dirtdealer, who had been feeding him information; and, of course, his colleagues in the newsroom, who had been asking him every day for the last three days if any new leads had turned up in the case.

"But people talk," E.G. said. "This Dirtdealer person could have said something to someone who may be afraid of me finding the truth. Nathanya Berns could be involved and could have hired someone to send the note and come here tonight to scare us. She certainly has the power and influence."

Rachel knew Nathanya Berns through her connection with E.G., having met her at various social functions which E.G. attended as a reporter but gained admittance free of charge. It was one of the luxuries of being married to a reporter with local influence, but one she didn't often take advantage of, especially because she didn't like listening to the rhetoric most politicians spewed, even in social circles.

"Do you think she's involved somehow?" Rachel asked.

E.G. shrugged his shoulders. "I don't know. From what I gathered, she knew Mickey was gay, but I don't believe she accepted his lifestyle. That doesn't mean she loved him any less to the point she'd want him dead."

"Unless he did something that we don't know about, something, obviously, that she's not going to tell you."

"Like what? Bring a lover home? That's no reason to beat the life out of your son."

Rachel hedged. "I wouldn't overlook that possibility. And what about the other guy who died? What do you know about him? Maybe he was cheating on his lover and the lover did it."

E.G. stared at Rachel with a dumbfounded look on his face. "This isn't General Hospital. Besides, I was with the other guy's lover tonight. That was the one whose bedroom I was in when the police called."

"Oh," Rachel said, absorbing the information she had just heard. "So someone who goes by the name of Dirtdealer is feeding you information about a certain man who happens to be the lover of one of the men who was killed?"

Yes, that's what's going on," E.G. said.

"It sure sounds like General Hospital," Rachel replied. "He may be setting you up. He could have had someone leave the note and come here tonight."

"Who? The man I was with tonight?"

"Yes."

E.G. shook his head. "No, that's not it. I spent about two hours with him and he has no idea my true identity. And he was drunk and willing to say anything. If he were involved, in his state tonight, he would have slipped somehow. I'm sure of that."

When silence filled the air between them, Rachel released her hand from E.G.'s and moved to the front window, drawing the drapes back just slightly to see into the street. E.G. watched her, longing to again hold her around her waist, to kiss the back of her neck, tasting the hair that would brush against his lips.

They were perfect together, he thought, and used their dialogue as a perfect example of how they worked as a team. Rachel, he knew, was frightened, but he also knew she had come to thrive on playing detective when E.G. presented her with scenarios of news stories he was developing. Whether the stories were about crime or politics, Rachel liked to put the players in place, create motives, and conclude why people act the way they do. Yet as many times as she was wrong, he always credited her efforts for trying.

"It's quiet out there," she said when she turned back around. "Do you think they'll be back tonight?"

"I can't say for sure, but I'm not leaving," E.G. replied. "I'll get up at six and head back to where I was tonight so my friend will think I stayed the night, and then I'll go to Steven Conroy's funeral with him. Hey, I might learn some more while I'm there."

"I'll get Erin's room ready for you," Rachel said, heading for the stairs.

"I thought it would be nice if we could just sit in the back for a while, watch some TV," E.G. responded.

It was what she wanted to hear, although Rachel would never acknowledge it. To prepare Erin's room would mean bedtime, which also would mean she would be alone in her own room when being alone was the last place she wanted to be. "Sounds like a good idea," she said, as she moved away from the stairs and led the way toward the family room.

E.G. pulled the drapes back and ensured the lock on the sliding doors was fastened. He panned the deck and the small yard that lay behind it. Nothing moved, as if the serenity E.G. had hoped for had descended on the home, at least for the night. The small juniper tree in the center of the yard lay still, like the few toys that lay scattered atop the lawn. By the time he turned around, Rachel had already taken a seat on the couch, in the center, and E.G. sat beside her. He put his arm across her shoulder and pulled her close to him.

She didn't resist. Instead, she rested her head against his chest and curled her body against his.

As Archie Bunker came to grips with having his life saved by a transvestite on an episode of "All in the Family," — NickatNite to the rescue — E.G. and Rachel drifted off to sleep, a scene that had such comforting familiarity to both of them.

CHAPTER TWENTY-TWO

Raymond opened his eyes and sat up in bed the moment the music began playing from the alarm clock on the dresser. He reached over and lowered the volume, turning his head back toward the bed to find out if the noise had awakened Liz.

She shifted slightly under the covers, but once she settled herself against the pillow again, she lay still, her hair cascading over the satin sheets.

Raymond pushed his legs over the side of the bed and stepped onto the floor. He unwrapped the end of the blanket that had fastened itself around his waist and pushed it back onto the bed. Naked, which is how he always slept during the summer despite Liz insisting that the room temperature of the house remain in the low sixties, he stepped into the bathroom, where the sound of the shower filled the air.

He had a funeral to attend this morning, and he wanted to be dressed and ready to leave before the rest of the family awakened.

But Liz wouldn't have that. By the time Raymond emerged from the bathroom, Liz had awakened and took her spot in front of the stove, the smell of sausage and eggs filling the kitchen. On the counter, a full pot of coffee sat next to two mugs.

Raymond kissed Liz on the back of the neck before filling his cup. He brought it to the table, where the daily newspaper waited, folded to the bottom of the front page where the latest of the murder stories appeared. "Officials virtually clueless in Essex murder case" was the headline.

From behind him, Raymond heard the announcement, but it was so normal, it was like the familiar hum of the refrigerator. "All knobs are off. Seven twenty-one a.m.," shouted Liz, and Raymond knew she was turning off the gas on the stove. It was a suggestion recommended by her therapist, a sort of game of association for her obsessive-compulsive behavior that served as a reminder if she was out of the house and couldn't remember if she had turned off the gas. It was a suggestion that apparently worked because recalling the time reduced the number of times she returned home to double check the gas. Or if she turned off the coffee pot. Or if she unplugged the toaster.

Raymond continued reading. Sensationalism, he thought, and scanned the article. Just because they had no clues didn't mean they were clueless, and Liz knew exactly what he was thinking when he pushed the newspaper to the side of the table.

"Don't let it bother you," she said, placing the breakfast dish in front of him.

"This is the media today," he replied with disgust. "There are two dead people with devastated families, one of whom is being buried today after a funeral Mass and the other after a private service, and we become the bad guys because we haven't found out who did it." He stuffed a forkful of sausage and eggs into his mouth.

"I said not to let it bother you. You'll solve the case. I have confidence in you."

Raymond nodded toward the upstairs. "When is E.G. coming for Erin?"

"I imagine sometime this morning. What do you suppose he had to do last night?"

Raymond shrugged. "Knowing E.G., he was probably snooping around with this case. The guy is fucking relentless when it comes to his job, so my guess is that he talked to some of his sources about Mickey Berns and Steven Conroy and was following up on those tips."

"Maybe it wouldn't hurt to talk to him. He may know something you don't know."

Raymond looked up at his wife. "And give him the satisfaction of knowing he knows more than I do? You're crazy. I wouldn't give that to him."

"I hope you're not upset about last night," Liz said.

"I was so looking forward to being alone with you. It's been so long."

"We'll get time," Liz said, rubbing Raymond's shoulders.

Raymond put the last of the sausage on the end of his fork and scooped the yolk off the plate. He wiped his mouth, kissed his wife, and slipped on the sport coat that he laid over the couch in the living room. Weddings and funerals. They were the only occasions he wore a jacket.

"This ought to be fun," he said, the sarcasm showing in the expression on his face.

CHAPTER TWENTY-THREE

He did all he could to slip into bed before the alarm clock sounded. And he did so with five minutes to spare.

At 6:25 a.m., E.G. removed the jeans and shoes he was wearing, pulled the shirt over his head and lay next to Travis, draping an arm over Travis' hip. He lay quietly although his breathing sounded rushed, and he knew it was more from anxiety than from overexertion.

Travis lay motionless on his side, and E.G. guessed that he had not moved all night. His breathing was even, and there was no sign that he had gotten sick while he slept.

An old Donna Summer song belted into the room, and even though he anticipated the radio to come on within a matter of minutes, the sound startled E.G. Donna was working hard for the money that morning, and from the volume, everyone on Travis' street probably knew.

He stepped out of the bed to lower the volume to a more reasonable level and when he returned, he leaned over Travis in the way only a lover would. He tenderly shook him on the arm and whispered his name.

Travis grunted, but did not wake up, so E.G. shook him a little harder and called his name again.

Travis rolled onto his back and opened his eyes, and E.G. instantly saw the pain that he must have felt in his head. His eyes closed as quickly as they opened, and he released a groaning sound that nearly drowned out Donna Summer.

"You feeling all right?" E.G. asked, resting his hand on Travis' bare stomach. If Patrick Crowe could see me now, he thought, and then let the rest of his thought drift away.

"I feel like my head is in a vice, and some sado-masochist is getting his jollies squeezing it," Travis groaned.

"Now there's a vivid picture," E.G. replied, trying to elicit at least a smile from Travis. "Where do you keep the aspirin?"

"Advil. The only thing that works is Advil. In the closet in the bathroom."

E.G. stepped out of bed, and just as he got to the door to the hallway, he heard Travis cry out behind him. "And bring some mouthwash back with you."

E.G. ran his tongue across his teeth and blew into his hand, which he placed inches from his mouth, to determine whether Travis wanted the mouthwash for himself or for E.G. Satisfied that it was for Travis, he gathered the bottles of aspirin and Listerine and a glass of water, and returned to find Travis holding his head. The blanket had come off, and E.G. could see the outline of Travis' erection as he lay in bed in his briefs.

The first thought that crossed his mind was Conor, and whether or not the two of them had awakened like this. Conor. How much did he not know about someone with whom he had been working for the last seven years?

E.G. sat next to Travis and fed him the Advil. When Travis swallowed the tablets and finished the water, he took a swig of the Listerine, gargled and spit into the empty glass, which he handed back to E.G.

"Thanks for staying with me last night," Travis said.

E.G. sighed, knowing for sure that Travis had not awakened during the night. He had no idea that E.G. had taken the key from his ring and slipped out during the night, only to return a few minutes before he was awakened. "You definitely needed the company."

"Listen, if we fooled around, I'm sorry, but I don't remember. The last thing I remember was sitting down there with you," he said, pointing to the bottom of the bed.

"It's all right. I'm not offended," said E.G., not confirming that they didn't fool around. "However, if you were sober and couldn't remember...Then that's a different story."

E.G. dashed to the closet, hoping to change the subject. "Do you have a preference as to what you want to wear today?"

Travis belched, and then shook as if the bile that raced to his throat left an unpleasant taste in his mouth. He paused before answering, waiting to see if the belch was just that, and nothing more. "Something dark," he replied. "I don't expect this will be a happy day."

E.G. returned with a navy blue pin-stripe suit, a white shirt and a red tie and hung them on the top of the door. It was an outfit he would have chosen for himself.

Travis slowly got out of bed, at first feeling dizzy when he planted his feet on the floor. Casually, as if he were the only one in the house, he removed the briefs and tossed them onto a chair in the corner of the room. The erection was gone, but Travis was pulling on himself as he left the room for the shower.

As the sound of the shower filled the second floor, E.G. rummaged through the closet once more, picking out a suit that he could wear himself. He also chose something dark. After all, he thought, this wasn't going to be a happy day.

CHAPTER TWENTY-FOUR

E.G. couldn't wait for Travis to get out of the car in the parking lot of The Lucky Leaf, where he slipped into the driver's side of his own car and led the way to the church in Montville. For the entire twenty minutes it had taken to get from Travis' house to The Lucky Leaf, Travis poured over E.G., thanking him for spending the night, for showing concern for a drunken man who mourned the loss of his boyfriend. At one point, he had even picked up E.G.'s hand and kissed it, then held it in his own hand for several minutes before letting go.

As they pulled into the church parking lot, a two-car funeral procession of their own, E.G. felt the guilt drip over him like maple syrup over the side of a mound of pancakes. He knew this was not what Patrick Crowe had meant when he questioned how far a reporter should go to get a story.

In essence, he was lying to get a story, becoming someone who did not exist in any other part of his life.

After spending the time he did with Travis the night before, E.G. was certain he was not directly responsible for the deaths of Mickey Berns and Steven Conroy. He was just as certain that the e-mails he was receiving from Dirtdealer were meant to push him in the wrong direction. And he was also certain that he had no idea who was sending the e-mails.

But the question that plagued him now was whether or not he should be up front with Travis, tell him who he really is, and why he was with him that morning and the night before. He wondered how Travis would react, expecting that he wouldn't be too happy, but that could change if he told him someone was out to frame him.

Travis stepped out of the Audi, and, under the sun that had crept through the scattered clouds, he saw a different person than the one he was with the night before. Travis stood taller, it seemed, and E.G. guessed it was probably the attire that made him look that way, and with his hair combed neatly and without the dent left around his head from the baseball cap he had worn, he could pass for a Fortune 500 businessman. It occurred to him that he had no idea what Travis did for a living.

The only thing that detracted from Travis' looks that morning were his eyes, the sadness that emanated from them as he looked toward the front of the church and saw the pallbearers lifting the cherry-colored coffin from the black hearse.

E.G. stepped out of his car and stood next to Travis. Instinctively — and he questioned why it was instinct — he placed an arm around Travis' waist and held him. Travis welcomed the gesture and leaned into his new friend, but just as quickly stepped away.

"We can't be seen like this," Travis said. "I don't want anyone to know, or even think, that I'm here because I was tied to Steven intimately. I want to be here as a friend, and nothing more. That's how he would have wanted it."

E.G. put his hands in his pants pockets, and the two walked slowly toward the church, giving the pallbearers time to climb the few steps and bring Steven inside. They waited outside the church until they heard the sound of the organ, and as they made their way to the front doors, they saw the pallbearers guiding the coffin up the center aisle.

They took seats in the back pew and both, at the same time, cast their eyes across the congregation. Most of the seats toward the front of the church were filled, while others, young and old, male and female, were scattered in the last half of the pews.

At the same time E.G. laid eyes on him, Raymond had turned and spotted his cousin. Both looked curiously at one another, and when E.G. watched his cousin's eyes dart toward Travis and back, he creased his brow in a pleading sort of way and shook his head, as if to urge Raymond not to ask questions.

Raymond turned back toward the front of the church and listened as the priest began the funeral Mass.

"How are you holding up?" E.G. whispered to Travis.

Travis gripped E.G.'s hand and whispered back, "I'll be all right," before letting go.

He watched as Travis scanned the church, and followed his eyes when they stopped on a figure on the left side of the church toward the back, about five pews behind Raymond.

A handsome man, he looked around 30 years old, the crew cut defining strong facial features.

"Do you know him?" E.G. asked, again in a whisper.

"That's Brian Winter, and for the life of me, I don't know why he's here."

It was as if Brian sensed that he was being talked about, because he turned and caught Travis' gaze. They both nodded at one another, then both dropped their eyes.

"How do you know him?" E.G. asked.

"Travel in the same circles. Played a few times," Travis said, not caring where he was. "If you ever just want to get your rocks off, Brian can be pretty hot."

"He's a good-looking man," E.G. said.

"No, he's hot," Travis quickly replied matter-of-factly. "But I would never let him hear me say that about him. I'm surprised his head fit in the church he has such a big ego."

E.G. ignored the remark. "Do you think he might have known Steven?"

"Don't know. Don't think so. But I know he knew Mickey. They went to school together, and had a thing going for a while."

"Why do you suppose he's here?" E.G. asked.

"I couldn't answer that. But I'll ask him afterward."

For the remainder of the service, they were quiet, even during the eulogies delivered by Steven's brother and an uncle, who spoke of the loving and caring person he had come to know in his nephew. They related stories from days past, when Steven was a prowess on the baseball diamond, named to the All-State teams each of his years in high school. They offered humorous anecdotes about Steven's dates during his college years and later, and both mentioned how much he had loved his fiancee, an auburn-haired woman in her twenties who sat in the front pew with the Conroy family, muffled sobs coming from behind her lips.

It should have been obvious to everyone in the church that descriptions of Steven's masculinity were presented to counter what everyone in the church most likely was thinking: that Steven died with another man in an area gay men frequented.

"This is making me sick," Travis whispered at one point. "The bottom line is that Steven was a wonderful person, and that's how he should be remembered."

Out of the corner of his eye, E.G. watched Travis as he wiped tears from his eyes, and he offered him a handkerchief that he found in the pocket of the suit jacket.

"As long as you remember him that way, that's all that counts," E.G. said.

As the priest descended the steps at the altar to lead the procession out of the church, several bursts of tears, those from Steven's parents and fiancee, echoed throughout the building. The coffin passed them, the cross-emblazoned cloth draped over the top. Now, standing behind E.G. in the pew, Travis held onto the back of the pew in front of them and quietly sobbed, hoping the family members and friends who were following the coffin out of the church wouldn't hear him.

E.G. looked across the church to where Raymond had been seated, and saw he was gone. He searched the back of the church, as well as the front, but he couldn't spot him anywhere. But he did see Brian Winter, who, when E.G. glanced his way, was already looking at him and smiled sadly when their eyes met.

When they stepped into the bright sunshine, E.G. squinted in his search for Raymond and found him leaning into what appeared to be the lead car in the funeral procession, the one, of course, behind the hearse that would be carrying Steven's body to the cemetery.

"I'm sorry for your loss."

The voice came from behind him, and when E.G. turned, he saw Brian Winter standing beside Travis. Travis turned at the same time, and acknowledged the gesture with a nod.

"I'm Brian," he said to E.G., extending his hand.

E.G. accepted his hand, but before he could say anything, Travis spoke. "Pardon my rudeness. This is my friend Caleb," he said.

Confused, E.G. shot a look at Travis, but just as quickly turned back to Brian. He smiled.

"Pleasure to meet you," they both said in unison.

"It's too bad it's under unfortunate circumstances," Brian added, and E.G. expected him to end with "Sir."

Brian had that look, E.G. thought, one that dripped of discipline and organization. He also noticed that Brian held his hand longer than what would be deemed normal for an introductory handshake.

E.G. glanced toward Raymond again as Travis asked Brian, "What brings you here today? Did you know Steven?"

More interested in Brian's answer, E.G. rejoined the conversation, comfortable knowing that Raymond was still talking to Steven's parents.

"We met on a few occasions, but I didn't know him well. I guess I was just taken by the whole situation, having known Mickey for as long as I did. I felt coming here would give Steven the respect he deserved, and I think Mickey would have appreciated my attendance."

"You hated Mickey," Travis retorted. "And he hated you, so where do you come off saying Mickey would have appreciated you being here?"

"Don't go bringing down the house because a piece of your furniture has rotted away," Brian said, and E.G. noticed the marked change in his behavior. When he had entered the conversation, Brian stood with his hands in his pockets, displaying all the attributes of a masculine, broad-shouldered man. Now, his hands rested on his hips and he threw back his head each time he wanted to emphasize a word. "House" and especially "furniture" were the two words he used to define Steven, and Travis fell for the goading.

Travis leaned in, standing only inches from Brian's face, and speaking in a low but gritty voice, said, "You have no idea how wonderful a man Steven was."

Brian leaned in just as closely, and their lips practically met. "Which, I suppose, is why he was fucking Mickey while you were calling him sweetheart."

E.G. stepped between the two, and, with his back to Travis, forced a smile and placed his hands on the shoulders of Brian's suit jacket, pretending to brush something from the lapel to prevent any of the remaining crowd from looking in their direction. "This is going to stop," he said sternly, loud enough for even Travis to hear behind him. "This is not the place for this."

Raymond had stepped away from the car, and E.G. caught him looking in his direction. He took his hands off Brian, but continued to face him. "Can you please leave?" he asked in a calm yet forceful tone.

"I love a dominating man," Brian whispered. "Too bad you're with him."

Instinct dictated that E.G. should tell Brian he was wrong, that they weren't a pair, but his admission, he knew, could jeopardize the trust he was developing in Travis. So he remained silent, yet stared until Brian backed away.

"Sorry about your loss, Travis. I really am," he said, looking beyond E.G. And then looking E.G. directly in the eyes, he said, "I hope to see you around."

Brian descended the front steps of the church and, walking to his car, he passed Raymond, who did a double take, then looked back, perplexed to say the least, at E.G. Discreetly, E.G. signaled with his index finger that he wanted Raymond to wait for him.

Raymond returned to his car, taking note of the Grand Cherokee in which Brian pulled out of the parking lot, then watched E.G. and Travis walk to their own cars.

"Caleb?" E.G. asked when they were alone.

Travis laughed nervously. "Sorry about that. Call it jealousy. I saw the way he looked at you. And then said he hoped to see you again. I didn't want him to know your name because somehow, he would track you down, and I don't want that to happen."

"Jealousy? You've known me for less than a day."

"But I like you. You're different. I can sense that already."

E.G. looked away out of guilt, and Travis misread his gesture.

"See. You have that boyish shyness that I like."

E.G. changed the subject. "Why don't you get some more sleep? I'll come by later if I have a chance."

They returned to their cars, and E.G. started his engine just as Travis did. He waited for Travis to pull out of the parking space, then slowly pulled out of his own space, giving Travis enough time to exit the parking lot before he turned the Tercel in the direction of Raymond's car.

By the time E.G. had gotten to his cousin, Raymond was already out of his car.

"You want to explain this?" Raymond asked through the Tercel's open window.

E.G. turned off the engine and got out of the car.

"I tried to talk to you the other day," E.G. shot back. "In your office. But you didn't want to listen to me."

The late morning sun pierced Raymond's eyes and he held a hand over his forehead to block the brightness. "How are you involved in this?" he asked.

"The same way you're involved. That's all," E.G. said, wondering if when Raymond said "involved," he meant more than as a journalist.

"How do you know those two guys?" he demanded.

"One I met yesterday; the other I met twenty minutes ago. And don't talk to me this way. I'm not a child."

Raymond turned and slapped a hand against the hood of his car. Who's the child now, E.G. thought.

"I can bring you in, E.G., for interfering with an investigation."

"Oh, bullshit," E.G. responded. "I'm not interfering with squat, and you know it. If I had information that could lead to an arrest in this case, I'd give it right to the police, and you know I would."

"So how do you know those two guys?" he asked again.

"To answer that, I would have to reveal sources, and I'm not about to do that. The information I have, and it's not necessarily from either of the two guys you saw me with today, hasn't gotten me anywhere. When, or even if, it does, I'll let you know."

Raymond wouldn't give up. "How do these two factor in? Who are they?" he asked, recognizing Brian from the yearbook photo, but declining to reveal that he knew his name.

"Do you know either one of them?" E.G. asked. "The way you keep focusing on them, it seems as if you do."

"Should I know either of them?" Raymond asked.

"Why would you think I should know?" E.G. asked, and the answering of questions with questions became enough for Raymond.

"Let's cut the shit, E.G. I don't have to know you for thirty-three years to know how you operate. You're good. I'll grant you that. Maybe you're too good. And because of that, I wouldn't be surprised if you have a lot of information that I don't have. But remember this. This is a police investigation, not some local yokel newspaper's crusade. If I have to, I'll use the law to force you to reveal what you know."

E.G. waited a moment before speaking. "Are you done?" When Raymond only stared back at him, E.G. continued. "You do what you have to. But let me remind you that I know that you know how much time it would take before I'm forced to reveal anything to you or any court in this state. Let me also remind you that you don't have that time because I know that once you start something, it becomes a project, and nothing can get in the way of that project until you've completed it."

The two men stood by the Tercel without saying anything, and E.G. felt the same awkward silence that he felt on a telephone call when neither party spoke. The last of the cars had left the parking lot on their way to the cemetery, where Steven Conroy's family would say their final good-byes to a man, it turned out, that many of them did not really know.

Travis declined the ride to the cemetery, knowing he again would be left to stand in the background and watch. He had told E.G. that he would visit on his own, perhaps in a few days, and say his last good-bye to Steven alone.

"Were you hoping to find something here?" E.G. said, breaking the silence between them.

"I didn't know what I would find," Raymond responded. "I really came to talk to Mr. and Mrs. Conroy."

They were both speaking in level tones, as if they were in one of their living rooms watching a Yankees game together and the subject had just happened to come up.

"Must have been a shock to them, huh?"

"If one of my kids was gay, that's the last way I'd want to find out," Raymond said. "They're absolutely beside themselves."

"So they had no idea?"

Raymond shook his head.

"Not even who Mickey Berns was?"

Again, he shook his head. "But I promised them I'd find out who did this."

"I know you will, Ray. You're good. Are you at least even close?"

"Not by a long shot."

It was an admission that E.G. never expected to hear from his cousin.

"Well, I know you'll get close, and eventually nab whoever did it. You've got a record to maintain," E.G. said, smiling and patting his cousin on the shoulder. "I'm going to head out of here. I have to pick up Erin, who should be at Rachel's house by now. And by the way, thanks for letting her stay at your house last night. I appreciate that."

Raymond shrugged it off as if it meant nothing, but he was looking forward to cashing in the rain check Liz promised him for a night to make up for the unexpected company the night before.

"And listen, E.G., I was serious about what I said before. If you get any information about this case, I want to hear about it first-hand, not read about it in the newspaper."

"Will do," E.G. said, getting back into his car. Once inside, he reached under the seat and removed a notebook he had placed there to hide from Travis. He flipped open to a blank page and scribbled: *According to a top law enforcement official involved with the case, the Conroy family had no knowledge of Mickey Berns and were not aware of their son's association with him. The official also said the*

Prosecutor's Office was nowhere near naming a suspect in the two murders.

He closed the notebook, tossed it onto the front passenger's seat and smiled and waved to Raymond as he pulled out of the parking lot. "I'll give you a local fucking yokel newspaper," he muttered.

As Raymond smiled and waved back, he did some muttering of his own. "I'll put your ass in a cell so fast, you'll be singing everything you know to a judge."

CHAPTER TWENTY-FIVE

He wasn't ready to pick up Erin yet, so instead of making a left off South Orange Avenue to Rachel's house, E.G. continued along the main avenue for approximately one-half mile, stopping at the Dunkin' Donuts before going a few more blocks to the office of *The Sentinel*.

As he expected, the building was empty, and as he entered, the only sound he heard was the clock ticking on the wall inside Mel's office. It was rare that anyone would be in the office on a Saturday afternoon, especially a hot Saturday afternoon in August. It was rare because there was an unwritten edict among editors and reporters at *The Sentinel* that Saturday was their day away from the office, even if they happened to be covering something that day.

Sunday was another story, however. At least seven of the twelve reporters and editors found themselves in the office on Sunday nights, either planning for the following two deadline days or filing the stories they couldn't file by Friday because other assignments got in the way. As much as they didn't want to come in on Sundays, they knew, as weekly newspaper reporters, their schedules were so erratic that if they didn't put in the time on Sundays, they likely would put in sixteen- to seventeen-hour days on Mondays and Tuesdays.

Most didn't mind, though. After awhile, Sunday became like any other day — a part of the normal work week.

As normal as one could get working for a weekly newspaper, E.G. thought. Unlike at daily newspapers, reporters at weekly newspapers could find themselves conducting an interview at 9 a.m. and covering a town meeting at 7:30 p.m. the same day. And the gap in between was filled with more interviews and filing stories. That's how it went at *The Sentinel*. You weren't fulfilling your objective as a reporter unless you were writing at least nine stories per week.

From time to time, E.G. would compare the work of his colleagues, as well as his own, against the work of reporters at the daily newspaper that circulated in the area. He wasn't surprised to find that in all cases, the daily reporters averaged four to five stories per week, while he and his colleagues averaged ten per week.

It also wasn't a management decision either that required *Sentinel* reporters to file that many stories on a weekly basis. Mel, E.G. knew, would be happy to accept those same four or five as the dailies give. Indeed, it was a desire among the staff to write as much as possible, living the philosophy that if there's news to tell, it will be in *The Sentinel*.

E.G. hated the "local yokel" reference the weekly newspapers shouldered. Not only was it Raymond's perception, but it was the perception of a majority of people across the country. To the average reader, the weekly newspaper is supposed to be the cheerleader for the towns it serves, and reporters who work for them are using them only as springboards to what the public has called "better" jobs.

E.G. believed, though, that through the 1990s, the majority had shrunk and more people, especially in Essex County, looked forward to *The Sentinel* every week because of its reporting, design and editing. The paper's circulation grew consistently throughout the decade, reaching more than one hundred twenty thousand readers on a weekly basis into the year 2000.

Sure, it was an ego builder to be honored with the Excellence in Journalism award from the state press association four consecutive years, but what was more important to E.G. and his colleagues was that they had the respect of their communities.

It was why E.G. didn't mind being in the office on a hot Saturday afternoon in August, holding a cup of coffee that was hotter than the blazing sun, and wearing a suit that belonged to someone who, he was certain, was being used as a guinea pig.

Perhaps Travis was involved in some way, E.G. thought as he slipped into his cubicle and turned on the computer. It could be why Raymond was so curious to know how he knew him — and Brian, for that matter.

He signed on as Stetson165, hoping to have at least received an e-mail from Matt. When he checked the member list, he got something better. Musicat62 was on line.

E.G. sent a private talk invite. "Hi, Matt. How have you been?"

It took a few minutes, but Matt responded. "Been okay. U?"

"I've been concerned about you. I know that sounds strange coming from someone you've only talked to less than two days, but it's true."

"Thanks," Matt replied. "I knew from the first time we talked that U were much different than most of the guys I've talked to."

"So why can't we meet?" E.G asked.

There was a longer response time, and E.G. wondered if Matt refused to answer the question, but just as he was about to ask Matt if he was still there, a response appeared on his screen.

"I guess I'm afraid to meet. It's so easy to remain anonymous here that I think I prefer that."

It was not what E.G. wanted to hear.

Another message followed.

"Besides, things are getting too complicated."

E.G. responded. "What things?" He wasn't apprehensive about asking the question because it was obvious Matt wanted to talk. The security of anonymity, E.G. thought, as he awaited a reply.

"I lied to you the other day, Barry," Matt said.

"About what?"

As he waited, E.G. heard the ticking of Mel's clock, and it was as if ten minutes had passed before he received a response.

"I know who did it."

E.G. dropped against the back of his chair and stared at the words, which seemed to glow at him in one-hundred forty point headline size, the kind that appear on the front pages of the *Daily News* and *New York Post*.

"I know who did it," he envisioned the front page stating, with a picture of a blurred face, blurred because it belonged to Matt, being rushed into a courthouse.

Now it was Matt's turn to ask if E.G. was still there.

E.G. typed. "Yes, still here. You caught me totally off guard with that one."

He sent another message before Matt could respond. "Are you serious? You're not pulling my leg, are you?"

"Not about this. I don't know what to do."

"What are you afraid of, Matt? Let's talk for a little bit, and if you can define what you're afraid of, maybe I can help you overcome that obstacle."

"Are you a psychologist?" Matt asked.

"No," E.G. replied. "Just a firm believer in common sense."

"I'm afraid of a lot," Matt finally wrote.

"The person we're talking about...Does he or she know you?"

"Yes."

"Does he or she know you were in the Reservation when this happened?"

"Not sure. But he may suspect that I know something."

So we've narrowed it to a male, E.G. thought. Probably a lover. "How?"

"It's too complicated to go into. But I bet the look in my eyes gave it away when I saw him."

"You've seen him since the murders took place?"

"Yes."

"And did he respond to any weird look in your eyes?"

"Not sure what you mean."

E.G. rephrased the question. "You said you might have given it away based on the look in your eyes when you saw him. Did that look prompt a reaction from him?"

Matt took a few moments before responding. "We ran into each other on Wednesday night. When I first saw him, I guess I looked startled. He asked why I jumped, and I made up an excuse that I didn't see him standing there. I don't know if that satisfied him."

Ran into him, E.G. thought. Maybe not a lover. He thought of Conor. Where was Conor Wednesday night, he wondered.

"I can certainly understand the fear," E.G. wrote, "but why should that stop you and me from meeting?"

"If he suspects I know something, he may be following me. I wouldn't want to put anyone else in harm's way."

E.G. thought of the next question, wondered whether or not he should type it, then decided to throw caution to the wind. "Can you tell me who it is?"

Instantly, a response came back. "NO!!"

"I was only trying to give you an opportunity to take the burden from your shoulders," E.G. wrote. "I figured if you told me, and I could do something about it, that would help you."

"I understand that, and I thank you, but I need to do things my way."

"Are you going to the police with this information?" E.G. asked.

"I reported the incident Wednesday morning. Today is Saturday. Don't you think I would have said something to the police by now?"

"Why won't you?"

"Because it's all too complicated."

He continued to chat with Matt, but realized shortly that there was no way Matt was going to reveal who killed Mickey Berns and Steven Conroy.

E.G. wanted desperately to meet Matt, but knew that too much pressure at this point in the conversation could result in losing him altogether.

He typed: "Are you familiar with South Orange, or just the area around the Reservation?"

"Very familiar with South Orange," Matt replied.

"Then I'll offer this to you," E.G. said, thinking Matt may be from town. "I will go to the entrance to the train station every night at 9 p.m. and stay until 9:30 p.m. If you feel like meeting and unburdening yourself to a friend, you can show up and we can talk."

Matt responded. "I'll keep your offer in mind. I may just call on you."

"I hope you do. It's funny, isn't it, that we've never met, yet I feel something for you," E.G. wrote, hoping to cement the trust that he knew he had built in Matt.

"I feel the same way about you too," he replied.

And then another message. "I have to sign off now. Have too much to do today."

"I understand," E.G. wrote back. "Same here. And don't forget my offer."

"I won't. Cya."

Before E.G. could interpret the "cya," Matt was gone. "Cya," he learned through phonics, was short for "See ya."

He finished the last of the coffee, which turned cold, and tossed the cup into the empty garbage can on the side of his desk. The cleaning crew had been in, he noticed, seeing nothing but an empty plastic bag wrapped inside the can.

When the cell phone rang, he instinctively reached up to the shelf where he laid it when he came into the office.

It was Rachel on the other end, demanding to know if E.G. was coming to pick up Rachel.

"I stopped at the office to check messages, etc.," he told her. "I can be there in about ten minutes."

"She's antsy," Rachel said. "She keeps asking for you as if she hasn't seen you in months."

"She loves her daddy," E.G. said, a smile so bright on his face that it lit the entire cubicle. "Tell her I'll be there shortly."

*** *** ***

"Daddy!" Erin yelled as she ran down the front steps into her father's arms.

E.G. picked her up and spun her in the air once before standing her back on her feet on the front lawn of his former home. "Did you miss me that much?" he asked, realizing Rachel was not kidding when she said Erin was antsy for him to return.

She nodded and looked back at the front door mischievously to see if her mother was in the doorway. When she saw the coast was clear, she whispered, "I went on a mission just like we did yesterday at that man's house."

"You did?" E.G. asked. "And where did you go?"

She continued to whisper. "I can't tell you yet. I don't want mommy to hear."

Now E.G. whispered back, realizing she was playing a game. "Okay," he said. "When we blow this place, we'll swap information and see if it gets us the jewels."

E.G. looked behind Erin to find Rachel emerging through the front door. He turned Erin toward the house and patted her in that direction. "Get your back pack and overnight bag so we can get ready to leave."

Erin ran around her mother as Rachel descended the steps. "Did you learn anything this morning?" she asked.

E.G. knew her question was more of a concern for her own safety and not because she was interested in him getting details for a story.

He shook his head. "Not really. I met someone new. Not sure if that will take me anywhere, but I did see Raymond. He was there." He waited a moment before asking, "Did anything happen around here while I was gone?"

Rachel shook her head. "I was out most of the morning before I picked up Erin at Liz's. I guess I came back expecting to find the house ransacked, but it wasn't. It was just as I had left it."

"I can stay again tonight," E.G. offered, but Rachel again shook her head. "I'm not going to live in fear," she said.

Erin emerged from the house carrying an overnight bag over her arm and dragging her backpack along the floor and porch as she stepped outside. "I'm ready to go, mommy," she said hurriedly, lifting her head and puckering her lips for the expected good-bye kiss.

Rachel bent and kissed her daughter as E.G. reached over and took the backpack from her. "What do you have in here, a rock collection?" he asked, throwing the bag over his shoulder.

Erin ignored the question and ran toward the car, getting into the rear passenger side and strapping herself in the seat belt.

"I'll have her back tomorrow night," E.G. told Rachel. "And if anything happens here, call me."

Without responding, Rachel walked back inside the house, waving at Erin one more time before she disappeared.

E.G. placed the backpack on the back seat next to Erin and slid into the front seat. As he pulled out of the driveway, looking in his rearview mirror, he watched Erin reach for the backpack. She pulled it closer to herself and then pulled the zipper from one side of the bag to the other. "I've got the jewels, daddy," she said.

In the rearview mirror, E.G. saw her struggle to remove a folder and a book from the backpack. His curiosity got the best of him, and just as he turned out of Meadowbrook Lane, he slammed on the brakes and pulled the car to the curb.

"What is that?" he asked.

"The priceless jewels," Erin said. "The answer to the riddle."

"I'm not kidding around," E.G. replied, reaching back and taking the book from her. It was a Columbia High School yearbook. "Where did you get this?" He also retrieved the folder, which displayed a label on its tab that indicated it was the Berns-Conroy file from the prosecutor's office.

Erin wasn't kidding when she said she went on a mission.

"You took this from Uncle Raymond's house," he said. "You can't do that. That's stealing."

That didn't occur to Erin. "I thought you would want this, daddy, to help you in your mission," she replied as if that was justification enough to take the items.

"No, no, no, honey. It doesn't work that way. This has to go back."

"But won't it help you?" Erin asked, obviously not understanding the difference between stealing and borrowing.

"I'm sure it could," E.G. said. "I'm sure it very well could, but we don't do things like that."

E.G. placed the two items on the front seat next to him as he pulled away from the curb and into the traffic around the park. He tried to explain to Erin that the items were the property of her uncle, and more importantly, a part of a police investigation.

But as he spoke to her in the mirror, his eyes continuously darted back to the book and folder. As he reached the top of the park and the intersection that would lead him to South Orange Avenue, he pulled the car to the curb once more, threw it in park and reached for the yearbook.

Two pages were book-marked with sheets of paper, and when he opened to the first one, he scanned the page and saw the picture of Mickey Berns. The second book-marked page left him confused until he looked closely at the picture in the bottom right corner — Brian Winter, the man whom he stood in front of earlier that day to prevent a fight between him and Travis.

Brian Winter. Why would Raymond have Brian Winter book-marked, he thought, remembering how curious his cousin was in the church parking lot when he saw E.G. standing with Brian. At the time, E.G. thought Raymond's curiosity developed because of Travis.

He closed the yearbook and turned to the folder. He held it in his hands as if it were a close friend's diary, something sacred and an act of betrayal if he were to look inside.

But how much could be inside, he asked himself, after only two days of investigation? Raymond was running around attending funerals, holding press conferences — hell, even babysitting for his daughter. All that surely put a dent into those forty-eight to seventy-two hours.

He opened the folder and scanned the few legal size pages of notes that he knew were in Raymond's handwriting. "Old Man Winter" was noted on one page, and how he was able to gain entry to the Reservation despite police barricades. Another page regurgitated dialogue he had had with Nathanya Berns apparently the same day E.G. had talked to her. A pair of breasts were drawn on another sheet of paper, one that contained an array of doodling that included the words, "Be home by 6. Be laid by 9." At the top of the sheet of paper was the date of the day before, and it didn't take long for E.G. to guess why Raymond was irritated when he dropped off Erin.

"Hey, if I can't get any, you can't get any," he said, reviewing the rest of the notes.

He closed the folder and returned to the yearbook and the page with the picture of Brian Winter. Brian Winter. Old Man Winter.

"Daddy, are you supposed to be looking at that?" Erin asked.

"No, I really shouldn't be," E.G. said, staring out of the windshield but seeing only the face of Brian Winter in front of him. "Come on. I need to get this stuff back to Uncle Raymond."

E.G. entered the traffic on Ridgewood Avenue and made a right turn when he came to South Orange Avenue. He spent the rest of the ride trying to imagine Raymond's expression when he showed up at his front door with the file on the Berns-Conroy case. Better yet, he tried to imagine Raymond's expression when he discovered the file missing, knowing his doodling and best laid plans were in someone else's hands.

CHAPTER TWENTY-SIX

E.G. found the office as quiet on this Monday morning as he had found it on Saturday. Then again, he wasn't used to being in his cubicle by 8:45 in the morning any day of the week.

He hadn't planned it that way on this day, either. At 6 a.m., when he had opened his eyes for at least the ninth time that night, he decided to get out of bed and get ready for work. He had many to blame for his tossing and turning, and Conor was tops on his list.

He hadn't heard from Conor all weekend, and intentionally did not reach out to him. That was unusual for Conor, because for as long as E.G. had known him, Conor checked in at least once either on Saturday or Sunday.

Each time he had awakened, his thoughts went back to the picture he had found under Travis' alarm clock, and he could see the two of them beside one another, arms draped across the other's shoulder.

So naturally, when he thought about Conor, he thought about Travis. He hadn't talked to Travis either since the funeral and felt more guilt about that than he did for avoiding Conor during the weekend.

He had tossed another time when Brian Winter entered his dream. They were in a department store of some kind, perhaps even a mall. E.G. remembered running around big display windows filled with clothes. Men's apparel. Some kind of men's store. But he remembered the running and how, even without looking back, he knew Brian was on his trail, gaining ground despite E.G.'s efforts to run faster. Obviously, he couldn't run any faster than he already had been running, and even told himself that he was probably dreaming. Suddenly, he was in the rafters, sitting on the large pieces of wood that stretched across the length and width of the store. So much wood, he thought.

He held onto one of the pieces of wood that rested between his legs for support as he leaned forward to find Brian. For a moment, there was no sign of him, and E.G. felt safe. But just as quickly as the feeling of security drifted over him, Brian appeared, his back to him looking around the department store. Brian was shirtless and holding what E.G. guessed was a newspaper, a rolled up newspaper that he held at his side in his left hand. Brian searched, peering through racks of shirts here, and racks of pants there. E.G. watched, sweat beginning to form on his forehead and his heart beginning to race. For some reason, Brian was angry, and he could tell from the way he used the rolled-up newspaper to swing at the hanging clothes.

Finally, Brian looked up, and they stared at one another for a moment before Brian lunged toward him.

That was at 4:12 a.m., forty-five minutes after the last time he had awakened. E.G. sat up and folded his arms over his knees, then rested his forehead against his arms. His heart was racing, just like in the dream, and his legs, which had been covered by a light blanket, were dripping in sweat. The urge to pee lured him from the bed, and as he stood over the toilet, bent slightly as his erection began to fade, he felt his breathing returning to normal. It had taken another fifteen minutes before he finally fell back to sleep, only to be awakened two more times before deciding he had had enough and stayed up for the day.

He searched the daily newspaper for a story about the murders, but found none. E.G. wasn't surprised. When it came to the *Herald Times*, he didn't expect enterprise on the part of the reporters. A press conference? Sure it would be covered. It was an easy story. A press release? It doesn't take much to add a couple sentences and put a byline on an already prepared story. But that's what he expected from the reporters and the *Herald Times*.

By now, he had four articles that he planned to write for that Thursday's edition and he was waiting to present the ideas to Mel once he arrived. One of them was the interview he had had with Nathanya Berns, which he had conducted in anticipation of other media converging on her home like fighter planes dive-bombing the enemy. But the *Herald Times* had no expansive coverage of Nathanya Berns, just notes in stories identifying the victims' families. Neither did the broadcast news reports.

He had told Nathanya that he would treat her respectfully, unlike what other newspapers might do to her name. But the other newspapers didn't touch that angle to the article, and he wondered if initiating the story in *The Sentinel* would lure other reporters to town. He'd discuss that with Mel, E.G. thought. A second story would be coverage of the funeral Mass for Steven Conroy and the brief, private memorial service held for Mickey Berns. The third would be the standard follow-up story to the murder investigation, and the fourth would be an expose about the Reservation itself and why it had become a popular place for sexual activity among men. That one ought to go over well, E.G. thought, knowing how protective Maplewood residents were of their reputation. It was bad enough that they were getting bad press because of the murders in their town. But it would be another thing to air the kind of laundry E.G. was prepared to air with his expose, and he hoped Mel wouldn't trash the idea.

He had a busy Monday ahead of him, and he wished Conor would get to the office before it was time to leave. It was a little after nine, and some of the advertising staff had filtered in, as well as Margaret, who greeted E.G. with a surprised look when she saw him in his cubicle.

"Did I not set my clock correctly?" she asked.

"No, you're right on time, Margaret," E.G. said, folding the *Herald Times* and tossing it on the floor near the trash can. "I have a busy day today. I want to get an early jump."

"Any update on the killings? Did the police catch anyone?"

"No, they haven't." E.G. remembered the notes he had seen in Raymond's folder. "It's my guess that they're not even close."

"And what about you? How close are you?"

E.G. handed her a perplexed look. "What do you mean?"

Margaret smiled coyly. "You wouldn't be the E.G. Lord I know if you told me you've been sitting at that desk waiting for the police to write the news for you." She paused before continuing. "But I know when not to ask any more questions," she said, finally leaving the entrance to the cubicle to answer the telephone.

Kelly Kelly had passed his cubicle, and as she did, she waved without looking in. Instead, E.G. saw the huge yawn escape from her mouth. He laughed. He guessed Kelly had been in the office the night before and lost track of the time, something she was notorious for, only to be punished for it the following morning.

"Hey, Kel," E.G. yelled over the cubicle.

"Yeah," Kelly yelled back.

"Were you in last night?" E.G. couldn't stifle the yawn he knew he caught from her.

"Was it Sunday?" she asked rhetorically.

E.G. got up from the chair and approached her cubicle. He leaned in to catch Kelly primping her hair in the small round mirror she had hung on the wall above her computer. He remembered when she had first hung a mirror. It wasn't the one that hung there now, which was affixed to the wall with some kind of adhesive that came stuck to the back of the mirror. It was the first time Kelly had tried to hang a mirror that he remembered so well. She had gotten the nail in the wall, even had the mirror hung on the nail the right way. But by the time she had moved her desk back in place and set all the books and file folders on top of that, she realized how crooked she had hung it. Instead of removing everything from the desk and then moving the desk to get behind it in order to straighten the mirror, Kelly decided to climb atop the desk and do it from there.

The crash was deafening and drew not only other reporters who had been writing stories or interviewing people on the telephone, but also drew staff from other departments.

E.G. was one of the first to arrive and one of the first to find Kelly on the floor, the computer and monitor in her lap, books spilled all over the floor, and the desk standing on its side.

But the mirror remained on the wall.

"My God, are you all right?" E.G. had asked, lifting the computer off her. She had a gash on her left arm.

Tears gushed from Kelly's eyes, but they fell more from embarrassment than from pain. When she looked up, all she saw was a doorway filled with the heads of co-workers laughing at her. She stood in anger and swung at the air in an effort to frighten them away, but the force of her swing twisted her body and she hit the mirror on the wall, cracking it and knocking it to the floor.

There was more laughter outside the cubicle, but it faded as each of her colleagues went back to their own desks.

And every time E.G. entered her cubicle, he thought of the mirror, but never dared remind her of that day.

"Did you see Conor last night?" he asked her.

"As a matter of fact, no," she said. "By eleven o'clock, I figured he wasn't coming in. And I wound up staying until about two."

And she wonders why the dark circles under her eyes drop to her cheeks, E.G. thought.

"Did you need him for something?" she asked.

"No, I'll catch him when he comes in," E.G. replied, then returned to his cubicle.

It was an hour later when Conor showed up, and in that time, Mel also had come in and he and E.G. had gone over the story ideas about the murders in the Reservation. Mel approved all of them, including the expose, and by ten-thirty a.m., he was ready to leave for the park when he met Conor in the parking lot.

"Hey, guy," he said as Conor got out of his car. He tried to be as normal as possible around his friend, but he couldn't help but imagine him in the clutches of Travis Boesgaard.

"Morning. Heading out?"

Conor looked tired, even depressed, and E.G. asked if he was okay.

"Yeah, why?" Conor asked, a strange smile and look on his face.

E.G. wanted to ask him about the photo, about how he knew Travis, and, hell, if he was going to go that far, if he knew either of the deceased men who were found in the Reservation. But that wasn't a conversation he wanted to have in the parking lot of *The Sentinel* office. He also didn't want to interfere with his assignments and deadlines. "Are you free tonight?" he asked him. "Feel like having dinner?"

"We'll see," Conor said, again delivering the same strange smile. "I didn't get to come in this weekend, so I'm going to have an intense day today."

"Maybe beers will help then," E.G. said, feeling as if he was stating the obvious.

"They sure sound good."

E.G. waited, as if Conor was about to make a decision, but he remained quiet. After a few moments, he said, "Well, I've got to get out of here. Need to do some research."

"Research? Into what?" Conor asked.

"I'll let you know when I get back," E.G. said. "I should only be a couple hours."

"Where are you going?" Conor knew E.G. well, and knew that if E.G. was going to be doing research six days after a murder, you can be sure the research had something to do with the murder.

"I'll let you know that too when I get back," E.G. said, sliding into the front seat of his car.

He didn't pull out of the space until he saw Conor disappear around the corner toward the front of the building. And while he waited, he watched his walk. It was a slow walk, and very unlike Conor, who normally had more bounce in his steps than the super balls he played with as a kid.

***   ***   ***

On his way to the Reservation, E.G. was expecting to find the same barricade he had found the previous five days, but he was more than surprised when he got to the entrance and found it open to the public. Not only did he see the long stretch of road that eventually vanished into the trees, but cars had been going up and coming down the trail.

He was excited. In fact, he was so excited that he almost missed seeing the oncoming car and floored the Tercel until he was safely nestled inside the entrance to the Reservation. He gave the finger to the driver who blew the horn, but that driver had already continued around the bend in the road and could not see the gesture.

E.G. slowed as a car came down the trail. Both drivers looked at each other as their cars met, but while the other driver maintained a gaze, E.G. turned his head and continued up the trail.

About a quarter of a mile ahead, E.G. approached the first parking area. Driving slowly, he counted five cars in the twenty-five parking spaces. Two of them contained one figure each, and E.G. guessed they were men. The other three cars, from what he could see, were empty. He drove about another quarter mile and, at the end of the road, he made a right turn, pulled the Tercel into a spot in the second parking area he came to and got out of the car.

He walked back to where the road bent because that was where the bodies of Mickey Berns and Steven Conroy were found. The yellow tape that he had watched the police wrap around the trees was gone, and even the red paint they used to mark the location of the bodies was fading.

He removed the notebook he had stuffed into the back pocket of his pants and took notes. He was here to work on a story, he had to tell himself, not to try to solve a murder. He took note of the serenity of the Reservation, that despite the few cars that had driven passed him since he got there, there was a certain calm about the park. The towering trees all around him offered the perfect amount of shade on this hot August day, one that was already topping the eighty-degree mark at such an early hour.

He stepped into the grassy area just around the red lines that was... Who, he wondered. Mickey? Or was this one Steven? He imagined seeing the body of Steven Conroy within the circle, the lifeless body, naked, a gash on his head. Suddenly Travis came to mind, and he pictured Travis and Steven together. Then Travis alone. He had his telephone number, which he had gotten from the phone book when he looked up his address. He wanted to call him, but what would he say? Travis had not given him his last name, so wouldn't he wonder how he got the number?

But he wanted to talk to him, and he almost felt desperate.

He dialed the number from his cell phone anyway, making sure to enter Star 67 to block his number, and sighed when the answering machine connected.

"Hi, Travis, it's Craig," he said. "I looked up your address on the Internet and found your phone number." Legitimate enough, he thought. "Sorry for the vanishing act I pulled this weekend, but I had some personal things to take care of. I can explain when I see you again. That is, if you'd like to get together again. I also need to return your suit, so I guess there's no getting around seeing me." He laughed into the phone, hoping Travis would laugh in response when he heard the message. "I'll call you again later."

As he hung up the phone, he wondered if Travis would be led on by the message. It was not his intention.

He crossed the road and looked down the hill at the dirt path that led into more woods and, further down, property in Maplewood. He could see the roofs of several houses and made a note to determine which street below bordered the Reservation.

E.G. got back into his car and followed the road as it bent in a circle until he came back to where he started. Along the way, he saw several parked vehicles, mostly cars, but also a van that displayed the company logo of a security firm. In most of the cars, a male sat in the driver's seat, each of them looking into E.G.'s car as he passed. The driver of the van was not present. "I'm sure he's not here to install an alarm," E.G. said as he came to the end of the road.

From there, he could either make a left turn and head back down the trail and out of the Reservation. Or he could make a right and return to the first parking area, where he had seen the five parked cars. He chose to make a right.

He parked in one of the spaces — now there were seven cars — and got out. Across the road, where legend had it that George Washington rested during the Revolutionary War, eight benches faced the New York skyline. E.G. climbed the five steps that were made from rock and stood against the waist-high wall, also made from rocks, and looked out into the horizon.

He shielded his eyes from the sun, which burned bright as it rose above Manhattan. Directly on the other side of the wall, the mountain began to descend into more trees. The open grassy area just below him was unkempt, filled with weeds, burned grass and loads of empty beer and liquor bottles.

He jumped up on the wall and sat, trying to get as comfortable as he could, what with all the corners of the rocks poking him in the ass. Another car had pulled into one of the parking spaces. The driver got out, gave E.G. the once-over, and disappeared into the woods. The driver of one of the other cars stepped out and leaned against the driver's side door, glancing frequently in E.G.'s direction.

E.G. kept his notebook in his pocket. He wanted the man to approach him, but he knew that if he displayed the notebook, he most likely wouldn't come.

So he waited.

The blue Ford that passed him had already done so twice, and E.G. found that curious. A silver Nissan had done the same. And the brown Oldsmobile, now that he was taking notice.

But he focused his attention on the man standing next to his car. He had walked around the car, lifted and closed the trunk, and opened the rear door and fiddled around, and all the while kept glancing at E.G.

E.G. wondered if there was something he had to do, some kind of code, to inform the man that he was interested. Was that what he was waiting for? I should just grab my crotch, he thought, which he figured would ensure getting the man's attention, but it's not why he wanted him to come over. Instead, when he knew the man was looking at him, E.G. nodded once.

It worked.

The man pressed the transmitter on his key ring to set the alarm on his car and approached E.G., who remained seated on the wall. The closer he got, the more anxious E.G. became. The sun burned into the back of his shirt and he felt the sweat drip down his body.

The man climbed the steps and stopped at one of the benches off to the side of the steps. He glanced at E.G. again, and E.G. responded, "How's it going today?"

"Good," the man said and came closer. He wasn't very tall and could have shed a few pounds before putting himself in the market, E.G. thought. A shave wouldn't have hurt either.

"They finally opened the Reservation, huh?" E.G. said. "Must have been opened this morning, because I'd been by here this weekend, and it was still closed."

That was the truth. E.G. had driven by the Reservation both nights during the weekend after his attempts to meet Matt were unsuccessful. Both nights, the barricades were in place.

"You a cop?" the man asked and caught E.G. by surprise.

"No," he responded. "What makes you ask that?"

"You're talking."

"And that means I could be a cop?"

"Just not used to conversation." The man turned and faced the skyline. E.G. noticed the wedding band on his left hand. "What'cha lookin' for?"

"Is it safe up here?" E.G. asked.

"I can take care of myself," the man responded.

"I'm sure you can. But listen, I don't know you, and I don't know your history, so I think I'll pass," E.G. said.

"I'm very selective with who I go with," the man quickly replied, almost defensively. "I don't pick just anyone."

E.G. shook his head in disbelief. "So because you're picky when it comes to anonymous sex, I should feel safe. Is that what you expect me to believe?"

The man backed away from the wall and started to walk away. "I don't have time for games," he said.

The man didn't return to his car. He continued walking and disappeared into the woods, taking the same path as the man who had gone that way only five minutes earlier.

He told himself that was no way to get quotes for a story. E.G. slid off the wall and began to walk along the paved path toward the area where the two bodies were found. A couple runners had passed him, but he didn't take notice of them. It was through the trees that he was trying to look, trying to sight some activity, but he knew it would be a fat chance in hell to find it. If he wanted to see any action, he knew he would have to go into the woods, deep into the woods, where it would be least likely for anyone to get caught, literally, with their pants down.

Along the quarter mile of road that he had to walk, E.G. observed more traffic circling the Reservation. He looked at his watch. It was getting close to lunch hour and that probably played a factor, he thought.

From where he stood, he could see, in the near distance, the end of the road. He saw a figure in the area, the back of a man who, from E.G.'s perspective, was searching for something. His head was lowered and he paced the area between the two red circles where the bodies had been marked.

As he got closer, the figure grew familiar. His heart raced as he realized it was Brian Winter. Doing what? Coming back to the scene of the crime, he asked himself. Is this why his cousin had book-marked the page in the yearbook that contained his picture?

He pulled the tail of his shirt out of his pants and covered the top half of the notebook that was exposed in his back pocket. The last thing he wanted Brian to figure out was that he was a reporter.

No, this morning he was going to be Caleb, the man Brian met at the funeral on Saturday. The man who came between him and Travis on the steps of the church before the two came to blows.

Brian apparently didn't hear him coming, because when E.G. called his name, Brian jumped.

When he recognized E.G., Brian's first reaction was to look around. A sort of strange smile appeared on his face before he said, "Hi," followed by, "What are you doing here?"

He was obviously not comfortable seeing E.G., and E.G. watched him shift from one leg to another, put his hands in his pockets, pat the back of his crewcut-type hairstyle.

"This is where they found them, huh?" E.G. asked.

"Yes, I guess it is," Brian said, pointing out the red, spray-painted circles.

"Are you looking for something?" E.G. asked. "That's what it looked like you were doing as I was walking over here."

"No, not at all," Brian replied, but E.G. sensed that he answered too quickly, and besides, he wouldn't look him in the eyes when he responded. "This is the first chance I've had," he continued, "to see where it all happened. The place was swarming with police the last few days."

"So you come up here often?" E.G. asked.

"What does that mean?" He looked E.G. in the eyes this time, and E.G. felt the stare penetrate him.

211

"Don't make any inferences," E.G. replied. "It was the way you said it. As if you tried to get up here, but couldn't because of all the police in the area."

"I come up here once in a while," Brian offered. "But anything I do is safe. Now why are you up here?"

E.G. had his story prepared, creating one the moment he realized he was about to confront Brian Winter.

"Travis was hit pretty hard by this. I wanted to come up here and see for myself where it happened, try to get a better perspective on it."

Brian seemed to have bought the explanation. "How long have you been going with Travis? I mean, do you realize that he and Steven were a couple?"

"I knew that," E.G. said. "So to clarify, Travis and I are not an item. We're just friends." There was a pause before E.G. continued. "Apparently, you and Travis are not friends. You guys made that very clear on Saturday."

"Travis is a user." The hatred poured from Brian's mouth. "And once he's done using you, he'll toss you aside like yesterday's garbage. Here's some advice for you if you're thinking of pursuing more than a friendship with Travis: I was that garbage. Mickey was that garbage. And I would bet that Steven would have become that garbage if he lived long enough. It should have been Travis in that circle, not Mickey," he said, pointing to the red outline behind them. "It's all so fucked up!"

E.G. froze. He froze because he didn't know how to react. I'm in the company of a killer, he thought, and where are all the men when you need them? Not a car was in sight, not even the sound of an engine approaching. The silence that hovered seemed to magnify the sound of the birds and the rustling of the leaves in the light breeze.

Brian paced quickly, his anger controlling his direction. He kicked the base of a tree, swung at limp branches and began to sob.

E.G. slowly backed away and stepped from the grass and into the middle of the road. If a car comes, he thought, the driver would be forced to stop.

Brian leaned against a tree and bent over, the sobbing becoming uncontrollable. E.G. remained where he was, not saying a word. He had the cell phone with him and could dial 9-1-1 if he had to.

"Mickey was my friend," Brian cried. "It shouldn't have been him."

E.G. didn't want to appear afraid. He also didn't want to leave because that would surely prevent him from getting closer to Brian. He was too close now, he thought, to give it all up and hand the case to Raymond on a silver platter.

E.G. moved closer, stepping from the road onto the grass again, purposely avoiding stepping inside one of the red outlines as if it were sacred ground. Brian had stopped flailing his arms; he was now just sobbing.

E.G. moved even closer, close enough to rest a hand on his shoulder. Brian didn't pull away. In fact, he took E.G. by surprise when he reached out and put his arms around E.G.'s waist, continuing to sob into his shirt.

E.G. let him hold on, and in what he himself felt was a bizarre reaction, he reached around and embraced Brian. Around the back and above the chest, he justified. A manly embrace.

But then he thought of the notebook, which lay only inches from where Brian held him. "Pull yourself together," E.G. whispered, scanning the area for any cars or pedestrians. The last thing he wanted was to be recognized in the South Mountain Reservation with his arms around another man. The only car in sight was an empty Plymouth parked about one hundred feet away.

As Brian released his arms, his right hand brushed against the notebook, hidden behind the tail of the shirt, but he didn't acknowledge it. Hell, for all he knew, it could have been a wallet or any number of things. It was E.G.'s imagination that was getting the best of him.

Although he let go, Brian kept his head lowered and continued to sob. "I'm sorry. I'm really sorry for showing you this side of me," he said, again not looking E.G. in the eyes.

"It's understandable," E.G replied. "You just lost a very good friend. Are you going to be all right?"

Brian nodded and wiped the tears from his eyes. "I look kind of silly, don't I? A grown man crying like this."

"Not at all. It's healthy to let it out."

Brian shook his head. "I'm normally not like this."

"I know," E.G. said. "You were quite the opposite the other day, if you recall."

He mustered a smile, remembering how E.G. had to step between him and Travis after the funeral. "Travis does that to me. He really gets to me."

"I wasn't referring to that," E.G. said, leaving Brian to wonder what he meant. "I was talking about how bold you were when you told me you wanted to get together with me."

"Oh, that," Brian said, his cheeks turning red. "I did mean it."

E.G. wanted the story. He could taste it. "Maybe one night we could meet for a drink." He couldn't believe he was saying this to Brian. Only three days ago, he uttered similar words to Travis. He pictured Patrick Crowe rolling in his grave.

"I'd like that. But you're sure you're not with Travis?"

"I'm positive. But while we're on the subject of Travis, are you angry with him because he dumped you, or is there more?"

"There's a lot more," Brian said without hesitation. "But I can't go into it with you. Not now."

"Does it have anything to do with the deaths of Mickey Berns and Steven Conroy?"

Brian's eyes dropped to the ground. "Why do you ask that?"

"Because if Travis had anything to do with it, I think I have a right to know."

"What makes you think I know anything?" Brian grew defensive, and E.G. noticed it immediately.

"I didn't say that. But earlier, you got very angry at Travis when you were talking about Mickey."

Brian shook his head, and E.G. guessed that his delay in answering was to create a story. "I just know how Travis treated Mickey is all." He removed a business card from his wallet and scratched a phone number on the back of it before handing it to E.G. "Listen, I have to get going. This is my number. I really would like to get together with you some night. Feel free to call me. It's my personal phone."

E.G. took the card and read the name and telephone number before stuffing it into his shirt pocket. "I'll do that. Maybe tomorrow night."

"Tomorrow night is good," Brian said.

Brian didn't come to the Reservation in a car. He crossed the road and stood at the top of the dirt path that led down the hill into the streets of Maplewood. He turned and waved to E.G., then disappeared behind the trees.

E.G. approached the path slowly, thinking Brian might be able to see him if he looked back as he got to the top of the hill. But by the time E.G. got there, Brian was nowhere in sight, engulfed by the towering trees, and the first thing E.G. thought was, what an easy escape route out of the Reservation.

CHAPTER TWENTY-SEVEN

Raymond got the call a little after eight a.m. as he wound his way down the mountain on Route 280 in West Orange. A group of kids had been playing on abandoned property in Newark and they had come across two pairs of men's clothing dumped in a pile of garbage. It was clothing that belonged to adult males and while they could have belonged to anyone, the fact that there was blood on them caught the attention of the kids, who reported the finding to their parents.

The property was off Broad Street in Newark, and, conveniently, on his way to the office, so Raymond took an earlier exit and met the officers at the site.

By the time he arrived, the police had bagged and tagged the clothing as they had found it, rolled neatly like a sleeping bag. Raymond touched the plastic and took note of the jeans and shirt. Indeed there was blood, but until he got to the forensics lab, he wouldn't know how much.

Four hours later, he sat at his desk, begging the phone to ring with the results of the tests. While he waited, he flipped through the folder bearing the name of Brian Winter, the only suspect he had in the murder case, and he wasn't even sure he could label him a suspect. Does a strange look from a father mean the son is guilty of something, he asked himself. Instinct was something in which he took pride and netted him many suspects, and instinct told him the day he met Ian Winter that he needed to check out his son.

The folder contained the basics: date of birth, address, high school, college, employment, business dealings. An investigation revealed he had no criminal record. He was awaiting reports from the Internal Revenue Service and the New Jersey State Division of Taxation for a listing of any holdings he had and with whom.

He had received a report that morning that Brian was at the funeral Mass for Steven Conroy on Saturday, but Raymond already knew that. He made a mental note to reprimand Manning, the detective he had assigned to surveillance, for not noticing him there.

The phone rang, and he flinched. It didn't get a chance to ring a second time. "Vanderhoeven," he said into the mouthpiece.

The voice on the other end did not belong to the Forensics lab. It was Manning calling from the Plymouth. Raymond listened, shook his head in disbelief and slammed down the phone when the conversation ended.

Manning reported that he had just left Brian Winter in the Reservation. Brian, he said, departed through the brush but not before an encounter with, "I don't know how to tell you this, Ray, but the guy he was with was the 'splitting' image of your cousin. You know, the reporter," Manning said.

Yeah, the one who has a habit of 'splitting' all over the ground, he thought. But Raymond wasn't as surprised as Manning. In fact, he was more surprised that the detective didn't note in his report that E.G. was at the funeral on Saturday as well.

"They were huggin', I think," he said.

"Hugging?" Raymond asked.

"Yeah. Exactly where we found the bodies. The guy was cryin' like a baby, and this other guy, who I think was your cousin, was holdin' him. You know somethin' about your cousin that we don't?"

"My cousin is as normal as you and me," Raymond responded. "At least when it comes to his sexuality. I can't vouch for him otherwise."

Nor did it make him happy to know that E.G. was following the same route as he was. Raymond concluded that there was no other reason why E.G. and Brian Winter would be seen together. Knowing E.G. and how well he cultivated and used his sources, Raymond felt more confident that he was on the right trail with his investigation of the Winter kid.

But hugging? Raymond couldn't get beyond that one. "What the hell was he hugging him for?" he asked himself aloud in the empty office. "And why was Brian crying like a baby?" A confession. His adrenaline began to take over, and he got up from behind his desk. Did E.G. get a confession out of him, he wondered. He reached for the phone and dialed the Forensics lab.

"Do you guys have anything yet or what?" he demanded into the phone. He wanted it. He wanted the answers so badly he could taste them.

When the voice on the other end told Raymond to "hang on," he held the mouthpiece of the phone as if he were about to beat the wall with it. But he composed himself and returned it to the side of his head.

Shortly after, another voice came on the line. "Ray?" It was Bob Meyer, whom Raymond had known for at least seven years and whose work he respected. Bob was closing in on seventy years old, but had no plans to retire. Raymond had guessed that if he announced his retirement, no one would accept it and he'd be forced to work in the Forensics lab for the rest of his life.

"Yes, Bob. Do you guys have anything yet?" He didn't have to be specific. Bob knew why he was waiting.

"As a matter of fact, we do," he said, and Raymond could hear him shuffling papers as he spoke. Bob was meticulous. There was no doubt about that. And he knew Bob probably had everything in a folder by now. "The blood on the clothes is a perfect match to the blood of both deceased men. It was their clothes, that's for sure."

Tell me more, Raymond thought.

As if Bob could read his mind, he continued. "We also found a third, as yet unidentified, sample of blood as well as a couple strands of hair, which do not match the hair of either of the deceased men."

Bob knew what that meant. Until they had a suspect, the strands of hair were worth nothing. Raymond knew as well, but he wasn't prepared to tell Bob about Brian Winter.

"Get me a suspect, and I'll test the hair," Bob said.

"I will do my best, buddy," Raymond said. "Anything else?"

Bob spoke the obvious, telling Raymond about the traces of foliage on the clothing. "I knew you wanted the blood samples immediately, so that's what I searched for first. If anything else shows up, you'll be the second to know."

"Thanks, Bob. It's always a pleasure," Raymond said as he hung up the phone. He picked it back up and dialed three numbers. To the voice on the other end, he said, "I need a meeting."

Five minutes later, he was in the office of Essex County Prosecutor Sheila Timoni, the Berns-Conroy folder tucked under his arm.

Sheila was in her mid fifties and was appointed as acting prosecutor to fill the post after the death of the former prosecutor. That was four years earlier, and her work and dedication to the office during the first two years in the interim position garnered her the permanent title. Sheila wasn't someone to deceive, and her staff was among the first to learn that. That included Raymond, who, when Sheila was first named to the position, joined his colleagues, all but the female colleagues, in the typical denouncement of a female boss.

Sheila was the first female to be named Essex County prosecutor, and it was a title, along with the respect, she had to earn.

And she earned it quickly. Within the first year of her tenure, she cut what she called the bullshit jobs from the budget, giving her office higher salaries and the ability to add better investigators and attorneys to the staff. She didn't mince words when it came to Essex County politics and actually instilled fear into those who could make or break her career.

Sheila went public with everything. Some feared it. Others loved it. But in either case, both sides respected her work.

"This isn't Romper Room," she had told her staff during her first meeting with them. "And I'm not Miss Nancy. I have no time for games, political or otherwise. I have ideas, plans and goals to make this the most effective and efficient prosecutor's office in the state, and I plan to accomplish those goals - with or without you. And having known many of you for many years, I'd like to do it with you."

Her audience had sat up that day and listened. And Sheila's transition eventually became one of the smoothest in Essex County government.

Within her second year, she had accomplished one of her goals. Her office had recorded the most winning cases on a per capita basis in the state. She had created several task forces targeting domestic violence, identity theft and pedophilia on the Internet, among others, and was recognized for her efforts in her third year by being named New Jersey's top law enforcement official.

And now she sat in her office opposite Raymond Vanderhoeven, one of her top assistants, who was trying to convince Sheila that Brian Winter was his only lead in the case.

"I met his father in the Reservation while he was out for a jog," Raymond said. "I didn't like the look he gave me when he learned Mickey Berns was one of the men who was found up there. He told me he knew Berns through his son, Brian, but that his son and Berns had not been friends for a long time, drifting apart sometime after high school graduation. But his son was at Conroy's funeral. I found that odd. His son also was seen this morning at the Reservation, exactly where the bodies were found, and he was being consoled. I've had Manning assigned to him for the past couple days, and he gave me that report earlier today."

He didn't tell Sheila who was consoling Brian.

"The other link is that the Winters live at the bottom of a trail that takes you directly to the area where the two bodies were discovered," Raymond said.

"It's not enough," Sheila responded. "We can't bring someone in for questioning because they live near the Reservation. As far as having to be consoled, this Winter kid could have been upset over the loss of a friend, whether it was a recent friendship or not. I need more."

"How about instinct?" Raymond quickly responded, declining to tell Sheila that part of the instinct included his cousin's presence in the Reservation with Brian.

"Raymond, you're one of the best investigators I have on staff. And I don't doubt your instinct. It's worked well in the past, and I'm sure it will serve you equally as well in the future. But I can't allow this office to start rounding up people on the kind of information you're giving me." She pushed her hair behind her ears. "Keep

Manning on surveillance. Get me something solid, and I'll let you run with it."

Raymond passed her the notes he had taken on the telephone with Bob. "He's got hair samples that are unidentified. They could belong to this Winter kid."

Sheila glanced over the notes. "Get me something solid," she said when she finished.

Although Raymond was upset, he knew Sheila was right. He needed more. And he knew that it was decisions like this that made the prosecutor's office more respectable. He also knew that these decisions made the staff work harder and sharpen their investigative skills.

On his way back to his office, Raymond convinced himself that he could get that "something solid" for Sheila. After all, it was already in the palm of his hand. As he closed the office door behind him, he had reached his decision, one that he thought would be the last one he would make.

He picked up the phone on his desk and dialed the number by memory.

When it connected, he said, with an air of surrender in his voice, "May I please speak to E.G. Lord."

CHAPTER TWENTY-EIGHT

E.G. was on the telephone when Margaret slipped the note under his nose. "Do you want to talk to your cousin? He's on line three," she had written in handwriting that reminded him of the nuns who had taught him in grammar school.

He raised his index finger and nodded as he listened to Nathanya Berns pleading that he not publicize her relationship to Mickey. The other newspapers did not pick up on it, she was telling him, and it was not the responsibility of the local newspaper to dwell on the negative.

The biggest misconception of the local weekly newspaper was that it was supposed to be a cheerleader for the municipalities it served. E.G. had heard that hundreds of times from hundreds of people, and each time another person mentioned it, he grew as angry as he did the first few times he had heard it.

The misconception was out there, he believed, because industrywide, the local weekly paper was considered the starting ground for journalists. It was also not the first time he had heard it from Nathanya during his tenure at *The Sentinel*.

"I have a responsibility to my readers, Mrs. Berns. I certainly understand the situation in which you find yourself, but this is news, and I'm required to cover it," E.G. told her.

"I'll sue the paper for everything it's worth if you print a story," Nathanya retorted.

"Not to sound obnoxious, but you can't do that. And you know you can't do that or you would have sued us thousands of times in the past."

"I thought we had a good relationship, E.G. Apparently we don't. Your publisher will hear from my lawyer."

E.G. didn't have a chance to respond. The phone went dead in his ear. He sat for a moment watching the flashing red light on his telephone. Everybody wants to sue today, he thought, sincerely feeling guilty about what his stories in that week's edition would mean to Nathanya Berns and the privacy she enjoyed.

He pressed the light on line three. "Raymond?" he asked.

"E.G. Did I catch you at a bad time?"

"Never a bad time when the prosecutor's office calls." E.G. had a bad habit. Whenever he bullshitted a caller, as he was doing with Raymond now, he waved his arm as if he were masturbating an extremely large penis. The longer the arm movement, the bigger the jerk off, was how he explained it to those who caught some of his animation as they passed his cubicle. Then all of a sudden, he got serious. "Did you make an arrest?"

"No, we didn't," Raymond said, feeling slightly inadequate making the statement. It was only in his own head, he assured himself, a result of making the pronouncement to E.G. and not a reflection of his ability as a law enforcement officer. "I'm going to be in your neck of the woods this afternoon. Will you be in the office later today?"

"My neck of the woods?" he repeated sarcastically. "Should I heat the chitlins?" But then he grew serious as well as curious, and quiet when he didn't get a response from his cousin. "Yeah, I'll be here. I plan to write all afternoon, so, yeah, I'll be here. Come anytime you want." He paused. "What's this all about?"

Raymond was now quick to respond. "We'll discuss that when I get there," and he hung up.

E.G. tucked the pen over his ear, collected his coffee cup and went next door to Conor's cubicle. With a notebook to the left side of the computer, Conor was filing a story and, as he typed, referred to the scribbled notes that only he could read easily. He didn't hear E.G. come into the room.

Nor did E.G. make his presence known. Instead, he watched Conor. He watched to see if his friend maintained the focus he had always had when writing a story. To see otherwise, he'd know Conor was distracted by something.

But Conor didn't give E.G. enough time to scrutinize him. With a quick snap of the neck, as if he felt someone's presence, he turned his head. When he saw E.G. behind him, he turned all the way around in his chair to face him. "Dude," he said, stretching the word like a rubber band as he said it. "What are you doing there?"

E.G shrugged his shoulders as if it was no big thing. "Just watching you." He shrugged again. "I'm concerned about you. You haven't been yourself the last few days."

His eyes were still slightly puffy, the look one gets when they either haven't slept well the night before or when ragweed blooms and one is allergic to it, but this wasn't the season for allergies.

"There's nothing wrong with me." He started to turn back to his computer. "I have to get back to work. I have a ton of writing to do today."

E.G. leaned against the wall of the cubicle. "I wonder if they made an arrest in the case today," he said aloud, sharing his news as he always did with Conor.

Conor turned back around more quickly than the first time. Panic had replaced the worried look in his eyes and E.G. noticed it. "What do you mean?"

"My cousin is coming here this afternoon," E.G. said, knowing Raymond's visit would not be to announce an arrest. He wanted to get Conor's reaction to the statement. "And I'm sure it's not to talk about a family reunion."

Conor stood. "When's he getting here?" He couldn't look at E.G. when he asked the question.

"Look at you, Conor," E.G. stated directly, yet in a whisper. "Look at your wrist. It's shaking. What the hell is going on with you?"

Conor spoke as softly yet as directly as E.G. "Nothing is going on. Drop it!" He pushed passed E.G. and left the cubicle, heading for the front entrance of the building.

E.G. waited a moment before following him, then, as casually as he could, headed toward the back entrance, hoping not to create a distraction. The presses were quiet as he passed them. Taking a rest, E.G. thought, until Wednesday, when the sound of the newspapers being printed would drown the silence in the room.

He found Conor in the yard, leaning against the back of his car and smoking a cigarette. He looked angry, the angriest he had ever seen him, and E.G. was a little reluctant to approach him. Conor had heard the back door open and saw E.G. standing half in and half out.

The only movement between them was Conor's arm, as he brought the cigarette up to his lips and then back down to his side. "Do you plan to just appear everywhere I go and stand there?" Conor yelled across the yard.

E.G. stepped into the yard. "Maybe until you tell me what you're hiding."

"What makes you think I'm hiding something?" Conor demanded. "I show interest in the stories you're working on, and you think I'm hiding something."

"Interest? You almost shit your pants in your cubicle when I said there might be an arrest. The Conor I know would have picked right up on that and told me that's not why Raymond was coming here. That if they were going to announce an arrest, they'd summon us to them."

E.G. took a few more steps closer to Conor.

"I told you earlier, I have a lot on my mind and I don't care to discuss any of it." He took one final drag on the cigarette and flicked it into the air. But he didn't move from his spot against the car when he was done.

E.G. stood only a few steps away from him. "How long have we been friends, Conor?" he asked. "There's nothing that you can't tell me that would put an end to our friendship." He again imagined Conor with Travis, each with their arm across the other's shoulder.

Conor looked toward the sky and shook his head. "You won't let go, will you?"

"No, I won't. Because to let go would mean to give up, to let you have your way. And that won't make me a good friend. I wish you'd talk to me."

By now, E.G. was standing next to Conor, and they both leaned against his car. Neither spoke for several minutes, but both of them felt fulfilled in each other's company.

Conor broke the silence with quiet laughter. "Do you remember the night you caught me fucking that girl - I don't even remember her name - right here in this parking lot?"

E.G. sensed he was nervous, but laughed back. He remembered the night. "I pulled into the parking lot next door because I saw an unfamiliar car pull into our driveway."

"And then you crept over here through those bushes," Conor said, pointing to the overgrown yews that lined the border of the two driveways.

E.G. continued, "From where I stood, I couldn't see anybody in the car, so I'm thinking, where could this person have disappeared?"

"So, naturally, the first thing you did was come look into the only car in the parking lot," Conor said.

"Hey, you were stupid for making yourself so obvious," E.G. said. "You could have brought her inside and did her on the presses before anyone would have known you were even in the building."

Now they both laughed.

"I think if she saw you, she'd have invited you in for a threesome," Conor said.

"Think so?" E.G. asked, not having the faintest idea where Conor was going with this stroll down memory lane. "If she did, would you have agreed?"

Conor looked at E.G. quizzically.

E.G. shrugged. "Would have been interesting."

Conor continued to look at his friend. "Are you serious?" he asked.

"Sure," E.G. said nonchalantly, preparing the trap. "I hope this doesn't make you uncomfortable, but I think it would be pretty neat to be able to share something so personal with a best friend. Come on, in your entire lifetime, you never wondered, even the slightest bit, what it would be like to be intimate with a good friend?"

E.G. was baiting Conor, and by the look on Conor's face, it was working.

"I guess I could see it happening," Conor finally said. "Is that something you're interested in?" He was uncomfortable asking the question, and he instinctively reached into his shirt pocket for another cigarette.

"I've never tried it, but I think once you develop a strong emotion for someone, even if it's someone you've been platonic with, it's only natural to want to transfer those feelings to the physical."

"And you're saying you've felt that way about another guy?" Conor asked.

"It's no big thing," E.G. said.

"Would you ever act on it?" Conor asked.

E.G. thought for a moment, knowing he would have to be truly convincing. "That would depend on the person. If I wanted to act on those feelings, I would engage him in conversation about it. Get his take on it. See where it goes from there."

Conor was silent. He was tempted to ask E.G. if he was, at the moment, engaging him in that kind of conversation, but as much as he wanted to ask the question, he felt the same strong feeling to withhold it.

"I never would have thought someone like you would feel that way," he said instead.

"What do you mean, someone like me?"

"You were married for a good number of years. You have a kid."

E.G. laughed. "That doesn't mean anything today, my friend."

Conor took another drag on the cigarette. "Why are you talking like this?" he asked E.G., wondering if his friend was fishing for information. "We've never had this kind of conversation in all the time we've known each other."

E.G. shrugged. "You brought it up, inviting me into a threesome."

"I didn't invite you. You invited yourself," Conor was quick to point out. "You know, it hurts to love someone and not be loved in return, but what's more painful is to love someone and never find the courage to let that person know how you feel."

E.G. digested the words, realizing how serious Conor had become. He wondered if Conor was referring to someone he had kept hidden within his lifestyle. "Are you feeling that pain, Conor? I know there's something wrong."

Conor was about to answer when the sound of a car chugged into the parking lot. Will Edmond's 1980s model Buick LaSalle slowly made its way into the rear yard and docked four stalls away from where E.G. and Conor stood. Will sat in the car for a while, letting the engine idle, and fumes poured from the exhaust pipe, filling the parking lot.

"When you think of all the bright and beautiful kids on this earth with disabilities and other health problems, and you see this guy with not a care in the world, you can't help but wonder if there is a merciful God," E.G. said.

"Hey, Will," Conor yelled, waving smoke away with his hand. "Turn the goddamn thing off."

Turning slightly in the driver's seat, Will flashed his hand out the window in Hitler-esque fashion and the engine died.

"We must really have a fucking love affair with this business," E.G. joked. "This guy's car is ready to explode, Andrea's been wearing the same pants for the last three days, and half the reporters in the building can't afford to buy a new pair of shoes. Why the hell do we spend years in college only to get a full-time job where we can also qualify for welfare?"

E.G. asked the question rhetorically, and both he and Conor fell silent. But the silence didn't last.

"So why are you so concerned about my cousin's visit?" E.G. asked. "We talked about almost everything but that."

Will had gotten out of his car by this time and approached E.G. and Conor. Without even looking, they knew he was coming from the sound of the coins that jingled in his pockets.

"Gentlemen," Will said, nodding to both of them. "I'm on first base right now, and if my plan goes according to schedule, I will be rounding second by six o'clock this evening, and on my way to third by nine o'clock tomorrow morning. By two o'clock tomorrow afternoon, I should be rounding third base and on my way to home plate before deadlines hit. But I can't get there if I'm standing in the parking lot, so if you'll kindly excuse me..."

Without looking back, Will started for the rear entrance, then second guessed his decision and disappeared around the side of the building toward the front entrance.

"What a character," E.G. said, then turned back to Conor. "Would you please tell me what's going on? In all seriousness, I'm concerned about you."

Conor stuffed his hands in his pockets. "Do you think they're going to make an arrest soon?"

"I don't know, and I'm sure Raymond is not going to tell me what kind of progress he's made since this happened. You leave me no choice but to think you're somehow involved in this, Conor. I can't imagine any other reason you'd be this interested in this case."

"Involved?" Conor replied. "Involved, like in killing those two guys?"

"I didn't say that. But I don't know what to think based on the way you've been behaving. If you're involved, talk to me. I'm your best friend."

Conor started to talk, but the brown Buick that was pulling into the back of the lot caught his attention and he stopped. E.G. followed Conor's eyes and saw the car himself.

Raymond nodded through a closed window and rolled into a parking space near the back of the lot.

"Ah, shit," E.G. said and turned back to Conor, who visibly grew nervous at the presence of the investigator. "Go inside," he demanded. "And don't talk to a soul about this."

"You'll let me know what he says?" Conor asked, starting to walk toward the building.

"We'll talk later," was all E.G. would say.

By the time Raymond had parked and approached E.G., Conor was well inside the building. He was, unsurprisingly, without a jacket on this hot afternoon, and his shirt sleeves were rolled just above his elbows.

"It must be very hot today," E.G. said. "You're actually carrying a handkerchief in your hand."

"It's the humidity that kills me," Raymond said, wiping his temple with the cloth, "but I'm not here to talk about the weather."

"Then you're as unpredictable as the weather," E.G. said sarcastically, "because I was sure as shit that that's why you wanted to see me."

Raymond ignored the remark. "I want to talk off the record," he said.

"I'm listening," E.G. said.

Raymond paused before continuing as if he were carefully selecting his words. "We both want the same thing. We both want justice to be served. Two men are dead, and their killer is on the loose. I'm not naive, and I'm certainly not stupid. I've read your stuff throughout the years, E.G. You have a reputation that goes well beyond your circulation area because you dig and you dig and you dig until you get just the right information you need for a story.

"You brought down a mayor by exposing his corruption; you single-handedly destroyed our office's case against an alleged child abuser and got her free..."

"She was innocent," E.G. interrupted.

"...and you exposed a conflict of interest between a developer and a councilman and put an end to a major project."

"Don't stop there, Ray. I've done a whole lot more than that."

"You know that, and I know that," Raymond responded. "And that leads me to this case. You know more about this double homicide than you've been willing to tell me, and I want to know exactly how much you know."

E.G. leaned against Conor's car. "What makes you think I know more?" he asked.

"Instinct, first of all. Second, you were in the Reservation this morning."

"Today was the first time the Reservation has been open since last Wednesday. I went there to check things out for a story."

"You were with Brian Winter," Raymond charged. "The same Brian Winter I saw you with at Conroy's funeral Saturday."

"Are you having me followed?" E.G. asked, but before Raymond could respond, E.G. continued, knowing Raymond wouldn't waste taxpayers' money on having him followed. "It's not me you're having followed. It's Brian Winter, isn't it? Do you think he did it? Do you think he killed Mickey Berns and Steven Conroy?"

231

"Should I think that?"

"You're the detective. You're the one with all the useful tools at your fingertips. You know, the forensics, fingerprints, sole access to the Reservation right after the bodies were found. I don't have all those wonderful tools. So could it be that little ole reporter here might know a little bit more than the big bad cop?"

"I'm losing my patience, E.G. I came here hoping that you and I could work together. I see that can't be the case."

"Don't try to make it look as if I can't be cooperative," E.G. said. "I tried to pin you down Thursday before your press conference specifically to tell you what I know. You didn't have time for me then, so maybe I just don't have time for you now."

"You will find the time because if you won't do this voluntarily, you would leave me no choice but to bring you in for questioning. As an official act."

E.G. laughed aloud. "And ask me what? Am I giving head in the Reservation? Go ahead. Do that, Ray, and I would have a field day in next week's paper destroying you, your office and your investigation."

Raymond moved closer. "Do you think this is all a joke? I can get you on obstruction of justice, hindering an investigation, withholding information that could lead to the arrest and conviction of a suspect..."

"What suspect?" E.G. challenged. "You mentioned Brian Winter, and the fact that I was with him at the funeral and in the Reservation. You never said he was a suspect. I don't make it a practice of talking officially with police about casual acquaintances. Now if you tell me he's a suspect..." E.G. let his voice trail purposely, avoiding a promise to reveal any information as well as confirm that he knows anything.

Raymond was quiet.

"Is Brian a suspect, Ray?"

E.G. only wanted Raymond to confirm the information.

"Off the record," Raymond said. "And I mean completely off the record."

E.G. nodded. "Off the record."

"My gut tells me he should be questioned, but I don't have anything tangible to bring him in on. At this point, you're my only link to him. If you can tell me something, anything, that would connect him to Berns and Conroy the night of the murder, I could move this case forward."

E.G. shook his head. "I'm sorry, but I can't."

"Can't or won't?"

"Can't," E.G. emphasized. "I met Brian at the funeral. I'd never seen him before in my life. I went to the Reservation this morning to look around. For a story I'm working on. He was there. I said hello and reminded him that I met him at the funeral. He remembered me. We talked briefly. He became upset because he had just lost a friend in a horrible way. That was it."

"And he called himself a friend? He used that word? Meaning who? Mickey? Or Steven?" Raymond asked, recalling Brian's father stating that Brian and Mickey hadn't been friends for years.

"We were talking about Mickey," E.G. responded, believing he was answering an innocent question. "He said he didn't know Steven that well."

E.G. declined to reveal to Raymond the statement Brian had made at the site of the murders, that it wasn't supposed to be Mickey who died. All he wanted to know was that Raymond was considering Brian as a suspect.

"Will you be seeing him again?" Raymond asked.

"I may," E.G. replied. "But you would know that, wouldn't you? Just like you knew I was with him this morning."

Raymond smiled. "I have a job to do."

"Are you asking me to do something if I see him again?"

"If you can get some information from him that will help me with this case, I would appreciate it."

"I'll see what I can do," E.G. said, looking his cousin directly in the eye.

As Raymond started to walk back to his car, he yelled over his shoulder to E.G. "And I would be careful about what I write in the newspaper if I were you. I wouldn't want my job to put my wife's and kid's lives in jeopardy." He winked at him. "I have my sources too."

CHAPTER TWENTY-NINE

As he did fairly regularly, Conor had classical music playing from a small Bose stereo that he had hooked up himself in his cubicle. E.G. had no idea which composer was playing, but something piano-ish was playing when he interrupted Conor.

Conor stopped typing and spun in his chair to face E.G.

"Turns out he just wanted to know if I had heard anything on the streets about the murders," E.G. said, intentionally omitting any reference to Brian Winter. He wanted to trust Conor, to trust him as he had done for the last seven years, but Conor was holding out on him, and until he knew how he was involved, E.G. wasn't prepared to reveal too much anymore.

"So they have no suspects?" he asked.

"None whatsoever." E.G. watched a look of relief cross Conor's brow. "Does that make you feel better?"

A crooked smile crossed Conor's mouth. "We'll talk later."

E.G. nodded, not wanting to push Conor any more than he already had. "I'm holding you to that," he said. He backed out of the cubicle and returned to his own, where he turned on the computer and sipped on the coffee he had made for himself on his way back into the building.

He signed on to eglord2541 and had mail. Six e-mails greeted him and, recognizing each of the senders, he opened them in order, leaving the sixth piece, the one from Dirtdealer, until the end.

"Aren't you going to tell the police to question Travis?"

E.G. clicked reply and began pounding on the keys, as if he could convey his anger through the key strokes. "Aren't you going to tell me why I should tell the police to question Travis? I'm completely in favor of using anonymous sources - hell, it's my life - but I'm not about to take a tip and run with it. I need more information before I can go to the police. Tell me what you know."

He sent the mail, signed off, and returned as Stetson165. Only one piece of mail greeted him, and that was from Musicat62.

"I've been thinking of your offer. Sorry I haven't come to the train station, and I hope you haven't been feeling like you've been wasting your time. You really sound like a nice guy, and I'd like to meet you one of these nights. Maybe soon. Matt."

E.G. replied: "Thirty minutes of my time each night is nowhere near a waste. It would be nice, though, if it included you. I've gone to the train station each of the last few nights since we talked, and I've waited. Here's hoping I'll see you tonight. Barry."

As he sent the mail, he dialed Rachel at work. "It's me," he said when she answered.

"Is everything all right?" she asked with a certain urgency in her voice.

That was typical Rachel, E.G. thought. If it were up to her, everyone would feel the kiss of death. "Everything is fine," he replied. "At least on this end. How's the house? Any more incidents?"

"None," she said.

"I knew it was a scare tactic. But I want to talk to you about Thursday, when this week's paper comes out. I've got a few different stories I'm writing that could mean more threats."

"Thanks for the encouraging words. I can't wait."

"I'm sorry about this. I really am. Is Erin going to be at the babysitter's?"

"You're scaring me, E.G."

"I know, I know. Let's just take this one step at a time. How about if I pick up Erin early Thursday morning and bring her to Ray and Liz's for the day. I can ask my contacts at the Police Department to do some extra patrols on our - your street to make sure the house is safe."

"What are these stories about? You don't name people, do you?"

"You know me better than that. I don't name names until I'm one hundred percent certain I can. They're normal follow-ups to last week's story, and all that was was basic coverage of a murder."

"I'm putting the house up for sale," Rachel announced, and E.G. rolled his eyes on the other end of the line.

"No you're not. That's ridiculous, and you knew that before you even said it."

"I don't want to live like this, E.G. Since Friday, I haven't been able to walk out of the house without looking over my shoulder, checking the yard, searching for unfamiliar cars parked on the street."

"I do the same thing when I come to work, but I'm going to tell you something." His voice dropped to a whisper. "I have a strong feeling that the answer to this is so close that I can feel its breath on the back of my neck. I can't go into it here, but I think I'm closing in on something."

"Are you in danger?"

"I don't know. I would think there would be some amount of danger involved if I were to expose the person who beat two men and left them for dead."

"Did you think about what I said? About talking to Raymond?"

"Let's not go there," E.G. said. "Listen, I'll be in touch with you throughout the week to make sure everything's okay. Give Erin my love tonight."

As he lay the phone into the cradle, he said, "And keep some for you."

He looked at his watch. It was time to write. As he did with almost every story he wrote, E.G. created the lead to the article well before the time he sat in front of the computer to write it. The first article he chose to write was the one about the Reservation itself since that was freshest in his mind.

"Police barricades were removed Monday from the entrance to the South Mountain Reservation, but local officials won't go as far as to declare the park safe," he began.

"A segment of the park, a well-known area for cruising by men for gay sex, had been closed since last Wednesday after police found two men fatally beaten. It is believed their deaths are related to the activity that frequently consumes the park.

"While police had been investigating the double homicide, they closed the park, often using officers and vehicles as barricades. For five days, the usual hum of idling engines heard among the rest areas of the park was relegated to South Orange Avenue, where motorists who wanted to use the Reservation were asked to continue along the main thoroughfare."

E.G. continued with his observations in the park that day, describing for the reader how drivers circle the park several times before parking their car or leaving altogether. He detailed how men disappear into the woods, mostly alone but followed by another man, and how other male visitors will park their car and move from the driver's seat to the passenger's seat.

There were Jeeps, Hondas, Cadillacs and BMWs, and they came from New York, Maryland and Connecticut, as well as New Jersey. So the license plates on the vehicles stated, E.G. noticed, and hoped they didn't come that far for the menu. They pulled into the Reservation at an average of sixteen cars per thirty minutes, and E.G. wondered how he could calculate just how much sex was occurring and if there were enough trees to camouflage each of the encounters.

He wrote about the site of the murders, the outlines that identified where the bodies were found, and how, late into the day, after night had fallen over the thick woods, "even the blind had an equal chance of spotting the bodies."

Describing the night in the Reservation, he used Musicat62's recollection of being there when the car approached and dumped the bodies. In the second story he wrote that afternoon, he used the information Nathanya Berns had given him about Mickey, and wrote the article from the point of view of a mother who had just lost her son.

As he wrote, he paid special attention to objectivity and fairness, editing any of the adjectives and adverbs that might make the story more emotional than it already was.

When he wrapped them up and filed them for Mel, E.G. left his cubicle and dashed toward Conor's. He wanted to remind him of the beer they had earlier discussed for later that night.

238

But Conor's cubicle was empty. And the soft-leather briefcase he carried with him every day was gone too.

CHAPTER THIRTY

Raymond threw himself into the leather high-back chair and sucked in the cool air. There were few things he hated more than humidity, and Mother Nature was giving the East Coast an abundance of it that day. Expect more of the same for the remainder of the week, the man on the AM station told him on his way to the office that morning. That, as well as thunderstorms, which were as predictable on an August day in New Jersey as the melodrama of the metropolitan area meteorologists any day of the year.

Using a napkin he found in his desk drawer, he wiped the traces of sweat that remained on his arms, his still bare arms, that formed between the time it had taken him to walk from his car in the employee parking lot to the Hall of Records. Tossing the stained napkin into the trashcan, he reached into the drawer and removed another one. It was one of probably more than one hundred of them stuffed into the drawer, all bearing the logos of some fast food restaurants - Burger King, McDonald's and Wendy's, among the most popular, but not excluding Blimpie's. He loved his Blimpie's tuna fish with everything on it, including the mayonnaise, which you had to request. You can never have enough napkins, he had told himself each time he chose the drawer instead of the trashcan as a repository. His desk drawer was no different than one of the drawers of the cabinets in the employee kitchen. Open one of them and thousands of tiny plastic packages of duck sauce and soy sauce surely would begin to spill out onto the floor.

And each time that happened, someone always would suggest cleaning out the drawer, that they didn't need that much duck sauce and soy sauce. But no one ever did, and the number of packages grew. It was no different from his desk drawer. How much would it take to just stick your hand in, grab as many napkins as you could, turn slightly to the right, like the mechanical arm in the quarter machine at the A&P, and dump the napkins into the trashcan?

He wiped moisture from his forehead and temples, and almost returned the napkin to the desk drawer before realizing this one belonged in the trash. It was moisture, not sweat, since the coolness of the building took care of the perspiration that had dripped along the side of his face.

Angela tapped on the slightly open door and stuck her head inside. "Package for you, Mr. V.," she said, waving a FedEx envelope.

"I'll take it," Raymond said, about to get up and meet Angela halfway, but she was already inside and only steps away from his desk.

"Are you all right?" she asked. "You look like you're gonna have a stroke or somethin' with all that perspiring you're doin'." Angela obviously was not employed by the prosecutor's office the previous summer.

"I'm sure I'm going to be fine," Raymond said, taking the package and locating the sender. He had contacts everywhere, including at the Securities and Exchange Commission, where this package originated. He looked back up at Angela and couldn't help but be distracted by the word "Spoiled" emblazoned on the front of her tight, pullover shirt. "Thanks for your concern."

"Oh, you're welcome, Mr. V." Angela shimmied out the slightly open door rather than pull it open further and then close it behind her.

Raymond tugged at the tape at the top of the envelope and removed an inch-thick set of documents from inside. It was introduced by a cover letter, handwritten, from his source at the SEC. "This is what I was able to locate on Brian Winter and Mickey Berns. Hope it helps."

Below the man's signature, there was a postscript. "Read the part about Lubalin Cosmetics. Interesting stuff."

He scanned the documents, which included a listing of the financial holdings held by Brian Winter and those held by Mickey Berns. While Brian did not possess too many, Mickey had an abundance of them and clearly died a wealthy young man. He jotted a note to himself to investigate the beneficiaries in his will, if someone so young even had a will.

But it was, as his source promised, Lubalin Cosmetics that caught his attention. He didn't have to search for the section; it was book-marked with a yellow stickie. Based in New York, Lubalin manufactured and merchandised cosmetics throughout the United States and in four foreign countries. It was currently listed as a $16 million-a-year company, having grown from a $9 million-a-year company the year before.

Raymond slid his finger along the columns of each page, giving himself a history of the company. Michael Berns Sr. had co-founded the company some twelve years earlier with a partner and, until his death in 1992, was the major principal and stockholder, owning more than eighty percent of the shares of the fledgling corporation. That eighty percent was given to Mickey Berns as dictated in the senior Berns' will, and Mickey had become the primary stockholder owning eighty percent of the company.

But things changed in 1995, Raymond discovered, when Mickey reduced his ownership to sixty percent by selling twenty percent of his shares to Brian Winter. Most interesting, though, began in 1997, when Mickey held only twenty percent ownership of Lubalin Cosmetics, having sold forty percent to a Travis Boesgaard, making this newcomer the major stockholder but with less than half ownership.

As he read through the rest of the report, Raymond realized that he may as well have been reading Braille. New names appeared as stockholders, Travis' shares increased, Mickey's disappeared, and eventually, within the last year, Brian's disappeared as well.

He glanced over the history of the company one more time to try to make heads and tails out of it. He couldn't. So he picked up the phone and dialed. When he heard the voice on the other end, Raymond said, "I've got your report."

It was his contact at the SEC. "Four, three, two, one," he said in his normal British accent and laughed. "So I was four seconds off."

"Off?" Raymond asked.

"I was expecting your call."

"I'm lost. While I understand how things went down, I don't understand why they went down the way they did."

"At first, I didn't either," the man acknowledged. "That's what made the report interesting to me. At first. So I made a couple phone calls. It's amazing how much people will tell you - and how freely they'll say it - when you say you're from the SEC."

Raymond laughed more to humor his friend than at what he had said.

"Did you notice the Boesgaard tyke?"

"Yes, I did. Who is he?"

"Well, according to the report, he's a very wealthy man. And a very bad one at that. He single-handedly gained control of Lubalin Cosmetics within two, three years' time. And once he had control, he turned a company that was heading for bankruptcy into one of the strongest, most profitable cosmetics companies internationally."

Raymond was curious. "What makes him a bad man?"

"The manner in which he conducted his business. According to some insiders at Lubalin, Mr. Boesgaard and the young Mister Berns were, shall we say, extremely close. Once the young Mister Berns inherited Lubalin upon the elder Mister Berns' demise, he showed his generosity toward his then-companion, Mr. Winter, by selling him what most would consider a hefty share of the company for practically nothing.

"Then, as the grapevine reveals, Mr. Winter and the young Mister Berns faced an obstacle - Mr. Boesgaard. And he was very jealous of Mr. Winter. I was able to decipher that the young Mister Berns and Mr. Winter were equally as close for several years prior to Mr. Boesgaard's arrival. And that presented a problem for Mr. Boesgaard. From what I've learned, he was very manipulative. Did you notice all those other names that appeared out of the blue a few years ago?"

"Yes," Raymond said, scratching notes as his contact spoke.

"Dummies. That's all they were. Mr. Boesgaard created these dummies and sold most of his shares to them - in effect, selling them to himself."

"Why would he do that?" Raymond asked.

"At the time, he circulated a rumor that Lubalin was going out of business. He made it look as if these dummies purchased his shares for a song. And he was able to convince Mr. Winter to do the same. Poor naïve Mr. Winter took a tremendous loss, despite earning his shares for far less than what they were worth to begin with."

Raymond continued writing, flipping the page on the legal pad for the second time.

His contact continued talking. "Once Mr. Winter and the young Mister Berns had sold all their shares to these dummies, Mr. Boesgaard, quote unquote, bought them back and Lubalin became his. It grew by millions of dollars within the two years he had full control."

"Was that legal?" Raymond asked.

"Let's just say, there is no legal action pending in the courts by Mr. Winter. Nor is there any pending by the late young Mister Berns."

Raymond reviewed his notes. "I can understand the jealousy factor between Boesgaard and Winter. I guess. But why would Boesgaard set out to screw, figuratively, Berns?" he asked.

"That's something you'll have to ask him, if you choose to pursue this," his contact said.

"How do I find him?" Raymond asked.

"I'm only human, my friend. I haven't gotten that far." His contact chuckled on the other end of the phone. "But I would guess that if he's been involved - in whatever way - with both Mr. Berns and Mr. Winter, that he may not be too far away from them."

When Raymond hung up the telephone, he reached for the phone book and looked up Travis Boesgaard's name, checking the Suburban Essex edition first. The West Orange listing stood out as if he had been looking at it through a magnifying glass. "Some shit," Raymond said aloud, jotting the address and telephone number on the legal pad.

CHAPTER THIRTY-ONE

The train station was deserted. Sloan Street was a short street. It ran from South Orange Avenue to Third Street and in between was First Street and Second Street, two even shorter streets that housed restaurants and an apartment building and provided access to the two major parking lots for downtown shopping and commuting to and from the train station. The main firehouse stood in the center, its tall tower revealing the rich history of what was once a tiny hamlet.

E.G. entered Sloan Street from South Orange Avenue. On his right was the train station. To his left was the parking lot. As he drove by the front of the building, E.G. slowed his Tercel long enough to peer through the dark entrance for a figure, any figure that might be standing in the shadows. But there were none.

Disappointed because he actually believed that Matt, or Musicat62, would be there that night, he drove around the circular island that led to the parking lot. At night, since all of the stores in the downtown were closed, the lot was used mainly for restaurant parking, but being Monday night, the restaurants were closed and the lot contained only a few scattered cars.

E.G. moved into a stall near the entrance to the lot, across the street from the entrance to the train station and in front of a row of bushes that stood high enough to block the car from view. Dunkin' Donuts was only down the street, and as he did each of the last three nights, he parked himself inside at the corner booth with his large cup of coffee. From there, he had a clear view of the entire street, so he could see the entrance to the building as well as a secondary route upstairs to the tracks. Four cars had pulled into the parking stalls in front of the station, three having turned off their engines, the fourth leaving the car running with the lights on.

The faint sound of the whistle alerted him that a train would be pulling into the station momentarily. He looked at his watch. Ten minutes after nine. This one would be coming from New York, he knew, because if it were coming from the opposite direction, western New Jersey, he wouldn't have been able to hear the whistle from where he sat. Seconds later, he looked up toward the tracks and saw the light from the train as it pulled to a screeching stop. A few minutes later, the stairs of the secondary entrance, the one closest to the main avenue, were filled with people. At the bottom of the stairs, they scattered, some walking up the avenue, a few coming into the coffee shop, and others walking along the narrow street toward the front of the train station. From that entrance, several more passengers appeared, and each of them scattered in various directions. Within minutes, they had dispersed, including the passengers whose rides were waiting for them in the four cars.

But when E.G. thought everyone had disappeared, and it was safe to walk back to his car, a lone figure emerged from the darkness of the building. The figure stood within the shadows, and from where E.G. sat in the Dunkin' Donuts, he couldn't make out who it was. He guessed it was a male, unless it was one of the tallest women he had ever seen. The man paced, drifting from the shadows into the darkness and back again. E.G.'s heart raced.

He had thought about what he would do when the moment came that he would meet Matt. He'd get up from his seat, take his coffee, and casually walk along Sloan Street, pausing briefly outside the front entrance to the train station as if he were not there for a meeting, then making eye contact with the figure before confirming each other's presence. No different, he realized, than what they do in the Reservation.

And he had begun to do just that when the figure stepped from the shadows and stood under the street lamp. There was no mistaking it, even from the distance that separated the two men. The tall, lanky figure was Conor.

CHAPTER THIRTY-TWO

Once Conor crossed the street toward the parking lot, he disappeared from view. E.G. pressed his face against the glass of the window until he could no longer see him, then got up from the booth and left the coffee shop. Slowly, he made his way along Sloan Street until the parking lot was in front of him, but by that time, Conor had pulled out of the lot and was heading in the other direction toward Third Street.

E.G.'s mind raced faster than his heart. He pictured Conor in the Reservation on the night of the murders, hunched behind a tree in the darkness as the driver and passenger of a vehicle removed two bodies from the rear of their car. One was lifeless; the other was about to have what was left of his life beaten out of him. And Conor had watched that. He had seen who did it. It certainly would explain the change in Conor's behavior during the past few days, E.G. thought.

The anonymous phone call to the police. The online name. Where did he come up with the name Matt, or Musicat62, for that matter? He felt Conor's torment, his fear, as he expressed it in e-mails to him. Then he wondered if Conor had even the slightest idea that he was talking to his co-worker, revealing some truths to someone who sat only a cubicle away from him. E.G. wondered if they had talked online on opposite sides of the wall in the office of *The Sentinel*. Wouldn't that be a kick in the ass, he thought.

E.G. looked at his watch. It was twenty-five after nine. Why would Conor show up, but then leave before nine thirty? The answer stared him in the face as he approached his car, the turquoise colored Tercel with the license plate STET that Conor clearly would recognize as belonging to E.G. After all, they parked in the same lot. Conor would have been a fool not to have seen the car.

As E.G. pulled out onto Sloan Street and headed toward South Orange Avenue, his concern for his friend grew. And he knew he had no choice but to confront him.

He made the right turn from Sloan Street to South Orange Avenue and headed back to the office. It was twenty-seven minutes after nine, and had he given himself the three additional minutes that would have completed the half-hour, he would have seen a different figure step out of the shadows of the entrance to the train station and wait.

CHAPTER THIRTY-THREE

It wasn't until Raymond sat at the intersection of Livingston Avenue and Northfield Road for the traffic light to change that he decided to pay Travis Boesgaard a visit.

He was on his way to work and normally would continue straight on Livingston Avenue to the highway, but to visit Travis, he'd have to make a right onto Northfield. Since his car was in the center lane, and he was fifth in line with at least as many cars in the right lane, he waited for the light to change before flashing the emergency light on his dashboard and squeezing over in front of all-too-obliging motorists.

The address was written on a sheet of paper and was clipped to the rearview mirror. A map had told him how to get there.

He pulled up in front of the magnificent home and stepped out of the car, looking at the house once more as if seeing it from within the car could have been an illusion. The black Audi sat in the driveway, and he couldn't help but think of the black Audi he had seen at the funeral four days earlier. In fact, he recalled, the car belonged to someone who had attended the Mass with his cousin. He also recalled E.G. shaking his head when he saw Raymond that day, indicating he didn't want Raymond to blow his cover. He complied.

Raymond ascended the steps in the center of the property, and, by the time he reached the top and felt his breath leaving him, he reminded himself to count them on his way back down. If the number of steps is less than thirty, he told himself, it's time to get back to the gym.

Travis responded to the doorbell within seconds. He stood naked behind the storm door, blocked from view below the waist only by the pattern in the lower half of the door. Both men recognized one another instantly from the funeral.

"Mr. Boesgaard?" Raymond asked, wondering silently why E.G. was attached to each of the men he was questioning thus far.

"Someone who looks like you can call me Travis and not feel the least bit guilty about doing so," Travis said, presenting a smile that revealed a good amount of his money went into dental work.

Raymond didn't smile back. He reached into his front pants pocket and removed his badge, flipping it open as he addressed Travis. "My name is Raymond Vanderhoeven, and I'm an investigator with the Essex County Prosecutor's Office."

The dental work disappeared. "And here I thought you found me so irresistible that you went out of your way to look me up."

"Would you mind if I took a few minutes of your time?" Raymond didn't smile.

"What would this be regarding?" Suddenly, Travis' demeanor became as serious as Raymond's.

"I'm investigating the deaths of Mickey Berns and Steven Conroy, and I'd like to ask you a few questions."

"I don't know anything about it," Travis quickly responded.

Raymond hated when they said that. "I'd like to be the judge of that," he said. "As I said, I won't take up too much of your time."

"Judge me all you want, but keep the verdict to yourself," Travis said. He stood on his side of the storm door staring at Raymond through the screen that replaced the design in the upper half. Raymond stood on his side staring back. Neither was going away, so Travis unlocked the door and pushed it open slightly. "I was on my way out, so this can't take long."

Raymond stepped into the foyer and was greeted by Travis' buttocks as Travis turned and stepped into the living room. "Maybe it's just the detective in me, but if you really are on your way out, I'd say you forgot something."

Travis ignored the remark, and he didn't do anything to cover his body. "I saw you at Steven's funeral on Saturday, didn't I?"

Raymond glanced around the room before answering. "I was present."

"Did you know Steven?"

"I met him Wednesday, under some unfortunate circumstances. Would you mind putting some clothes on?" Raymond had looked around enough, and his eyes kept pulling in the direction of Travis' naked body.

"I would mind," Travis replied. "You're an unexpected visitor to my home, where I enjoy dressing this casually." He sat down on an easy chair and crossed his legs.

While he was still uncomfortable questioning a naked man, Raymond felt a little at ease as long as Travis' legs were crossed. He sat on the sofa across from him, separated by a long, narrow coffee table. Among the magazines that lay on top, Playgirl caught Raymond's eye. "I understand you were in business with Mr. Berns," Raymond began.

"The operative word being 'were'," Travis said, raising his index finger and pointing it toward Raymond. "He left Lubalin more than a year ago, sold everything he owned of it."

"Why was that? A company as lucrative as Lubalin, and he just dumps his share of it?"

"A poor business decision? Unfortunately, we can't ask Mr. Berns, can we?" Travis said, and Raymond saw that there were no good feelings between the two men — at least from Travis' perspective.

"Did Brian Winter make the same poor business decision?" Raymond asked.

Travis creased his brow. "You did some homework before coming to see me," he said. "I'm impressed."

"My job is not to impress those I question," Raymond said, although he felt the feather drift neatly into his cap. "I'm investigating a double murder, and I want answers. I hope you would be cooperative with me."

Travis uncrossed his legs and leaned slightly forward. "If you expect me to sit here and tell you some gushy stories about how wonderful a man Mickey Berns was, I'm afraid I'm going to disappoint you. Mickey and I were involved at one time, but that relationship ended. Simple as that."

"Why did it end?" Raymond not only wanted answers, he was also curious.

"I'm sorry to be so blunt, but as it turned out, I wasn't enough to satisfy him," Travis said.

"Is that when he turned to Brian Winter?"

"Did someone write a book about my life and leave it on some used book sale table for you to pick up?" Travis asked. "How do you know all this stuff about me?"

"Did I tell you I graduated at the top of my class?" Raymond asked. "Does that impress you more?"

"It's scaring me." Travis looked Raymond directly in the eyes when he said it. "Where is this investigation leading? Should I have a lawyer present?"

"If you're asking whether or not you're a suspect, I would tell you I don't rule anyone out until they've convinced me otherwise."

"Then I suggest we stop talking," Travis said. "I can be as cooperative as you'd like, but not when I have this kind of a weight tied to me."

"So convince me otherwise," Raymond said. "Why would anyone want to kill Mickey Berns and Steven Conroy?"

As Travis was about to speak, the phone on an end table rang. Instinctively, he reached over and picked it up. "Craig," he said with a smile when he realized who it was. "Yes, I got your message yesterday, and was a little disappointed that you didn't call last night like you said you would." After a pause, he continued. "I understand. I'm teasing."

Raymond got up from the sofa and stretched near the front window. Travis watched him, his eyes locking on the outline of Raymond's ass through his dress pants.

"But can I call you back?" he said into the phone. "I have some unexpected company this morning."

After another pause, he said, "No, nothing like that, although I would be very tempted," emphasizing the word "very" and continuing to look at Raymond. As if on cue, Raymond turned and was greeted by a smiling Travis. "It's actually a police officer, but he was just about ready to leave. Give me ten minutes and call me back."

Travis returned the phone to the cradle and stood. "As I said, Mr. Vandawindawin, or however you say it, I would like to cooperate, but I would prefer to do so in the presence of an attorney."

Raymond turned. "Very well. I will be arranging that soon."

Travis followed Raymond to the front door and remained behind the screen door as Raymond descended the steps.

Although he promised he would count the steps as he returned to his car, Raymond was distracted. He couldn't help but feel Travis' eyes on him, and when he stepped around the car to get to the driver's side, he looked up at the house. As he predicted, Travis was still at the front door and remained there until at least by the time Raymond pulled away from the curb.

Raymond could have played his trump card that afternoon and revealed his relationship to E.G., the man with whom Travis attended the Conroy funeral. He also could have told Travis that E.G. was a reporter, betting his life that E.G. hadn't identified himself as such.

But doing so, he knew, only would have created a distraction that he didn't need or want. The way Raymond felt, he wanted Travis all to himself, wanted him to be a cooperative participant in his investigation. He wanted to nail Brian Winter for the crimes, and he was sure Travis held the answers.

He reached into his shirt pocket, removed his cell phone and dialed. Sheila Timoni picked up on the first ring.

"I'd like to bring someone in for questioning this afternoon," Raymond said, lowering the fan on the air-conditioner so he could hear her response. "His name is Travis Boesgaard, and he is a principal in a cosmetics company that once included Brian Winter and the late Mickey Berns as owners. He also was involved personally with both Winter and Berns. Winter and Berns were duped into selling their shares, and Boesgaard wound up with almost everything. The whole deal is fishy, and I can't help but wonder if the takeover has something to do with Berns winding up dead."

"Can we find him?" Sheila asked.

"No problem there. I just left his house. He didn't want to talk anymore without an attorney present. And I strongly recommend that we question him downtown, not at his house," Raymond said without explaining his remark.

"Are you classifying him as a suspect?" Sheila asked.

Raymond turned the air-conditioning vents toward him and placed a hand in front of them to absorb the coolness that flowed from them. "You know, Sheila, I don't get the feeling that he's involved, but I also don't want to rule him out. I think he may be able to give us some information we need."

"You have my okay on that. Bring him in," Sheila said.

Raymond hung up and dialed the telephone number from the sheet of paper that clung to the rearview mirror. "Damn it," he said when he got a busy signal.

He turned his car onto Central Avenue, a route he normally avoided on his drive into Newark, and by the time he pulled into the employee parking lot in the rear of the Hall of Records complex, the temperature had reached eighty-four degrees. He rolled up his sleeves before turning off the air-conditioner and looked up into the clear blue sky, where not a cloud could be found.

"Another hot one," he said, stepping from the car. "Son of a bitch."

CHAPTER THIRTY-FOUR

E.G. waited the ten minutes Travis had requested before calling him back. "Is the cop still there?" E.G. asked when Travis answered the phone.

"No. He left, but I'm afraid that's not going to be the last I see of him," Travis said, concern etched in his voice.

"Where was he from?" E.G. asked.

"The prosecutor's office. Some kind of investigator looking into Mickey's and Steven's murders. I don't know if you remember, but we saw him at the funeral Saturday."

E.G. played dumb. He knew it was Raymond. "Which one was he?"

"The hot one I pointed to and said I didn't recognize. Until this morning, I thought he might have been another one of Steven's friends that I didn't know about, but I guess I was wrong. Funny, I almost feel relieved."

"How did he come upon you? Did he say? Are you part of his investigation?" E.G. asked.

"Through a business deal I had with Mickey and Brian Winter, the guy I almost belted outside the church."

E.G. didn't know about that, and slid an empty notebook closer to him to jot down the information. "What kind of business deal?" he asked.

"We were co-owners of a cosmetics company. Did you ever hear of Lubalin Cosmetics?"

E.G. couldn't say that he had. "I'm sorry. I don't know it."

"It originally belonged to Mickey's father. After he died, Mickey inherited it, invited Brian into partnership and the two practically ran the damn thing into the ground. Then I got involved and realized that the only way I could make it profitable, no less successful, was to do it myself. So that's what I did. I took the company right from under their feet."

"And where is this company today?" E.G. asked.

"Where have you been?" Travis asked. "It's only one of the top cosmetics companies in the world."

E.G. was silent for a moment, but Travis filled the void. "Well, at least I know you're not after me for my money," he said with a chuckle.

E.G. returned the chuckle. "That's certainly the truth." He continued to jot in his notebook. He doodled the word Dirtdealer a few times, trying to decide whether or not Dirtdealer could be Brian Winter. After all, Brian had reason to deflect suspicion from himself and probably would take pleasure throwing suspicion on someone such as Travis Boesgaard. But he wasn't prepared to buy the "small world" theory yet.

"So when am I going to see you?" Travis asked. "I want to wake up next to you again very soon."

"I'll call you tonight. Will you be home?"

"Awaiting your call," Travis said. He heard a tone on his end of the phone. "Can you hang on? Another call is coming in."

He clicked into the other call without waiting for E.G.'s consent. While he waited, E.G. checked his e-mails. Neither Dirtdealer nor Musicat62 sent him one. "Musicat62," E.G. said aloud, wondering how Conor could have come up with a name like that. He doesn't play any musical instruments, at least to the best of my knowledge, he thought, and the last thing E.G. would consider him to be is a cat. At least with Stetson, E.G. justified, someone could extract the word Stet and tie the copyediting word to a person in the newspaper business.

E.G. looked at his watch. Travis had been on the phone for four minutes, and he debated whether or not he should hang up and call back. But before he could make his decision, he heard Travis' voice on the other end of the phone.

"Still there?" he asked.

"Yes, I'm here. I was just about to issue an all-points bulletin for you," E.G. said, chuckling.

But Travis didn't laugh back.

"Is everything all right?" E.G. asked.

"Strange phone calls usually leave me speechless," he replied.

"Strange? In what way?"

"I don't know what's going on here, and quite frankly, it's beginning to worry me. First, a visit from the police and now this phone call."

"What's with the phone call?" E.G.'s curiosity was peaked.

"Nothing I'd want to go into," Travis said.

"If you're in some kind of trouble, I'd like to know that. I'd like to help." Somewhere between the time Travis returned to the phone and making his last statement, E.G. had removed his reporters' garb and donned the cloth of friendship.

"And you're a doll for feeling that way," Travis said, "but I'd like to see this through myself."

E.G. rolled his eyes. Call him odd, but he didn't like being called a doll by another man. He skipped over the remark, however. "Does it have anything to do with Brian Winter?"

The question apparently hit a nerve because Travis remained silent. After a moment, he asked, "Why would you ask that?"

"Probably because I felt the tension between the two of you on Saturday. It was obvious that you hadn't seen one another in quite some time. My guess is that if the police came to your house to discuss your business dealings with Brian and Mickey, then they already did the same with Brian. Hence, the phone call from Brian."

"I wish I could tell you one way or another," Travis said after another moment of silence. "But I can't."

"Well, then when can I see you again?"

"You're more than welcome to come by now," Travis said, a tease in his voice.

"Wish I could, but I'm at work, and I really need to get back to it."

"You never told me what you did," Travis said. "Or maybe you did, but I was too drunk to remember."

E.G. was ready for the question, and had been ready since Saturday, when he thought Travis might ask it. "I'm in publishing," he said and left it at that.

"Book? Magazine?" Travis asked. "Do you work in the city?"

"Too many questions," E.G. said, chuckling to try to reduce his importance in the world. "Let's get to know each other first before I start revealing my personal life."

"You're married, aren't you?" Travis asked. "Ah, what the hell. That doesn't mean a whole helluva lot to me. I've been with marrieds, straights, bi's, you name it."

"I was married," E.G. offered. "Divorced a little more than five months now."

"You came to your senses," Travis responded, laughing.

"Something like that," E.G. said. And the guilt for lying once again choked him. "It would be tough for me to get together tonight, too, because of work, so maybe tomorrow or Thursday."

"Call me," Travis said. "I'll make the time."

The moment he hung up the telephone, E.G. darted for Mel's office. He knocked on the half open door and peered in to find his editor staring at the computer monitor. He didn't wait for Mel to acknowledge him. "I've got another story I want to put together today. It would be something along the lines of a reporter's notebook, in which I detail everything that's happened during the last week. You know, the online conversations, the mysterious meetings, the funeral, the threatening notes to my wife, the e-mails sending me on the wrong path. What do you think?"

Mel completed the passage he had been reading and turned toward E.G. "Are you sure that's a wise move?" he asked. "Once we publish that piece, you're putting yourself out there as E.G. Lord, reporter, and giving up these personas you've created."

Without an invitation, which he didn't expect, E.G. stepped into Mel's office and sat in the chair on the other side of his desk. "I've thought about that. Probably because of the guilt I've been feeling having been lying to many people. People who, by the way, seem to be decent souls. I'm a journalist, and one of the first things we're taught as journalists is to be honest, accurate and fair. I haven't practiced all those virtues while trying to investigate this story. In less than a week's time, I've manipulated a close friend and colleague. I've been leading on a guy simply to get information from him. I'm trying to befriend another guy to find out what information he can give me. And I've obstructed justice because of some old rivalry that I have with my cousin. This isn't where I wanted to go with this story, and by doing a notebook-type piece, I can become E.G. Lord again. I can go about getting the story the right way. My name is Barry to one person, and while another person knows me as Craig, he referred to me as Caleb as he introduced me to a third person. I can't remember who the hell I am when I'm talking to these people."

The room became silent except for the sound of the clock. Mel studied his fingers as if they had somehow changed in appearance overnight and it was the first time he was discovering it. "I read the two stories you filed yesterday," he said. "Dynamite stuff, I have to admit, but I think you're right as far as personality and tone. Those stories could have been written by anyone assigned to them. But they don't have E.G. Lord's insignia, the kind of stories I would expect you to write having done what you've been doing for the past week." Mel grabbed four of his fingers on his left hand with his right hand and cracked his knuckles. "File the other two stories we discussed first, and give yourself the afternoon to work on the notebook piece."

E.G. cracked a smile and winked at Mel. "Thanks," he said, getting up from the chair. "Since last night, I've been writing it in my head. I know where I want to go with it, so I should have no problem putting it together."

On his way back to his cubicle, he paused in front of the opening to Conor's cubicle and glanced in. Conor was not in yet, and he felt almost relieved. But that feeling passed quickly, because he knew that if he was about to reveal himself to the public through his story, he was going to have to confront Conor before the piece was published.

By noon, he had completed his third story, coverage of Saturday's funeral for Steven Conroy. It was a brief piece in which he quoted from the eulogies delivered that morning as well as remarks made by the priest officiating the Mass. He pulled the quotes from the microcassette recorder he had kept in his pocket, but which he kept hidden from Travis while they were in the church. By noon, Conor still had not come into the office, and his absence became a distraction to E.G.

But he kept writing anyway.

The fourth story, an update into the investigation of the murders, was a breeze to put together. Nothing but the facts as they were presented to him, E.G. kept in mind as his fingers pranced along the keyboard. And as far as he knew when it came to the facts, there was not much more that he could write than the story that had appeared in the edition the week before. The one he reminded himself was a scoop on all the dailies and weeklies in the region. During his press conferences, Raymond had merely confirmed what E.G. had published a day before the press conferences began. Even the daily newspapers didn't have anything new to report.

And that excited him. In another two days, *The Sentinel* would publish another edition, and his newspaper would be thrown on the desks of reporters from other newspapers who would look up to find angry editors standing over them. Those editors would have traces of foam on the sides of their mouths as they demanded to know why their staffers, supposedly better trained and accessible to more resources, couldn't compete with someone from a weekly newspaper.

How misguided, E.G. thought, as he developed the lead and then used details from the press conferences to flesh out the story. He made sure to note that some of the facts had already been reported in *The Sentinel*, but he was sure Mel would delete those references, knowing it was E.G.'s way of grandstanding. And it wasn't grandstanding in front of his readers. No, it was his way of making the daily newspaper reporters jealous. Perhaps there would be another press conference. Perhaps another reporter would charge that E.G. got all his information because Raymond was his cousin. And perhaps the entire room would break into laughter once again, as they did a week earlier.

By one-thirty, he completed the story and let Mel know he was finished with his work for the week with the exception of his notebook piece. On his way to Mel's office, he checked Conor's cubicle, and it was still empty.

"Hey, Mel, what's with Conor today? I haven't seen him. This isn't like him for a Tuesday," E.G. said.

Without looking up from the computer monitor, Mel reached for the piece of paper that sat on a corner of his desk and waved it in front of E.G. "He's already been in today. He wanted to check out the courthouse this morning, so he came in at five and wrapped up his assignments for the week."

Kelly Kelly interrupted and stood next to E.G. in the doorway to Mel's office. "I'm done with the water story," she said, placing her hand on E.G.'s ass, unbeknownst to Mel.

E.G. looked over, and Kelly winked. But she didn't remove her hand.

"How many towns are affected?" Mel asked.

"Officials from the water company say twelve from Essex County," Kelly responded, referring to the notebook she held.

"What's with the water?" E.G. asked.

"Did you drink any today?" she asked, removing her hand from his ass as Mel turned toward them.

"I'm sure I did. I made coffee several times today," E.G. said.

"There was a flood in a substation this morning, and our water might be contaminated."

Here comes the drama, E.G. thought.

"You were supposed to boil the water for three minutes before drinking it." Kelly rapidly flipped the pages of the notebook until she found the part of the notes to which she wanted to refer. "Officials haven't had a chance to perform tests on any water yet. They expect to do so later this afternoon," she read and then looked up at E.G.

"You couldn't remember that bit of information without having to look in your notebook?" E.G. asked.

"E.G., this could be very serious. Some residents couldn't even shower this morning, never mind drink their water. It could be dangerous."

E.G. rested his arm on Kelly's shoulder. "If I feel the onset of diarrhea, you'll be the first person I'll tell, and you can have the exclusive." He started to back out of the office, but turned his attention to Mel as he did. "I'm getting to work on my last piece. I'll let you know when I'm done."

As he walked back to his cubicle, E.G. turned back and watched as Kelly discussed the story with Mel, referring to pages upon pages of notes. She certainly was thorough, E.G. thought, expecting that she and Mel would still be discussing the water story even after he completed his last article.

And what about Conor coming into work at five in the morning to complete his assignments? E.G. threw his legs on the corner of the desk as he sat back in his chair. He picked up a pencil and inserted the eraser end into his mouth, gnawing slightly about an inch below it while he thought. Conor had never, to the best of his knowledge, gotten up that early to finish his assignments. He reached for the keyboard and called up Conor's menu of stories for the week. Six stories, all indicating they've been completed and were ready for the copy desk. Beside his keyboard sat his Rolodex, and with a flip of his fingers, E.G. found the entry he was seeking. He picked up the phone, dialed and waited for the familiar voice to pick up on the other end.

"It's E.G. Lord from *The Sentinel*," he said. "How are you?" After a pause, he said, "Good, good, glad to hear that. Listen, I have a question. Has Conor been floating around the courthouse today?" He didn't have to be specific and give Conor's last name. Everyone at the courthouse knew him. "I see," he said after another pause. "No, no message. But thanks very much for your help."

He hung up the phone and instantly wondered where Conor had been all day. His source at the courthouse had said he had not been there at all that day. He replaced the menu of his stories on the computer with the Internet window and saw that he had mail. He realized he must have received the mail while he was talking to Mel, and confirmed that information when he opened the lone piece from Musicat62.

"You must have left before I got there last night," the e-mail stated, "because no one approached me in front of the train station. Were you there at all? I need to talk to someone because I think something is going to come down in the next couple of days."

"On a fucking Tuesday I have to get this?" E.G. said aloud to his monitor. He swung his legs back to the floor, picked up the phone again and dialed Conor's number. After five rings, his answering machine connected. "Conor, this is E.G. It's Tuesday at about two o'clock. Please give me a call as soon as you get this message. It's very important." He tossed the phone back into the cradle and headed to the kitchen for a cup of coffee. Passing Mel's office, he overheard Kelly relating more facts for the article she had written about the substation flood. But by this time, Mel must have subtly pushed her out of his office because she was standing outside his door, while he stood in the doorway.

On his way back, Kelly spotted him with the coffee and stopped him. "That could be contaminated, E.G. Our coffee machines don't boil water..."

"Fuck the water, Kelly," E.G. yelled, refusing to let her continue. Kelly brought her notebook to her chest as if she were using it as a shield. "I don't want to hear one more thing about the water today."

He laid the coffee cup on his desk once he got back to his cubicle and darted toward the front of the office, the eyes of all in the editorial department descending upon him. Margaret greeted him with a look of concern when he got there, having heard the outburst from her side of the partition.

"Was Conor here when you got in this morning?" he asked her.

Margaret replied over the sound of the telephone ringing. As she answered it, she said, "No. I haven't seen him all day." And without skipping a beat, said, "*Sentinel*. How may I help you?" She raised an index finger toward E.G. "May I tell him who's calling?" She placed the call on hold and turned to E.G. "I have a Travis Boesgaard on the line," she said, indicating that he was calling regarding "the case in the Reservation."

E.G. froze. "He asked for me specifically?"

"Uh huh. I can tell him you're on deadline and that you'll call him back," Margaret offered.

E.G. shook his head, not sure if Travis wanted the reporter for *The Sentinel* covering the murder investigation, or if he had discovered E.G.'s identity. "No," he said. "I'll take it."

"It's on line two," Margaret said, answering another incoming call.

Back in his cubicle, E.G. stared at the red light that flashed on his phone. He cleared his throat and picked up the line. He announced his name, but in a voice much deeper than his own voice.

"My name is Travis Boesgaard," he said, "and I got your name from the newspaper article last week about the two guys who were killed in the South Mountain Reservation."

"Okay," was all E.G. said in the same deep voice. British accent, he thought. I should have used a British accent. But he was satisfied that Travis hadn't made a connection between himself and Craig.

"I'm calling to give you a tip on something," he said. "I've been summoned to the prosecutor's office for questioning because they have me as a suspect. I didn't do this, and I want the newspaper to write a story about how my rights are being violated."

"When is this questioning going to take place?"

"As soon as my attorney gets to my house, we'll go together," Travis said.

"Have you told your attorney that you were going to call me?"

"No, I haven't. I'm so angry about this."

"What is your attorney's name?" E.G. asked, hoping he could continue to get away with the phony voice. He jotted the name of the attorney in his notebook and said, "I would prefer to call him and speak directly with him. I'm sure he is going to ask you not to comment on this."

"Call him. I'll tell him I spoke to you, and that he should expect your call," Travis replied. "I don't want anyone else in your office to know that I gave you this tip. This is for you."

Odd, E.G. thought, knowing he meant to withhold the information from Conor. If a story is published about Travis Boesgaard being a suspect in a murder case, Conor is going to find out anyway. "I won't say a word," E.G. said, indulging him as he wrote the phone number under the lawyer's name. "While I have you on the phone, if you didn't do it, do you have any idea who might have done it?"

"None whatsoever," Travis replied. "My lawyer's here. I have to run. Call him, and I mean that."

E.G. hung up the phone and dialed Raymond's number. Angela answered. "Is my cousin available?" he asked.

The prosecutor's office had the worst music a person could listen to while on hold. E.G. didn't think it could even be categorized. But normally when he called, he didn't have to wait long, because either

Raymond or Angela would return to the phone moments after he was placed on hold. And today, they didn't let him down.

"What's up, E.G.?" It was Raymond's non-committal voice.

"I understand you may have a suspect in the murders," E.G. said.

"I'm not prepared to comment on that."

"Can you confirm whether or not Travis Boesgaard is a suspect? I understand he's on his way to your office as we speak for questioning."

"Is he a friend of yours, E.G.? You were with him at the funeral, and now, less than an hour after I call him in for questioning, you're aware of our visit with him. I can't figure out yet if I'm on the right track with this guy, but knowing that you're involved - in whatever way you're involved - it makes me think I am."

"I'll take that as a compliment."

"This is no joking matter. We're dealing with a double homicide. The person who did this, E.G., isn't stable. You piss me off as a reporter, and you sometimes piss me off as my cousin, but the bottom line is that you're my cousin, and I don't want to see anything happen to you. Be straight with me, huh?"

The son of a bitch was right, E.G. said to himself. Putting aside all of the competition, the past and the rivalry, the two of them were cousins, and that's the only thing that wouldn't change.

"Ten to one, this Boesgaard guy doesn't know you're a reporter, does he?" Raymond continued.

"No, he doesn't."

"You fucking guys in the news business really don't give a shit about people, do you? You'll do whatever it takes to get a story, and not give two shits about the people you hurt along the way."

"That's not true, Ray. At least I'm not like that."

"Bullshit," Raymond responded. "You were in the Reservation yesterday with Brian Winter, and he didn't know you were a reporter. You were at a man's funeral Saturday with Boesgaard, and he didn't know you were a reporter. You're possibly putting your ex-wife's and daughter's life in jeopardy because you have information that others don't want revealed. And you're going to try to tell me that you do give a shit about the people you write about?"

"You're in law enforcement, Ray. You do the same thing."

"I can't do the same thing. There's already a word for that. Entrapment. And I'd blow every case in which I used those tactics."

He had him, E.G. knew. Raymond would face legal ramifications, while E.G. would face ethical issues. "Please don't reveal my identity to Travis," E.G. said. "Not yet anyway. I'm doing a story for Thursday's paper that's going to do that for me. And I'm prepared to accept whatever happens. But I do have to tell you that my gut says Travis didn't do it."

"How do you know that?"

"I was with him Friday night, the same night Rachel got the scare in the mail and at the house. He was not involved in that."

"How do you know Boesgaard?"

"I've been receiving e-mails, anonymously, from someone pushing me in Travis' direction. Whoever is doing it is setting me up. I realized that after spending time with Travis that night, and after a conversation I had with him this morning. I was the one who called while you were at his house. For what it's worth, he thinks you're good looking."

"Tell me about it."

E.G. laughed, and it prompted a laugh from Raymond. E.G. continued. "Travis called here a few minutes before I called you. He was calling for E.G. Lord, the reporter, not knowing he was talking to the guy he befriended this week. He wants me to do a story about how his rights are being violated. A guilty man is not going to bring the · press into this. That's common sense, Ray. Trust me on this one."

Raymond was silent. "I'll take what you say into consideration."

"And I beg you not to tell him who I am. Not yet. *I* need to do that."

"Fine," he said. "But I think you and I need to talk again. Maybe together, we can solve this mystery. Look how much we accomplished in the few minutes we've spent on the phone."

"Yeah, we did have a good chat, didn't we?"

"I'll call you later, after I talk with Boesgaard. I'll keep you posted."

"Thanks, Ray. I mean that."

CHAPTER THIRTY-FIVE

E.G. didn't know what to expect when he pulled the Tercel into the Reservation for the second time in two days. He slowly drove up the narrow path, discreetly eyeing the faces of the motorists coming in the opposite direction. Each of them was male, as he anticipated, and each looked back at him as their cars brushed by one another.

The sun was still in the sky, but hardly. It had passed overhead hours ago, and as it began to set behind the tall trees, he was forced to turn on his headlights. His watch read ten minutes after seven, and while he expected to have at least another ninety minutes of daylight, he knew he wasn't going to get that where he was heading. If they were lucky, he and Conor could talk for about thirty minutes before they would become silhouettes against a dark canvass.

The top of the path opened into the parking area, and E.G. searched for Conor's car. It was there, parked between a Cadillac and a Honda, neither of which contained occupants. Nor did Conor's car. E.G. looked toward his left, toward the rest area with the benches and the large rock that stood in the middle just at the top of the steps. Conor was sitting on the back of one of the benches, his legs resting on the seat, and he stared at the view of the New York skyline. His chin was cupped in his hands, his elbows firmly planted on his thighs.

E.G. slipped the Tercel into an empty stall four to the left of where Conor parked and got out. His looks and his build drew the attention of a passing motorist, who braked to a near crawl to get a glimpse of E.G. and make eye contact with him. E.G. ignored the driver and walked around the vehicle toward Conor. The driver waited a moment, curious to see where E.G. went, and when he saw the figure of another male on the bench, stepped on the accelerator and moved on.

E.G. approached Conor cautiously, not really sure what he was going to say to him. Conor was his best friend, and E.G. knew he was hurting.

He moved up the steps slowly, hoping Conor would see him out of the corner of his eye, but Conor only stared straight ahead. E.G. stopped one step before he would have reached the top of the landing.

"You can come all the way up," Conor said, still staring straight ahead.

E.G. chuckled. "Very little gets by you, doesn't it?" he asked, climbing the last step and moving toward the bench. E.G. maneuvered next to him and sat on the back of the bench, just as Conor was seated. "I wasn't sure if you saw me coming."

"Did you finish your stories for the week?" Conor asked.

"Wrapped them up about half-an-hour ago." Now E.G. gazed at the New York skyline, the one missing the Twin Towers of the World Trade Center.

"I'm glad. I'd hate to have you come out here without having your work finished," Conor said, referring to his invitation to meet in the Reservation. Conor still had not looked at E.G.

"Wouldn't have mattered. You're more important to me than any story I could write. It's why I've been asking you to talk to me the last couple days. I knew something was bothering you, and it bothered the shit out of me that I couldn't do anything to make you feel better."

Conor didn't respond.

"But now that I know what's been bothering you," E.G. continued, "I want to help you. I got your e-mail this morning."

Conor turned for the first time and looked at E.G. He left his chin cupped in his hands. "What e-mail?"

"I know you didn't realize this, but you've been writing to me, telling me all about the last week of your life. I'm Stetson," E.G. admitted, waiting for the look of surprise on his friend's face. But the look didn't appear. Instead, one of confusion caused Conor's brow to crease.

Conor shook his head. "I have no idea what you're talking about. I've never heard of Stetson."

Now it was E.G.'s turn to be confused. He looked deeply into Conor's face for a sign of denial, but couldn't find it. "You haven't been talking to me online for the last week? You didn't see everything that occurred up here last Tuesday night?"

"What would make you think that?"

"You were at the train station last night. I saw you."

"And that makes me a witness to a murder?" Conor asked.

"Then why were you there?"

Conor turned back to the skyline. The lights of New York City were glowing, and the view was breathtaking. He straightened his back. He responded, but his voice was muffled. E.G. asked him to repeat himself.

"I followed you there," he said more clearly. "But once I got there, I couldn't find you."

"Why would you do that?"

Conor obviously was uncomfortable, but at the same time, seemed to be seeking the courage to answer E.G, who waited and gave his friend the time he needed.

Finally, Conor said, "I thought you might have been meeting someone I know. I guess you were there for another reason."

"I was there because, for the last week, I have been communicating with someone, apparently not you, who said he saw what happened up here last Tuesday night. I've been at the train station each night since Friday because I told him I would be there during a certain time period, and if he wanted to meet me and talk about it, he could do that. I saw you there last night and assumed it was you who has been talking to me online." Something occurred to E.G. "I guess I missed the real person because he e-mailed me this morning telling me he was there and I wasn't. I left after I saw you leave."

Neither knew what to say next.

After a moment, Conor spoke. "What did he say? The guy who was e-mailing you. What did he say he saw?"

"He described the entire incident. He said he saw who did it. In fact, he said he knows the person, and he was afraid to go to the police."

"So why would you place me here? I can understand your assumption after seeing me at the train station, but why would you think I'd be up here? Did I ever give you reason to think that I would frequent this place? Especially at night when you can't see your hand in front of your face?"

"You have to admit you've been acting very strangely this week. Conor, I've never seen you like this, and I've known you for about seven years. When my cousin came to the office yesterday, your reaction was so bizarre that I thought for a moment you committed the murders." E.G. chuckled, but below the surface of the laugh, he was serious. "And there's something else." E.G. balked, and Conor looked back at him.

"What?"

"Can you tell me how you know Travis Boesgaard?"

Although Conor didn't respond immediately, E.G. knew he was cornering him. Conor was nervous, and, with his right hand, he grabbed the pinky finger of his left hand and began massaging it. "Who?" he asked.

"Is that who you thought I was meeting last night at the train station?"

"No," Conor quickly answered.

"Then who?"

Conor bent back his pinky and a knuckle cracked.

"You did," E.G. pushed. "You thought I was meeting Travis. I know about the two of you, Conor."

Conor faced E.G., shifting his body on the bench. "What do you know? How do you know Travis?"

"You have nothing to be upset about." E.G. intentionally spoke in a soothing voice. "Nothing is going to change the way I feel about you. You're my best friend, and I love you, guy."

Conor stepped off the bench, put his hands in his pockets and inched toward the wall of the rest area. Once there, he looked out at the skyline, but said nothing. E.G. stayed on the bench and waited.

If it weren't for Conor's white T-shirt, he would have faded into the darkness.

Finally, Conor turned. "Since we're being honest here, how do you know Brian Winter?" he asked.

"I really don't know him that well at all," E.G. replied. "I met him this week. At a funeral."

"For someone you've known less than one week, you seemed to be very intimate with him yesterday. I saw you over there."

For all E.G. knew, Conor could have pointed to the area where he and Brian had met the day before or he could have simply indicated with a nod. It was too dark to tell. He got up from the bench and joined Conor near the wall. "You were here?" he asked. "You're making it a habit of following me."

"I knew you were on to something. I wanted to learn what it was."

"Because you have some personal interest in this. I know that."

"The last thing I expected to see was you holding Brian," Conor said.

"He was upset. He was standing at the spot where..." E.G. stopped. "Wait a minute. You know Brian Winter. That's why you followed me last night, wasn't it? You thought I was meeting Brian Winter. And that's because you saw the two of us up here yesterday afternoon." E.G. waited for Conor to confirm or deny what he had said, but Conor remained quiet. "Are you and Brian...?" He let his voice trail off.

Conor turned back toward the skyline.

"You have nothing to be jealous of," E.G. said. "I met Brian on Saturday at the funeral for Steven Conroy. I came back up here yesterday for a story I was writing for this week's newspaper, and Brian was here. We talked about Mickey and Steven, he got upset, and he hugged me. That was it."

"Why would he hug a reporter?" Conor said. "What else has he told you?"

"He doesn't know I'm a reporter. He thinks I'm a friend of Travis. I was with Travis at the funeral Saturday, and he was the one who introduced me to Brian. Travis doesn't even know I'm a reporter.

And besides," he continued as if it were an afterthought, "And here's a revelation. I'm not gay."

Conor looked back. "Who the hell do you think you are? Clark Kent? One day I'm a reporter, the next day I'm Superqueer," he said, beating his fists against his chest.

"I'm sorry. I had no idea about you and Brian. In fact, I had no idea about this side of your life until this week after I met Travis."

Conor looked back at E.G. "What did he say about me?"

"He didn't say anything - although he did refer to a former lover who, I guess, could have been you. But not by name. I saw the two of you in a photograph that he keeps on the dresser in his bedroom."

"You were in his bedroom?" Conor asked incredulously.

"Friday night," E.G. replied.

Now it was Conor's turn to look at E.G.

"Nothing happened," he said, anticipating what Conor was thinking. "Well, almost nothing." He knew he had to explain so he continued. "I met Travis Friday night at a bar and by the time we were ready to leave - separately - he had had too much to drink, so I offered to drive him home. I wanted to know more about him because I thought he was involved in these murders, so I pretended to be interested in him. When we got back to his house, he got all touchy-feely with me, and I guess I let him do it. For a story. But before it got heavy, I convinced him he was with me for all the wrong reasons. He was seeing Steven Conroy before Steven died, and I guess I persuaded him that he was using me to be with Steven.

"I lay next to him until he fell asleep — actually he passed out — and then I left. I got a call, and wound up at Rachel's. I got back to his house the next morning before he woke up, so he thinks I stayed the night."

"You're no better than those TV journalists, are you?" Conor asked.

E.G. got defensive. "What was I supposed to do? I get tips that Travis is somehow involved in the deaths of Mickey and Steven. Was I supposed to go up to him and ask, 'Hey, did you kill two people this week?' Of course I couldn't do that."

"You have tons of sources in police departments all throughout this county," Conor said. "You could have called any number of them. They could have handled it from there. That was the intent."

E.G. froze. "What intent?"

Out of the darkness, the figure of a man approached the rest area and casually stood against the wall, not too far from E.G. and Conor. He watched the two of them. Conor started to walk away, and E.G. followed. "Conor, what intent?" E.G. had lowered his voice. He grabbed Conor by the arm to stop him and turned him around.

Conor looked back toward the man before answering, feeling comfortable that he was far enough away that he couldn't hear. "I'm the one who sent you those tips," he said in a whisper. "I'm Dirtdealer."

E.G. released Conor's arm, not so much voluntarily as much as he lost the energy to hold on any longer. "What?" he asked, although he knew it to be true; otherwise, how would he know the name. "Why?"

Conor again looked back to see if the man was still far enough away. In the darkness, he couldn't see him at all. "The minute I knew you'd be working on this story, the minute I knew Mel gave this to you as your only assignment, I was afraid you'd find out the truth. I needed time, so I tried to distract you. And that's why I directed you toward Travis. I figured I could also get some payback for how he treated me."

"The truth. Time. What truth? Time for what? If I had followed your intended course, an innocent man could be in police custody right now." He waited for a response from Conor, but got none. "Travis is innocent, isn't he?"

After a moment, Conor nodded. "Yes," he said, his voice still as low as a whisper.

"Then who are you protecting, Conor? Yourself?" E.G. asked.

Conor looked back at E.G. and shook his head slowly. "No. Not me."

"Brian?" E.G. asked, remembering the fear that enveloped him the day before in Brian's presence.

As if someone had lifted a weight from his shoulders, Conor dropped his head and began to sob. E.G. put his arms around Conor's waist and drew him closer to his own body. "I didn't realize how much you were in the middle of this." Conor laid his right hand on E.G.'s left bicep and squeezed, as if the touch of his friend's body would make him feel more secure. "When did you learn Brian did all this?"

"I realized it Thursday night," Conor replied.

"How long have you two been seeing each other?" E.G. asked.

"A few months. We got together after Travis dumped me, and he screwed Brian out of his share of a company they owned together. I guess you could say we had something in common at that point. It wasn't too long after that that I found out Travis had hooked up with Steven Conroy. Brian kept talking about him, non-stop, saying things like, 'He wants to take something away from me. I'll show him what it's like to lose something important.' He wouldn't let go of it."

"So Brian was out to get Steven?" E.G. asked. "I thought Mickey was the target. He seemed the more likely of the two to be a target. Did Brian confess to you?"

"I had no idea that these murders took place until you called me Wednesday night after you went to press with the story," Conor said. "I got your message about wanting to meet for a few beers and your exclusive, but I couldn't meet you. I had gotten a call that day from Brian, and he sounded frantic. I was at the courthouse all afternoon, so by the time I got both messages, his sounded more important. I was home when you called back. I was screening calls waiting for Brian to get back to me. But he never did. I tried him at work on Thursday, and he wasn't there. I tried several times on Thursday at home, but he either wasn't home, or wasn't taking calls. So Thursday night, I went to his house. I sat in my car on Sagamore Road until I saw his father leave. His father has no clue about us. It's not as if I can go up to the front door and ring the bell, and ask if my lover is home."

By this time, E.G. had released his arms from around Conor's waist, and they both stood against the wall of the rest area.

"Brian answered the door, and from the moment he saw me, he started to cry," Conor said.

Conor pushed his way into the house and held Brian. "What's going on?" he asked.

Brian hugged him back. "You can't stay. My father is coming right back."

"You left me a message yesterday and haven't gotten back to me. Why are you so upset?"

"Not now. Please leave."

Conor let go and held Brian by the arms. "If I leave, you're coming with me. Come back to my place. Tell me what's going on."

"I can't. I don't have the time. My father will be back, and I don't want him to see you here."

"Dammit, Brian, why would you leave me a message telling me you have to talk to me, and then when I try to do just that, you push me away?"

"You read the damn story in your paper today," Brian said. "Call off that mother fucker who's writing it before I have to do it."

Conor froze. This was a side to Brian that he had only seen when Brian talked about Travis Boesgaard and Steven Conroy. "What does that story have to do with you?" he asked. "Where were you Tuesday night?"

"We can't see each other anymore," Brian said flatly. "You have to get out of here."

"You don't mean that, and we both know it. Don't do this to me. You'd be no better than Travis."

"If he didn't start all this, we wouldn't be in this mess."

"What did you do? Please tell me, Brian."

"The Reservation. Mickey. Steven. I…" His voice trailed off when he heard the sound of the car coming up the driveway. "He's home. Get out of here," Brian said, ushering Conor to the slightly opened door.

Conor had no choice but to leave. Not only did he want to protect Brian from his father, he wanted to protect his own anonymity in the relationship. He dashed down the front steps and crossed the street, glancing back to be sure Ian Winter hadn't come around to the front of the house. When he got to the other side, he walked casually to his car, watching the front window for any sign of Brian. There wasn't one, and he didn't know then that that would be the last time he would see Brian until he spotted him in E.G.'s arms in the Reservation.

Conor pushed himself off the wall and walked to the center of the rest area, taking in the view of New York City at night. E.G. followed him. "Old man Winter came blowing in just when Brian was about to tell me everything," Conor said. "Just as you've been concerned about me all week, I've been feeling the same way about Brian. Except he won't even see me. So when I saw you yesterday with him, and then with the talk about threesomes, I went nuts. I didn't know what to think."

E.G. was silent.

"What did Brian say to you?" Conor asked.

"He obviously hates Travis. And he did say something along the lines of Travis losing something valuable. I didn't know what that meant then. But now it makes sense."

"I didn't want to go to the cops," Conor said. "I've been wanting to talk to Brian to convince him to turn himself in, but I can't even get to see him. On my way home that night, I thought of things I could do to honor his request to call you off the story, as he said. I had a sick feeling earlier in the day about all this. Too many coincidences. Brian's urgent message. The announcement that Mickey and Steven were the two who were killed. Where they were killed and how close it is to Brian's house. That's when I came up with the bogus e-mail account and began sending you the e-mails. It was supposed to be a distraction. Get you to go to the police and tell them to investigate Travis. I'd kill two birds with one stone: distract you and get even with Travis for what he did to me and to Brian."

"Setting up someone for murders they didn't commit is criminal in itself," E.G. said. "We need to convince Brian to turn himself in. If you want me to do that, I will. He's apparently more willing to talk to me than he is you. He gave me a card yesterday when I saw him. I can call him."

"As E.G. Lord, or some fictitious friend?" Conor asked.

"As E.G. Lord. If he reads the paper on Thursday, he's going to find out the truth about me anyway. He may as well learn it beforehand."

Conor nodded.

"C'mon. Let's get out of here," E.G. said. "No offense, but even you have to be turned off by this endless parade coming through here in the dark."

CHAPTER THIRTY-SIX

E.G. slipped into his cubicle unnoticed. Reporters had been filing back into the office after covering Tuesday night town meetings, and were filing their stories when he returned from the Reservation. Most of the editors, including Mel, had left for the night, only to return by seven the next morning to read the voluminous accounts of local government action the night before.

The sound of fingers against keyboards always raised E.G.'s adrenaline. Each tap of the finger meant another letter, word, sentence, paragraph. Before long, a story would be told, some dry, some exciting, but a story nevertheless. The bottom line was that it reflected a writer at work. Within twenty-four hours, those stories would be dipped in ink, run on the press and be delivered to the more than one hundred thousand people living in Essex County who waited weekly to be told those stories.

For the less patient, the newspapers would be ready on most newsstands in convenience stores on Wednesday night. But for most readers, they'd wait until Thursday, when *The Sentinel* flag would greet them from their mailboxes.

E.G. had calls to make, and the first was to Raymond, who had called earlier and left a message on his voice mail.

"How'd it go with Travis?" he asked when Raymond came to the phone.

"I let him go," Raymond responded. "We had nothing to hold him on."

"I told you that. I had a gut feeling Travis didn't do it. And now I know for sure he didn't do it."

"How can you be sure?"

"Remember I told you about the tips I was getting? That someone was pushing me in Travis' direction?"

"Yes."

"Well, whoever it was told me tonight that he was trying to distract me. It wasn't Travis after all. Thanks for seeing that, Ray. You didn't tell him who I am, did you?"

"No. I'll leave you to your games. Did this tipster tell you anything else? Like his name? Or why he was implicating Travis Boesgaard?"

"No, he didn't," E.G. lied. "He just left another short message."

"I want his account information. I want to know who this person is," Raymond insisted.

But E.G. held him off. "Give me until tomorrow. I need to follow up on something, and then I can tell you the whole story."

Raymond agreed, but he promised he would use legal means to get the information he wanted from E.G. if his cousin didn't provide it by the end of the afternoon.

E.G. ended the conversation and dialed Travis' number seconds after hanging up with his cousin. Travis picked up on the second ring.

"How did things go at the prosecutor's office?" he asked.

"I'm so happy I want to celebrate," Travis said. "How would you like to help me?"

E.G. ignored the invitation. "What did they say? Obviously, they didn't arrest you."

"Of course they didn't. I didn't kill anyone, and they believed me." Travis re-extended the invitation. "Why don't you come up to the house? It's a little lonely here, and tonight's not the night to be alone."

E.G. balked. He remembered his promise to reveal his true identity, but he didn't want to do it yet. He wanted to be with Brian Winter first, to get the truth from him and then confess to Travis.

But Travis was right. It wasn't a night to be alone. He had just been questioned about his involvement in a double murder and was given a clean bill of health. "I'll be up in a couple minutes," he said.

It was more like fifteen minutes by the time E.G. arrived at Travis' house. The way Travis opened the door and greeted him reminded E.G. of Faye Dunaway as Joan Crawford in "Mommie Dearest," when she opened her front door and greeted reporters on the front lawn the night she won an Academy Award. Travis reached out and embraced E.G., who reluctantly put his arms around Travis' waist and pushed him into the foyer. Travis laid a kiss on E.G.'s mouth and said, "I feel as if I am reborn."

Travis stepped into the living room, and while his back was to E.G., E.G. wiped his lips and followed him. He was greeted by a glass of champagne, which already had been poured and was waiting on the glass coffee table. "To my new, mysterious friend," he began, "who came into my life when I needed him desperately, and who, I hope, will remain in my life for a long, long time." He raised his glass in the air, and E.G. did the same before they both sipped from their glasses.

"To freedom," E.G. said. "Here's hoping you never have to have yours in jeopardy again. And to truth. Here's hoping that when the cloud of mystery is removed from our relationship, things will be easier."

"I'll drink to that!" Travis said with enthusiasm. "Everyone on my Caller ID has a name but you. You're known as Mr. Private Number."

They both drank from their glasses until they were empty. "Just give me a couple more days," E.G. said. "It takes time for me to open up to people, and although I feel very comfortable with you, I just need a little more time."

Travis approached E.G. and put his arms around him again. "Take all the time you need. Just don't disappear from my life. You're kind, understanding, and honest, and it's so refreshing to find that in a person today."

E.G. rubbed Travis' back, more out of guilt than anything else. "And honesty is what you'll get." He pulled away from Travis. "How about another glass of that champagne?"

As Travis poured, E.G. eyed the Caller ID box next to the phone on the end table. As he handed the glass to E.G., Travis said, "Do you want to take this upstairs?"

E.G. smiled, but shook his head. Step one of the truth was about to spill from his lips. "I have to be up front with you. I've never been with a guy."

"Don't say another word," Travis said. "I understand. You're either married or divorced, and this is something you've wanted to try for a very long time."

"Divorced," E.G. said.

"I'm enjoying your company," Travis said. "We'll move slowly."

"Thanks for understanding."

"You know how many times I've heard that line from married or divorced guys? To you, this is something new. To me, it's not. Don't worry about it."

"Can you get me a glass of water?" E.G. asked, moving to the chair next to the telephone.

Travis left the room, and once E.G. heard the water running, he checked the Caller ID box. No new calls were posted, but there were twelve old numbers logged. He pressed the Review button, noticing the first call went back about five days ago. He pressed Review several times until he came to calls placed the day before, hoping to locate the telephone number of the call which Travis described as "strange." He remembered being on the phone with him early in the day, but there were no calls from that time period. Then, he remembered, Travis had used Call Waiting, so the call did not appear on the Caller ID. He continued to press Review, and two calls later was a number E.G. recognized. It was Brian Winter's cell phone number, even though the name attached to it stated "New Jersey." He pressed Review until all the saved telephone numbers had been displayed and the box announced "End of List."

Within seconds, Travis returned with a glass of water and handed it to E.G. He then sat on the arm of the chair in which E.G. sat and sipped from his glass of champagne.

"Yesterday when we were on the phone, you received a call. You put me on hold, and when you came back, you told me the call was strange. What was that all about?"

Sliding his tongue along the lip of the champagne glass, Travis stared at the floor for a moment before answering. "I received a business proposition. And we set up a meeting for tomorrow. That's all."

"What's so strange about that?" E.G. asked. "As I recall, it was enough to distract you from hearing what I was saying on the telephone."

"It was the person making the business proposition. And it was strange in the sense that I'm particularly curious to hear his offer. Why are you so interested?"

"With everything that's gone on during the last week - Steven, the police questioning you - I just want to make sure you're thinking about yourself."

"That's very sweet of you," Travis said, laying a hand on the side of E.G.'s face.

It wasn't so much that Travis' hand rested on his face that bothered E.G. as much as it was that he pictured Conor doing the same. And so caught up by the image was he that he reached out and laid his own hand over Travis'. His mind raced. He thought of Conor and of some of the times he spent with his friend. The back rubs from Conor, the hand over his body the night they fell asleep in the same bed, the expressions of love written in birthday cards to E.G. They were images that touched down in his head like a tornado and erased every other thought in his mind. Those were signs from Conor, he told himself, not gestures of friendship.

"Earth to Craig," Travis said, finally interrupting E.G. He had to say it three times before E.G. returned to the room. "Where the hell were you?" Travis asked.

E.G. smiled dumbly, knowing he wasn't about to reveal where his head trip took him. He wiped the bottom of the glass of water with his hand before placing it on the end table. He stood, almost knocking Travis off the arm of the chair. "I have to go. I just realized I was supposed to be somewhere."

Travis stood as well. "Oh, don't leave," he said, almost pleading. "We don't spend enough time together. I don't think I'll ever get to know the real you."

Walking toward the front door, E.G. stopped and turned. "Oh, yes you will. Eventually, you'll know everything there is to know about me. I assure you."

Travis put down his champagne glass and embraced E.G., who returned the gesture. "Call me tomorrow," he said.

E.G. agreed and left, leaving Travis watching from the door as he made his way down the long flight of steps to his car.

Within twenty minutes, E.G. stood in the hallway of Conor's apartment building, tapping the buzzer three times before pausing, then tapping it four more times. It was a code he used to save Conor from getting on the intercom and asking who it was. Once he heard the code, Conor would press the door-lock release and allow E.G. to enter, like he did that night.

He climbed the stairs two, sometimes three, at a time until he reached the third floor, and by the time he arrived at Conor's apartment, the door had opened and his friend stepped into the hallway. He seemed to be nervous, almost afraid of the reason E.G. had come to his apartment.

"I didn't know," E.G. said. "Until tonight, I didn't know how you felt about me."

Conor didn't move, nor did he change the expression on his face.

"You're in love with me, aren't you?"

Still, Conor did not move, but his eyes welled.

E.G. slowly approached him. "Were you ever going to say something to me?"

"And risk losing the best friendship I've ever had?" Conor shook his head. "I wasn't prepared to do that." He lowered his head rather than wipe the tear that had fallen from his eye.

But E.G. wiped it for him. And then he led him inside the apartment and closed the door behind them.

CHAPTER THIRTY-SEVEN

E.G. opened the lap top computer in the middle of the coffee table in his living room, and, while it booted, sipped from a cup of coffee. It was nearly 8:30 a.m., and he had returned home from Conor's apartment only a few minutes earlier. But he couldn't spend too much time online that morning because he had a full day ahead of him.

He removed a sheet of paper from his shirt pocket and reviewed his calendar for the day. He wanted to check the layout of that week's *Sentinel* before it went to press. Mel had become known for slapping together the front page of the newspaper, and with the four stories he had written for that week's edition, E.G. wanted to be sure that they were presented in such a way that readers would be interested in reading them. He also wanted to reach out to Brian Winter, and he wanted to do that early enough so that he could tail Travis for the day.

E.G. signed on as Stetson165 and had mail. There was one piece, and it was from Matt.

"Apparently, you don't take me seriously," Matt wrote. "I sat in front of the train station from 8:45 to 10 o'clock tonight, and nobody approached me."

"Damn," E.G. said to the computer. "Oh, Matt. I completely forgot." He continued to read.

"I have proof that something's going down tomorrow," Matt wrote. "I'll take matters into my own hands. It's about the only option I have right now. Ciao, buddy. It was nice knowing you."

E.G. clicked Reply. Tomorrow meant today, he thought, and short of seeing Matt online, his only option was to send him an e-mail and hope for a reply before anything happened. Matt must know Brian, but how? E.G. wondered.

"I'm sorry I didn't meet you last night," he wrote, "but please don't think it's because I don't care. I'm praying that you receive this e-mail before you take matters into your own hands, whatever that means. That's dangerous, Matt!! And I don't want to see you doing anything that could put your life in danger. Give me one more chance, and I'll help you. If you get this e-mail this morning, meet me at the train station at one o'clock. I'll be there. If you get this after one o'clock, meet me at the train station at three o'clock. In any event, here's my cell phone number. Call me as soon as you get this e-mail."

He typed his cell phone number into the e-mail and sent the mail.

E.G. shut down the computer and headed for the shower, but was stopped by the ringing of the telephone. He picked up the cordless phone in the living room.

"Where the hell have you been all night?" It was Rachel's voice and she was hysterical.

"What's wrong?" E.G. replied.

"You didn't get my messages?" she asked.

He carried the phone into the bedroom with him and saw the red flashing light on his answering machine. "I just got in a few minutes ago. I haven't checked messages. What's wrong?" he asked again with more emphasis.

"I'm standing here in front of three broken windows in my house," Rachel said. "Erin is scared witless, and you're nowhere to be found. All I get is that goddamn answering machine, and your cell phone tells me you're not available!" Rachel's anger turned to fright, and she began to sob. "I thought you were injured or, God forbid, dead."

"Where's Erin now? Did you call the police?" E.G. asked.

"She's right beside me. She won't leave my side."

"Did you call the police?" E.G. asked again.

"Yes. I called them immediately after it happened. Which was last night," she said, stressing "last night" as if it would spit guilt.

It worked. "I was out with Conor last night, and wound up staying at his place," E.G. quickly said, forgetting for a moment that he and Rachel were divorced and he could stay anywhere he wanted to stay. "What time did this happen?"

"About eleven o'clock. I had the TV on in the back and all of a sudden, I heard a crash. I ran to the front window and heard another crash, and by the time I got to the living room, there was a third crash. Bricks and rocks were in the living room. I ran upstairs to Erin's room to make sure she was all right, and looked out the window up there, but there was nobody outside. I heard a car screeching away."

"I don't want Erin going to the babysitter today."

"She's not," Rachel interjected. "She's staying right here with me all day. I'm not going anywhere."

"Do me a favor, Rachel. Take Erin to Ray and Liz's today and stay there with her. Not that I expect anything to happen at the house today, but something's going on today, and I just don't want you guys near the house."

"I'm supposed to leave the house with three broken windows?" she asked. "Why don't I just put all my valuables on the front porch with a sign that says, 'Free merchandise.' I can't leave until I can get someone here to replace these windows."

"I'll call Conor…"

"Conor fixes windows?" Rachel asked, interrupting E.G.

"No, I'll get him to meet you at the house, and he can stay until someone gets there. Did you call anyone to fix the windows?"

"I called while the police were here and left a message. They called this morning, and said they'd have someone out shortly. What's going on today?" Rachel asked. "You said something was going on. Are you in danger, E.G.?"

"I'll be fine. Let me call Conor, tell him to meet me at your house, and I'll be there as soon as I can." He paused before continuing. "Tell Erin I love her."

He hung up the phone and dialed Conor's number. When he got the answering machine, he cursed. "Conor, this is E.G. I really need you, buddy. If you're there, please answer." He waited, but no one picked up the phone. He continued. "When you get this message, call me at Rachel's house. You have the number. It's important that you either call me there or meet me there this morning. I'm leaving now."

He hung up the phone, and without checking the messages on his answering machine, left the house.

***   ***   ***

Conor closed the door to his apartment and set the dead bolt. He wasn't ten steps toward the stairs when he heard the phone ring. He stopped, debated whether or not to go back and answer it, and decided it could wait. He had somewhere to go, something to do, and there would be no interruptions.

***   ***   ***

A white van displaying the name of a local glass company sat in Rachel's driveway when E.G. pulled in front of the house. He got out and crossed the lawn, pausing only to let a heavyset man in overalls pass him on his way, he assumed, back to the truck. At the front door, he peered into the house and heard Rachel demanding Erin to finish getting dressed.

"I don't care which shoes you wear. Just put something on your feet."

"Will daddy be going with us?" Erin asked.

"Daddy thinks he's Clark Kent and wants to save the world. We'll be going by ourselves."

"Is he going on another mission?"

"I don't know what he's doing."

"Is it for the newspaper?"

Rachel had had enough. "Stop with the questions!" she demanded. "Jeez, talking to you is like talking to your father."

E.G. couldn't help but smile. Reputation, he thought. If he had anything, it was a reputation. He slipped through the open front door and crossed the living room before either of the two women in his life saw him. Erin saw him first.

"Daddy!" she called and broke away from her mother. She ran into her father's arms and he held her, smelling her hair, kissing her cheek.

"How's my girl?" he asked.

"They broke the windows," Erin said, in the event, E.G. guessed, that he didn't notice it on his way into the house.

"And I bet they made a mess on mommy's rug," E.G. said. "We'll have to get them for this."

"Do you know who did it?" Erin's eyes lit up, as if she expected E.G. to have the answer.

"Not yet, but we'll find them. I promise you that."

"We're going to Raymond's house today. Mommy's not going to work."

"I know. I want you guys to spend the day there."

"Can you come with us?"

"I'm afraid I can't, baby. I have a whole bunch of things to do today, and it's going to take probably all day. But I'll come by later and make sure you're okay."

When E.G. winked and smiled, Erin held him again, this time holding tighter. "I love you, daddy."

"And I love you too," he said, holding her tighter.

Rachel's voice interrupted them. "He said it would take about an hour before the windows are replaced. Is Conor coming here?"

E.G. put Erin down, and she returned to the couch, where she put on her shoes. "I couldn't reach him. I got his answering machine and left a message for him to call here. Can you stay here until he finishes the job, and then go to Ray's?"

"You're not staying?" Rachel asked.

"You'll be fine. Nobody's going to come back with this guy here. But as soon as he leaves, I want you to leave."

"Where will you be?"

"I can't say. I honestly don't know. I need to follow someone today."

For a moment, E.G. and Rachel stood facing one another. Neither spoke, but all the words that could be spoken were done through their eyes. Finally, Rachel approached E.G. and embraced him. He held her back, tighter than he could remember in all their years of marriage.

"You have a seven-year-old daughter who wants to see you tonight," she said. "You'd better not let her down." He heard the fear in her voice.

"I won't," he said. "I guarantee you'll see me later."

Through one of the broken windows, Rachel watched the Tercel disappear out of Meadowbrook Lane. "I want to see you tonight too," she whispered.

CHAPTER THIRTY-EIGHT

Raymond closed the manila folder and spoke into the telephone. "The person who said follow the money is perhaps the smartest man in the world." He was talking to his source at SEC, who had sent him additional information about Brian Winter and his ownership in Lubalin. "This will help."

He saw a figure move into the doorway and he looked up. It was Angela, and she was tapping her watch. Raymond excused himself and placed a hand over the mouthpiece of the phone. "Your appointment is here," she whispered. Raymond nodded and returned to his caller. He listened for a few more minutes before ending the conversation. He slid from behind his desk and moved to his door. He looked into the outer office and beckoned his visitor inside.

Through the door walked Conor, and he entered slowly, as if with each step, he wondered if this was really where he wanted to be. He followed Raymond's extended hand to a chair near his desk and sat. Instead of taking the chair behind his desk, Raymond sat in the chair next to Conor. "Your phone call peaked my interest. What can I do for you?"

If it had taken any longer for Conor to answer, Raymond would have sworn the reporter had come to his office just to sit and relax. But he was used to behavior such as this. So he gave Conor all the time he needed. Finally, after what seemed an eternity, Conor looked over at him. "I want to turn in a killer."

CHAPTER THIRTY-NINE

E.G. turned the Tercel into Sagamore Road and brought the car to a halt in front of the Winter residence. Instinctively, he removed his notebooks and press cards from the front seat and tucked them under a sweatshirt on the floor of the back seat. The Grand Cherokee that he remembered Brian driving the day of Steven's funeral sat in the driveway, and it was the only car parked there. The sun, creeping over the tall trees that lined the street, burned into the back window of the truck, and he was reminded of his youth, when he burned bugs with a magnifying glass that absorbed the heat of the sun. It was going to be another hot one today, E.G. thought, as he climbed the driveway.

Brian opened the door before E.G. had a chance to ring the bell. And he was smiling. E.G. couldn't figure out the look, because it didn't seem to be a happy smile. It was more like one of relief. "I saw you from the window," he said, pointing upstairs with one hand as he used the other to open the screen door. Brian stood to the side and allowed E.G. inside. He looked once up and down the street before closing the screen door as well as the front door and following E.G.

"What brings you here? How did you know this is where I live?"

"I wanted to see you, and you're in the phone book." E.G. looked around the living room. "Nice place you have here. Do you live alone?" he asked, already knowing the answer.

"I live here with my dad," Brian said. "But don't worry. He's not in right now."

E.G. turned to face Brian. "Why would I worry?"

"He's not too thrilled with some of the choices I've made with my life. He sees me with a guy, and he thinks we're more than friends. As long as I'm living under his roof, he gets to decide who can and who cannot visit."

"Sounds like a tough man," E.G. said.

"I still love him, though," Brian said. The bright blue eyes seemed to dim as he disappeared behind them in thought. "I love him very much. He's always been there to protect me."

Or perhaps covering up, E.G. thought. Could Old Man Winter know what his son did and be protecting him, he wondered. "Where is he now?"

"He said he had to run an errand. I don't expect him back for a while."

"When I saw you at the Reservation the other day, you were very upset. Do you have anyone you can turn to?" E.G. asked, wondering if Brian would acknowledge his relationship with Conor.

"I did have someone," he said. "But I guess I fucked up that relationship this week." He looked directly at E.G. "I pushed someone away, so no, there really is nobody."

"Why did you push him away? Assuming it was a he," E.G. asked.

"There's just a lot going on in my life right now, and I can't be tied to anyone."

"Is that fair to him? I mean, did you let him know why you pushed him away?"

Brian shook his head. "I think he knows what's going on in my life, so I'm sure he has an idea why I've backed away, but no, I haven't told him. Why are you so interested in my relationships?"

"Not necessarily interested as much as hoping you have someone who can help you through your grief."

Brian smiled. "Maybe you can. Why don't you come upstairs with me," he said, winking.

E.G. did not respond.

"I find you very attractive." Brian was straightforward. "At least I'm being honest with you."

"But what about your companion? Are you being honest with him? Doesn't he deserve more than you're giving him?" He wanted to tell Brian that Conor was his best friend, and he deserved to be treated better. But now was not the time.

"Fuck the companion shit," Brian yelled, slapping a hand against the wall. The outburst caught E.G. off guard and he froze. "The fucking guy is in love with someone else. Do you know what it's like to constantly hear about how wonderful this guy he works with is? I'm so sick of hearing about him." With one swift move, Brian cleared the end table of pictures and knick-knacks, and then turned to face E.G., who had begun to back away. "Try advancing a relationship when you have that to deal with."

E.G. had never seen a look of anger on anyone's face like he saw on Brian's. He's cracking, E.G. thought. But just as he was about to push his way toward the front door and leave the house, he heard a car pull up the driveway. Brian heard the same and panicked. He dropped to his knees and gathered the picture frames and small items that he had thrown to the floor and began replacing them on the end table. "You have to get out of here," he said. "Goddamn it, he wasn't supposed to be home this soon."

E.G. brushed passed Brian. There were no good-byes or invitations to dinner or the theater. Only E.G.'s desire to get out of the house, and Brian's desire to see him leave.

As he approached the door, E.G. saw the shadow cross the small squares of glass that adorned the top of the door. E.G. had a choice: retreat to a rear exit or stand firm and meet Ian. While his feet told him to retreat, his heart told him to stay. His heart won.

The front door opened and Ian Winter stepped into the house. The look of confusion that rested upon his face turned into one of recognition, and once that occurred, the look returned to confusion. It took him a minute to realize where he knew E.G. from, and as soon as he placed him, he dropped the bag he was carrying and glared at his son. "What the hell is going on here?"

Brian shook. He had been warned about transient guests. "Dad, it's not what you think. Caleb is a friend of Travis, and he just stopped by to give me a message."

Ian's eyes darted from Brian to E.G. and back at least three times trying to decide how he was being deceived. He knew E.G. from the newspaper, and knew he was writing about the Berns murders. He realized his son had been duped. "This is the fucking reporter from *The Sentinel*," Ian said to Brian. "Can you be so stupid?" Ian rushed E.G. and pushed him against the wall in the living room. "What are you doing in my home?" he demanded, his face only inches from E.G.'s. "Looking for a story? How about 'Reporter arrested for trespassing.' If you don't leave my property, that's what your headline will be."

E.G. grabbed the hand that Ian used to hold him against the wall and pushed him away. Ian fell back against the couch, and Brian ran over to him, catching him before he fell. Brian looked at E.G., and E.G. saw the combination of confusion and hurt in his eyes, but, crazy enough, he saw a look of hope on Brian's face. E.G. moved along the wall until he reached the open door. Brian followed him and stopped him on the front walkway.

"Is it true?" he asked. "Are you a reporter?" Brian didn't need words. The look on E.G.'s face revealed it all. "What do you know? What are you after?"

"Conor told me everything," E.G. replied. "You need to go to the police."

Before Brian could reply, Ian's voice stopped him. "Get the hell off my property," he yelled to E.G., at the same time grabbing hold of Brian and pushing him back toward the house. "Get inside now," he said to him.

Brian shook him free. "No, dad. I'm not a child anymore. I'm a man. Maybe not the kind of man you want me to be, but I am a man."

Ian froze, while E.G. watched the two men with fright.

"*You* get in the house," Brian said to his father in one of the strongest tones Ian had ever heard from his son. "I can't carry this burden anymore."

Ian shifted his gaze from Brian to E.G. and then back to Brian. He realized Brian knew everything. "Don't say a word to him," he muttered.

"Get inside!" Brian's demand was nothing short of a howl, and the strength of the tone pushed Ian into the house, but not before one more glaring look at E.G. Brian turned to E.G. "I don't know what Conor told you, but he doesn't know anything. If he's trying to set me up..."

"He's not," E.G. interrupted. "He cares about you, and he's very concerned. You've pushed him away."

"He brings you into this, and sends you here pretending to be someone else? That's his way of showing concern?"

"He didn't send me here. Yes, I'm a reporter, but I had been gathering information before Conor said anything to me. I'm here to tell you how much he cares about you, and to convince you to find him and listen to him. He wants to do what's in your best interest."

Brian descended the steps and approached E.G., who had already backed further toward the street when Brian turned on his father. "Conor doesn't know what's in my best interest." And then it dawned on him. "It's you. I'm competing against you for Conor. And the funny thing is, you're lovers with Travis." He stopped and thought a moment, then continued to walk toward E.G., who had backed far enough that he was nearing his car at the foot of the property. "Is this all a set-up with Travis too?"

"Travis is a good person," E.G. said.

"Travis stole my company from under my feet," Brian shouted, adding in sarcasm, "*That* must make him wonderful."

"Do you hate him?" E.G. asked.

"More than any person on this earth."

"Enough to want him dead? Is that what you meant the other day when you said it should have been Travis lying in the Reservation and not Mickey?"

"Mickey was a good person."

"Then it was a mistake, wasn't it?" E.G. said. "Mickey wasn't supposed to be in the Reservation last week. You knew Steven Conroy better than you've admitted, didn't you? You expected Travis to be with Steven, and it turns out Mickey was with him. You didn't know about the two of them, did you?"

"Why do you think I was at Steven's funeral?" Brian asked. "Of course I knew about the two of them. Every time I saw Mickey and Steven together, I had a laugh on Travis."

"But…" E.G. was distracted. From where he stood, he could see Ian Winter in the rear yard, carrying the same bag he had with him when he came into the house and heading into the woods beyond the property.

"But nothing," Brian answered for him. "I've had enough of your deception. I don't know what kind of story you want here, but I'm not giving you one. If you don't get off my property, I'll have the police remove you." He turned and started for the house. "Ciao, buddy," he said.

It took a moment before E.G. realized he had heard those words not too long ago, and by the time Brian reached the top of the stairs, it dawned on him where they came from. Impulsively, he called back, "Matt?"

Brian stopped and turned. "What did you call me?"

Instead of retreating, E.G. moved slowly toward the house. "You're Matt," he said. "From online. You were in the Reservation the night Mickey and Steven were killed. But you didn't do it."

"You're Barry too?" Brian asked.

"Stetson165," E.G. replied.

"How many fucking people are you?" Brian shouted.

"We were supposed to meet at the train station. Several nights I showed up, but you weren't there. You were there the night before last, but Conor showed up, and I thought he was Musicat62. I thought he was in the Reservation the night Mickey and Steven were killed. You showed up at the train station last night, but I wasn't there. And that pissed you off. You sent me an e-mail last night telling me you didn't have time for my games. And then you signed off by saying 'Ciao, buddy.' You were the one who saw Mickey and Steven die."

Brian sank to the concrete on the porch. E.G. placed a hand on his shoulder, but Brian pulled away.

"Take your hands off me," he demanded.

E.G. began reciting some of Brian's e-mails. "You didn't want to go the police because you were afraid," he said. "You were afraid because you knew who did it."

"Keep your voice down," Brian said. "I don't want my father to hear you."

"You were afraid because you thought the person who committed the murders had an idea that you knew."

"I told you to keep quiet," Brian said.

"Your father's not going to hear me," E.G. said. "I saw him run to the back of the yard."

Brian looked up. "When?" he asked, concern etched in his voice.

"Three minutes ago," E.G. said. "Where was he going with the bag? Burying the instruments he used to kill Mickey and Steven? It was your father, wasn't it?"

Brian pushed passed E.G. He looked into the yard but didn't see his father. "Did he go into the woods?" he asked.

"Yes. What's in there?"

"It's how he gets into the Reservation. And I think he's supposed to meet Travis there today."

CHAPTER FORTY

Brian reached the top of the hill before E.G. did. And what amazed E.G. was that Brian wasn't the least bit out of breath. By the time he reached the top, E.G. was panting and grabbed hold of the bark of a tree while he got his bearings.

"You climb this often?" he asked.

"It's nothing once you get used to it," Brian replied, looking around for signs of his father.

"How do you know your father was supposed to meet Travis here?"

"I don't. I'm guessing."

"You made me climb this mountain on a hunch?" E.G. asked.

Brian crossed the road, and once on the other side, continued to look for his father. It was quiet in the Reservation that morning, and the only sounds E.G. could hear were those belonging to their feet as they trampled across dried leaves. They stood only a few yards from where the bodies of Mickey and Steven were found.

"It's not really a hunch. I heard my father on the phone the other morning, and based on his side of the conversation, I figured he was talking to Travis. Something about a business proposition and it would be easiest to meet up here. I heard him say eleven o'clock."

E.G. glanced at his watch. It was fifteen minutes before eleven.

"We have one of those phones that displays the last number dialed, and sure enough, it was Travis' number that he called."

"You called Travis later that afternoon," E.G. said.

"I watched my father and another person beat two men to death last week," Brian said. "It wasn't likely that he was calling Travis to shoot the bullshit over a couple beers. I called Travis to warn him, to tell him not to meet my father, but he wouldn't talk to me."

"I'm not surprised," E.G. said. "There was more tension between the two of you at the funeral than there is in the bottom of the ninth of a tied Yankees-Red Sox game." E.G. followed Brian along the trail. "But why? Why did your father do this?"

Brian stopped. "Classic case of revenge. He...Oh my God."

E.G. bumped into Brian as he looked in the same direction. "What?"

"That car," he said, pointing to the black Camaro parked in one of the spaces near the murder scene. "That's the car they used that night. I saw them drag Mickey and Steven out of that car." His voice broke and his legs began to shake. Standing behind Brian, E.G. held him by the arms and led him behind a closely grouped set of trees.

E.G. also recognized the car, or maybe he only pictured the kind of car Rachel described as being in front of her house the night she saw the man on her rear deck trying to get into the house through the sliding door. But he was sure he had seen it somewhere before that. "Stay down," E.G. said, crouching beside Brian and resting an arm over his shoulder. "I don't see Travis' car, so maybe he's not here yet."

"But where could my father be?" Brian asked. "We need to call the police."

"Well, unless you have a cell phone with you, we can't because mine died last night and I haven't had a chance to charge it."

"We left the house in such a hurry that I didn't bring it with me. I didn't even think of it."

"Then we're on our own," E.G. said.

The sound of tires on the hot pavement drew their attention, and both men recognized Travis' black Audi as it pulled onto Crest Drive and coasted into the parking area. Travis paused in the middle of the road before deciding to pull into one of the spaces. If there were twenty spaces, three of them were occupied with vehicles, but none of them contained drivers or passengers.

Travis got out of the car, walked to the back of it and leaned against the trunk. He looked around behind dark sunglasses. His hair was slicked back with gel, and he wore shorts and a pullover shirt. He dangled a cigarette between his lips for a few moments before he lit it. He looked more like he was in the Reservation to cruise than he was for a business meeting.

Brian whispered to E.G. "Do we just sit here?"

"We can't go out there yet," E.G. said in the same whisper. "If we warn Travis, we'll blow the chance of witnessing whatever your father and whoever owns that car are planning. Stay tight. Take it from a pro."

"Do they teach you this in journalism school?" Brian asked.

"Yeah, that, and how to alter your personalities." E.G. looked at Brian. "I'm really sorry for making you believe Barry was real. I was lured onto the board you were on, having no idea you were there. When you started to talk to me, I couldn't reveal my true identity. Especially after you sounded as if you knew more than anybody else about what happened up here. I created Barry for the same reason you created Matt - to remain anonymous. I'm really not a bad guy."

"Who lured you?"

"Conor. But he didn't know he was luring me."

E.G. peeked around the tree to be sure Travis was still near his car. "I've seen such a big change in him during this last week, and it's because of you. You gave him no choice but to believe you were responsible for all of this. You owe him big time."

"What did he expect me to do?" Brian said, lowering his voice after starting the question in a shrill. "It's not every day you watch your father kill two people."

"He didn't know that. He was more concerned that you felt you couldn't confide in him, whether you did this or not. How many people in your life can you say that about? How many people in your life can you say would be there for you if you told them you committed murder? Dammit, he tried to send me in a different direction to stop me from finding out that you could be a suspect."

"But he loves *you*."

"No he doesn't. He cares a great deal about me, and I feel the same way about him. But he knows there could never be anything more between us than friendship. That's where I was last night when you were waiting for me at the train station. We talked for hours. Hours. I didn't get home until this morning." He looked around the tree once more. Travis was flicking his cigarette into the air. "Give him a chance. You're a lucky guy. Don't go looking for someone else like you were planning to do with me."

The sound of a car door closing drew their attention. Travis had gotten back into his car and started the engine, had shifted it into reverse when Ian stepped from the woods in front of him. He turned the engine off and got out of the car.

From where E.G. and Brian hid, they couldn't hear the exchange between Ian and Travis, but they both could tell Ian wasn't happy. His arms seemed to accompany every word he spoke, including the times he poked Travis on the shoulder. Travis had backed away each time, but that didn't stop Ian from moving closer. Finally, Travis pushed back and with enough force that he knocked Ian against the Audi. The passenger door of the Camaro opened, and a tall man who looked to be in his early forties stepped from the car. Ian stretched his arm toward the man, signaling with his hand that he didn't need his assistance.

Travis turned his head in the same direction, aware now that he had men on either side of him. He stepped back, almost into the road, to give himself a better view of both men at the same time. Ian got back on his feet and came closer. The man from the Camaro did the same.

Travis stepped back some more, and by this time, they were close enough to E.G. and Brian that they could hear Ian. "I want every penny of it back."

"Sue me for it. You'll walk out of court with less than what you had going in."

Travis could be a cocky son of a bitch, E.G. thought, when he wanted to be.

"You know that," Travis continued. "That's why you arranged this little get-together up here, so you could try to muscle me into a deal. You morbid bastard. This is where Mickey and Steven were murdered. Did you think I'd get sentimental up here? Is that why you asked me to meet you here?" He looked at Ian's accomplice and taunted him as well. "And you brought your big bad ass friend to do what?"

"Shut up," Ian demanded.

"I'm shaking, Ian," Travis said.

"You cost me six hundred thousand dollars," Ian said, moving closer to Travis.

E.G. looked at Brian, who nodded. "He fronted the money. I didn't make anything to pay him back."

"Bad business deal, Ian," Travis said. "You weren't watching your investment."

Travis could see the anger building to feverish pitch on Ian's face, yet he continued to taunt him. "And we couldn't rely on your son to watch it for you, could we? Brian may be adorable but he hasn't a brain in his head. Nice piece of ass, though. Always good for a fuck."

The anger got to him. "Grab him, Gavin!" Ian shouted to his accomplice, who darted for Travis.

As agile as a cat, Travis leaped into the woods, only yards from where E.G. and Brian hid. E.G. held Brian by the arm after it seemed Brian was about jump from cover. He placed his index finger against Brian's lips to keep him quiet.

Gavin grabbed Travis and held him against a tree as Ian neared. Through the trees, they could see an emerald green Mercedes pull into the parking lot and slip into the stall next to the Camaro. Nathanya Berns stepped out of the car and looked around. As Gavin held Travis, Ian stepped from the woods and called her name. Nathanya followed Ian back into the woods, where she, Ian and Gavin surrounded Travis. And then E.G. remembered where he had seen the black Camaro: It was the vehicle that had nearly pushed him off the road as he left the Berns residence two days after the murders.

"This is my story," E.G. whispered to Brian.

"And this is my father," Brian whispered back. "How could he do this?"

Nathanya stepped within inches of Travis' face. "My son is dead because of you," she said without a trace of emotion in her voice.

"Because of me?" Travis asked, looking from Nathanya to Ian and back. "Is that why we're all up here? You think I killed Mickey and Steven?"

Brian whispered to E.G.: "And he says I don't have a brain?"

"You've got it all wrong," Travis continued. "I had no idea about the two of them, and even if I did, I'm not a killer."

"Shut up!" Nathanya demanded. "It should have been you and Steven lying over there, not my son. So now we have to do it this way."

Ian stuck his hand in the waistband of his pants and removed a handgun, draped with a silencer. He pointed it against the head of Travis, who finally began to understand what was happening. "Mickey wasn't supposed to die, was he?" he asked Nathanya, keeping an eye on the gun pointed at his temple. "You think you can get away with this?"

"We will get away with this," Nathanya said. "Because you're going to help us."

Ian interjected. "We've drafted a few documents we want you to sign before you take a vacation," Ian said. "They in effect turn Lubalin over to us, kind of similar to the way you took Lubalin from my son and Mickey Berns."

"I didn't kill anybody for the company," Travis said.

"You may as well have," Ian said.

"And how long do you think it will be before someone wonders, after this sweetheart deal of ours, when I'll be coming back from this vacation you've planned for me?"

"No one will have to wonder," Nathanya said. "You're going to tell all your investors, all your employees, everyone affiliated with Lubalin, that you've taken an extended vacation for personal reasons, and the decision to sell your company to us was one that you had been pining for a long time."

"Mrs. Berns, you've been an upstanding member of this community for many years," Travis appealed. "You don't want to do this."

"You've left me no choice."

"We can work out a deal," Travis said the moment he heard Ian cock the gun. He trembled. "It doesn't have to end like this." He glanced at Gavin and then back at Nathanya. "Will you be able to trust that Slick over here can keep a secret?"

Nathanya stepped back. "We're not concerned about Slick," she said, using Travis' word. "In fact, we can assure you right now that Gavin won't utter a word about this."

Ian turned his arm and put a bullet in the middle of Gavin's forehead, dropping him to the ground with a thud. Travis gasped as he clung to the tree. Ian turned the gun back to Travis.

"Dad! No!"

Brian emerged from behind the brush. Tears fell from his eyes as he stared at his father in disbelief. E.G. stood as well, just to the right of Brian, and surveyed the scene. Ian turned toward them, pointed the gun, and fired.

CHAPTER FORTY-ONE

Brian grabbed his arm where the bullet grazed him and blood spilled between his fingers. He would have looked at his wound, but he couldn't take his eyes off his father.

For a moment, Ian stared at his son. The look on his face asked Brian's forgiveness, his understanding. Then, as the blood saturated his shirt, his body jolted once and then fell forward, landing at Travis' feet.

Nathanya, confused, watched Ian drop as Brian ran to his father's side. Travis, frozen against the tree, stared down at them. E.G. looked through the trees, just as Nathanya did, to determine where the bullet had come from that struck Ian. She began to slowly back out of the woods before they heard the familiar voice call out, "Hold it. Police."

The voice was familiar to Nathanya because she had heard it several times during the last week. The voice was familiar to E.G. because he had heard it many times throughout his life. Raymond stepped from the brush on the other side of the tree where Travis stood and held his gun on Nathanya. She obeyed his order and held her hands out to indicate she wasn't carrying a weapon.

He patted her down regardless, and then called to E.G. "Cover her until back-up arrives. I've radioed for assistance." As Raymond moved toward the bodies of Gavin and Ian, E.G. stood near Nathanya, who dropped to the ground and began to sob. E.G. looked at Travis, who had been looking back at him with a confused look on his face. He was still frightened and had begun to shake. He moved toward E.G.

E.G. held his arms out, and without understanding why, Travis slipped into them and held him. "Who are you?" he asked, his face pressed against E.G.'s sweat-stained shirt.

"He's one of the best reporters the newspaper business has ever had."

E.G. and Travis looked behind them, as Brian looked up from where he knelt next to his father. Conor stood alone a few feet away from them. He looked into E.G.'s eyes. "And he's the best friend a guy could ever have."

E.G. smiled at Conor, and nodded toward Brian, who had stood. Conor held out his arms to Brian, and he rushed into them, holding Conor as if it would be the last time he would ever do so.

Sirens wailed in the background, and as each minute passed, they grew louder and seemed to scream into the woods. Raymond beckoned Conor. "Go out and let them see you. Let them know our location."

Conor assisted Brian out of the woods, assuring him the wound was a flesh wound and that he'd live. Raymond returned to Nathanya and removed a pair of handcuffs from a back pocket. He helped her up from the ground and led her out of the woods and into the parking area, where scores of police vehicles had begun to converge on the area. A uniformed officer from the local police department stepped from one of the first cars to arrive and approached Raymond.

"This is Nathanya Berns," he told the officer as he placed the handcuffs on Nathanya's wrists. "I am placing Mrs. Berns under arrest for her involvement in the murders of Mickey Berns, Steven Conroy, and a third victim who is identified from his driver's license as Gavin Preston. Mrs. Berns, you have the right to remain silent..."

"You're really a reporter?" Travis asked, slowly pulling away from E.G.'s hold.

E.G. nodded. "We didn't meet by chance. When I met you at The Lucky Leaf, it was because I had followed you there. I got a tip that you may have been involved in this murder. I was doing my job. I write for *The Sentinel*. I'm E.G. Lord, and you spoke to me the other day on the telephone when you called the office."

Travis was quiet for a moment. "You stayed at my house. You slept in my bed. You accompanied me to a funeral. You had me believing you were my friend. Is it any wonder people don't trust reporters."

"I was doing my job," E.G. repeated. "But the more time I spent with you these last few days made me realize that you weren't involved in this. Raymond is also my cousin. I told him you weren't involved, and he believed me. You had become my friend, but I couldn't tell you who I really was because I was investigating this murder, and it could have put your life in jeopardy. I created this persona to get to the truth, and I'm sorry if it hurt you along the way. I'd like us to be friends."

Travis looked through the trees and watched as a police officer assisted Nathanya into a patrol car. A female paramedic treated Brian's wound as Conor stood near him. Officers had entered the woods and were standing over the bodies of Gavin and Ian. "I suppose you're not gay either," Travis said.

"No, I'm not," E.G. replied.

"Not even for a day?" Travis asked, a flirting smile crossing his mouth.

E.G. chuckled. "Sorry."

"Well, that's okay. If I'm to be your friend, I'll have to accept your flaws."

E.G. laughed, put his arm around Travis and led him to the parking lot. A plain-clothed officer approached them, and asked to take a statement from Travis. As the two men walked to a patrol car, E.G. sought out Raymond, who was talking with a colleague outside the car where Nathanya sat in the back seat. He didn't have to interrupt because Raymond saw him coming.

"Thanks, man," E.G. said to his cousin, extending his hand.

Raymond took it and held it tightly. "You can thank Conor. He's the one who confirmed everything for me this morning."

"I'll be sure to do that," E.G. said. He nodded toward the woods. "Thanks for showing up when you did. I'd hate to think I'd be carried out of here in a bag too."

"I have one bit of advice for you," Raymond said. "Leave the detective work to the detectives. You worry about the journalism."

"In that case," E.G. said, removing his notebook from his back pocket, "I have a few questions for you. And this time, everything is on the record."

CHAPTER FORTY-TWO

Two more dead in Reservation
Two suspects in double homicide fatally wounded

By E.G. Lord
Sentinel Staff

SOUTH ORANGE - Two men who police believe were part of a three-person ring responsible for the double homicide in the South Mountain Reservation last week were fatally wounded yesterday after they returned to the scene of the crime allegedly to commit another murder.

The third member of the group, prominent South Orange resident and business woman Nathanya Berns, was arrested at the scene. Formal charges were expected to be levied against Berns this morning during an arraignment in Superior Court in Newark. She was expected to be charged with two counts of conspiracy to commit murder, one count of attempted murder, one count of kidnapping, and one count of extortion. Berns' son, Mickey, also of South Orange, was one of the victims of the double homicide, which, according to an investigation by *The Sentinel*, was a plan gone awry by Nathanya Berns and her two accomplices.

Those two accomplices, Ian Winter of Maplewood, who at one time sought election to the town's governing body, and Gavin

Preston, both died from gunfire that erupted in the usually serene South Mountain Reservation. Winter died from a single bullet fired from the gun of an investigator from the Essex County Prosecutor's Office, after Winter had fatally wounded Preston from a single shot to the man's forehead with his own gun.

Raymond Vanderhoeven, lead investigator for the Essex County Prosecutor's Office, called the murders and subsequent attempted murder a "classic case of revenge" by Winter and Nathanya Berns against the owner of the Lubalin Cosmetics company, a company once part owned by the suspects' sons.

"We have enough evidence against Nathanya Berns that we expect this case will come to a speedy conclusion in our justice system," Vanderhoeven said yesterday in the Reservation as officers from the Sheriff's Department transported Mrs. Berns to the Essex County Jail in Newark.

Vanderhoeven was expected to hold a press conference this afternoon in Newark announcing the arrest and the events that surrounded the shooting deaths of the two men yesterday. The bullet that killed Winter came from Vanderhoeven's gun. The 10-year law enforcement veteran said yesterday he will voluntarily surrender his weapon to authorities, who are expected to conduct an investigation into the shootings.

Mickey Berns, who lived with his mother, and Steven Conroy, a Montville resident, were found dead in a grassy area along Crest Drive in the Reservation last Wednesday after police received an anonymous call that morning alerting them to the murders. Police said the two men died the night before.

Because the Reservation is a frequent cruising spot for gay men, initial speculation indicated that foul play resulted from homosexual-related activity. But as *The Sentinel* investigation reveals, the two men were intentionally lured to the site. Only one obstacle got in the way: The suspects believed the owner of Lubalin Cosmetics was one of the men they were luring, and not the son of one of the suspects.

Held hostage

Travis Boesgaard, the West Orange man who wrested control of Lubalin Cosmetics from Mickey Berns and Brian Winter only a year ago and who was reportedly supposed to have been one of the murder victims last week, was held hostage in the Reservation yesterday by Nathanya Berns, Ian Winter and Preston. Boesgaard was lured to the site yesterday, where, it was learned by *The Sentinel*, he was expected to involuntarily sign over control of the company to the elder Berns and Winter. Winter revealed that he had lost more than $600,000 when Boesgaard bought out his son in a covert takeover deal.

Winter revealed that information shortly before he and Preston held Boesgaard captive in a wooded area of the Reservation yesterday. It was not yet known how much, if any, of an investment was lost by Mrs. Berns.

Mrs. Berns had served on the South Orange Board of Trustees for a number of years, and remained politically active even after choosing not to seek re-election. She was the last to arrive in the Reservation yesterday, and she came with documents she had drafted for Boesgaard to sign before they were to allegedly kill him. Police confiscated those documents.

Son injured

But it was moments later that panic surfaced on Boesgaard's face. It was then, to prove how serious Mrs. Berns and Winter were, that Winter turned his gun on Preston and shot him to death with one bullet. Winter's son, Brian, who was present in the Reservation but who remained hidden, emerged after the gun was fired and implored his father to stop.

Winter turned on his son and fired his gun, grazing the younger Winter in the arm, but at the same time, the elder Winter was struck by the bullet fired from Vanderhoeven's gun. Both men were pronounced dead at the scene by the Essex County Medical Examiner's Office.

A trying morning

Boesgaard declined medical attention, while EMS technicians treated the younger Winter at the scene before transporting him to nearby Saint Barnabas Medical Center in Livingston for treatment of the flesh wound. Brian Winter was listed in stable condition last night at the hospital and was expected to be released this morning.

Police will question Winter this week about his knowledge of the murders because he admitted to law enforcement officials that he made the anonymous phone call the morning after the murders occurred. No charges are expected to be filed against him, according to Vanderhoeven.

Police will also investigate Boesgaard's takeover of Lubalin Cosmetics to determine whether or not charges should be filed against Boesgaard.

'Happy it's over'

A spokesperson for the Conroy family spoke to *The Sentinel* yesterday afternoon and, when informed of the events earlier in the day, said he and his family were "happy it's over," saying it brings closure to Steven Conroy's death.

"We're still trying to cope with the shock of Steven's death," the relative said. "Although there is so much we still don't understand, we take comfort in knowing that Steven was an innocent victim in this tragedy."

A funeral Mass was held for Conroy Saturday in Montville.

The silent accomplice

As of presstime, little was known about Preston, except for confirmation from the younger Winter that he was present the night of the Berns-Conroy murders.

It is also expected that he will be placed at the home of a relative close to the murder investigation. During the week, that person, whose identity is being withheld by *The Sentinel*, identified a black Camaro parked in front of her South Orange home. The driver, whose description matches Preston, reportedly attempted to gain entry into the home through a rear door on one occasion. He also may be the suspect who vandalized the home by throwing bricks through the front windows on another occasion.

The victim said she can identify the man who appeared at her rear door and will be asked by police to view the body.

A dedicated detective

Police closed the Reservation to vehicular traffic yesterday afternoon and are expected to keep the park closed for at least one more day as they continue their investigation into the incidents of the last week.

When asked for a comment about the handling of the investigation, Essex County Prosecutor Sheila Timoni said, "Investigator Vanderhoeven has a reputation in this office as being one of the most diligent and dedicated detectives in law enforcement today. He has a platinum record for bringing criminals to justice, and this case is just one example of how important he is to our office."

While not revealing how his investigation progressed, Vanderhoeven said he simply "followed the scents" that were laid out before him to solve the murders.

Recognizing that this newspaper was covering these murders at deadline, *The Sentinel* will publish a special "Extra" edition tomorrow and continue its expansive coverage of the murders in the Reservation. This will be the first time the newspaper will publish a special edition since its debut 80 years ago.

CHAPTER FORTY-THREE

E.G. put the newspaper down and stared at the one word that leaped from the middle of his story. "Exclusive."

The *Herald-Times* didn't have the story. The corner store was the first place he stopped before starting his day that morning, and while the man behind the counter watched him, E.G. tore apart the daily newspaper, section by section, looking for even a mention of the arrest and shootings. Even 1010-WINS, the "all news, all the time" AM radio station in the New York area, didn't include the incident in its morning reports. And, he convinced himself, even if the print and broadcast media did have the story, there was no way they could have reported the news as he did. Theirs would have had more attribution, less flavor. Theirs would have been riddled with "authorities said" and "according to officials." His didn't need that; he was there. And it always made his heart leap as a journalist knowing his career was built on sources and investigations that placed him where the news would be.

Margaret was the first to laud E.G. when he walked into the office that morning. The praise came, of course, after she literally had to be pulled from the newspaper when he tapped his fingers on the front counter. And then it was Kelly's turn, and then Will's turn, and other reporters and editors as well as Advertising Department salesmen and women, who mostly wanted to know if such a negative story would adversely impact their efforts to sell ad space in future editions. "They'll just never get it," E.G. told himself on his way back to his cubicle.

As he scanned the story once again, his computer indicated that a piece of mail had arrived. It was from Musicat62. "Dear Barry," it began. "I want to thank you for all you've done for me. Whether you realize it or not, you've taught me many things: the courage to stand up for myself, the ability to trust in friends, and never to take true love for granted. I have all of these things now because of you. Most important is the true love."

E.G. turned his head toward the opening of his cubicle to be sure Conor wasn't standing there, silently, as he did many times. "I'm sure you'll hear all about that," Brian continued, ending the sentence with the online symbol for a smile. "I'd be interested in getting together with you from time to time. There was a certain amount of trust I developed in you during our brief period together. Funny, isn't it, how you build a trust in someone you've never met, and to make it worse, realize, after you've met, that the personality wasn't real. Go figure. Maybe one day you can formally introduce me to E.G. Lord. We met briefly yesterday, and he seems like a real nice person. Well, I have to go. Today is the first day of my new life, and I can't wait to get it started." He signed the e-mail "Brian, aka Matt."

E.G. clicked Reply and typed the salutation. But before continuing, he decided to ignore it. "Time to lay Barry to rest," he said aloud.

"Good idea. E.G.'s a better person anyway."

E.G. turned to find Conor in the opening of the cubicle, and for the first time in a week, saw a smile cross his face and the lines of concern disappear from his forehead. "Hey," he said, smiling back.

Conor came into the cubicle. "I read your story. It was excellent. Reporters at the daily are sucking your wind today."

"And it was a mean dose of wind I gave them."

"Sure did," Conor replied. "You were right in the middle of that story from the beginning."

"That's what journalism is all about."

"And what is this I hear that we're coming out with an extra edition tomorrow?" Conor asked.

"Yeah, can you believe it? First time in the history of the paper. I'll still be able to wipe my ass with the *Herald-Times* tomorrow morning. My prediction? They'll have one story, say forty inches long, credited to three or four staff writers, and all it will be is a repeat of what I had today. Mel redid the front page yesterday, so the stories I had planned for today's paper didn't make it. I'll rework those as well as do an update on anything that happens today. Raymond's got a press conference today, and I spent most of last night writing a follow-up to today's piece."

"Our work never ends," Conor said.

"No, it doesn't. Are things okay between you and Brian?"

Conor's face grew a light red and his smile broadened. "We got to know each other real well last night. We had a great talk, so, yes, things are okay between us. I would just ask, E.G., if you wouldn't say anything to anybody about us."

"I won't utter a word. And I'm happy for you. You look happy. I just have one question."

"Only one?" Conor asked.

"Today, yes. Only one."

"Shoot."

"When we were in the parking lot the other day, you reminded me of the night I caught you and your girl in your car. Why did you bring that up?"

Conor smiled. "I was trying to tell you about me. And I thought I would start with the night that turned out to be the last time I was with a woman. That was the night."

E.G. nodded his understanding. "Got it." And then he excused himself. "I have to get back to work on this special edition. Maybe we can grab a beer later tonight."

"I'd like that," Conor said, looking toward the reception area. "Unless you have other plans."

E.G. followed his eyes. Coming toward them were Rachel and Erin, who was tugging on her mother's arm. E.G. crouched and realized he was at eye level with Conor's crotch. He looked up and said, "Don't think your dearest wish is going to come true here." Conor laughed as E.G. turned toward Erin and held his arms out. His daughter ran into them and he hugged her, kissing her hair.

"The bad guys got caught, daddy? That's what mommy said."

"Yes, the bad guys got caught so I don't want you worrying another minute."

Erin looked directly at E.G. "I wasn't worried, daddy," she said, as if she were offended, and then leaned in to whisper in his ear. "I had to protect mommy. She was worried."

"She was?" E.G. locked eyes with Rachel and he put Erin on the floor.

Conor interjected and spoke to Erin. "I have about five boxes of popsicles in the freezer just in case we got weather like today. You want one?"

Erin looked from her father to her mother for approval, and when they both nodded, she disappeared with Conor toward the kitchen.

E.G. led Rachel into his cubicle.

"My source tells me you were worried about me," he said.

"I can send your source to bed tonight without a snack for revealing information I told her off the record." She paused before continuing. "Are you all right? Raymond told us last night what happened. I tried reaching you, but I couldn't get through on your cell phone, so I left a couple messages on your voice mail."

E.G. glanced at the phone and saw the message light flashing. "I haven't checked messages yet, and I haven't recharged my cell phone. I spent yesterday afternoon writing today's story, and then last night writing another piece for a special edition we're publishing tomorrow."

"Yeah, I saw that at the bottom of your story."

"So you've read it?"

"It was wonderful," Rachel said. "Frightening too, knowing you were in the middle while all this was going on."

"It's my job," he said, shrugging it off.

"Something that always made me jealous. Like today, I see how happy you are, and that makes me jealous. I know that's dumb."

"What's important is that you were worried. To me, anyway."

"It was strange last night because as I was sitting with Liz and we talked about what we knew, I had such a nagging feeling that you weren't coming home last night. You haven't come home in about a year, so I don't know why this felt so pressing." Rachel lowered her head to hide the tear that had welled in her eye, the one had that fallen onto her cheek.

E.G. saw it and couldn't control the love that he still felt for her, the love that he knew was born the day he met her and the love that had not died. He wrapped his arms around her and held her, and she returned the embrace. As his head rested against her hair, E.G. tried to recall the last time he had felt such a return of affection from Rachel. It had been a long time, he knew, but it remained so strangely familiar to him.

"I can come home tonight, if you'll have me," he said.

Before Rachel had the chance to answer, Mel popped his head into the cubicle. "E.G., I need stories to read, you've got a press conference this afternoon, and we've got a special edition to finish tonight. Good morning, Mrs. Lord." E.G. waited for a clap of the hands, the hop-to-it rhythm. It was all that was missing to accompany the tone in his voice. Then Mel disappeared.

They both looked at each other for what seemed like an eternity. Both knew it was times like this that had driven them apart.

"I understand," Rachel said sadly, freeing herself from E.G.'s embrace.

"No, you don't understand," E.G. said. "If you want to make dinner tonight, I will be home by six o'clock. Guaranteed. And the three of us can sit down to a nice family dinner." He rubbed her hair and kissed her forehead.

But Rachel wouldn't have it. "I wouldn't want to make you begin choosing all over again. You know what I mean."

And Mel's voice, from somewhere in the outer office, pierced the moment.

"E.G.!" he yelled. "I need your stories!"

30-30-30

Printed in the United States
42224LVS00005B/1-87